THE INTENDED VICTIM

"When I called to check with the candy company, they told me that their stores provide pre-paid mailers to any customers who buy two-pound boxes if the customer asks for one," Mike said. "At some point, someone must have thrown away the mailer, but I don't know when."

"Sounds like you've had a frustrating morning so far," Hannah said.

"I still have no idea when that candy was mailed and when it arrived at KCOW."

"So what you're telling me is that since you can't pin down the arrival of the candy, you can't identify the intended victim."

"Right."

"And that means you have to investigate anyone who might have had a reason to kill either Ross or P.K."

"Exactly. I'll need to ask you some questions about Ross's background, Hannah. I've got to find out if there's anyone who might have wanted to kill him and why . . ."

Books by Joanne Fluke

Hannah Swensen Mysteries
CHOCOLATE CHIP COOKIE MURDER
STRAWBERRY SHORTCAKE MURDER
BLUEBERRY MUFFIN MURDER
LEMON MERINGUE PIE MURDER
FUDGE CUPCAKE MURDER
SUGAR COOKIE MURDER
PEACH COBBLER MURDER
CHERRY CHEESECAKE MURDER
KEY LIME PIE MURDER
CANDY CANE MURDER
CARROT CAKE MURDER
CREAM PUFF MURDER
PLUM PUDDING MURDER
APPLE TURNOVER MURDER
DEVIL'S FOOD CAKE MURDER
GINGERBREAD COOKIE MURDER
CINNAMON ROLL MURDER
RED VELVET CUPCAKE MURDER
BLACKBERRY PIE MURDER
DOUBLE FUDGE BROWNIE MURDER
WEDDING CAKE MURDER
CHRISTMAS CARAMEL MURDER
BANANA CREAM PIE MURDER
RASPBERRY DANISH MURDER
CHRISTMAS CAKE MURDER
CHOCOLATE CREAM PIE MURDER
JOANNE FLUKE'S LAKE EDEN COOKBOOK

Suspense Novels
VIDEO KILL
WINTER CHILL
DEAD GIVEAWAY
THE OTHER CHILD
COLD JUDGMENT
FATAL IDENTITY
FINAL APPEAL
VENGEANCE IS MINE
EYES
WICKED
DEADLY MEMORIES
THE STEPCHILD

Published by Kensington Publishing Corporation

RASPBERRY DANISH MURDER

JOANNE FLUKE

KENSINGTON BOOKS
www.kensingtonbooks.com

KENSINGTON BOOKS are published by

Kensington Publishing Corp.
119 West 40th Street
New York, NY 10018

All Kensington titles, imprints and distributed lines are available at special quantity discounts for bulk purchases for sales promotion, premiums, fund-raising, educational or institutional use. Special book excerpts or customized printings can also be created to fit specific needs. For details, write or phone the office of the Kensington Special Sales Manager: Kensington Publishing Corp., 119 West 40th Street, New York, NY, 10018. Attn. Special Sales Department. Phone: 1-800-221-2647.

ISBN-13: 978-1-61773-226-3
ISBN-10: 1-61773-226-5
First Kensington Hardcover Edition: March 2018
First Kensington Mass Market Edition: March 2019

ISBN-13: 978-1-61773-225-6 (e-book)
ISBN-10: 1-61773-225-7 (e-book)

10 9 8 7 6 5 4 3 2 1

Printed in the United States of America

This Hannah book is for John.
I couldn't have written it without him.

Acknowledgments:

Heartfelt thanks to Doctor Richard Niemeyer, our "Doc Hockey."
John and I will miss you so much.
(And so will Doc Knight.)

Hugs and kisses to my family for their patience when I'm on deadline.
An extra cookie for all of you!

Hugs to Trudi Nash for going on all those book tours with me and doing countless things to help. Thanks for being able to identify ingredients simply by tasting something we like and helping me create a recipe to make it. And more important than anything, thanks for being my friend.

Thank you to my friends and neighbors: Mel & Kurt, Lyn & Bill, Gina, Dee Appleton, Jay, Richard Jordan, Laura Levine, the real Nancy and Heiti, Dr. Bob & Sue, Dan, Mark & Mandy at Faux Library, Daryl and her staff at Groves Accountancy, Gene and Ron at SDSA, and everyone at Homestreet Bank.

Hugs to Richard Jordan for going on tour with me for *Banana Cream Pie Murder*. You were great company and a big help.

Thanks to Brad, Eric, Amanda, Lorenzo, and Meg for *Just Desserts*.

Hello to my Minnesota friends: Lois & Neal, Bev & Jim, Lois & Jack, Val, Ruthann, Lowell, Dorothy & Sister Sue, and Mary & Jim.

A big thank you to my brilliant editor, John Scognamiglio.

Thanks to all the wonderful folks at Kensington Publishing who keep Hannah sleuthing and baking yummy goodies.

And a special thank you to Robin, who makes everything perfect.

Thanks to Meg Ruley and the staff at the Jane Rotrosen Agency for their constant support and their sage advice.

Thanks to Hiro Kimura, my talented cover artist, for his delicious cover art.
(No, you can't eat that Raspberry Danish!)

Thank you to Lou Malcangi at Kensington for designing Hannah's gorgeous book covers. They're always just perfect.

Thanks to John at ***Placed4Success.com*** for Hannah's movie and TV placements, his presence on Hannah's social media platform, the countless hours he spends helping me, and for always being there for me.

Thanks to Rudy for managing my website at **www.JoanneFluke.com** and for giving support to Hannah's social media. And thanks to Annie for help with social media and everything else.

Big thanks to Kathy Allen for the final testing of the recipes. And thanks to Kathy's friends and family for taste testing.

A big hug to JQ for helping Hannah and me for so many years.

Hugs to Beth for her gorgeous embroidery and for telling me about the "Moishe flop."

Thank you to food stylist, friend, and media guide Lois Brown for her invaluable assistance with the launch parties at Poisoned Pen and the TV baking segments in Phoenix.

Hugs to the Double D's and everyone on Team Swensen and the Hannah Maniacs who help to keep Hannah's Facebook presence alive and well.

Thank you to Dr. Rahhal, Dr. and Cathy Line, Dr. Wallen, Dr. Koslowski, and Drs. Ashley and Lee for answering my book-related medical and dental questions.

Grateful thanks to all of the Hannah fans who share their family recipes, post on my Facebook page, **Joanne Fluke Author**, and read Hannah mysteries.
This one's for you!

Chapter One

Hannah Swensen Barton glanced at the clock in the bedroom that she now slept in alone. There were tears in her eyes as she put on her warmest sweater. Her new husband, Ross Barton, had been gone for two weeks now and even though her youngest sister, Michelle, was staying with her at the condo, Hannah still felt terribly alone. It was easier during the day. When the sun had risen and it was no longer time to cuddle with Ross on their new couches or sleep beside him in their new king-size bed, she managed to convince herself that everything was going to be all right, that Ross was planning to come back to her. Then, with the sun shining brightly, it was possible to believe that the reason he'd taken their condo key and left all his other keys behind was proof that he planned to come home. But now, at five in the morning after spending a restless night, it was doubly difficult to convince herself that all would be well if she just waited patiently.

"Keep a positive attitude," she said aloud to her image in the mirror. "Ross will be home very soon and he'll explain everything." The words she spoke formed the mantra that she repeated every morning, even though she was fast losing hope. There had been no phone calls from Ross at The

Cookie Jar, her bakery and coffee shop in Lake Eden, Minnesota, and no calls at night at their condo. She had no clue to his whereabouts or the reason he had left in the first place. It was as if her new husband had disappeared off the face of the earth and vanished into thin air without a trace.

A tear rolled down Hannah's cheek and she wiped it away with the back of her hand. It was a good thing she didn't wear makeup because the tears she'd shed during the long days and nights would have surely ruined it. As she picked up her hairbrush and attempted to tame her unruly red curls, she wondered if her appearance was at fault for Ross's defection. If she'd worn perfect makeup like her mother, Delores, and her fashionable sister, Andrea, would Ross still be with her? And if she'd been born with beautiful hair that looked cute in any style like her youngest sister, Michelle, would he be watching her admiringly as she got ready for work? Perhaps she should have tried harder to lose weight so that she could attain a perfect figure like the rest of the women in her family.

"If he'd just told me what was wrong, I could have fixed it," she told Moishe, turning to face her twenty-three pound, orange and white cat, who was nestled on Ross's pillow.

"Rowwww!" Moishe responded, and to Hannah's eyes, he looked outraged at the critical direction her mind was taking.

"Sorry, Moishe," she said, walking over to the bed to give him several comforting scratches and pats. "It's just that I keep trying to find answers and there aren't any."

"Rrrrrow," Moishe yowled again, and Hannah interpreted his response as an expression of sympathy. She was sure that Moishe missed Ross, too.

"I have to leave for work now," she told him. "But don't worry. Michelle and I will be back home in time to feed you your dinner."

Hannah shrugged into her parka and left the bedroom. She was just passing the guest room door as Michelle came out. Her youngest sister was holding a key ring in her hand. "Are these keys yours, Hannah?" she asked, handing them to Hannah.

Hannah examined the keys and shook her head. "They're not mine, but they look like the keys to Ross's car. I knew they must be here somewhere since it's still in his parking space. Where did you find them?"

"They were in the top drawer of the dresser in the guest room. They were sitting right on top of my warmest winter scarf. I never would have found them if I hadn't decided to use that scarf this morning."

"Well, I'm glad. I never thought to look there."

"That's understandable. I was really surprised when I found them. Why did Ross put them there?"

Hannah began to smile as her mind latched on to the obvious conclusion. "It's simple, Michelle. Ross wanted you to drive his car while he was gone. There's no other explanation."

"Are you sure?"

"The more I think about it, the more positive I am. He took the time to go into your room and put his car keys in your dresser drawer. There's no other reason he would have done that."

Michelle still looked doubtful. "But how do you feel about it? Do you want me to use Ross's car?"

"Why not? It should be driven. If it just sits there, it's not going to start when Ross comes home. He obviously wanted you to keep his car running for him."

"Well . . . if you're sure . . ."

"I'm sure."

Michelle began to smile. "I was going to ask Mother if I

could borrow her car, but now I won't have to do that. It's a big relief!"

"Because Mother would say yes, but then she'd figure out some way to make you pay a couple of pounds of favors for the privilege?"

"Exactly!" Michelle headed toward the rug by the door where they kept their winter boots. She pulled on hers and then she slipped her shoes in the tote bag she was carrying.

"Take your time, Hannah," she said as she opened the outside door. "I'll help Lisa bake the dough we mixed up last night and get things ready in the coffee shop. Have another cup of coffee before you leave, and enjoy being a lady of leisure for a change."

"Thanks," Hannah said as Michelle went out and closed the door behind her. Then she shrugged out of her parka, draped it over the back of the couch, and went into the kitchen to pour herself another cup of coffee. The coffee was still hot enough to drink without reheating.

"A lady of leisure," she repeated Michelle's phrase to Moishe, who had followed her into the kitchen and seemed to be staring at her curiously as she took a seat at the kitchen table. "I'm not exactly sure what that is."

Moishe made no comment. Instead, he headed for his food bowl. As her feline roommate crunched kibble, Hannah stared out the window at the snow blowing past the pane. It had been less than three minutes since Michelle had walked out the door, and Hannah was already feeling guilty for not putting on her boots and following her sister to work.

"Either I'm not a lady, or I don't know the meaning of leisure," she told Moishe. "If you don't mind, I'm going to gulp down this coffee and drive to work."

* * *

A biting wind hurtled icy snow against Hannah's cheeks as she left the condo and hurried down the covered staircase to ground level. As she passed her downstairs neighbor's window, she noticed that the kitchen light was on. That meant Sue Plotnik was up fixing breakfast for her three-year-old boy, Kevin. His father, Phil Plotnik, would be home soon from his night supervisor shift at DelRay Manufacturing. Phil would eat breakfast with them and then Sue and Kevin would leave for her teaching job at Kiddie Korner, Lake Eden's preschool. Once they'd left, Phil would go to bed and sleep until Sue and Kevin got back home. It was a demanding schedule, but Sue and Phil had worked it all out. They'd spend the rest of the day together with Kevin until Phil went back to work again at eleven that night.

When Hannah started her Suburban, she noticed that the engine sounded a bit sluggish. It was time to start using her engine block heater and plugging her cookie truck in every night. The garage had a strip of outlets on the wall in front of the parking spaces for that purpose. There was also a strip of outlets in the parking lot at The Cookie Jar.

As Hannah drove to work, she thought about the busy days ahead. It was Monday, and Thanksgiving would arrive soon. That meant they had to prepare for the Thanksgiving baking. The orders for pumpkin pies, pumpkin scones, pumpkin cookies, and sugar cookies decorated with turkeys and pumpkins were already pouring in. The pumpkin pies could be made no more than a day in advance and the same was true for the scones and cookies. They could, however, mix some of the ingredients together ahead of time and have everything ready for the marathon of baking that was necessary on the two days before the November holiday.

For the most part, things had gone smoothly the previous year, but there were more orders this year. Hannah was thankful that she had help. Her partner, Lisa, was a dynamo in the kitchen. They also had Jack and Marge Herman, Lisa's father and stepmother, to handle the business in the coffee shop while they baked in the kitchen. This year, they had two additional bakers, Lisa's aunt Nancy, who was a genius at coming up with new recipes, and Michelle, who would pitch in when she wasn't busy with rehearsals. Part of Michelle's college curriculum was work study, and she was in town to direct the Thanksgiving and Christmas plays that their local community theater group was performing, and also to direct the high school junior class play, which would be performed between Thanksgiving and Christmas.

There was no traffic at this time of the morning, and Hannah pulled into her parking spot in back of The Cookie Jar much sooner than she'd expected. She got out of her cookie truck, locked the doors, plugged in her block heater, and hurried to the back kitchen door. When she came in, both Lisa and Michelle looked surprised.

"I thought you were going to take time for coffee," Michelle said by way of a greeting.

"I did, but coffee by myself was boring. I thought I'd have another cup with you two here."

"I'll pour some for you," Lisa offered. "And since we already have bar cookies in the oven, Michelle and I can take a break."

"How about a piece of Raspberry Danish?" Michelle asked Hannah. "Lisa was here early and she baked some company-size ones." She turned to Lisa. "It's cool enough to cut, isn't it?"

"It should be." Lisa turned to Hannah. "Aunt Nancy baked it for us when Herb and I went to her house for brunch last weekend. She gave me the recipe and I wanted to try it here."

"Is it difficult to make?"

"Not at all! I thought that if you like it, we could serve it here."

"That's a really good idea. We've never served any kind of Danish before, and I'm sure our morning customers would appreciate it. Personally, I just love Danish!"

Michelle smiled. "So does almost everyone I know. I think it would go over great, Hannah."

Lisa hurried to the bakers rack, removed a pan from one of the shelves, and carried it over to show Hannah. "Doesn't it look pretty?"

"It certainly does," Hannah told her. "And it smells wonderful, too. I love the scent of raspberries. If they could bottle it, I'd be tempted to use it as perfume."

Both Lisa and Michelle laughed. Then Michelle warned, "That would be dangerous, Hannah."

"Why?"

"Strangers everywhere would follow you around just so they could sniff you."

"I know Herb would," Lisa told her. "He ate three pieces at Aunt Nancy's brunch."

"Is it made with puff pastry dough?" Hannah asked.

"Yes, and I like it a lot better than the raspberry Danish you can buy in the bakery aisle at the store. Those taste like sweet rolls with raspberry jam on the top."

Hannah frowned. "The puff pastry could be a problem. I read through a recipe for that once, and it took hours to make. You had to mix it up and roll it out, put chunks of butter on the top, fold it up, and refrigerate it for a while, before you rolled it out again. I don't remember how many times you had to do that, but it was a lot. The recipe said that all the buttering and rolling was what made the dough tender and flaky."

"We don't have to make the dough from scratch," Lisa told her. "I used the frozen kind this morning. Aunt Nancy said she made puff pastry from scratch once, and the frozen dough is just as good."

"How about the raspberries?" Michelle asked her. "It's really hard to find a source for fresh raspberries in November."

"You can use either frozen or fresh. I used frozen and so did Aunt Nancy. She told me she uses fresh berries when she can get them, but frozen work just fine."

"Don't tease us by talking about it, Lisa," Michelle told her. "Cut the Danish and give us a piece. I've been dying to taste it ever since you took it out of the oven. The way I feel right now, I could eat the whole thing, all by myself."

Both Hannah and Michelle watched eagerly as Lisa placed the large Raspberry Danish on the stainless steel surface of the work table and picked up a knife to cut it. "Who wants the end piece?" she asked.

"I do!" Hannah said a split second before Michelle spoke.

"But so do I!" Michelle looked disappointed.

"Relax," Lisa told them. "Both of you can have an end piece. And I bet I know why you both wanted end pieces. You think there's more raspberry filling on the ends."

"Isn't there?" Hannah asked.

"No, but it looks like it. The raspberry filling is the same in every piece."

Once Lisa had cut the large pastry into pieces, she gave one end piece to Hannah and the other to Michelle. She took a middle piece, and there was silence for several moments as the three women sipped coffee and enjoyed their breakfast treat.

"What do you think?" Lisa asked when only a bite or two of her piece was left.

"I think I want another piece!" Hannah told her, and Michelle nodded agreement.

"So do I," Lisa admitted, getting more for all of them.

"I think our customers will want a second piece once they taste the first," Michelle said quickly. "Hannah and I have to test that theory."

Hannah looked thoughtful. "I wonder if there's a way we could make them individually."

"Good idea!" Lisa said. "Aunt Nancy and I will experiment. And we'll have a taste test to see if the individual Danish are as good as the large ones. Dad just loves Raspberry Danish and so does Marge. And Aunt Nancy's friend Heiti is crazy about her Danish."

"Check on the time it takes to make the individual Danish as compared to the large ones," Hannah told her. "The individual ones might not be cost effective."

"Good point," Lisa responded. "I didn't even think of that. I'll know after next weekend. Herb and I are having everyone over for Sunday brunch, and I'll tell you on Monday morning."

"One more piece, Lisa?" Michelle begged. "It was so good!"

Hannah stared at her youngest sister in awe. Michelle loved sweets and she ate cookies and other sweet treats whenever she wanted. If the world were fair, Michelle would weigh three hundred pounds by now. But her youngest sister somehow kept her perfect figure. Perhaps if she'd gone to the gym every day and worked out for an hour or so, or jogged miles in the morning, Hannah could understand it. But Michelle only went to the gym when she wanted to go, and Hannah had never seen her jog. Hannah had asked Doc Knight about it once, and he'd told her that the only explanation for Michelle and Andrea's failure to gain weight had to do with body chemistry, an active metabolism, and luck of the draw. He'd also said that no doctors he knew could really explain it and perhaps it was simply hereditary. Hannah figured that whatever it was, she didn't have it. It seemed as if she could simply walk by the bakers rack, glance at the cookies, or pies, or cakes cooling on the shelves, and she would gain weight. There were times when life just wasn't fair and there wasn't anything she could do about it.

RASPBERRY DANISH

DO NOT preheat your oven yet. You must do some preparation first.

Hannah's 1st Note: Frozen puff pastry dough is good for all sorts of things. When you buy it for this recipe, buy 2 packages. You'll only use one package in this recipe, but keep that second package in your freezer for later. Thaw it when you want to dress up leftovers by putting them inside little puff pastry packets and baking them, or make some turnovers from fresh fruit. Puff pastry can also be used for appetizers.

The Pastry:

One 17.5-ounce package frozen puff pastry dough ***(I used Pepperidge Farm, which contains 2 sheets of puff pastry)***
1 large egg
1 Tablespoon water ***(right out of the tap is fine)***
White ***(granulated)*** sugar to sprinkle on top

The Raspberry Sauce:

¾ cup fresh raspberries ***(you can also use frozen, but you'll have to thaw them and dry them with paper towels so they won't have an excess of juice)***
2 Tablespoons water ***(right out of the tap is fine)***
¼ teaspoon ground cardamom ***(if you don't have it, use cinnamon)***
1 and ½ Tablespoons cornstarch
½ cup white ***(granulated)*** sugar

The Cream Cheese Filling:

8-ounce package brick cream cheese, softened to room temperature ***(I used Philadelphia)***
⅓ cup white ***(granulated)*** sugar
¼ teaspoon vanilla extract

The Drizzle Frosting:

1 and ¼ cups powdered ***(confectioners)*** sugar ***(pack it down in the cup when you measure it)***
¼ cup whipping cream ***(that's heavy cream, not Half & Half)***
1 teaspoon vanilla extract
⅛ teaspoon salt

Thaw both sheets of puff pastry dough according to package directions. Do this on a floured surface ***(I used a bread board)***. To prepare the surface, sprinkle on a little flour and spread it around with your impeccably clean palms.

While your puff pastry sheets are thawing, make the raspberry sauce.

In a medium-size saucepan, combine the raspberries with the water.

In a small bowl, combine the cardamom, cornstarch, and sugar. Stir with a fork until they are thoroughly mixed.

Sprinkle the contents of the bowl on top of the raspberries and water in the saucepan. Stir everything together until all the ingredients are well mixed.

Cook the contents on the stovetop at MEDIUM HIGH heat, stirring constantly with a wooden spoon until the mixture reaches a full boil. Continue to stir for 2 minutes. Then pull the saucepan over to a cold burner, turn off the burner you used, and let the raspberry sauce cool to room temperature.

While your raspberry sauce is cooling, make the cream cheese filling.

In a microwave-safe bowl, combine the softened cream cheese with the sugar and the vanilla extract. Beat the mixture until it is smooth and creamy. Cover the bowl with plastic wrap and leave it on the counter.

Hannah's 2nd Note: If your forgot to soften your cream cheese, you can do it by unwrapping the cream cheese, placing it in a microwave-safe bowl and nuking it for 10 seconds or so in the microwave.

Hannah's 3rd Note: You will not be making the Drizzle Frosting yet. You will do this after your Raspberry Danish are baked and cooling on racks.

Preheat your oven to 375 degrees F., rack in the middle position.

While your oven is preheating, prepare 2 baking sheets by lining them with parchment paper.

Check your sheet of puff pastry to see if it is thawed. If it is, it's time to prepare it to receive its yummy contents.

Unfold one sheet of puff pastry on your floured board. Sprinkle a little flour on a rolling pin and roll your puff pastry out to a twelve-inch square.

Hannah's 4th Note: I use a ruler to make sure I have a 12-inch square when I'm through.

Use a sharp knife to make one horizontal cut through the middle of the square and one vertical cut through the middle of the square. This will divide it into 4 equal ***(or nearly equal)*** pieces.

Break the egg into a cup. Add 1 Tablespoon of water and whisk it up. This will be your egg wash.

Transfer one of your cut squares of puff pastry to your prepared cookie sheet.

Use a pastry brush to brush the inside edges of the square with the egg wash. This will make the edges stick together when you fold the dough over the cream cheese and raspberry sauce.

Measure out ¼ cup of the cream cheese filling and place it in the center of the square.

Spread the cream cheese over the square evenly to within ½ inch of the edges.

Spread 2 Tablespoons of the raspberry sauce over the cream cheese.

Pick up one corner of the square and pull it over the filling to cover just a little over half of the filling.

Then pick up the opposite corner and pull that over to overlap the first corner.

Since the egg wash you used on the square of puff pastry dough acts as a glue, that second corner should stick to the first corner. If it doesn't, simply use a little more of the egg wash to stick the two overlapping corners together.

Hannah's 5th Note: This sounds difficult, but it's not. You'll catch on fast once you complete the first one. It takes much longer to explain than it does to actually do it.

When you've completed the first of the 4 squares, cut your second sheet of puff pastry and repeat the process to complete those.

Once you have all 8 Raspberry Danish on the cookie sheets, brush the top of the pastry with more egg wash and sprinkle on a little granulated sugar.

Bake your Raspberry Danish at 375 degrees F., for 25 to 30 minutes, or until they're golden brown on top.

Remove the cookie sheet from the oven to a wire rack and let the pastries cool for 10 minutes. While

your Raspberry Danish are cooling, make the Frosting Drizzle.

Place the powdered sugar in a small bowl and mix it with the cream, vanilla extract, and salt. Continue to mix until it's smooth and thoroughly combined.

Use your favorite method to drizzle frosting over the tops of your Raspberry Danish. A pastry bag ***(or a plastic bag with one of the corners snipped off)*** works well for this.

Hannah's 6th Note: If you don't want to use a pastry bag to do this, simply mix in a little more cream so that the frosting will drizzle off the tip of a spoon held over the pastries.

When all the Raspberry Danish have been decorated with the frosting drizzle, pull the parchment paper and the Raspberry Danish off the cookie sheet and back onto the same wire rack.

These pastries are delicious eaten while slightly warm. They're also good cold.

If any of your Raspberry Danish are left over ***(I don't think this will happen!),*** wrap them loosely in wax paper and keep them in a cool place.

Aunt Nancy's Note: I've made these pastries with many other fruits including strawberries, blackberries, blueberries, peaches, pears, and apricots. If you use large pieces of fruit, puree them and use ½ cup of the puree to make the sauce.

Lisa's Note: I was in a hurry one day and I used seedless raspberry jam instead of making the sauce. I took off the lid and heated it a little in the microwave, just enough so that I could spread it on top of the cream cheese filling. Since pineapple is Herb's favorite fruit, I'm going to try it with pineapple jam next, if Florence can order it at the Red Owl. I'm pretty sure that Smucker's makes it.

Chapter Two

It was ten minutes past eleven when Hannah took the last pan of Cherry Chocolate Bar Cookies out of the oven. She'd just slipped the cookie sheet onto the bakers rack when there was a knock at the back kitchen door. The first knock was followed by two more slightly louder knocks in quick succession.

"Mother?" Michelle asked.

"Mother," Hannah agreed. "You're getting better at recognizing knocks, Michelle. I'll pour the coffee and cut a pan of bar cookies. You can answer the door and let Mother in."

"Any news?" Delores called out to Hannah as she hung her coat on a hook by the door and headed for her favorite stool at the work station.

"Not a word," Hannah replied, knowing exactly what Delores meant. She wanted to know if Hannah had heard from Ross. She asked the same question every time she came in the door at The Cookie Jar or called Hannah on the phone.

"Thank you, dear," Delores said as Michelle served her coffee. Then she noticed what Hannah was doing and asked, "What are you cutting, Hannah? Whatever it is, it smells like chocolate and . . . cherries?"

Michelle began to laugh. "You have a great nose, Mother. We just finished baking six batches of Cherry Chocolate Bar Cookies."

"Thank you, dear. No one's ever called my nose *great* before." She turned to Hannah again. "If those chocolate cherry creations of yours are cool enough to cut, does that make them cool enough to sample?"

"Of course." Hannah finished transferring the bars she'd cut to a serving plate and carried them to the stainless steel work island. "Here you go, Mother. Tell us if you like them."

Delores picked up one of the bar cookies, took a bite, and began to smile. "Heavenly! Ten stars out of ten, dear."

"Thanks, Mother," Hannah said, taking the stool across from her mother. She noticed that Delores was wearing full makeup and one of the designer suits she'd purchased from Claire Rodgers Knudson at *Beau Monde Fashions*. Her dark hair was stylishly arranged, and the ruby ring on her finger mirrored the color of her suit. Although Delores always looked fashionable, today she was dressed to the teeth. This caused Hannah to assume that her mother was going somewhere important.

"Are you headed for somewhere special, Mother?" Michelle asked, just as if she were reading Hannah's mind.

"Yes. I have a meeting with the Rainbow Ladies at the hospital." Delores named the group of volunteers she'd founded over a year ago.

"Is it a special occasion?" Hannah asked. Usually, when Delores met with the Rainbow Ladies, she wore black slacks and one of the brightly colored jackets the ladies wore to set them apart from the rest of the hospital staff.

"Yes, but it has nothing to do with the Rainbow Ladies. I'm spending the afternoon with Doc at the hospital and then we're going out to dinner. It's our anniversary."

Hannah and Michelle exchanged puzzled glances, and

Hannah was the first to speak. "But, Mother . . . this is November and you got married in September. Are you celebrating an anniversary every month?"

"What a lovely thought!" Delores smiled at her eldest daughter. "But no, dear. This is a real anniversary. Doc first asked me to marry him in November."

"And you married him nine months later?" Michelle asked.

"No, dear. We got married almost two years later. I wasn't sure I wanted to get married again, but Doc convinced me."

"And you're glad he did," Hannah stated the obvious.

"I certainly am!" Delores reached out for another bar cookie. "Sally's making a special anniversary dinner for us tonight at the Lake Eden Inn. We're having duck with cranberry sauce and a chocolate soufflé for dessert. That's what we had the night that Doc first proposed to me."

Michelle looked confused. "But . . . I thought you didn't like duck."

"I don't, but Doc does and it's a tradition. We have it every year on the anniversary of the night he proposed to me."

"And you eat it?" Michelle followed up on her former question.

"Of course. That first night, I was so shocked at Doc's proposal, I ate everything on my plate without even tasting it. And now that we do this every year, I think I might actually learn to like it."

Hannah couldn't help bursting into laughter and neither could Michelle. Delores stared at them in confusion for a moment, and then she joined in the laughter. They were still laughing when there was a knock on the back door.

"I'll get it," Michelle said as she got up to answer it. A moment later, she ushered her friend P.K. into the kitchen and gestured to a stool next to Delores at the work station.

"Hello, P.K.," Delores greeted Ross's assistant at KCOW Television. "I was going to call you this morning to thank you for calling Hannah every day to let her know if Ross had called you. And thank you, too, for doing those commercials for Michelle's plays."

P.K. smiled at her. "Please don't let anyone at the station hear you call them *commercials*, Delores."

"But why?"

"Because I'd have to charge for them if they were commercials."

Delores looked confused. "But what are they then?"

"They're *public service announcements*."

Delores laughed. "I see. And the station doesn't charge for those?"

"Of course not. We produce and air them as a community service."

P.K. smiled and Hannah was struck by how much he'd changed since he had run footage of the Hartland Flour baking contest for her. Then, he'd been the long-haired, rebel-type night tech guy from KCOW-TV. Now he was older, more mature, and very capable as Ross's assistant videographer.

"I thought you'd be at work by now, P.K.," Delores said.

"I should be, but I had to take my car in to Cyril's garage. Turns out it needs a new alternator." He turned to Hannah and Michelle. "I was wondering if somebody here could give me a ride to the station."

Michelle locked eyes with Hannah, and Hannah knew exactly what her youngest sister was asking. The question Michelle was asking was, *Is it okay if I let P.K. use Ross's car?* Hannah gave a nod and Michelle smiled.

"You can use Ross's car," Michelle told him. "I found the keys this morning and it's parked in back of Claire's dress shop. Keep it until your car is ready."

"Thanks, Mickie. But how are you going to get to work?"

"I'll ride in with Hannah. I've been riding with her all along, and another couple of mornings without a car won't kill me."

"Thanks!" P.K. said, as Michelle drew the keys from her sweater pocket and handed them to him. "I promise I'll be really careful with it, and it'll only be for two days. Cyril said my car will be ready the day after tomorrow."

When P.K. started to rise to his feet, Hannah waved him back down. "Have a couple of bar cookies before you leave. And warm yourself up with coffee. It's cold outside today."

"You have to stay for at least ten minutes," Michelle told him. "Then I have to go over to Jordan High for rehearsal and you can give me a lift."

"Sure thing." P.K. reached for a bar cookie and took a huge bite. "These are good," he said. "Are they new?"

Hannah nodded. "We're going to call them Cherry Chocolate Bar Cookies. And they're not all that's new. Lisa's Aunt Nancy gave us the recipe for Raspberry Danish this morning."

"We're thinking about serving it here if we can bake individual portions," Hannah added. "I'll give you one of the large Danish to take home for breakfast tomorrow."

P.K. smiled in appreciation. "If it's as good as these Cherry Chocolate Bar Cookies, it might not last until tomorrow."

"I don't suppose you have . . ." Delores started to speak.

"Don't worry, Mother," Michelle interrupted what she knew would be a request from their mother. "I know exactly what you're going to say. Hannah and I remembered that Doc loves Raspberry Danish so we saved one for you."

CHERRY CHOCOLATE BAR COOKIES

Preheat oven to 350 degrees F., rack in the middle position.

1 cup white ***(granulated)*** sugar
¾ cup salted butter ***(1 and ½ sticks, 6 ounces),*** softened
1 large egg
½ teaspoon vanilla extract
2 cups all-purpose flour ***(pack it down in the cup when you measure it)***
¼ teaspoon baking powder
½ cup chopped walnuts ***(measure AFTER chopping)***
1 jar ***(12 to 15 ounces)*** cherry preserves ***(that's jam with cherries in it)***
2 cups flaked coconut, chopped into smaller pieces
2 cups ***(12-ounce package by weight)*** semi-sweet chocolate chips

Hannah's 1st Note: If all you can find in your store is 11-ounce packages of chips, that's close enough.

Hannah's 2nd Note: You can mix up these bar cookies by hand with a wooden spoon in a large bowl, or with an electric mixer. Either way will work just fine.

Prepare a 9-inch by 13-inch cake pan by spraying it with Pam or another nonstick cooking spray. Alternatively, you can line the cake pan with heavy-duty foil and spray that.

Place the white sugar in the bowl of an electric mixer. Add the softened butter and mix until light and creamy.

Beat in the egg, and the vanilla extract. Continue to mix until everything is well blended.

In another bowl, combine the all-purpose flour and the baking powder. Mix until well blended.

Hannah's 3rd Note: You can mix the flour and the baking powder with a fork.

Gradually add this flour mixture to the sugar and butter mixture. Beat until everything is well combined.

Mix in the ½ cup of chopped walnuts. Continue to mix until they are well incorporated.

Press ¾ of the dough into your prepared cake pan.

Hannah's 4th Note: You can set aside one cup of the mixture and press the rest in the cake pan. That's close enough.

Flatten the mixture in the cake pan with a metal spatula or with the palms of your impeccably clean hands.

Open the jar of cherry preserves. Take off the lid and place the glass jar in the microwave.

Heat the jar on HIGH for 20 seconds. Let it cool in the microwave for 1 minute.

Spread the cherry preserves evenly over the mixture in the cake pan. Smooth it out with a rubber spatula.

If you haven't already chopped your coconut flakes into smaller pieces, do it now. ***(If you have a food processor, use the steel blade to chop your coconut.)***

Sprinkle the chopped coconut over the cherry preserves as evenly as you can.

Sprinkle the chocolate chips over the top of the coconut flakes.

Crumble remaining dough mixture over the top of the chips.

Press down lightly with your impeccably clean palms.

Bake at 350 degrees for approximately 30 to 35 minutes or until the top is golden brown.

Remove the Cherry Chocolate Bar Cookies from the oven and place the pan on a wire rack.

Cool completely and then cut into brownie-sized bars.

Serve with plenty of strong coffee or tall glasses of cold milk.

Yield: Approximately 3 dozen delicious cookie bars.

Hannah's 5th Note: These are Mother's favorite cookie bars and our customers at The Cookie Jar loved them so much, they've become a permanent part of our cookie menu.

Hannah's 6th Note: Sometimes, just to please my chocoholic mother, I frost these cookie bars before I cut them into pieces. I usually use my Neverfail Fudge Frosting recipe because it's so quick and easy.

The Neverfail Fudge Frosting recipe follows:

NEVERFAIL FUDGE FROSTING

½ cup ***(1 stick, 4 ounces, ¼ pound)*** salted butter
1 cup white ***(granulated)*** sugar
⅓ cup heavy cream ***(that's whipping cream)***
½ cup semi-sweet chocolate chips
1 teaspoon vanilla extract

Place the butter, sugar, and cream into a medium-size saucepan on the stovetop.

Turn the burner to MEDIUM-HIGH heat and bring the mixture to a boil, stirring constantly.

Continue to stir and turn the heat down to MEDIUM. Stir for 2 minutes.

Add the half-cup of chocolate chips. Stir them in, and then move the saucepan to a cold burner. Don't forget to turn off the heat on the original burner!

Let the mixture cool, without stirring, for one minute and then stir in the vanilla extract.

Pour the frosting on the top of the cake pan and spread it out quickly with a heat-resistant rubber spatula.

Cool the frosting completely before you cut and serve. If you wish, you can place the pan in the refrigerator, uncovered, until the frosting is cool and has "set".

Chapter Three

When Michelle came in the back kitchen door at three in the afternoon with cheeks rosy from the cold, Hannah rushed to get her a cup of hot coffee. "I thought you were going to call me to pick you up."

"I was, but I decided to walk."

"You're shivering," Hannah said, turning to glance at the indoor-outdoor thermometer mounted on the kitchen window as she carried the mug of coffee to her sister. "It's twenty-two degrees out there, and that doesn't take the wind chill factor into account."

"I knew that it was cold, but it felt wonderful at first. The cold air was nice and bracing, and I enjoyed it for almost a block. Then I started to shiver and the cold air began to hurt my throat."

"Did you tie your scarf around your face and breathe through that?"

"Yes. And I had a real problem doing it with my mittens on. I had to take them off to tie on my scarf."

"Why didn't you walk back to the school and call me?"

"Because I was halfway here. I figured I'd be just as cold when I arrived back at the school as I'd be when I got here.

Besides, the wind was at my back when I walked here. If I'd turned around, it would have been blowing in my face."

Hannah gave a little laugh. "I can't argue with your logic. You're absolutely right, but if it's this cold tomorrow, don't do it again. I'll be happy to drive you to the school for rehearsal and pick you up when you're ready to come back here."

"But you're really busy here during the day."

"True, but if I'm busy, Marge, or Aunt Nancy, or Lisa will come to get you. We can always spare one of us, and I don't want you walking in weather like this and getting sick."

"Doc says there's no medical basis for that. You can't catch a cold from the cold."

"I know, but I still don't want you walking. Just call, okay?"

"Okay. If it stays this cold, I'll take you up on that. But it's really not all that cold. It's just that the wind cuts right through you."

"The wind robs your body of heat. That's what the wind chill factor is all about. It would be interesting to know how long it would take a cup of water to freeze on the top of my truck."

Michelle cupped her hands a little tighter around her coffee mug. "You can try it if you want to. I'm not going out there again . . . at least not until it's time to go home. And then I'm going to sprint for your cookie truck."

There was one knock on the back door, but before either one of them could get up to answer it, the door opened and Norman rushed in. "Sorry, girls. I would have waited for you to answer the door, but I was so cold, I just wanted to get inside where it was warm."

"You walked here?" Michelle asked him.

Norman nodded. "I didn't think it was *this* cold. Maybe I'm just not acclimated to winter weather yet, but it feels like it's below freezing out there."

"It is," Hannah told him. "I just looked at the thermometer and it's twenty-two degrees."

"I thought so!"

"And it feels like it's even colder with the wind chill," Michelle added. "I'll get you a hot cup of coffee."

"And I'll take your coat," Hannah said. "You'll warm up faster without it." She waited until Norman had handed it to her. "Now sit down, cup your hands around that mug of hot coffee Michelle just poured for you, and I'll get a couple of cookies."

The words were no sooner out of her mouth than there was another blast of cold air as the back door opened and Mike came in. "Brrrr!" he said, closing the door behind him. "Winter's here, that's for sure. I'm switching to my parka tomorrow."

Hannah glanced at his uniform jacket. It was wool, but it certainly wasn't as warm as a parka would be. "I think that's a very good idea. You look chilled to the bone."

"I am and I only walked in from the parking lot." He turned to see Norman sitting at the work station and walked over to take the stool next to him. "That wind is brutal."

"Tell me about it. I walked here from the clinic."

"Well, I'll give you a ride back when I leave. It's too cold to walk today."

Hannah placed a plate of cookies in front of the two men. She sat down across from them and gave Mike a questioning look. Her questioning look meant, *Did you find out anything about Ross?* Mike gave a slight shake of his head and Hannah knew that meant, *Nothing yet, but I'll find him eventually*. The words were unspoken, but both of them knew what the other meant. It was the unspoken ritual they'd gone through ever since Ross had left and Mike had told Hannah that he'd use every means at his disposal to find her new husband. Hannah knew that Mike was still searching and he wouldn't stop until he'd found out why Ross had left her and where he'd gone.

"These cookies are great, Hannah," Norman said as he finished his first one and reached over for another. "What do you call them?"

"Marge brought in a recipe for Light Fandango Cookies, but that wasn't very descriptive. I asked her if we could change the name and we're calling them Pineapple Crunch Cookies."

"I think they're some of your best," Mike commented, proving that he was sincere by reaching for another cookie. He had just taken a bite when his cell phone began to vibrate against the metal surface of the work station. "I have to check this," he said, grabbing the phone and glancing at the display.

Hannah watched as Mike began to frown. His frown deepened as he finished reading the text. "What is it?" she asked him.

"Bad accident out on the highway. Two fatalities, four injuries. They're calling for backup, and I have to get out there right away." Mike turned to Norman. "Take the rest of your coffee with you. I'll drop you off on my way to the highway."

Hannah was on her feet immediately. She grabbed two takeout bags from the stack on the counter and dumped half of the remaining cookies in each bag. "Take these with you."

"Thanks, Hannah," Mike said, grabbing his bag of cookies. "Be careful when you drive home tonight. The roads are icing over."

"I will be," Hannah promised.

"Better yet, let me take you home," Norman offered. "I

just got new snow tires on my car and the back tires on your truck look like they need to be replaced. The tread's worn down to practically nothing."

Hannah shook her head. "Thanks, but we'll be okay. I'm a very careful driver."

"Take these with you," Michelle said arriving at the work station with another, even larger bag. I filled a bunch of coffee's to go and I threw in some sugar and creamers. You can give them out at the scene."

"You guys are great," Norman said, as Michelle poured the rest of his coffee into a takeout cup, clamped on the lid, and handed it to him.

Less than a minute later, the back kitchen door closed behind the two men. Michelle went to make another pot of coffee, and Hannah sat back down on the stool she'd so quickly vacated. "It was nice of Norman to offer to drive us home, and now I'm wondering if I should have said yes."

"It's not too late," Michelle pointed out, returning to her own stool. "You can always call him at the clinic."

"I know. It's just that Norman is going to want to take us out for something to eat and . . . well . . ."

"You want to be alone."

"Yes. I know I'll be tired and I don't think I'll have the energy to be good company, if you know what I mean."

"I know exactly what you mean. I'm like that during finals week. I don't want to see anybody, including Lonnie. I just want to relax and get a good night's sleep. Let's stop at the Corner Tavern for a hamburger on our way home. It's tiring to drive in blowing snow, especially if it comes straight at you. If we stop to eat, we'll have a break halfway home."

"That sounds good. We'll do that, Michelle."

"Except we'll have to leave here at five-thirty. We need to be back at the condo by seven-thirty."

"You have a date with Lonnie?" Hannah guessed.

"No. P.K. filmed another advertisement for the Thanksgiving play. He said that since it's for the Lake Eden Players, the big boss said they'd run it tonight. It's going to air between eight and eight-thirty."

"He just filmed it today and they're running it tonight?"

"Yes. He was going to go straight back to the station, edit it, and turn it in. I don't know if I should believe him, but he said that it was no trouble at all."

Hannah took a sip of her rapidly cooling coffee. She didn't really want it, but she wanted to be sure that what she was about to say would be received in the right way.

"What?" Michelle asked, noticing the thoughtful expression on Hannah's face.

"Don't take this the wrong way, Michelle, but I wonder if P.K. is beginning to develop . . . *feelings* for you."

Michelle looked surprised. "You mean you think that he might be falling in love with me?"

"That's exactly what I mean. I just wasn't sure how to say it. It's fine if you feel the same way about him, but it could become a problem if you don't."

"I don't, and if you're right, it might become a problem. P.K.'s a friend, but that's it." Michelle stopped speaking and began to look worried. "You don't think I'm *using* P.K., do you? Because of the commercials he does for the plays I'm directing?"

"No, I don't. You wouldn't do that, Michelle. I'm just hoping that P.K. doesn't perceive your interest in him as something more than it is."

"I see what you mean. I'll have to be very careful that I don't give him any encouragement on the romance front. It just never occurred to me that he might be developing those kinds of feelings for me."

Hannah gave a little shrug. "I could be wrong. I just thought I sensed something. And as your big sister, I wanted to warn you."

"Thanks. Now that I think about it, you could be right, Hannah. Just last week, P.K. told me that he was engaged to the girl he'd been dating since high school, but they'd broken up. I asked him why, but he said it was still painful and he didn't really want to talk about it."

"Okay." Hannah got up and gave her sister a little hug. "It's like Great-Grandma Elsa used to say, *Forewarned is forearmed*. Let's forget about it for now and concentrate on what we're going to bake next. We've got a lot of cookies to make and a lot of bowls of dough to mix up before we can drive out to get those burgers."

"And fries."

"And onion rings. And stop it right now, Michelle. I'm getting hungry and we still have a couple more hours to go!"

"Just what I wanted!" Hannah said, biting into her juicy, mustard-, mayo-, and pickle-laden burger.

"Oh yes!" Michelle said with a happy sigh as she dipped a crispy French fry into the side of blue cheese dressing they'd ordered. "I'm really glad we stopped here, Hannah, and it's not just because of the food. It was really nasty out there."

"I know. The snow was blowing so hard, it was almost impossible to see the side of the road. Let's hope it lets up a little while we're eating."

"Here are some complimentary onion rings," their waitress announced, placing a paper-lined basket on the table between them. "They just came out of the fryer. I haven't seen your mother at the Red Velvet Lounge lately, Hannah."

"Maybe we'll all come in for lunch on Saturday," Hannah said, smiling up at the waitress, who also worked at the restaurant in Delores and Doc's condo building. "Thanks for the onion rings, Georgina."

"Don't thank me. Thank the fry cook. He put up that order by mistake and I nabbed it for you two. How's Ross doing, Hannah? I heard that KCOW-TV sent him out to do a special program. Where is he, anyway?"

"The last time he called, he was in New York," Michelle jumped in before Hannah was forced to tell the lie that their whole family had devised. She turned to Hannah. "You didn't hear from him today, did you, Hannah?"

"Not yet," Hannah responded truthfully.

"Well, when you talk to him, tell him we're all really curious about that program he's doing."

Hannah smiled. This she could handle. "I'll do that, Georgina."

"Now eat up those onion rings before they get cold." Georgina turned to face Michelle. "I heard you're coming along great with the Thanksgiving play. Everybody says it's going to be wonderful."

"Thanks for telling me, Georgina. You got tickets, didn't you?"

Hannah was secretly amused. She'd heard Michelle ask The Cookie Jar customers the very same question.

"I got mine the first day they went on sale."

"They're going to run an ad for the play on KCOW tonight," Michelle told her. "P.K. just filmed it today."

"What time?"

"Between eight and eight-thirty."

Georgina looked disappointed. "I'm on until ten tonight."

"Maybe they'll put it on in the bar and you can sneak away to see it," Hannah suggested.

"I'll tell the bartender about it," Georgina promised. "And I'll call my sister. She can always record it for me."

She turned to look at another table. "I'd better go. They probably want coffee at table sixteen. Bye, girls."

They were both hungry, and it didn't take long for Hannah and Michelle to finish their meal. Georgina brought them coffee and the check, and Hannah gave her a generous tip. Once they'd finished their coffee, Hannah glanced at her watch. "We'd better go. If it's still windy out there, it might take a while to get home."

"Good idea," Michelle agreed, standing up and slinging her purse over her shoulder. "Hurry up, Hannah. I'm going up to the register to pick up coffee to go for us. Your truck is going to be cold."

In less than five minutes, they were in Hannah's cookie truck, pulling out of the parking lot. The wind was still blowing, but visibility was much better than it had been when they'd driven in.

"What smells so good?" Michelle asked, after they'd turned on the access road to the highway.

"It's probably the Pineapple Crunch Cookies. I packed up the ones that were left so that we could take them home."

"Brilliant," Michelle complimented her. "I'll make a pot of coffee once we get to the condo, and we can eat cookies and drink coffee while we're waiting for P.K.'s commercial to air. There's only one problem with that."

"What's that?" Hannah asked her.

"I want a cookie right now," Michelle said, leaning over the back of her seat to see if she could reach the cookies that Hannah had packed for them.

Hannah just smiled, deciding not to voice the thought that was running through her mind. *You just ate two double double cheeseburgers with bacon, a side of French fries, a side of coleslaw, and most of the onion rings that Georgina gave us. And now you're rummaging around in the back of the truck for cookies?*

PINEAPPLE CRUNCH COOKIES (LIGHT FANDANGO COOKIES)

Preheat oven to 350 degrees F., rack in the middle position.

1 can ***(8 ounces by weight)*** crushed pineapple ***(I used Dole)***
1 cup salted butter ***(2 sticks, 8 ounces, ½ pound)***
1 cup white ***(granulated)*** sugar
1 cup brown sugar ***(pack it down in the cup when you measure it)***
2 teaspoons baking soda
1 teaspoon salt
2 teaspoons vanilla extract
2 large beaten eggs ***(you can just beat them up in a cup with a fork)***
2 and ½ cups all-purpose flour ***(not sifted – pack it down in the measuring cup)***
2 cups corn flakes ***(I used Kellogg's)***
1 to 2 cups white chocolate ***(or vanilla)*** chips

Open the can of crushed pineapple and drain it in a strainer. Save the juice if someone in your house likes pineapple juice.

Place the butter in a microwave-safe bowl or measuring cup. Heat it on HIGH in the microwave for 1 minute. Let it sit in the microwave for an additional minute and check to see if it's melted. If it's not, heat it in 20-second increments until it is.

Place the white sugar in a large mixing bowl.

Add the brown sugar and mix both sugars together until they are a uniform color.

Pour the melted butter on top of the sugar. Mix it in thoroughly.

Sprinkle in the baking soda, salt, and vanilla extract. Mix until everything is thoroughly combined.

Feel the mixing bowl to make sure it's not so hot it could cook the eggs. If it's still hot, let it cool for a few minutes.

Mix in the beaten eggs. Continue mixing until everything is smooth and combined.

Add in the flour in half-cup increments, mixing it in thoroughly after each increment.

Pat the crushed pineapple with a paper towel and add it to your mixing bowl. Beat until it's thoroughly mixed in.

Measure out the corn flakes and put them in a sealable plastic bag. Seal up the bag and crush the corn flakes with your hands, by squeezing the bag, or by rolling it with a rolling pin. Continue to crush until the corn flakes are the size of crushed gravel.

Add the crushed corn flakes to your bowl and mix until they are well combined.

Take the bowl out of the mixer, if you used one, and get ready to add the white chocolate or vanilla chips by hand.

Add the 1 to 2 cups of chips, mixing in enough to satisfy your family's sweet tooth.

Let the dough sit on the counter for a minute or two to rest. ***(It doesn't really need to rest, but you need time to prepare your cookie sheets.)***

Spray your cookie sheets with Pam or another nonstick cooking spray, or line them with parchment paper. ***(I prefer parchment paper so that I can simply pull the paper off on a wire rack, cookies and all, when they're baked.)***

Form the cookie dough into walnut-sized balls with your fingers and place them on your prepared cookie sheets, 12 to a standard-size sheet.

Hannah's Note: I baked a test cookie first. If it spreads out too much in the oven, either chill the dough in the refrigerator before baking, or turn the dough out on a floured board and knead in approximately ⅓ cup more flour.

Press the dough balls down just a bit with your impeccably clean hand so that they won't roll off on the way to the oven.

Bake your Pineapple Crunch Cookies at 350 degrees F. for 10 to 12 minutes or until they are golden brown.

Remove the cookie sheets from the oven and place them on cold stove burners or wire racks.

Let your cookies cool on the cookie sheets for 2 minutes. ***(If you remove them from the cookie sheets right after they come out of the oven, they may bend and/or break.)***

Use a metal spatula to remove the cookies to a wire rack. ***(The rack is important—it makes them crisp.)***

Yield: approximately 6 to 8 dozen, depending on cookie size.

Chapter Four

Michelle was smiling as she turned to Hannah. They were sitting in front of the giant-screen television, and they'd just watched the commercial that P.K. had made for the Thanksgiving play. "I loved it! How about you?"

"P.K. did a super job. Everyone who saw it is going to come to the play."

"Irma's keeping track of advance ticket sales. I'll check in with her to see if there's a jump in sales tomorrow. The cast really looked good, didn't they?"

"The cast looked really great," Hannah agreed. "I loved those costumes."

"I'm really glad we took the time to do makeup and get into our costumes." Michelle gave a little smile. "At first, I was upset when P.K. suggested it because it takes so much time, but he was right. It looks so much better than seeing the characters in their everyday clothes."

Hannah was about to go to the kitchen to get more coffee when Michelle's cell phone rang. "That's probably P.K. to see if you liked his commercial," she speculated.

"I bet you're right," Michelle said, reaching out for her cell phone. "I'm going to record it to see if he liked his commercial." She answered the call, and almost immediately began to frown.

"What is it?" Hannah asked quickly as a distressed expression crossed Michelle's face.

"It's P.K. There's something wrong, Hannah! Look!"

Hannah glanced at the display and realized that she was watching a video of P.K. driving Ross's car.

"It's real time," Michelle said quickly. "He's got his phone in the dashboard holder Ross has in his car."

"Mic . . . kie," P.K. said, giving a lopsided smile. "How . . . you, girl?"

"He sounds drunk!" Michelle exclaimed.

"Or drugged. Can you ask him if he's okay?"

"Are you okay, P.K.?" Michelle asked.

"Mic . . . kie." P.K. reached up to rub his face. "Pret . . . ty Mic . . . kie. Doan feel goooood."

P.K.'s phone was positioned so that they could see his face and also the driver's side window. As the two sisters watched, the edge of the road appeared to move forward and then recede.

"Tell him to pull over!" Hannah said, grabbing Michelle's arm. "Hurry! He almost went in the ditch!"

"Pull over, P.K.!" Michelle said loudly. "You shouldn't be driving. Pull over right now!"

Hannah moved closer so that she could listen for his response, but there was no response at all. "Please, P.K.," she shouted. "Pull over!"

"It's no use," Michelle told her. "Either he's got our audio off or he's too drunk or stoned to listen to us."

"Noooo," P.K. said, and both sisters could see that his eyes looked vague and unfocused. "Thought I . . . juss hung . . . gry. Ate Rossss . . . hiz . . . desk. Can . . . dees . . . sickkk."

"Pull over!" Hannah shouted again as the car veered toward the center of the road and then lurched back toward the ditch again. "Pull over, P.K.!"

"Please pull over!" Michelle added, the panic clear in her voice.

There was no response to their pleas and Michelle shook her head. "He can't hear us, Hannah."

"You're probably right, but at least he's back on his side of the road again."

"No . . . more . . . can . . . dees," P.K. mumbled, and then his eyelids began to lower. "Got . . . ta get . . . Doc . . . hos-pit . . . uh . . ."

Both Hannah and Michelle watched in horror as the car weaved from one side of the road to the other, barely missing a county road sign. They had just given sighs of relief when the car began to drift toward the wrong side of the road again.

"Wake up, P.K.!" Michelle called out, leaning close to the phone. "Listen to me! You've got to stay awake!"

Again, there was no response from P.K. The only thing they heard was the sound of the engine growing louder and louder.

"He's stepping on the gas!" Hannah said in horror.

"I know! I can hear it! And he's . . . oh no!"

Michelle's last word was an anguished cry, and Hannah felt as if it had come from her own throat. P.K.'s eyes were closed now, but the car was going faster and faster.

The scene outside the driver's side window appeared to bounce up and down as the pine trees rushed past at break-neck speed. Then there was a loud blaring sound.

"The horn's on!" Michelle identified it. "P.K. must be blowing it for help."

Or he's wedged on the steering wheel, Hannah thought, but of course she didn't say what she was thinking.

"Look!" They watched as the bakery box with the Raspberry Danish that they'd given P.K. that morning flew past the screen as if it had suddenly grown wings.

"He's in the ditch!" Michelle gasped. "And the car's still going!"

Her horrified words were no sooner spoken than the screen on Michelle's cell phone went black.

"His phone shut off, or broke, or something!" Michelle gasped. "We have to do something, Hannah!"

Hannah thought fast. "You said you were going to record the call."

"I did!"

"Can you send that video to Mike's cell phone?"

"I . . . yes, I think so."

"Do it right now. I'll call Mike and tell him it's coming."

While Michelle figured out how to retrieve the video and send it, Hannah placed a call to Mike. Then she ducked into the kitchen to speak to him in private. Michelle was upset enough already. There was no way Hannah wanted her to overhear the conversation she was about to have with Mike.

Luckily, Mike answered on the second ring, and Hannah told him the video was coming. "It looked really bad, Mike, and I recognized a couple of landmarks. I think P.K. went off the road right before Abe Schilling's back pasture, the one where he keeps his bull in the summer. Do you know where that is?"

When Mike had assured her he knew the particular pasture she'd described, Hannah added her final sentences, the ones she hadn't wanted Michelle to overhear. "Hurry out there, Mike. There may be a chance that P.K. is still alive, but . . . I really doubt it."

Before she left the kitchen, Hannah poured the rest of the coffee into a thermos and carried it out to the living room. "Did Mike get the video?" she asked Michelle.

"Yes. He just texted me."

"Good. Now go get your parka and your boots. We're going out there."

"How? We don't know where P.K. went off the road!"

"I recognized some landmarks and I think I know where it happened. Hurry up, Michelle. And don't forget your warm scarf and mittens."

"Is that the county road sign we saw?" Michelle asked as Hannah drove down the winding road.

"I think so. And if I'm right, we only have a mile or two to go." Hannah slowed for another bend in the road. "Do you hear a siren?"

Michelle lowered her window. "Yes. I hear it, too."

"It's probably Mike."

"Or the paramedics," Michelle added. "I think I hear two sirens now."

When they rounded the next bend, they could see lights in the distance across the expanse of snow. Right after they passed an old yellow and black MINNESOTA BREEDERS ASSOCIATION sign nailed to a tree, Michelle drew in her breath sharply. "I saw that sign on the video," she said, her voice shaking slightly.

"I know." They rounded another curve, and Hannah saw more lights in the distance. "Hang on, Michelle. We're almost there."

"Doc's car," Michelle identified the car that was parked on the side of the road.

"And Mike's cruiser." Hannah pulled past it and parked behind another car that was on the shoulder of the road. "That's Doctor Bob's car. Let's go, Michelle."

As they opened their car doors, two figures materialized

through the blowing snow. At first it was impossible to identify them, but as they reached the crest of the ditch, Michelle rushed forward. "Mother?" she called out.

Hannah was right behind her sister. It was obvious that their mother must have been riding with Doc because her car wasn't there.

"Take your mother back to my car, Michelle," Doc said. "I left it running, and the heater is on. Make her take off her wet shoes and wrap her in a blanket. And stay with her until I come back, okay?"

"Of course. But . . ."

"Not now, Michelle," Doc interrupted what was certain to be a question about P.K. "Just take care of your mother for us. There's nothing you can do to help out here."

Hannah watched as her sister's face crumpled into a mask of sorrow and loss. Michelle had also caught the message behind Doc's words. She slipped an arm around Michelle's shoulders, gave her a comforting squeeze, and leaned close. "I'll take care of everything out here," she said. "You take care of Mother."

Michelle swallowed hard. And then she nodded. "I will," she promised, reaching out to take their mother's arm and leading Delores to Doc's car.

Hannah waited until Michelle and her mother had left, and then she turned to Doc. "Bad?" she asked him.

"Yes. Mike's down there now and he filled me in about the video. What do you want to know?"

"Was P.K. drunk?"

"No."

"Drugged?"

Doc gave a slight nod. "That's my guess. I'll know more after I take your mother home and get back to the hospital. They'll be here to transport him soon."

Hannah asked the question she knew Michelle would have asked. "Was P.K. in pain?"

"That's very doubtful." Doc reached out to pat her shoulder. "I'll know more later, but I'm almost certain he was already gone when he went off the road."

"Did Doctor Bob find him?"

"No. Bob delivered a calf at Karl Schilling's farm. He said it was a breech birth and Karl called him to help. Bob was just driving out when he heard a car horn. As he rounded the bend, he heard the sound of branches breaking and he knew that someone had gone in the ditch."

"So he stopped to help?"

"Of course. And that's when he saw the deer by the side of the road."

"P.K. hit a deer?"

"He sideswiped a deer as the car went into the ditch. Bob was about to climb down in the ditch when your mother and I pulled up. I told him to take care of the deer and I'd take care of anyone who was in the car."

"Is the deer dead?"

"No, just stunned. Nothing broken, no major injuries. Bob thinks it'll be up on its feet in a couple of minutes and hightailing it back into the woods."

Doc rubbed his hands together, and Hannah realized that he was cold in his dress coat and thin leather gloves. "Do you want some hot coffee, Doc? I've got a thermos in my truck."

"I can wait until I get back to the hospital, but I'll bet Mike and Lonnie could use some. If you give me the thermos, I'll take it down there to them."

"I'll take it. I've got on snow boots."

"Not on a bet, Hannah. I know the real reason you want to take that coffee down to Mike and Lonnie."

Hannah did her best to look perfectly clueless. "What do you mean?"

"You want to go down there because it'll give you a chance to pump them for information. Isn't that right?"

Hannah sighed. "You know me too well, Doc."

"That's because I delivered you. I'm the first person you ever saw. And that means I've known you all your life."

Hannah smiled at the predictable line. Doc told all three of the Swensen sisters the very same thing. "How about Mother? Will she be all right if you take her back to the penthouse and go back to the hospital?"

"She'll be fine. You underestimate your mother, Hannah. She's a lot stronger than you think she is."

"But she's had a nasty shock. Except for Doctor Bob, you and Mother were first at the scene, and it must have been . . ." Hannah paused to think of the right word. ". . . an *upsetting* sight."

"It would have been if I hadn't blocked your mother's view. Car accidents are never pretty. The human body is no match for asphalt and metal. Now go get that thermos and I'll take it down to Mike and Lonnie. Then I want you to take Michelle away before my paramedics arrive. She doesn't need to see them take P.K. away."

"But really, Doc," Hannah began to protest.

"Forget it, Hannah." Doc took her by the shoulders and turned her around. "Mike always comes over to your place after something like this happens, and you can pump him for information later."

Chapter Five

When the alarm clock began its predictable high-pitched electronic beeping at four-thirty the next morning, Hannah sat up in bed. She'd been plagued by dreams of cars skidding off roads covered in ice and crashing into fences and snowbanks. It didn't take a genius to know why her dreams had featured winter driving accidents. She gave a sorrowful sigh for P.K. and the fate that had befallen him, and then she threw back the covers and swung her feet over the side of the bed. Michelle might want to talk about P.K.'s death and she wanted to be there for her sister.

Hannah turned to look at the pillow on the opposite side of the bed. It was where Moishe usually slept unless he'd stolen her pillow. There was no orange and white, twenty-three pound cat nestled on the expensive goose down. She gave a fleeting thought about how much she wished that Ross were sleeping there, and then she pushed that unhappy notion from her mind and got up to find Michelle.

The moment she was on her feet and fully awake, Hannah smelled the enticing scent of berries. She wasn't sure whether the berries were raspberry, strawberry, or something else, but she knew that Michelle was baking. Her sister must be making breakfast, and it smelled delicious.

A quick shower later, she put on the fluffy robe Delores had given her as part of her trousseau. Then she found her slippers under the bed and padded down the carpeted hallway to investigate.

She found Michelle taking something from the oven, something that caused her taste buds to wake up and beg for a bite. "What is it?" she asked, bypassing the usual *good-morning* greeting.

"Which is it?" Michelle replied, gesturing toward the kitchen counter. Two wire racks were in evidence, one of them filled with something that looked like muffins. The other was waiting to hold the pan that Michelle had just taken out of the oven.

"Some kind of muffins, and . . . cheese and eggs?" Hannah hazarded a guess.

"Close. I made Mixed Berry Muffins and Chili-Cheese Omelet Squares. Mike called to say he was coming over to talk to you before you left for work, and I invited him to breakfast. I hope that's all right."

"It is, but that was a lot of work for you. How long have you been up?"

"Since two. I couldn't sleep. I kept thinking about P.K. and how unfair everything is. I really liked him a lot, Hannah."

"More than you thought you did?"

"I . . . yes."

A tear ran down Michelle's cheek, and Hannah wished she hadn't asked the question. She hurried over to her sister and hugged her gently. "I'm sorry. I shouldn't have brought that up."

"It's okay." Michelle's voice was shaking slightly. "It's true, but I didn't know it until . . ." she stopped and swallowed hard, ". . . until he was gone and I realized I'd never see him again. I wasn't in love with him, but I loved him. And I'll miss him, Hannah."

"I'll miss him, too. What time is Mike coming?"

Michelle glanced at the apple-shaped kitchen clock on the wall. "He'll be here in ten minutes."

"And he'll be on time because you promised him breakfast and he knows what a good cook you are." Hannah turned toward the doorway. "Please pour me a cup of coffee, Michelle. I'm going to go get dressed and I'll be back here before it cools."

"But don't you want me to wait until you're back here?"

"No. That cup of coffee will be like the carrot in front of the donkey. I'll hurry so that I can get back here to drink it."

True to her word, Hannah was back in the kitchen in less than five minutes. She'd already chosen her outfit for the day, and it was a simple matter to slip into her clothes and run a brush through her hair.

"That was fast!" Michelle commented, as Hannah came into the kitchen.

"That's because I had an incentive." Hannah headed straight for the kitchen table and the mug of coffee that was waiting for her. "Thanks," she said, picking up the mug and taking her first sip of the bracing brew.

"Would you like a muffin to go with your coffee?" Michelle asked.

Hannah thought about that for the space of a nanosecond. "Yes, please. They smell wonderful!"

Michelle plucked a muffin from the cooling rack and brought it to Hannah. Then she brought soft butter and a knife. "Let me know how you like them," she said.

"I will." Hannah peeled the paper from the muffin and bit into it without benefit of butter. It had just the right amount of berries, and it was fragrant with cinnamon and nutmeg.

She gave Michelle a nod and a smile, took another bite, and finished the muffin in no time flat.

"My guess is you liked it," Michelle commented.

"It was wonderful, Michelle. I want another one right away, but I'm going to hold off until Mike gets here. Do you have any idea what he wants besides breakfast?"

"Not really. He just said he needed to talk to you, but he didn't go into detail."

"Okay." Hannah drained her coffee mug and got up to pour another. She'd just seated herself again when the doorbell rang.

"I'll get it," Michelle volunteered.

"Thanks. Don't forget to look through the peephole. Mike's a real stickler for that. If you don't, he'll lecture you about it."

"Something sure smells good," Hannah heard Mike say as he stepped inside. A moment later, he came into the kitchen. "Hi, Hannah," he greeted her, and then he turned back to Michelle. "What did you make for breakfast?"

"Chili-Cheese Omelet Squares and Mixed Berry Muffins. Sit down and I'll get you some coffee and a muffin to start. The omelet squares need to cool for another couple of minutes."

"Wow!" Mike commented, twenty minutes later when his plate was empty for the second time. "That was the best breakfast I've had in years!"

Hannah exchanged amused glances with Michelle. Mike said that every time he finished a breakfast that one of them had made for him. But even though they'd heard it before, they knew it was sincere. The proof was in the eating and both sisters had been watching as Mike had eaten his breakfast. He'd wolfed down five muffins and four Chili-Cheese

Omelet Squares that were more than liberally slathered with Slap 'Ya Mama hot sauce. Mike had eaten like he'd been starving, and both of them knew that wasn't true. It was a wonder that his uniform still fit him!

"I'm glad you enjoyed your breakfast," Michelle told him. "How about another cup of coffee?"

"That'd be great!" Mike held out his mug. "And then I want to talk to both of you about something serious."

Hannah felt her pulse begin to quicken. This was the moment she'd dreaded. Was Mike about to bring up the horrid suspicion that had occurred to her during the night?

"What is it, Mike?" she asked after Michelle had filled his coffee cup and returned to the table.

"Doc called me this morning. P.K. ingested a lethal dose of a drug that constricted his striated muscles."

Michelle gasped. "The heart contains striated muscles, doesn't it?"

"You're probably right. Doc said that in layman's terms, P.K. had a fatal heart attack caused by the drug he ingested."

Hannah swallowed hard. "From the candy he ate?"

"Doc said it was likely, but he doesn't know for sure yet. P.K. didn't take any cookies with him when he went back to work, did he?"

"No. We gave him a Raspberry Danish, but we know that he hadn't eaten it yet. We saw it on the video he sent to Michelle, and it was still in the original packaging."

"But he ate cookies with you before that?"

"Yes," Hannah answered. "When he borrowed Ross's car, he ate some Cherry Chocolate Bar Cookies, but so did Mother, Michelle, and I."

Mike made a note in the small notebook he always carried in his pocket. "What time did he eat your cookies?"

"I don't remember, but I know it was before Michelle left for her rehearsal at the school." Hannah stopped speaking and began to frown. "You don't think our cookies were drugged, do you?"

"No. I'm just getting a timeline here. Doc told me that the drug would have worked within an hour or two so it couldn't have been in your bar cookies."

Hannah took a deep breath and blurted out the nightmarish thought that had plagued her sleep. "Do you think the drugs were in the candy that was in Ross's desk?"

"Yes."

Michelle reached out for Hannah's hand and gave it a comforting squeeze. And then she asked the question that was uppermost in Hannah's mind. "Do you think that the drugged candy was meant for P.K.?"

"I don't know yet." Mike glanced at his watch. "KCOW's offices open in twenty minutes. I'm going out there now to talk to the office staff when they come in. We confiscated the candy last night and Doc's running tests in his lab, but I need to find out when and how that candy got into Ross's desk."

"And then you'll know if P.K. was the intended victim," Michelle said, drawing the obvious conclusion.

"Maybe, but maybe not. It all depends on when and how the candy got there."

Hannah swallowed hard. "What if you can't pin it down? What if the candy was there before P.K. moved into Ross's office?"

"I think you already know the answer to that," Mike told her, and then he reached out to pat her shoulder. "Sorry, Hannah."

Hannah somehow managed to maintain her composure. Whatever happened, she couldn't avoid reality. "If you can't pin down the timing on the candy, you'll have to run two murder investigations, one for P.K. and one for . . ." Hannah stopped for a second to collect herself. "And one for Ross, just in case he was the intended victim."

"Exactly right. I'm sorry I can't tell you that it wasn't intended for Ross."

Hannah gave a little nod. "So am I. If it was, do you think that could be why Ross disappeared without a trace?"

"It's certainly a possibility, especially if someone knew what was going to happen and warned Ross that his life was in danger."

Hannah swallowed hard. "P.K. told us that Ross got a phone call right before he told P.K. that he had to leave, that it was a family emergency."

"That constitutes a family emergency in my book. And if Ross was afraid that you or your family could be in danger too, it could explain why he didn't tell you where he was going."

MIXED BERRY MUFFINS

Preheat oven to 375 degrees F., rack in the middle position.

The Muffin Batter:

⅔ cup white ***(granulated)*** sugar
½ cup salted butter ***(1 stick, 4 ounces, ¼ pound)***, softened
2 large eggs
1 teaspoon vanilla extract
2 teaspoons baking powder
½ teaspoon baking soda
½ teaspoon ground cinnamon
¼ teaspoon salt
¾ cup whole milk
2 cups all-purpose flour ***(pack it down when you measure it)***
1 cup quick-cooking oats ***(I used Quaker Quick 1-Minute)***

The Fruit:

1 and ½ cups frozen mixed berries
⅛ teaspoon ground nutmeg

1/8 teaspoon ground cinnamon
1 cup all-purpose flour
1/8 cup brown sugar ***(pack it down in the cup when you measure it)***

Prepare your muffin pan by spraying the cups with Pam or another nonstick cooking spray or lining the cups with double cupcake papers. This batch will make 12 to 18 muffins so you will need 12 to 18 muffin cups.

In the bowl of an electric mixer, beat the sugar and butter together at MEDIUM speed until they are light and fluffy.

Add the eggs, one at a time, beating after each addition.

Add the vanilla extract, baking powder, baking soda, ground cinnamon, and salt. Mix them in thoroughly.

You will now add the milk and the flour in three parts, beating after each addition.

Pour in 1/4 cup of the milk and 1/2 cup of the flour, mixing both in thoroughly.

Pour in another ¼ cup of the milk and another ½ cup of the flour. Mix until they are thoroughly combined.

Add the final ¼ cup of the milk and the final cup of the flour, mixing both in thoroughly.

Process the cup of quick-cooking oats with the steel blade in your food processor or grind them in a grinder. You should end up with ¾ cup of finely ground oats.

Add the ground oats to your bowl and mix them in thoroughly.

Measure out 1 and ½ cups of frozen mixed berries. Cut the large berries into several pieces while they are still frozen and place them in a small bowl.

Sprinkle in the nutmeg, cinnamon, flour, and brown sugar. Mix them into the frozen fruit until everything is evenly combined.

Fill the muffin cups one-third full with the muffin batter. If the batter is too sticky, first dip the spoon or scooper in water so that the batter will slide right off.

Spoon half of the berries on top of the muffin batter in the cups, dividing it between all the muffins as evenly as you can.

Spoon muffin batter over the fruit, filling each muffin cup ¾ full.

Add the rest of the mixed berries on top, dividing them between the muffins as evenly as you can.

Bake your Mixed Berry Muffins at 375 degrees F. for 35 to 40 minutes or until a toothpick inserted into the center of a muffin comes out clean with no muffin batter clinging to it.

Place the muffin pans on a cold stovetop burner or a wire rack and cool for at least 10 minutes. Then either tip them out of the muffin cups or lift them out by their cupcake papers.

Transfer the muffins to a wire rack to cool to slightly above room temperature.

Place the muffins on a pretty platter and serve them with plenty of soft butter. They can also be cooled completely, covered with foil or plastic wrap, and reheated in the microwave for later enjoyment.

Yield: 12 to 18 delicious muffins that everyone will love.

CHILI-CHEESE OMELET SQUARES

Preheat oven to 350 degrees F., rack in the middle position.

2 cups shredded cheddar cheese ***(I like to use sharp cheddar)***
4-ounce can chopped green chilies ***(I used Ortega)***
2 cups shredded Havarti cheese ***(Monterey Jack will also work)***
1 and ¼ cups whole milk or half-and-half
3 Tablespoons all-purpose flour
½ teaspoon salt
¼ teaspoon cumin powder
3 large eggs
8-ounce can tomato sauce
¼ teaspoon chili powder

Prepare an 8-inch square pan with sides 2 inches high by spraying it with Pam or another non-stick cooking spray.

Layer half of the shredded cheddar cheese in the bottom of the pan.

Drain the chopped green chilies and sprinkle half of them over the cheddar cheese.

Sprinkle half of the shredded Havarti or Jack cheese over the chilies.

Repeat, using the rest of the cheeses and the green chilies.

Pour the milk into a bowl. Sprinkle the flour, salt, and cumin powder on top of the milk.

Crack the eggs and mix them into the bowl. Beat the eggs until you have a smooth, fluffy mixture and the ingredients are well-combined.

Pour the egg mixture into your prepared pan.

Bake your Chili-Cheese Omelet Squares for 40 minutes or until the top is golden brown.

Take the pan out of the oven and place it on a wire rack on the counter.

Cool the omelet for 10 minutes before cutting and serving it.

While you are waiting for your omelet to cool, pour the tomato sauce into a microwave-safe container.

Stir in the chili powder and heat the mixture on HIGH for 1 to 2 minutes or until it is bubbling hot.

Cut your Chili-Cheese Omelet Squares into 8 pieces and serve it with the tomato-chili sauce.

Yield: 8 tasty servings

Hannah's Note: If you invite Mike for breakfast, be sure to put Slap 'Ya Mama hot sauce on the table for him.

Michelle's Note: When I make this for my roommates at college, I always double the recipe and use a 9-inch by 13-inch cake pan. We like leftovers because we can reheat them in the microwave.

Chapter Six

"We need to bake, Hannah," Michelle said as they stepped into the kitchen at The Cookie Jar. "Baking always calms us down."

"That's true. And I have a new cookie I want to try. Do you have rehearsals today?"

"Yes, I have two rehearsals, back-to-back. We're going to run through the junior play at noon, and the Lake Eden players come in at two. At least their rehearsal is shorter and I should be back here by three-fifteen." Michelle moved a little closer. "I can cancel both rehearsals if you need me here, Hannah."

Hannah shook her head. "No, Michelle. Thanks for offering, but I'm like you. . . . I'm better off if I stay really busy."

"Okay, but I'll have my cell with me. Just call if you need me and I'll come straight back here. I want to work with you in the kitchen, though. I don't want to work in the coffee shop."

For a moment, Hannah was puzzled, and then she thought she understood. "Is Lisa going to tell the murder story?"

"Yes. I sent her a text last night and said I'd tell her all about it when I saw her in the morning."

"Are you sure you want to do that?"

"I'm sure. I certainly don't want to listen when Lisa tells the story, though."

Hannah began to frown as an unwelcome thought crossed her mind. "I want you to be completely honest with me, Michelle. Are you encouraging Lisa to tell the story because you think it'll increase our cookie sales?"

"That's part of it," Michelle admitted. "But Lisa loves to tell stories and everyone's going to want to know the details anyway. If they don't get them from Lisa, they'll find out about the video and ask us."

Hannah gave a reluctant nod. "You're probably right. But it may be really difficult for you to fill Lisa in on the details."

There was silence for a moment, and then Michelle sighed. "You're right. It *will* be difficult, but it may be cathartic. And if I talk about it, I might not have any more nightmares like the ones I had last night."

"Okay then." Hannah gave a slight nod. "Do what you think is best, Michelle. But if you decide that you really don't want Lisa to tell the story, I'm sure she'll understand."

"She will. That's exactly what she said to me in her text message last night. There's only one thing I'm wondering about. Do you think I should show Lisa the video?"

Hannah took a moment to think about that. Then she shook her head.

"Okay. I already decided that I wasn't going to tell Lisa what Mike brought up this morning."

"You mean that P.K. might not have been the intended victim?"

"Exactly. I thought it might interfere with our investigation." Michelle stopped speaking and looked up at Hannah. "We *are* going to investigate, aren't we?"

"Yes."

"And we're going to investigate both possibilities . . . aren't we?"

"Yes, but I'm not sure how we'll find out if Ross was the intended victim since no one knows where he is."

"You'll find a way. You're really good at investigating murders."

"Thanks." Hannah turned to look at the kitchen coffeepot and saw that the green light was on. "The coffee's ready, Michelle. Let's have a cup and then we'll bake. If Lisa tells the story today, we'll need as many cookies as we can make."

"I know."

Hannah got up to pour two cups of coffee and carried them over to the work station. "What shall we bake first?" she asked as she took the stool across from her sister.

"I've got a bar cookie recipe that Aunt Nancy gave me the last time I came home from college. She said it belonged to Heiti's mother, and I'm dying to try it."

"Don't say *dying*," Hannah told her. "There's already been enough of that around Lake Eden."

Hannah was just taking the last pan of bar cookies she'd baked from the oven when someone knocked on the kitchen door. Michelle was in the coffee shop, giving Lisa the background for the story that she would tell after their customers came in, so Hannah rushed to let her visitor in the back door.

"Hi, Mike," she said even before she checked to make sure that it was him.

"How did you know it was me?"

"I know your knock."

"My knock is different than everyone else's?"

"Yes," Hannah said, choosing not to elaborate. She didn't

want to say that Mike's knock was rapid and authoritative. It practically screamed, *It's the police. Open the door! Now!*

"Something sure smells good in here," Mike told her, hanging his uniform parka on one of the hooks by the back door.

"I know. Michelle and I have been baking. Sit down and I'll get you a cup of coffee and a couple of cookies."

"Great! I'm starving!"

There was an amazed expression on Hannah's face as she went to pour Mike's coffee. Two hours ago, he'd been sitting at her kitchen table, inhaling the breakfast that Michelle had made.

He's a bottomless pit, she thought, but didn't say it. Instead, she said, "Here's your coffee," and set it down in front of him. "I'll cut some bar cookies for you."

"What kind are they?"

"Blueberry Shortbread Bar Cookies. We've made them before. It's one of Aunt Nancy's recipes."

"Then they're bound to be good. Aunt Nancy's recipes are always great. And if you and Michelle baked them, that's another plus."

"Thanks," Hannah said, going to the bakers rack to remove a pan of bar cookies. "It'll just take me a minute to cut these."

"I think I can wait, but I've got to warn you. My stomach's already growling."

Of course it is. With you, it's a permanent affliction, Hannah thought to herself as she tipped the bar cookies out of the pan and began to cut them into brownie-sized pieces. "How many do you want?" she asked.

"I could eat the whole pan if you'd let me."

Hannah laughed. It was the answer she'd been expecting. "I'll give you eight for now. Just ask if you want more. How's that?"

"Fine with me."

Hannah waited until Mike had eaten two of the bar cookies and then she got up to refill his coffee cup. She sat back down on her stool, but she simply couldn't wait any longer to ask what he'd found out at KCOW Television.

"So what did they tell you about the candy?" she asked him.

Mike gave a loud sigh. "Nothing definitive. The receptionist was out the day the mail room brought up the candy and a temp accepted the package."

"Did it come by mail?"

"Yes, and the mail room handles a lot of mail. I asked and no one there even remembers it. Since it was a prepaid mailer and it didn't look personal, it's entirely possible it could have been sitting in the mail room for a while before someone took it upstairs."

"Does the temp remember the day it came in?"

"Yes. She asked and someone said to put it on Ross's desk."

"Why were they putting things on Ross's desk when he wasn't there?"

"Because everyone thought he'd be back any day. No one knew that Ross had disappeared. They all thought that he was out in the field taping something for their special programming."

"Who told them that?"

"P.K. He was covering for Ross. And you and your family substantiated that story by telling everyone in town that Ross was out on location."

Hannah groaned. "So you still don't know if Ross or P.K. was the intended victim."

"That's right. And that's the problem, Hannah. The temp remembers that the mailer had a return address, but it was the address of the candy company's corporate headquarters.

When I called to check with the candy company, they told me that their stores provide pre-paid mailers to any customers who buy two-pound boxes if the customer asks for one. At some point, someone must have thrown away the mailer, but I don't know when. The cleaning crew empties the trash every night and it's collected three times a week. Paper trash is recycled daily, so now there's no trace of it."

"Sounds like you've had a frustrating morning so far."

"That's right. I still have no idea when that candy was mailed and when it arrived at KCOW. That avenue's a dead end, Hannah."

Hannah began to frown. "So what you're telling me is that since you can't pin down the arrival of the candy, you can't identify the intended victim."

"Right."

"And that means you have to investigate anyone who might have had a reason to kill either Ross or P.K."

"Exactly. I'll need to ask you some questions about Ross's background, Hannah. I've got to find out if there's anyone who might have wanted to kill him and why. And since Michelle was P.K.'s friend, I'll need to ask her if he told her anything that might suggest a motive for his murder. Is it okay if I drop by the condo to see both of you tonight?"

Hannah made up her mind instantly. "Of course. Come by for dinner at seven and bring Lonnie with you. I'll invite Norman, too. He spent time with Ross and P.K. when they worked together covering sports events at Jordan High. Norman may know something personal about Ross or P.K. that could help."

"Great." Mike stood up and grabbed a paper napkin. He dumped the remaining bar cookies inside and folded it into a packet. "I'll take these with me to eat on the way out to the sheriff's station. That's okay, isn't it?"

"Of course it's okay."

"Thanks, Hannah. I'll see you tonight."

When Mike had left, Hannah sat back down at the work station for the space of several seconds, and then she jumped up. Lisa could handle opening the coffee shop alone while Michelle baked in the kitchen. She had to get over to Florence's Red Owl Grocery to pick up something she could put in the slow cooker for dinner!

Chapter Seven

Hannah had just returned to The Cookie Jar after buying the ingredients for Jambalaya and was driving back to the condo to start their dinner when Michelle came through the swinging restaurant-style door that separated the kitchen from the coffee shop.

"Oh, good! You're back," she greeted Hannah. "Lisa says to tell you that you had two calls while you were gone. One was from Cyril Murphy at the garage. He wants you to call him about Ross's car."

"I hope it's good news and it's still in fairly good shape. How about the second call?"

"It was from Sally at the Lake Eden Inn, and she told Lisa that it was important."

"Thanks, Michelle. I'll call Sally first and then I'll talk to Cyril."

"There's one other thing. Andrea's out front and she wants to talk to you. Should I send her back now, or wait until you've returned your calls?"

"Send her back now. I need to talk to her anyway. I'll give her a cup of coffee and a couple of cookies and then I'll make my calls."

A phrase their great-grandmother Elsa had been fond of saying popped into Hannah's head. "*It never rains, but it pours*," she said, smiling at Michelle.

Michelle looked at her blankly for a moment, and then she began to smile back. "I don't exactly remember it, but that sounds like Great-Grandma Elsa."

"You're right."

"It means that everything happens at once, doesn't it?"

"It does," Hannah said, and then she glanced at the clock. "Today, that's a good thing."

"Why?"

"Because Andrea arrived in time to take you to your rehearsals. I'll make sure she leaves in about thirty minutes."

"Great! I looked at the thermometer and it's really cold out there. But that's not the only good thing about Andrea coming in."

"What do you mean?"

"She's brought her new whippersnapper cookies for you to taste. She gave a sample to Lisa, Aunt Nancy, and me, and I know you'll like them. They're really good!"

"I'm sure they are. Andrea loves to make whippersnappers. Go tell her to come back here and I'll taste one before I make my calls. And if Lisa starts telling the story, just come back here with Andrea and me."

Hannah had just poured a cup of coffee for her sister when Andrea breezed through the swinging door. She was carrying a plastic container, and she set it down on the stainless steel surface of the work station. She was wearing a powder blue cashmere sweater and skirt that looked stunning with her shining blond hair. Andrea was the perfect picture of the highly successful real estate agent that she actually was.

"You look lovely, Andrea," Hannah complimented her.

"Thanks."

Hannah somehow managed to keep the amused smile off her face. Usually, when someone received a compliment, they responded with a return compliment in kind. Of course, Hannah couldn't really fault Andrea for not returning the compliment, since she was wearing a pair of old jeans, a green sweater that had seen better days, and her voluminous white chef's apron.

"I brought you something," Andrea said, motioning toward the container. "I baked a new whippersnapper cookie."

"Your reputation has preceded you."

"What?"

"Your whippersnappers. Michelle already told me that I was going to love them." Even though she wasn't really hungry, Hannah's mouth started to water as Andrea took off the lid and the scent of pineapple wafted through the air. "They smell delicious," she said.

"Come and taste one. So far, everyone likes them, but your opinion matters the most to me."

Hannah was pleased. As far as she was concerned, what Andrea had just told her was even better than a return compliment.

"If they taste as good as they smell, I'm sure I'm going to love them." Hannah walked over and plucked a cookie from the container. "They're pretty, Andrea. I like the cherry on top."

"Thanks. They looked a little plain, and I thought they needed something for color."

"Well, you picked the right something. Half a maraschino cherry always reminds me of holidays or special occasions." Hannah bit into the cookie and smiled as the flavor she'd smelled became a reality. "Oh, my!" she said.

"Does that mean you like them?"

"I *love* them! What do you call them?"

"Pineapple Raisin Whippersnapper Cookies. I start with a spice cake mix and add the Cool Whip, crushed pineapple, and golden raisins."

"Will you give me the exact recipe? I know our customers will love them. They love *all* of your whippersnapper cookies."

Andrea looked extremely pleased even though Hannah had told her that before. "Then I guess that it's a really good thing I have more cookies in the car. I'll go get them before I leave, and you can try them out on your customers."

"That'll be fun. I'll be happy to pay you for the cookies, Andrea."

"Don't be silly!" Andrea waved away Hannah's offer. "Consider it a favor. You do lots of things for me."

"I do?"

"Yes. The biggest favor is that you're teaching Tracey to bake. And I think Bethie's old enough to have a small part in it."

"Oh, good!" Hannah said. It was the one thing that she could do for Tracey and Bethie that Andrea or Grandma McCann didn't have the time or the inclination to do.

"I wish you would give me more so I could do for you," Andrea said. "Sometimes I feel like I take and take from you, and I never give back."

An idea flashed like lightning through Hannah's mind and she gasped aloud. There *was* something that Andrea could do for her!

"What is it?" Andrea looked concerned.

"I just thought of something that only you could do for me. But I'm not sure that you have the time."

"I'll make the time. What is it, Hannah?"

"I want you to investigate a murder."

"But *you* do that."

"I know, but I can't investigate this one. People wouldn't tell me the truth."

"Are you talking about P.K.'s murder?"

"No. This investigation is about Ross."

Andrea's mouth dropped open. "Ross is *dead*?!"

"No! Or at least I don't think he is. It's just that Mike doesn't know whether the drugged candy in Ross's desk was meant for Ross, or for P.K. And that means Mike has to investigate both possibilities in order to catch the killer."

Andrea thought about that for a moment, and then she nodded. "I get it. I knew that P.K. ate drugged candy. Mother saw the autopsy report when Doc's secretary typed it up this morning. She called to tell me about it and she said to tell you when I got here. But it sounds as if you already knew."

"Mike told me."

"He's sharing information this time?"

"He told me that when he described his meeting he had with the KCOW office staff. The candy was addressed to Ross's office number so a temporary receptionist took it to his office."

"I get it!" Andrea said. "I knew that P.K. was using Ross's office, but I didn't even consider that the candy might have been intended for Ross!"

The two sisters were quiet for a moment, and then Andrea reached out for Hannah's hand. "That's just awful, Hannah! How can you live with the knowledge that someone might have been trying to murder your husband?"

"What choice do I have? The reality is that it could have happened that way. I need to find out if it's true. And that's where you come in."

"I see. You can't question people about Ross because he's your new husband and nobody would admit it if they had a grudge against him. Tell me exactly what you want me to do, and I'll do it."

"Thanks, Andrea. Can you stick around while I make a couple of calls? Then we can talk about it."

"Yes. I don't have anything to do except pick Tracey up when school's out for the day. Is there anything else you need?"

"Actually, yes. Could you give Michelle a ride to Jordan High for her rehearsals? It's cold out there, and I don't want her to have to walk."

"I can do that, no problem."

"Thanks. And don't ever think that I don't appreciate the fact that you've already helped me a lot."

"How?"

"Just by loving me and being my sister."

Andrea looked surprised, but then she smiled. It was a slow smile, almost as if the clouds had rolled back and the sun had peeked through. "Go make your calls, Hannah. I'll run out to the car and get my second container of whipper-snappers for your customers. Do you care if we pass them out right now?"

"Not at all. You can judge their reactions that way."

"Okay. Then that's exactly what I'll do. Come out to get me when you finish your calls, and we'll talk about exactly how you want me to investigate."

When Andrea left the kitchen, Hannah walked to the phone. A few seconds later, she had Sally Laughlin on the phone. "Hi, Sally. It's Hannah. Michelle told me you called and she said it was important. What's up?"

"Did you see the article Rod ran in the Sunday *Lake Eden Journal* about the Holiday Gift Convention I'm going to hold in our convention center this weekend?"

"Yes. It sounds like a wonderful idea."

"It's even more wonderful than I thought. I checked the vendor roster this morning and we have almost a hundred."

"Wow!" Hannah was impressed. Sally's gift show was going to be larger than any convention they'd ever held at the Lake Eden Inn.

"They're all selling Christmas and Thanksgiving decorations and gifts. Most of their items are handmade, and if they're not, they're personalized. I think the customers will appreciate that."

"You're right, and I'll certainly be there. It's hard to find gifts for Mother. If she likes something, she buys it for herself. I'm always looking for something new and different."

"You're exactly the kind of customer we want to attract. We're competing with the Tri-County Mall and the catalogues. Our gifts and decorations have to be unique."

"The paper said the convention starts on Friday and lasts through Sunday. That's right, isn't it?"

"Yes. Friday is the opening day and I think it'll be big. Everyone's very excited about it and the phone at the Inn has been ringing off the hook. Some of my vendors are already here, setting up their booths."

"And they're staying with you, of course. That's good for your winter business, isn't it?"

"You bet! This is a slow time of year for us, and it should bring in quite a few hotel guests. Anyone who's not a vendor and stays at the Inn can get into the convention an hour before we open to the general public."

"That's very smart, Sally."

"Thank you. There's something else, too. Our vendor food service doesn't start until tomorrow so they've all been eating in the restaurant or ordering from room service."

"You have a food service just for the vendors?"

"Of course. We offer three meals a day in the dining room

attached to the convention center. Brooke and Loren do a great job running it. They're a really cute couple and sometimes I wonder when they'll get around to getting married. All you have to do is look at them to know they're in love." Sally stopped speaking and gave a little laugh. "I bet you're wondering why I called you."

"Actually . . . yes. Michelle said it was important."

"It is. Would you like to run a cookie booth on the three days of the convention? Brooke and Loren planned to do it, but we didn't expect this many vendors and they're going to have their hands full. They won't have time to bake cookies, too."

Hannah thought about it for a moment. It was a great business opportunity. "How much does it cost for the booth?"

"Absolutely nothing. All you have to do is set it up with cookies and coffee before we open the doors. Charge whatever you think is a good price."

"But you'll take a percentage of the profits, won't you?"

"No. You'll be doing me a favor, Hannah. We're going to set up tables and chairs in the center of the convention hall so people can sit down and take a break. They'll want a cup of coffee or tea to perk them up and something sweet to have with it. That's what your booth will provide."

Hannah didn't hesitate. They were always looking for expansion, and this opportunity was a natural for them. "I'm in, Sally. Just let me check with Lisa and make sure that we have the personnel to do it. How many cookies do you think we might need every day?"

"As many as you sell per day at The Cookie Jar and perhaps a few more. You'll be able to judge that after the first full day. Call me back and tell me if Lisa says it's a go, Hannah. I really need you to do this and I think it'll be good for The Cookie Jar, too."

"I already know it would be good for us, but that's a lot of extra cookies to bake."

"What do you think, Hannah?" Sally prompted. "Can you handle selling cookies in two places?"

"I think so, but I'll get back to you for sure within the hour," Hannah promised. "If we can handle the extra volume, this could be a very good thing for both of us."

PINEAPPLE RAISIN WHIPPERSNAPPER COOKIES

DO NOT preheat your oven yet. This dough needs to chill before baking.

8-ounce can crushed pineapple ***(I used Dole)***
1 cup golden or regular raisins
Approximately ¼ cup water
1 box ***(approximately 18 ounces)*** spice cake mix, the kind that makes a 9-inch by 13-inch cake ***(I used Duncan Hines – 18.5 ounces net weight)***
1 large egg, beaten ***(just whip it up in a glass with a fork)***
2 cups Original Cool Whip, thawed ***(measure this – a tub of Cool Whip contains a little over 3 cups and that's too much!)***
1 teaspoon vanilla extract

½ cup powdered ***(confectioners')*** sugar ***(you don't have to sift it unless it's old and has big lumps)***

Small jar of maraschino cherries, drained and cut in half vertically ***(optional for decorating your cookies)***

Use a strainer to drain the pineapple.

Place the raisins in a microwave-safe measuring cup that is large enough to contain the raisins with room to spare for the water.

Pour the water over the raisins.

Hannah's 1st Note: If you prefer, you can use rum instead of water.

Heat the raisins and the water for 1 minute on HIGH in the microwave. Let the cup sit in the microwave to plump the raisins for an additional minute.

Remove the cup to a folded towel or pot holder on the kitchen counter. Give the raisins a stir and then cool the cup to room temperature. DO NOT drain the raisins yet. Leave the liquid in the cup.

Pour HALF of the dry cake mix into a large mixing bowl.

Use a smaller bowl to mix the two cups of Cool Whip with the beaten egg and the vanilla extract. Stir gently with a rubber spatula until everything is combined.

Add the Cool Whip mixture to the cake mix in the large bowl. STIR VERY CAREFULLY with a wooden

spoon or a rubber spatula. Stir only until everything is combined. You don't want to stir all the air from the Cool Whip.

Pat the crushed pineapple dry with paper towels and then add it to the large mixing bowl.

Drain the raisins, pat them dry with paper towels, and add them to the large mixing bowl.

Sprinkle the rest of the cake mix on top of the fruit and gently fold everything together with the rubber spatula. Again, keep as much air in the batter as possible. Air is what will make your cookies soft and give them a melt-in-your-mouth quality.

Cover the bowl with plastic wrap and chill the cookie dough for at least one hour in the refrigerator. It's a little too sticky to form into balls without chilling it first.

Hannah's 2nd Note: Lisa and I mix up this dough before we leave The Cookie Jar for the night and bake it when we come in to work the next morning.

When your cookie dough has chilled and you're ready to bake, preheat your oven to 350 degrees F., and make sure the rack is in the middle position. DO

NOT take your chilled cookie dough out of the refrigerator until after your oven has reached the proper temperature.

While your oven is preheating, prepare your cookie sheets by spraying them with Pam or another nonstick baking spray, or lining them with parchment paper.

Place the powdered sugar in a small, shallow bowl. You will be dropping cookie dough into this bowl to form dough balls and coating them with the powdered sugar.

When your oven is ready, take your dough out of the refrigerator. Using a teaspoon from your silverware drawer, drop the dough by rounded teaspoonful into the bowl with the powdered sugar. Roll the dough around with your fingers to form powdered sugar coated cookie dough balls.

Hannah's 3rd Note: If you coat your fingers with powdered sugar first and then try to form the cookie dough into balls, it's a lot easier to accomplish.

Place the coated cookie dough balls on your prepared cookie sheets, no more than 12 cookies to a standard-size sheet.

Hannah's 4th Note: Work with only one cookie dough ball at a time. If you drop more than one in the bowl of powdered sugar, they'll stick together. Also, make only as many cookie dough balls as you can bake at one time. Cover the remaining dough and return it to the refrigerator until you're ready to bake more.

If you decide you want to decorate your cookies, press half of a maraschino cherry, rounded side up, on top of each cookie before you bake them.

Bake your Pineapple Raisin Whippersnapper Cookies at 350 degrees F., for 10 minutes. Let them cool on the cookie sheet for 2 minutes, and then move them to a wire rack to cool completely. ***(This is a lot easier if you line your cookie sheets with parchment paper—then you don't need to lift the cookies one by one. All you have to do is grab one end of the parchment paper and pull it, cookies and all, onto the wire rack.)***

Once the cookies are completely cool, store them between sheets of waxed paper in a cool, dry place. ***(Your refrigerator is cool, but it's definitely not dry!)***

Yield: 3 to 4 dozen soft, delicious spice and fruit cookies, depending on cookie size.

Chapter Eight

Hannah glanced at the bakers racks standing by the oven. They were almost empty, and that meant it was time to bake again. Lisa was telling her story about P.K., and customers were lining up to hear it. Some of them, like Grandma Knudson, the first lady of Holy Redeemer Lutheran Church, had been in the coffee shop for three performances. Grandma's granddaughter-in-law, Claire Rodgers Knudson, had come in several minutes ago from her dress shop, and it looked as if Grandma would be staying for a fourth performance.

Once Hannah had explained what she wanted Andrea to do and Andrea had left with Michelle, Hannah had checked with Lisa, Aunt Nancy, and Marge. All three had agreed that Hannah should accept Sally's offer and Hannah had called Sally back with the good news. She'd thought about returning Cyril's call, but she decided that it could wait and that she would work on replenishing their cookie supply first.

Nothing in their thick volume of tried and true cookie recipes appealed to Hannah, and she decided to come up with a recipe for a new cookie. Their customers loved lemon, and there was no reason why she couldn't combine their recipe for lemon cookies with their recipe for oatmeal cookies. A quick check of the pantry and cooler assured her that she had all the ingredients she needed on hand. This was good, because she really didn't have time to run out for missing ingredients. She collected everything she needed, quickly mixed up the cookie dough, and now she was waiting for her Oatmeal Lemon Cookies to come out of the oven.

There was a knock on the back kitchen door and Hannah glanced at the timer. There was one minute to go and she hurried to answer the door.

"Hi, Norman," she greeted him and motioned him in. "I have just enough time to get you a cup of coffee before my new cookies come out of the oven."

Norman hung his parka on a hook by the back door and took his usual seat at the work station. Hannah had just delivered his mug of coffee when the timer began to buzz. "Thanks, Hannah. You have perfect timing," he told her.

"So do you. I was going to call you, but now you're here. Hold on a second while I take the cookies out of the oven and brush on the topping."

"Take your time," Norman said as he picked up his mug of coffee.

When Hannah opened the oven door, the scent that rolled out caused her to smile. She breathed in deeply and took the first pan of golden brown cookies from the oven shelf.

The warm cookies had to be glazed immediately, and Hannah had already mixed up the glaze. She brushed the glaze on each pan of cookies before she slid the cookie sheets onto the bakers rack.

"What smells so good?" Norman asked her.

"Oatmeal Lemon Cookies. They'll be cool in a couple of minutes, and then we can sample them."

"I've never tasted those before," Norman said.

Hannah laughed. "Neither have I. It's a new recipe I just tried. I have no idea if they're good or not."

"They smell good," Norman commented. "I'll be happy to help you test them."

"You're always happy to test something, Norman."

"I know. I'm just a nice guy that way."

Hannah smiled as she poured herself a cup of coffee and sat down across from Norman. "I was going to call you at the clinic to invite you to dinner tonight, but now I can ask you in person."

"Thanks, Hannah. I'd love to come. Can I bring anything?"

"Yes. Bring Cuddles. Moishe loves it when he can play with a friend, especially when the friend is Cuddles."

"My pleasure. And it'll be a pleasure for Cuddles, too. What are we having for dinner?"

"Jambalaya."

"You've never made that before, have you?"

"No. This is the first time."

"Well, I'll be happy to test that for you, too. Would you like me to pick up anything to go with the Jambalaya?"

Hannah thought about that for a moment, and then she nodded. "I could use some ginger ale. I think I'm all out. Or anything else you want to drink. I know I have beer, but I doubt Mike will drink since he's on-call. And since Mike is Lonnie's boss, I'm almost certain that Lonnie won't have anything with alcohol. I already have white wine for Michelle if she wants it, and of course I'll make coffee."

"I'll pick up some ginger ale. I have to run out to the mall, and there's a new store out there called the Pop Shop. They bottle their own sodas, and if you buy a case, you can mix and match."

"I wonder if they have red cream soda. It was Grandma Ingrid's favorite, and she always had it in her refrigerator."

"If they have it, I'll put a few bottles in the case for you," Norman promised.

"Great! That would be like a trip down memory lane. Now, if I could only find lemon ice cream, I'd have everything that Grandma Ingrid loved."

"Including you, of course."

"Yes," Hannah said, remembering how her grandmother used to hug her every time she visited.

"What's in your Jambalaya, Hannah?"

"Chicken, shrimp, tomatoes, rice, garlic and onion, and seasonings. And that reminds me, I brought a big bag of frozen shrimp and I'm not going to use it all, so Moishe and Cuddles will have shrimp for a treat."

"Perfect. Those two always appreciate shrimp."

"I know. Shrimp and salmon are their favorites." Hannah got up from her stool. "I'm going to remove the cookies from their sheets and put them on wire racks so they'll cool faster."

"Good idea." Norman watched while Hannah removed the cookies with a wide metal spatula and placed them on racks on the counter. "How long will it take for them to cool?"

"Not long at all if I put one rack in the cooler." Hannah carried a rack filled with cookies to the walk-in cooler and opened the door. She went in with the cookies and was back a few seconds later. "Can I top off your coffee, Norman?"

Norman picked up his cup and held it out as Hannah approached with the coffee carafe. When she'd added fresh coffee to his mug, he smiled. "Thanks, Hannah. Are you sure those cookies aren't cool enough?"

Hannah laughed. "They've barely been in the cooler for a minute."

"I wouldn't mind tasting a hot one."

"All right. I'll go check."

Hannah went back to the cooler, and when she returned, she was carrying a paper plate full of cookies. "They're still pretty warm, but that should be all right," she said, setting the plate down between them. "Help yourself, Norman."

Norman didn't need any further encouragement. He reached for a cookie and bit into it.

Hannah reached for her own cookie and took a bite. "Mmmm," she said.

"*Mmmm* is right," Norman agreed. "These are incredible, Hannah. The lemon flavor just explodes in your mouth, and I love the combination of oatmeal and lemon. They're tart and sweet at the same time."

"I like that, too," Hannah concurred.

They sat in silence, munching the cookies, until each of them had eaten three. Then Hannah sighed. "Go ahead and ask me, Norman."

"You know why I came here today?"

"I think so. It's P.K.'s murder. You want to ask me if I'm going to investigate."

Norman reached across the stainless steel surface, took her hand, and shook it. "Congratulations! You're a genius. And you're right, of course. Are you?"

"Yes."

"That brings up another question. It occurred to me the minute I heard exactly what happened to P.K. and Doc Knight confirmed that he was fatally drugged by the candy that was delivered to Ross's office. You know what I'm trying to say, don't you?"

Hannah gave a reluctant nod. "Yes, I do."

"Is Mike investigating both murders? I know that sounds weird, but that candy could have been intended for Ross."

"Unfortunately, that's true."

"And both you and Mike are investigating both murders? The one that could have happened and the one that did?"

"That's right."

"What can I do to help you, Hannah?"

"Come over for dinner tonight."

Norman looked surprised. "I already told you I'll come."

"Yes, and coming for dinner will help me investigate."

"How?"

"I want you to tell Mike and me anything you know about P.K.'s personal life. And then I want you to tell us what you know about Ross's background that I don't know."

"You probably know more than I do, Hannah."

"Not necessarily. We really didn't discuss his family or his past. When I was in college and we were all living in the same apartment building, he told me that his mother died giving birth to him and he lived with his grandmother until his father got married again. Ross's fiancée, Linda, showed me his mother's photo. It was sitting on a table in their living room."

Hannah stopped and sighed. "That photo was one of the things Ross didn't take with him when he left. It's still sitting on the dresser in the bedroom."

"What else do you know about his background?"

"After Ross moved back here to go to work for KCOW, he said that when he grew up, his family lived next to Senator Worthington's family."

"That could be important, Hannah."

"I don't know if it is, or not. Mike knows that Ross knew Senator Worthington. They talked about it."

"Do you know why Ross's family didn't come to your wedding?"

"No. Ross said he asked them and they couldn't make it, but I was so busy with the Food Channel Contest and all, I didn't think to ask why. And looking back on it now, I realize that I have no idea how many relatives Ross has or where they live."

Norman patted her shoulder. "That's all right, Hannah. Everything happened very fast."

"Yes," Hannah said, and then something very surprising happened to her, something that had never happened before. Two tears rolled down her cheeks and she had to swallow hard before she could speak again. "Engaged couples usually ask questions of each other like, *Where do you want to live after we're married?* And, *Do you want children?* We never did that. There just wasn't time. I know I loved him and I think he loved me. But . . . I'm beginning to think that I really didn't know Ross very well at all!"

OATMEAL LEMON COOKIES

Preheat oven to 350 degrees F., rack in the middle position.

The Cookie Dough:

2 cups brown sugar ***(pack it down in the cup when you measure it)***
1 cup ***(2 sticks, 8 ounces, ½ pound)*** salted butter, softened
1 large egg
¼ cup whole milk
¼ cup sour cream
1 teaspoon baking soda
1 teaspoon baking powder
½ teaspoon salt
1 teaspoon lemon zest ***(the finely grated yellow part of the lemon peel)***
2 and ½ cups all-purpose flour ***(pack it down in the cup when you measure it)***
1 and ½ cups quick-cooking oatmeal ***(I used Quaker 1-minute)***
1 teaspoon lemon extract ***(if you don't have it, use vanilla extract)***

The Topping:

¼ cup lemon juice
¼ cup white ***(granulated)*** sugar

Prepare your cookie sheets by spraying them with Pam or another nonstick cooking spray or lining them with parchment paper.

Place HALF of the brown sugar in the bowl of an electric mixer.

Add the 2 sticks of salted, softened butter.

Sprinkle the other half of the brown sugar on top of the softened butter.

Beat on MEDIUM speed until the mixture is light and fluffy.

Continue to beat and add the egg to your mixing bowl. Beat the brown sugar, butter, and egg mixture until it is lighter in color and thoroughly blended.

With the mixer running on MEDIUM speed, add the milk and the sour cream. Mix thoroughly.

Add the baking soda, baking powder, and salt. Then add the lemon zest and beat until they are well combined.

Add one cup of the flour and mix it in thoroughly on LOW speed. Then add the second cup of the flour. Once that is mixed in, add the remaining half cup of flour and mix it in. The dough should be fairly stiff.

Turn off the mixer and scrape down the bowl with a rubber spatula.

Sprinkle in the quick-cooking oatmeal, turn the mixer back on LOW speed, and mix in the oatmeal.

With the mixer still running on LOW speed, mix in the lemon or vanilla extract.

Take the bowl out of the mixer, scrape it down again with the rubber spatula, and give your cookie dough a final stir with a wooden spoon.

Drop by rounded spoonful onto your prepared cookie sheet, 12 cookies to a standard size sheet.

Moisten the palm of your hand and press the cookies down slightly. You can also do this with a metal spatula dipped in water to keep the dough from sticking to the spatula.

Bake at 350 degrees F., for 12 to 15 minutes, or until they are a nice, golden brown. ***(Mine took 14 minutes.)***

While the first pan of cookies is baking, mix up the topping.

Heat the lemon juice just a bit in the microwave. ***(The sugar will dissolve more easily if the juice is warm.)*** Add the sugar and stir until it is dissolved. Place the topping next to your wire cooling racks, along with a pastry brush.

When the cookies come out of the oven, remove them to a wire rack with a piece of foil placed under the rack to catch the drips when you brush on the topping. If you've used parchment paper, just pull the paper with the cookies on it from the cookie sheet onto the wire rack. Leave the cookies on the parchment paper and there's no need for a piece of foil under the rack.

Brush the Lemon Topping onto the hot cookies. The faster you do this, the quicker the topping will dry into a glaze.

Yield: Approximately 5 dozen sweet and tart cookies, depending on cookie size.

Chapter Nine

After Norman left, Hannah composed herself, and then she returned Cyril Murphy's call. Mike had told her that when the crime scene investigators released Ross's car, he would call Cyril and one of his mechanics would go to pick it up and assess the damage.

"Hi, Cyril," Hannah said when the owner of Cyril's Garage and Shamrock Limousine Service came on the line. "It's Hannah. My sister Michelle told me you'd called?"

"Hello, Hannah," Cyril responded, and Hannah began to smile. Even though Cyril had never lived in Ireland, his parents had immigrated from the Emerald Isle and there was still a slight trace of an Irish brogue in Cyril's voice.

"It's about the car. I had my top mechanic go over it, and there's surprisingly little damage. Mike told me that he'd hit a deer and that usually does all sorts of damage."

"He just sideswiped it, Cyril."

"Oh, then that explains the dent in the fender that my guys popped out. There was a scrape on the side that we took care of with touch-up paint and that's the extent of the body damage. Good thing there was a lot of snow in that ditch. The car had a soft landing, and it still runs just fine."

"That's good, I guess," Hannah said, shuddering slightly.

She knew she would never want to drive it, and she was almost certain that Michelle wouldn't either. Neither one of them could forget the fact that P.K. had died behind the wheel.

"What do you want me to do with it, Hannah? I can have a couple of my mechanics drop it off in your extra space at the condo."

"I . . . I don't think that's a good idea, Cyril. If it sits right next to my cookie truck at the condo, it's just going to make us sad every time we see it. Since Ross isn't here to make a decision, I'm not sure what I should do with it."

"I understand. But it's not Ross's decision, Hannah. It's yours."

Hannah was confused. "What do you mean? It's Ross's car."

"No, it's not. The pink slip was in the glove box, and Ross signed it over to you."

Hannah pulled out the chair by the phone and sat down hard. "He did?"

"Yes. He signed it and dated it."

"Dated it?"

"Yes. I've got it right here on my desk. Do you want to know the date?"

"Yes, please."

Cyril read the date to her and Hannah came close to gasping. It was the day that Ross had left Lake Eden. She drew a deep breath to steady herself, but that didn't keep the deep wave of grief from washing over her. Ross had signed his car over to her and put the keys in Michelle's dresser. Had he feared that he wasn't coming back anytime soon? Or perhaps not at all?

"Do you want to think about it and call me back, Hannah?" Cyril asked her.

"Um . . . no. I know what I want to do with it, Cyril. Make

it look as good as you can and sell it. And I'll use the money to buy a nice used car from your lot for Michelle. Give her a couple of options and I'll bring her out to choose what she wants tomorrow morning."

"I'll do that this afternoon, Hannah. I've got someone in Long Prairie who's looking for that exact make and model. I can send one of my mechanics over on his break to bring you the pink slip so you can sign it."

Hannah made another instant decision. "That's fine, Cyril. I'll send back some cookies for you. It's really nice of you to do this."

"No problem. I'll run the price past you before I make a deal with the buyer."

"Don't bother," Hannah said instantly. She knew that Cyril would never cheat her. "Just sell it and pick out some used cars you think Michelle would like. And thanks, Cyril. You're making things easy for me."

"My pleasure, darlin'."

Hannah smiled. Cyril's brogue was thick when he said the typically Irish phrase. "Bye, Cyril. And I won't forget to send those cookies."

Hannah was smiling as she hung up the phone. Talking to Cyril always put her in a good mood and she decided to make something special for him. Perhaps she could bake an Irish Potato Cookie. He'd really like that. And somewhere, in her voluminous recipe collection at the condo, she thought she had a recipe. Since Michelle had scanned all the recipes and put them on her home computer, and she now had access to her files on the cloud, she'd be able to search for the recipe from here.

Six pans of Multiple Choice Bar Cookies, six pans of Lovely Lemon Bar Cookies, and six pans of Rocky Road

Bar Cookies later, Hannah had climbed into her cookie truck and driven to Jordan High to pick up Michelle from her two play rehearsals. She pulled up to the curb and idled there while she used her cell phone to text her sister, and then she leaned back in the driver's seat and shut her eyes for just a moment.

"Hannah!"

Hannah woke up to the sound of someone tapping her driver's side window. She blinked several times, and then she smiled as she saw Michelle standing there.

"Get in, Michelle," she called out, unlocking the passenger door. And after her sister had slid into the seat, she said, "Sorry, Michelle. I must have dozed off for a moment."

"That's not surprising. Neither one of us got much sleep last night. How's the baking coming, Hannah?"

"Good." Hannah put the truck in gear and drove to the corner. "I took on another project, Michelle."

"Really? What project?"

"Sally asked us to run a cookie booth at her Holiday Gift Convention. I talked to Lisa, Aunt Nancy, and Marge, and they said they could handle the baking for the coffee shop by themselves if I wanted to do it."

"How many cookies do you think Sally's cookie booth will need?"

"Sally thinks we'll sell about the same number as we sell at the coffee shop."

Michelle looked surprised. "That's a *lot* of cookies!"

"I know. But we get to keep all the profits. Sally doesn't want a thing. And she's not charging us rent for the booth. She told me she wanted to provide it as an on-site service so that the attendees can come to our booth, buy cookies and coffee, and carry them to the tables and chairs that they're going to set up in the center of the space."

Michelle gave a little nod. "That's a smart idea on Sally's part. It'll be almost like a food court."

"Yes, except we'll be the only food booth. Brooke and Loren are so busy catering breakfasts, lunches, and dinners for the vendors, they won't have time to supply cookies for the cookie booth. Sally said she expected about fifty vendors and almost a hundred have signed up."

"That's great. And I want to help you in the booth. We don't have any rehearsals over the weekend, and Friday's a half day at school. I'm available on all three days."

A delighted smile spread over Hannah's face. "That's the best news I've gotten all week. And you'll have your own transportation to come and go as you please."

"What do you mean?" Michelle drew a deep breath and began to frown. "It's very generous of you, Hannah, but . . ." She stopped and swallowed. "Well . . . I hope you'll understand, but I really don't think I can drive Ross's car again, not after . . . you know."

"Of course not! I feel the same way. I wouldn't be able to stop thinking about what happened. And that's why I decided to sell it."

Michelle looked puzzled. "But, Hannah . . . how can you sell it? It's Ross's car."

"Not anymore. It's my car now. Cyril found the pink slip, and Ross signed it over to me on the afternoon he left."

"Oh, Hannah!" Michelle sounded as if she wanted to cry. "Do you think that means Ross knew he wasn't coming back?"

"Maybe. I guess that's the obvious conclusion. If he hadn't taken the condo keys with him, I'd be convinced of it. But he did, and now I'm not quite sure what all this means."

Michelle thought about that for a moment. "It means he was looking out for you. Otherwise he wouldn't have taken the time to sign the pink slip."

"He was looking out for you, too. He left the keys in your top dresser drawer."

"You're right. And Ross had no way of knowing that P.K. would be killed in his car and neither one of us would want to drive it again."

Both sisters were silent for a moment, and then Hannah sighed. "Well, even if he didn't know it was going to happen, Ross managed to solve a problem for you."

"What problem?"

"Transportation. Cyril has a buyer for Ross's car, and I told him to pick out a couple of used cars that would be good for you. If everything works out all right, we'll just do an even trade."

"But . . . Ross didn't intend to buy me a car," Michelle objected. "He intended to give his car to you."

"The keys were in *your* dresser drawer, not mine. That settles it for me. Ross wanted you to have a car so we're going out to Cyril's Garage tomorrow morning and you're going to choose which car you think is the best for you. I don't want any argument on this, Michelle."

"Well . . . if you're sure . . ."

"I'm sure." Hannah pulled into her parking spot in back of The Cookie Jar. "Now let's bake some cookies for Cyril. I told him I'd send some out to the garage when his mechanic came here with the pink slip."

"What are we baking?"

"Irish Potato Cookies. He should like those."

Michelle nodded, and then she reached across the seat of Hannah's cookie truck to hug her sister. "Thanks, Hannah. You're the best sister in the whole world!"

IRISH POTATO COOKIES

This dough must chill before baking.

1 and ½ cups white ***(granulated)*** sugar
1 cup salted butter ***(½ pound, 2 sticks)***, softened to room temperature
3 large eggs
2 teaspoons cream of tartar
1 teaspoon baking soda
½ teaspoon salt
1 teaspoon vanilla extract
1 and ½ cups all-purpose flour ***(pack it down in the cup when you measure it)***
3 cups instant mashed potato flakes ***(I used Hungry Jack Original)***
1 cup finely chopped walnuts ***(measure AFTER chopping)***
½ cup powdered ***(confectioners')*** sugar in a bowl for later

Place the white ***(granulated)*** sugar in the bowl of an electric mixer.

Hannah's 1st Note: This recipe is a lot easier to make if you use an electric mixer. You can do it by hand, but it will take much longer.

Add the softened butter and mix until the two ingredients are well combined and the mixture is light in color and fluffy.

Add the eggs, one by one, beating after each addition.

Add the cream of tartar, baking soda, and salt. Mix until everything is well combined.

Add the vanilla extract and mix it in.

Measure out the all-purpose flour in a separate bowl.

Mix it into the sugar, butter, and egg mixture in half-cup increments at LOW speed, mixing well after each addition.

Add the instant mashed potato flakes in half-cup increments, mixing well after each addition. Beat until everything is well incorporated.

Mix in the chopped walnuts. Beat for at least a minute on MEDIUM speed until everything is thoroughly combined.

Hannah's 2nd Note: At this point, you can add several drops of green food coloring if you are making these cookies for St. Patrick's Day. Try to achieve a nice pale green.

Scrape down the sides of your mixing bowl and give your Irish Potato Cookie dough a final stir with a wooden spoon by hand.

Prepare your cookie sheets by spraying them with Pam or another nonstick cooking spray, or covering them with parchment paper.

Scoop out a small amount of cookie dough with a spoon from your silverware drawer and try to form a dough ball with your impeccably clean hands. If this is too difficult because the dough is too soft, cover your bowl with plastic wrap and refrigerate it for 30 minutes to an hour. ***(Overnight is fine too, but then don't forget to shut off the oven!)***

When you're ready to bake, preheat the oven to 350 degrees F., rack in the center position.

While your oven is preheating, place the powdered sugar in a small bowl. You will use it to coat the cookie dough balls you will form.

Form balls of cookie dough 1 inch in diameter with your impeccably clean hands.

Roll the dough balls in the bowl of powdered sugar, one at a time, and place them on the cookie sheets, 12 dough balls to a standard-sized sheet. Flatten the dough balls a bit with a metal spatula or the heel of your impeccably clean hand.

Bake at 350 degrees F. for 10 to 12 minutes, or until your cookies are golden around the edges.

Take your cookies out of the oven and cool on the cookie sheet for 2 minutes and then remove them to a wire rack.

If you've covered your cookie sheets with parchment paper, all you have to do is grasp the edges of the paper and pull them, cookies and all, onto the wire rack.

Yield: Approximately 8 dozen tender and delicious cookies, depending on cookie size.

Chapter Ten

Hannah glanced in her living room window as she followed Michelle up the covered staircase that led to her condo. Usually Moishe was sitting on the sill staring out at her, but he wasn't there today. Perhaps he was sleeping and hadn't heard them climb the stairs. Now that she thought about it, Moishe had been sleeping a lot lately.

"I'll catch him if you open the door, Hannah," Michelle offered as Hannah reached the landing.

"Okay. Brace yourself." Hannah pulled out her keys and waited until Michelle was standing within a foot of the door with her body braced for the impact.

"Here we go," Hannah warned, inserting her key in the lock, unlocking the door, and opening it.

Both sisters stood there for a moment waiting, but there was no sound from inside. The door was open, but Moishe was nowhere in sight.

"Where do you suppose he's . . ." Michelle began to ask when an orange and white blur bolted out the door and jumped into her arms. She made a sound that was halfway between a groan and an exclamation, and then she laughed.

"He answered your question," Hannah told her.

"I guess!" Michelle was smiling as she carried Moishe

inside and placed him in his favorite spot on the back of the couch.

Hannah watched as her feline roommate played his usual game with Michelle. He looked up at her with an expression that Hannah could only describe as pathetic and gave a plaintive meow. Then he reached out with his paw, claws drawn in, and plunked it on the top of her hand. Hannah knew exactly what her cat wanted, but did Michelle know?

"Okay, you got it," Michelle said with a laugh. "Just hang on, Moishe. I'll get your kitty treats."

Convinced that her sister had all the bases covered, Hannah set the box she was carrying on the table and walked over to check the phone to see if there were any messages. The red light was blinking and the numeral five was displayed. That meant five people had called while she'd been at work. She pressed the button to play the messages, and was treated to a quintet of sales calls from a roofer, someone who called himself a handyman, a woman who wanted to sell her long-term health insurance, and someone she'd never heard of who warned her that it was time for the annual checkup of her heating and air-conditioning system. The last call, the fifth one, was the most interesting. It was a survey, supposedly, to find out if she had a home security system. If she already had a system, the caller wanted to know which make and model she had and how recently it had been installed.

Hannah was laughing out loud as she erased the messages, and she turned to see Michelle standing next to her.

"What's so funny?" Michelle asked her.

"That last message. Did you hear it?"

"Yes. I know they said it was a survey, but it was really a sales call, wasn't it?"

"Not necessarily. Mike warned me about calls like that. Sometimes they're more sinister than simple sales calls. The caller is gathering information about your home. If you tell them which kind of security system you have, they can compile a list for criminals who want to defeat your security system and break into your house."

"Oh! I didn't think of that. Did Mike tell you to just hang up, or what?"

"He said to tell them that you just installed a state-of-the-art system. And then, before they can ask any more questions, to hang up."

"I'll do that from now on and I'll tell my housemates to do the same. The Jambalaya smells great, Hannah. Do you have to add anything else to it before we serve it?"

"Yes, but it's easy. About a half hour before everyone comes, I'll thaw the shrimp and add it to the slow cooker. And then I'll cook the rice so it's all ready to add to the crock right before serving."

"I'll help you with that. Do you want me to bake some Cheesy Garlic Crescent Rolls to go with our salad? I noticed that you had a can of crescent rolls that's about to expire in the refrigerator."

"That would be great. Do I have everything you need to make them?"

"Yes. There's some shredded cheese on the second shelf, and you have garlic in the mesh basket with the onions. What are we having for dessert? Do you need me to make something quick?"

Hannah shook her head. "No, I've got that covered. I baked an Ultimate Fudgy Chocolate Bundt Cake while you were at the school."

"Is that what was in the box you carried up the stairs?"

"Yes, but I didn't have time to frost it."

"I'll frost it now. You have a tub of Cool Whip in the refrigerator and I know how to make Cool Whip Fudge Frosting."

"You're doing all the work, Michelle."

"Not really. You shopped, drove back here to put up the Jambalaya, and baked the cake. All I'm doing is throwing together the rolls and frosting the cake."

"But you must be tired, Michelle. You didn't get much sleep last night. Wouldn't you rather use the time before everyone comes to take a nap?"

"I don't need a nap. I'm all jazzed up about getting my own car in the morning. You look like you need a nap much more than I do. Why don't you go stretch out on your bed for twenty minutes or so? I'll wake you a few minutes before they come so you have time to freshen up."

Hannah was about to refuse when she reconsidered. She'd worked hard all day and she *was* very tired. A short nap was exactly what she needed.

Hannah opened her eyes. It was dark outside her bedroom window and for a moment, she thought it was morning. Then she remembered that she had stretched out to take a nap before Norman and Mike arrived. Had Michelle forgotten to wake her up? Or had she awakened on her own? Since she couldn't hear the sound of voices and Moishe was still with her and not playing with Cuddles, she assumed it was the latter.

"Time to get up, sleepyhead," she told the cat who was stretched out on half of her pillow. It was amazing how long Moishe was when he slept in her bed. There were times when he ended up with both pillows and she found herself sleeping on the very edge of the mattress. "Let's go, Moishe. You're getting company tonight. Norman is bringing Cuddles to play with you."

At the sound of his best friend's name, Moishe lifted his head. Then he sat up, gave a little shake, and watched her as she washed her face, brushed her hair, and changed to a clean sweater.

"Let's go see how Michelle is doing in the kitchen," Hannah said, and Moishe jumped off the mattress to pad down the hallway after her as she walked toward the kitchen.

As Hannah passed her desk in the living room, she noticed her personal checkbook sitting next to her daily calendar. She paused to pick it up, and put it in her saddlebag purse. She knew her balance because she subtracted the amount of every check she wrote and kept a running balance. She had three hundred and seventy-six dollars in that account, and she might need some or all of that money if Michelle's car cost more than Cyril could get from the sale of Ross's car. If the car Michelle chose cost more than that, she would pay it off on Cyril's time-payment plan.

As she entered the kitchen, Hannah began to smile. The Jambalaya she'd made smelled wonderful. She moved to the slow cooker, peered through the glass lid, and saw that Michelle had thawed the shrimp and stirred it in.

"You're up," Michelle said. "I made coffee if you want some."

"Coffee would be great," Hannah told her, taking her favorite cup from the cupboard and heading for the coffeepot to fill it. Then she sat down at the kitchen table and watched Michelle as her sister carried a covered pot to the crockpot and set it down on a folded kitchen towel.

"Rice?" Hannah made an educated guess.

"Yes. I made a mixture of brown rice, red rice, and white. Is that all right?"

"That's perfect. Variety's always nice when it comes to food. Did you have time to frost the cake, or shall I do it?"

"It's frosted, and I put it in the refrigerator. It should be refrigerated for at least thirty minutes so the frosting will set."

"When did you have time to do all that?"

"While you were sleeping. You needed the rest, Hannah. I checked on you a couple of times and you were out like a light." Michelle reached down to pet Moishe, who was looking at his food bowl expectantly. "Moishe was out like a light, too. He was even snoring."

At that instant, Hannah had an unwelcome thought. Did she snore and was that why Ross had left her? She was almost afraid to ask, but she had to know. "Was I snoring, too?"

"No. At least I don't think you were. You had the blanket pulled up over your face so I'm not sure I would have heard it."

"I was just curious," Hannah said, deciding it was best to change the subject. "I'll set the table."

"Sounds good." Michelle went to the counter, finished rolling up the last Cheesy Garlic Crescent Roll, and carried the pan to the refrigerator. "I'll put these in the oven when they get here."

As Michelle opened the refrigerator door, Hannah spotted her Ultimate Fudgy Chocolate Cake. Michelle had frosted it perfectly, and it looked delicious. There was a large salad bowl on the middle shelf, and she asked, "What's in the salad bowl?"

"I made a cut green bean, chopped hardboiled egg, and crumbled bacon salad. There's a sweet vinegar and ginger dressing in the bottom of the bowl, and I'll toss it when the guys arrive."

"But . . . I didn't buy any green beans. How did you . . . ?"

"You had a package in the freezer," Michelle explained, anticipating the rest of Hannah's question. "All I had to do was cook them. And you had a couple of hard-boiled eggs in the refrigerator."

Hannah got out a clean tablecloth and walked to the dining room table. As she folded the matching cloth napkins, she thought about how much easier it was to entertain when Michelle stayed with her. She went back into the kitchen to gather dishes, bowls, glasses, and silverware, but before she opened the cupboard door, she went to Michelle and gave her a hug.

Michelle smiled and hugged her back. "What was that for?" she asked.

"That was because I love you. And it was also a thank-you for all the work you did while I was sleeping."

JAMBALAYA

(Make this recipe in a 3-and-a-half or 4-quart slow cooker.)

12 ounces of boneless, skinless chicken breasts
2 green bell peppers
1 medium onion
2 stalks crisp celery
4 cloves of minced garlic ***(approximately 5 Tablespoons of jarred minced garlic)***
1 can ***(14 and a half ounces by weight)*** canned whole tomatoes
⅓ cup tomato paste
1 can ***(14 and ½ ounces by weight)*** beef broth ***(I used Swanson)***
1 Tablespoon dried parsley ***(or fresh parsley, but cut it up and use 2 Tablespoons)***
¼ teaspoon powdered oregano
¼ teaspoon powdered sage
1 teaspoon salt
1 teaspoon tabasco sauce ***(I used Slap 'Ya Mama because I like it much better)***
1 teaspoon cayenne pepper
1 pound shelled and deveined shrimp ***(I used***

frozen salad shrimp – it's already cleaned, and Moishe and Cuddles love it)

3 cups cooked rice

Hannah's 1st Note: Traditionally, white rice is used in this recipe, but you can use brown or mixed rice if you prefer – just follow the package directions to cook it.

Spray the inside of the slow cooker crock with Pam or another nonstick cooking spray.

Hannah's 2nd Note: This will make it much easier to wash later.

Cut the chicken into 1-inch pieces and put them into the bottom of the crock.

Clean the green bell peppers by taking out the seeds and stems. Chop them in pieces and add them to the crock.

Chop the onion and add it to the crock.

Chop the celery into slices ***(you can use the leaves if your stalk has them)*** and add them to the crock.

Add the minced garlic to the crock.

Add the whole tomatoes ***(and their juice)***. Also add the tomato paste to the crock.

Open the can of beef broth and add the broth to the crock.

Sprinkle in the parsley, oregano, sage, and salt.

Add the tabasco sauce ***(or your favorite hot sauce)***.

Stir in the cayenne pepper.

Hannah's 3rd Note: You will add the cooked rice and shrimp shortly before serving after the rest of the ingredients above have cooked together.

Turn the slow cooker to LOW and cook for 8 to 10 hours.

When the cooking time is up, thaw the shrimp by putting it in a strainer and running cold water over it.

Add the shrimp to the crock and cook for another 15 to 30 minutes.

Hannah's 4th Note: DO NOT ADD FROZEN SHRIMP to your crock. It could crack a hot crock and your whole meal would be ruined.

While your shrimp is cooking, cook the rice on the stove ***(or in the microwave if you bought the kind in pouches)*** according to the package directions.

Add the rice to the crock and stir it in right before serving the Jambalaya.

Hannah's 5th Note: I usually put all the ingredients except the rice and the shrimp in the slow cooker the night before and store the crock in the refrigerator. In the morning, I return the crock to the pot and turn it on LOW to cook all day while I'm gone. When I get home, all I have to do is add the shrimp to the crock, cook the rice on the stove, and stir it into the crock right before serving.

Michelle's Note: There is a hurry-up way to make this dish. If you turn the temperature dial to HIGH, it only has to cook for 3 to 4 hours. Then all you have to do is add the shrimp for 15 minutes, stir in the cooked rice, and you're good to go.

CHEESY GARLIC CRESCENT ROLLS

Preheat oven to 375 degrees F., rack in the center position.

2 eighteen-ounce (by weight) cans of refrigerated Crescent Dinner Rolls ***(I used Pillsbury)***
2 teaspoons crushed garlic
2 Tablespoons salted butter ***(1 ounce, ¼ stick)***, softened to room temperature
1 large egg, beaten ***(just whip it up in a glass with a fork)***
2 ounces finely shredded cheese ***(I used Kraft Cheddar)***

While your oven is preheating, prepare your baking sheets by spraying them with Pam or another nonstick baking spray or lining them with parchment paper.

Hannah's 1st Note: Parchment paper works best.

Open the cans according to package directions and unroll the dough on a lightly floured surface. DO NOT separate the rolls into triangles quite yet. Leave them in sheets for now.

Mix the crushed garlic together with the softened salted butter in a small bowl.

Spread the garlic and butter mixture evenly over the surface of the dough.

Mix the beaten egg with 2 ounces of finely shredded cheese.

Spread the egg and cheese mixture in a thin layer over the butter and garlic layer.

Separate the rolls into triangles and turn them so that they are point up, facing away from you.

Roll each triangle up from the base to the point and curve the resulting roll into a crescent shape.

Place your Cheesy Garlic Crescent Rolls on your prepared baking sheet.

Hannah's 2nd Note: If you'd like darker brown rolls, brush the tops of each crescent roll with melted salted butter.

Bake your rolls at 375 degrees F. for 10 to 12 minutes or until they are golden brown.

Leave the rolls on the baking sheet for 2 minutes and then transfer them to a napkin-lined basket and cover them with another napkin.

Serve your Cheesy Garlic Crescent Rolls warm.

Yield: 16 delicious rolls to serve with any entree.

Michelle's Note: If you invite Mike, Lonnie, and Norman to dinner, you'd better double this recipe!

Chapter Eleven

"More Jambalaya, Mike?" Hannah asked as Mike finished his third helping.

"Thanks, but I couldn't eat another bite." Mike leaned back in his chair and gave a satisfied smile. "You know something, girls?"

Hannah glanced at Michelle. They both knew what Mike was going to say. She gave a nod, Michelle nodded back, and they both spoke at once. "It was the best meal you've had in years!"

Mike looked shocked. "How did you know what I was going to say?"

"Just a lucky guess," Hannah replied, winking at Michelle.

"Yes, just a lucky guess," Michelle echoed her older sister. "The coffee's all ready to go, and I'll turn it on. Does anyone want dessert now?"

"We'll wait until Lonnie and I get through interviewing you," Mike decided for all of them. "Hannah? You're up first. Let's go in the kitchen where it's private. Then I want to talk to Michelle, and after that, we'll interview Norman."

"Just let me bring the carafe of coffee out here before you

start," Michelle added. "Then I won't have to come back in the kitchen to get anything."

Once the carafe, cups, and cream and sugar were on the table, Hannah followed Mike and Lonnie to the kitchen table. She wasn't looking forward to this interview because she'd have to admit that she hadn't really known much about her husband's background. Since she knew even less about P.K.'s private life, at least her interview shouldn't take long.

As it turned out, Hannah was wrong. Mike had wanted to know everything about Ross's life, including anything he'd told her about P.K. and even what she'd learned about Ross in college. Then Mike wrapped up her interview and sent her back to the table to tell Michelle to come in.

Once Michelle had left, Norman reached out for Hannah's hand. "You look exhausted. Were they that hard on you?"

"No, not at all. It's just that Mike wanted to know everything I knew about Ross in college and . . ." She paused and took a sip of her lukewarm coffee. "Those memories brought everything back."

"Just as if everything were happening again?"

Hannah sighed. "Yes, and it made me realize how naïve I was. When I was in college, I took everything at face value, including anything that anyone told me. And I never compared what I thought I knew about Ross then with what he told me later."

"There were discrepancies?"

"Yes. And I didn't realize it until Mike pointed them out to me. Ross told me that he'd grown up in Minnesota, but Mike checked his college records and he was an out-of-state student. And back then Ross said he was an only child, but when we talked about the wedding, he mentioned that his sister couldn't come because she worked in London. I guess it's possible that his father got divorced and remarried and his third wife had a daughter, but Ross has only been out of college a few years and his half-sister would be too young to move to London and work there."

Norman shrugged. "Perhaps Ross's father did get divorced again and his third wife had an older daughter from a previous marriage. Or they could have adopted an older child."

"It's possible, I guess, but there were other things, too. Little things that I didn't think about before. I . . . I really don't want to go into them now."

"Of course not." Norman slipped his arm around her shoulders. "You've had a long day."

"It's not that. It's just that . . . that I'm beginning to doubt my husband and everything he told me. I don't even know if that photo on our dresser is really his mother. Now I'm questioning everything, and that makes me feel disloyal."

"Then why don't you trust what Ross told you until it's proven false. Give him the benefit of the doubt, Hannah. There may be a reasonable explanation for all of these discrepancies."

"Yes, that's exactly what I'll do. That's what a good wife should do. At least I think it is."

"Loyalty," Norman said. "That's admirable, Hannah."

"That's true, unless that loyalty is misplaced and I'm wearing blinders. Then it's just plain stupid!"

"That was a great cake, Hannah." Mike shifted the box Hannah had given him to his other arm so that he could give her a hug. The box held three pieces of cake that Hannah suspected would be eaten by midnight. "Try not to worry, okay? We'll solve this case and find Ross."

Hannah nodded, even though she was beginning to doubt

that Mike could find Ross unless Ross wanted to be found. "Thanks, Mike."

"Bye, Shelly." Lonnie gave Michelle a quick hug. "I'll see you tomorrow morning. I'm going out to the garage to help Dad before I go to work . . . unless Mike needs me sooner, of course."

"Not until ten," Mike told him. "I have to make some calls when I get to the station and you can't help me with those."

Hannah turned to give Michelle a look that said, *I'll tell you later*. Their sisterly radar must have been working because Michelle nodded back.

"I'd better find Cuddles and head home," Norman said, after the door had closed behind Mike and Lonnie. He walked over to the couch, where she had been napping with Moishe, and then he turned back with a puzzled expression. "The cats aren't there."

Hannah smiled. "They're probably on my bed. Moishe's been going to bed early lately. Let's go look."

Hannah and Norman walked down the carpeted hallway and peeked in the open door to the master bedroom. It was clear that the cats hadn't heard them coming because Moishe was still sprawled out on Hannah's feather pillow and Cuddles was right next to him. Neither cat moved when they approached the bed or even twitched a whisker.

Hannah put her finger to her lips, and Norman gave a nod of agreement. Then both of them backed out of the room. When they got back to the living room, Hannah led the way to one of the soft leather sofas. "If you want to leave Cuddles, that's fine with me. You can always pick her up tomorrow."

"You do know she grows much longer during the night, don't you? And she also gains weight. Some nights, when I try to move her, she weighs three hundred pounds."

Hannah laughed. "That's okay. I'm used to that phenomenon. Moishe does the same thing."

"When you wake up in the morning, do you find yourself curled up into the smallest space possible so that Moishe can have the whole bed?"

"That's exactly what happens, but my offer still stands. Cuddles can have a sleepover with Moishe."

"Okay, as long as you know what you're getting into. You're leaving early tomorrow, aren't you?"

"No. I'm taking Michelle out to Cyril's garage, and he opens at seven for the people who want to leave their cars before they go to work. Michelle and I want to be there when he opens."

"What time will you leave here?"

Hannah did some lightning-quick calculating. "We'll leave here at six-thirty. Lisa said she'd come in early with Aunt Nancy and Marge to start the baking."

"Then I'll be here at six. That'll give me time to have a cup of coffee with you and pick up Cuddles. My first appointment's not until eight so I'll have plenty of time to take her home before I go to the clinic."

"Fine with me," Hannah said, smiling at him. "Thanks for your support, Norman. I really was a wreck after that interview with Mike."

"That's understandable." Norman stood up, pulled her into his arms, and gave her a hug. "I'll let myself out. Good night, Hannah."

"Good night, Norman."

After Norman had left, Hannah sat there for a moment, thinking. She wasn't sure just how she should feel if Ross had misled her about his background deliberately. Was that grounds for divorce? And did she really want a divorce? She considered it for a moment, and then she decided that she was borrowing trouble. As Norman had said, there could be a perfectly reasonable explanation for the discrepancies.

Feeling a bit better, Hannah got off the couch and headed for the bedroom. As she passed the door to the guest room, she glanced in and found Michelle already in bed, curled up on her side and sleeping. There was a slight smile on her face and Hannah wondered if her sister was dreaming about the car she would choose in the morning.

Five minutes later, Hannah was ready for bed and she climbed under the covers. A gentle nudge convinced the cats to move to the foot of the bed so she could reclaim her pillow, and before she could even think about how tired she was, she was in the exact same position as her youngest sister, fast asleep.

ULTIMATE FUDGY CHOCOLATE BUNDT CAKE

Preheat oven to 350 degrees F., rack in the middle position.

4 large eggs
½ cup vegetable oil
½ cup cold coffee ***(or water, if you don't want to use coffee)***
8-ounce ***(by weight)*** tub of sour cream ***(I used Knudsen)***
1 box of Chocolate Fudge Cake mix with or without pudding in the mix, the kind that makes a 9-inch by 13-inch cake or a 2-layer cake ***(I used Duncan Hines)***
5.1-ounce package of instant chocolate pudding mix ***(I used Jell-O, the kind that makes 6 half-cup servings.)***
12-ounce ***(by weight)*** bag of mini chocolate chips ***(11-ounce package will do, too—I used Nestle)***

Prepare your cake pan. You'll need a Bundt pan that has been sprayed with Pam or another nonstick cooking spray and then floured. To flour a pan, put some

flour in the bottom, hold it over your kitchen wastebasket, and tap the pan to move the flour all over the inside of the pan. Continue this until all the inside surfaces of the pan, including the sides of the crater in the center of the pan, have been covered with a light coating of flour. Shake out excess flour. Alternatively, you can coat the inside of the Bundt pan with Pam Baking Spray, which is a nonstick cooking spray with flour already in it.

Crack the eggs into the bowl of an electric mixer. Mix them up on LOW speed until they're a uniform color.

Pour in the half-cup of vegetable oil and mix it in with the eggs on LOW speed.

Add the half-cup of cold coffee and mix it in on LOW speed.

Scoop out the container of sour cream, and add the sour cream to your bowl. Mix that in on LOW speed.

When everything is well-combined, open the box of dry cake mix and sprinkle it on top of the liquid ingredients in the bowl of the mixer. Mix that in on LOW speed.

Add the package of instant chocolate pudding and mix that in, again on LOW speed.

Finally, sprinkle in the 12-ounce bag of mini chocolate chips and mix those in on LOW speed.

Shut off the mixer, scrape down the sides of the bowl, and give your batter a final stir by hand.

Use a rubber spatula to transfer the cake batter to the prepared Bundt pan.

Smooth the top of your cake with the spatula and put it into the oven.

Bake your Ultimate Fudgy Chocolate Cake at 350 degrees F. for 55 minutes.

Before you take your cake out of the oven, test it for doneness by inserting a cake tester, thin wooden skewer, or long toothpick midway between the sides of the circular ring. ***(You can't insert it in the center of the cake because that's where the crater is!)***

If the tester comes out clean, your cake is done. If there is still unbaked batter clinging to the tester, shut the oven door and bake your cake in 5-minute increments until it's done.

Once your cake is done, take it out of the oven and set it on a cold stove burner or a wire rack.

Let your cake cool for 20 minutes and then pull the sides away from the pan with impeccably clean fingers. Don't forget to do the same for the crater in the middle.

Tip the Bundt pan upside down on a platter and drop it gently on a towel on the kitchen counter. Do this until the cake falls out of the pan and rests on the platter.

Cover your Ultimate Fudgy Chocolate Bundt Cake loosely with foil and refrigerate it for at least one hour. Overnight is even better.

Frost your cake with Cool Whip Fudge Frosting. ***(Recipe and instructions follow.)***

Yield: At least 10 pieces of decadent chocolate cake. Serve with tall glasses of ice-cold milk or cups of strong coffee.

COOL WHIP FUDGE FROSTING

This recipe is made in the microwave.

8-ounce ***(by weight)*** tub of FROZEN Cool Whip ***(Do not thaw!)***
6-ounce ***(by weight)*** bag of chocolate chips ***(I used Nestle semi-sweet chips)***

Hannah's 1st Note: Make sure you use the original Cool Whip, not the sugar free or the real whipped cream.

Place the Cool Whip in a microwave-safe bowl.

Add the chocolate chips to the bowl.

Microwave the bowl on HIGH for 1 minute and then let it sit in the microwave for an additional minute.

Take the bowl out of the microwave, then stir to see if the chocolate chips are melted. If they're not, heat them in 30-second intervals with 30-second standing times in the microwave until you succeed in melting the chocolate chips.

Let the bowl sit on the countertop or on a cold burner for 15 minutes to thicken the icing.

When the time is up, give the bowl a stir and remove your cake from the refrigerator. Frost your Ultimate Fudgy Chocolate Bundt Cake with the frosting and don't forget the crater in the middle. You don't need to frost all the way down. That's almost impossible. Just frost an inch or so down the crater.

Return your cake to the refrigerator for at least 30 minutes before cutting it and serving it to your guests.

Hannah's 2nd Note: You can also use this icing on cookies. Simply frost and let your cookies sit on wax paper on the kitchen counter until the frosting has set and is dry to the touch.

Yield: This frosting will frost a batch of cookies, a 9-inch by 13-inch cake, a Bundt cake, or a round two-tier layer cake.

Hannah's 3rd Note: I always keep a tub of original Cool Whip and a bag of chocolate chips on hand to make this easy and delicious chocolate frosting.

Chapter Twelve

Grandma Knudson sat in her favorite chair as Hannah poured tea. The tea tray contained the teapot in a cozy, lemon, sugar, cream, and two bone china cups with saucers. The only thing missing on the tea tray was the pair of white gloves that Grandma said were passé.

"Thank you, Hannah," Grandma said, as she accepted the saucer and cup of tea from Hannah. "You do this beautifully, dear."

"Thank you. It's only because you taught me," Hannah returned the compliment.

Grandma Knudson looked pleased. She took a sip of her tea, smiled at Hannah, and asked, "Are you glad you're married, Hannah?"

"Oh, yes," Hannah said quickly, but she was a bit taken aback. Grandma wasn't usually this personal. "Ross is a wonderful husband."

"I'm glad to hear it, dear. To tell you the truth, I think you two make a perfect pair."

Suddenly, almost by magic, the scene changed to the Red Owl Grocery. Hannah was standing by the meat counter, trying to decide what she should buy for dinner.

"The salmon is good today," Florence told her, leaning

forward in her snow-white butcher's apron. "It just came in from Alaska."

Hannah smiled. She loved salmon. "That gives me a wonderful idea, Florence! Ross loves salmon so I'll take three pieces. And I'll make Salmon Wellington for Ross."

Florence nodded and began to wrap the salmon in butcher paper. "Then things are going well, Hannah?"

"Oh, yes!" Hannah replied. "Everything's just wonderful, Florence."

"That's good," Florence said as she handed the package to Hannah. "I think you two make the perfect pair."

The scene shifted again, and Hannah was the perfect pear, a lovely golden color with a slight rosy tint that proved that she was ripe for the picking. She was hanging from a branch on a lovely little pear tree in a beautiful garden. It must have been night because there were colorful Japanese lanterns hung from the other trees, and little twinkling lights decorated the trunks and branches. There was a stamped concrete square in the very center of the carefully manicured garden and it appeared to be a dance floor for balls and parties. An orchestra played on the far side of the square, and Hannah could see beautifully dressed couples dancing in the night.

One couple caught Hannah's eye. The man was Ross, and he was dancing with a lovely woman who looked exactly like Grace Kelly in *The Swan*. Her hair was golden, her white ball gown fit her perfect figure like a glove, and the image they presented was utterly breathtaking.

Even though the stellar couple was far away, Hannah found that she could hear their conversation. It was as if they were speaking directly into her ear.

"I love you with all my heart," Ross said. "I would move heaven and earth to make you happy. Your wish is my command."

His lovely partner smiled at him and held him close. "There's only one thing I really want."

"Anything," Ross promised. "What is it, darling?"

"The perfect pear. I'd like to have the perfect pear."

"If I knew where to find it, I'd get it for you," Ross said, smiling down at her.

"I see it. It's there on that little pear tree." The woman pointed to Hannah's branch. "Right there. Do you see it?"

"I do. I'll pluck it for you, my dearest. Just wait and you'll have it as a gift from me."

Hannah felt cold, as if something dreadful were about to happen. And then she began to tremble, but it was not from fear. Ross was standing directly below her branch, reaching up toward her. Since she was on the highest branch, he couldn't quite reach her, but he was shaking the branch, trying to make her fall right into his hand.

"Nooooooo," she screamed, terrified that she was about to lose the safe haven of her branch. "No, Ross! Please don't hurt me!"

But he didn't seem to hear her because he shook even harder. Her branch, her safe and secure home, began to sway back and forth, threatening to break. But her branch and her stem were strong. She had a fighting chance. If only he would stop trying to shake her down, she would be safe.

And then it happened. The heart of her, her strong and resilient stem, could not withstand such abuse. With a snap, it gave way and she was hurtling toward the ground, toward Ross and his waiting hand.

"Here you are, darling," Ross called out, carrying her to the beautiful woman who was waiting at the edge of the dance floor. "Let's eat this perfect pear together and pledge our love. You first."

Hannah screamed as the woman bit into her tender flesh.

Her life was over. Ross had betrayed her with another woman. He cared for her no longer. She was completely dead to him.

"Hannah? Hannah, wake up!"

The voice was familiar, and Hannah came out of her hideous dream with a gasp. "Wha . . . ?" She tried to speak, but tears were choking her throat.

"That must have been one heck of an awful nightmare," Michelle said, sitting down on the edge of Hannah's bed. "I should have realized that something was wrong when the cats came racing into the kitchen and tried to hide under the table. Cuddles was shaking, and Moishe's ears were flat against his head. Then I heard you screaming and I ran all the way to the bedroom to see what was wrong."

"Sorry," Hannah gasped as she sat up and began to breathe again. She hadn't been aware that she'd been holding her breath. "You're right," she said. "It was a nightmare and it was awful."

"Do you want to tell me about it?"

"Not really, but it was about a pear tree." Hannah stopped speaking and realized that she smelled something wonderful. "Do I smell pears baking?"

"You do. I've got two Upside Down Pear Coffee Cakes in the oven and another two cooling on the racks. Aunt Nancy and Lisa found the recipe in one of Heiti's mother's old cookbooks."

"It smells great!" Hannah said, chasing away the last vestiges of her nightmare. "No wonder I dreamed about perfect pears!"

"Maybe I'd better stop baking with fruit," Michelle said, still holding Hannah's arm. "First you dreamed about strawberries, then peaches, and now pears. I'd hate to think of what might happen if I baked a fruitcake!"

"You don't have to bake one," Hannah told her. "If I keep on having nightmares like this, I'll *be* one."

Michelle stood up. "Tell me about your dream later if you feel like it. My psych professor says that sometimes, if you tell someone about a nightmare, you don't dream the same one again."

Hannah considered that for a moment, wondered if it was true, and decided that she'd have to try it sometime. "Thanks, Michelle. I'll take a shower and be right out. That coffee cake smells so good, my stomach is growling."

The coffee cake was every bit as good as it smelled, and Hannah and Norman were full of compliments for Michelle. "I especially like the pears," Hannah said, accepting a second piece.

"So do I," Norman held out his plate for his second slice. "It's pretty, too. It's almost like the pineapple and cherry upside down cake that my mother used to make."

Michelle laughed. "Yes, except that my coffee cake doesn't have pineapple and cherries?"

"That might be it," Norman said with a laugh, and Hannah knew he was laughing at himself. "What made you decide to use pears, Michelle?"

"I thought about apple slices, but Hannah didn't have any apples. Then I thought about peaches, but she didn't have any of those either. I looked through her pantry, spotted a couple of cans of pears, and I decided to use them."

"Do you think you could make them with fresh pears, too?" Hannah asked her.

"I think so if I peel, core, and slice them. That's what I was planning to do with the apples. Let's stop by the Red Owl and see if Florence has any fresh pears. If she doesn't, I'll use canned pears again. I want to make another couple of coffee cakes for The Cookie Jar to see how your customers like it."

"Good idea. We can serve coffee cake at Sally's convention too, if we get some small paper plates and plastic forks," Hannah suggested. "The convention opens at nine and we could feature coffee cake as our breakfast treat."

"And muffins," Norman suggested. "You don't need plates and forks with those and they're good for breakfast, too."

"And Michelle makes great breakfast muffins," Hannah said.

"I've had the peach muffins and the strawberry muffins," Norman remembered. "You could make mini muffins in mini cupcake papers and people could mix and match them."

"Good idea," Hannah said, turning to Michelle. "The next time you come home on vacation, let's try it at The Cookie Jar."

"That would be fun," Michelle agreed. "Are you going to come out to help me pick out my car, Norman?"

"Yes, right after I take Cuddles home. Doc Bennett's coming in to help me today so I have the day off. And I'd like to take both of you out to dinner tonight at the Lake Eden Inn to celebrate."

"Thanks, Norman," Michelle said, accepting for both of them. "I'm really glad you'll be with us at Cyril's. I value your opinion, and I want to make sure I choose the right car."

Hannah could tell that Norman was pleased. "We can drink some of Cyril's bad coffee while we wait for Michelle to test-drive the cars," she told Norman. "That way, I won't be standing in the car lot alone."

"You're not going to look at the cars with me?" Michelle sounded surprised.

Hannah shook her head. "No. You don't need my help, and it's your decision. You'll be the one driving it."

"But . . . how can I be sure I get the right car?"

"It's easy," Hannah said. "All you have to do is pretend you're shopping for clothes. When you try something on, you know if it's right for you. A dress might look wonderful on the rack, but if it looks awful on you, you won't buy it. It's the same thing with cars. They can look good sitting there in the lot, but you have to try them on by test-driving them. I'm sure you have a good idea of what you want. When you see it and when you drive it, you'll know and you'll make the right choice."

An hour and a half later, Norman stood next to Hannah as Lonnie and Cyril showed the used cars they'd chosen to Michelle. "If you were the one buying a used car, which one would you choose?" he asked Hannah.

"Personally, I'd choose the blue one, but it's up to Michelle." Hannah was glad that Norman had arranged with Doc Bennett to take over his morning appointments. It was good to have company on a car-buying expedition like this.

Norman looked slightly worried. "She won't go for the convertible, will she?"

"It's really a nice-looking car, but I don't think so."

"Good. I had a used convertible when I was in Seattle, and it was awful in the winter. I was always cold, even when the heater was going full blast."

"That's why I'm glad it's winter and Michelle is test-driving the cars now."

"You're right. She'll get to test the heaters, too."

"A car with a bad heater can be miserable," Hannah replied, and that certainly wasn't an exaggeration. The heater in her cookie truck had never worked properly until Mike and Norman had paid Cyril to fix it for her as a surprise present.

One by one, Michelle climbed behind the wheels of the

cars that Lonnie and Cyril had selected. Lonnie went along on the test drives, and Hannah was glad to see that Michelle was shaking her head after she'd driven the convertible. She'd saved the blue car for last and Hannah found she was smiling as Michelle drove out of the lot.

"Do you think that's the one?" Norman asked her.

"I hope so. She saved it for last, and Michelle tends to save the best for last."

"How do you know?"

"I remember when she was little. She loved bacon and she always ate her pancakes first and saved her bacon for last. I've got my fingers crossed, Norman. The blue one would make a good car for her."

"Why?"

"It's not too large, and that means she wouldn't have any problem parking. And it's not so small that it wouldn't hold everything she usually carries with her. It has a back seat and that would be good for passengers, and it looks sporty, but it's also a sedan."

Five minutes later, Michelle was back. She parked the car and she looked very excited as she ran over to join them. "Is it okay if I choose the blue one, Hannah?"

"Of course," Hannah answered quickly. "You can have any car that you want."

"But what if it's a lot more than the money Cyril could get for Ross's car?"

"Don't worry about that. Cyril and Lonnie picked out the used cars that were an even trade, or very close to it."

Michelle gave them a big, happy smile. "Then I'll take the blue one! I've always wanted a car like that." She threw her arms around her sister and gave her a big hug. "Thank you, Hannah! Lonnie and Cyril both checked it out, and they said it runs perfectly."

"Then go tell them that you made your decision and you want it," Hannah urged her.

"I will! I can hardly wait to drive it to The Cookie Jar."

When Michelle ran off, Hannah turned to Norman. "I'm going to go talk to Cyril."

"That's fine with me. I'll leave, too. I really should get down to the clinic."

Hannah was surprised. "But I thought Doc Bennett was taking over your appointments."

"He is, but I have some paperwork to do. I'm way behind on my billing. I'll see you later, Hannah."

"Great. I'll be testing out some new cookies today and I'll save samples for you."

Once Norman had left, Hannah walked over to Cyril, Michelle, and Lonnie. "Could I see you for a moment, Cyril?"

"Sure thing." Cyril moved away from Michelle and Lonnie. "What's up, Hannah?"

"Two things. Let's go to your office. We can talk on the way."

Hannah waited until they were completely out of earshot, and then she broached the first subject. "Something occurred to me last night, but it was too late to call you. Did the man who bought Ross's car know that P.K. died in it?"

"No. There was no reason to tell him."

"But I thought you had to file a report when the car had been in an accident."

"You do if the damage is over a certain amount. This was less."

"I wonder if the man would have bought it if he'd known."

"I think he would have, but we weren't required to tell him so we didn't. I'm really sorry about P.K., Hannah. I liked him, and I liked his girlfriend, too."

"You knew his girlfriend?"

"I only met her once, but she left a lasting impression." Cyril gave a little chuckle. "P.K. bought one of my used cars for her as an engagement present. He said she'd always wanted a Jeep and we had a nice used Wrangler on the lot. It didn't have that many miles on it, but it needed to be repainted. P.K. told me that was fine because he was going to have it repainted in Pinkie's favorite color before he gave it to her."

"Her name was Pinkie?"

"That's what he called her, but I think it must have been short for something else. P.K. said that pink was her favorite color and she'd always wanted a pink Jeep. He was going to sign it over to her right before he proposed and gave her an engagement ring."

"That's a really nice engagement present."

"Yes, and it's unique. I've never seen a pink Jeep before."

"Neither have I!" Hannah gave a little laugh. "Did you paint her Jeep here?"

"No, P.K. took it to one of those places that paint your whole car in a day. He picked it up the next day and brought it back here. We put it up on the hoist so she wouldn't see it right away and it could be a surprise. They got engaged in bay two of my garage."

"She didn't know about the pink Jeep?"

"She didn't know about any of it, including the ring P.K. hid in the glove box. We lowered the hoist and you should have seen her face! P.K. handed her the keys, told her that the Jeep was his present for her, and said that there was another present for her in the glove box. They got in, she opened the glove box and found the engagement ring, and they kissed for what must have been a whole five minutes. My mechanics still talk about how much fun we had that day."

"I can see why." Hannah was still amused at the idea of a pink Jeep. "Did she love her pink Jeep?"

"She surely did. She was totally in love with the paint job, and she even noticed that they painted the inside of the glove box and all four wheel wells. That was a great day, Hannah. We toasted them with champagne for us and sparkling apple juice for them because P.K. had told us that they didn't drink. We closed the shop early that day, and all the customers who came in to pick up their cars joined in the party."

"I wish I'd been here."

"So do I. We really had a good time. We ordered pizza and made sure we got a special chicken and mushroom one for her because she doesn't eat meat. And when a couple of the mechanics' wives came to pick them up, we turned on the radio and danced to the music. Then Bridget came in with the engagement cakes she'd baked for them."

"Cakes?" Hannah asked, noticing that Cyril had used the plural to refer to his wife's contribution to the party.

"That's right. She made three of them, exactly the same. When I asked her why, she told me that she just knew it was going to turn into a big party."

"What kind of cake was it?"

"Chocolate. Everyone who was here had a slice with ice cream on top because she didn't have time to frost them. She told me that she got the recipe from you."

"Did she call it Ultimate Fudgy Chocolate Cake?" Hannah asked him.

"That sounds right. It was so good, I asked her to make it for all my birthdays from then on."

"Tell Bridget I'll give her the recipe for my chocolate frosting. It's fast and easy to make. And it's the perfect frosting for that cake."

Hannah and Cyril arrived at the outer door to the garage

and they walked to his office. Once Hannah had seated herself in the chair in front of his desk, she drew out her checkbook.

"I want to write you a check for whatever I owe you on Michelle's car. And if it's more than I have in my checking account, I want to pay off the rest on time."

"That's nice of you, Hannah, but you don't owe me anything. As a matter of fact, I owe *you* five hundred dollars." Cyril laughed at her astounded expression. "That's right, Hannah. I got a great price for the car Ross signed over to you. Even adding in the registration and insurance, you still came out five hundred bucks to the good."

"Really? Are you sure that includes everything?"

"I'm positive. This isn't the first car I've sold, Hannah."

"I know. It's just hard to believe you got that much for Ross's car. You must be a great salesman!"

"Of course I am. I'm Irish." Cyril gave her a smug grin. "Some people might call it Irish blarney, but I call it Irish charm."

"You're wonderful, Cyril. Thank you so much for your Irish charm. Between you and Ross, Michelle has a great gift."

"Maybe I shouldn't ask you this, but what's happening with Ross, Hannah? Is he coming back? I know the word on the street is that he's out on location for a special project, but the fact he signed his car over to you makes me wonder."

Hannah took a deep breath, readying herself for the explanation her whole family had urged her to make. She opened her mouth to speak the rehearsed words, but she just couldn't do it.

"Truthfully, I just don't know," she admitted. "I can't explain why he signed his car over to me, and I can't ask him until he comes back."

"Fair enough, Hannah. Maybe he was planning to get a new car, or maybe he had some sort of premonition that something was going to happen to him and he wanted to provide for you, just in case. People do have premonitions, you know. They call it the gift of second sight."

"Anything's possible, Cyril," Hannah responded, even though she didn't want to think about it.

"Keep the faith, darlin'," Cyril told her, patting her shoulder. "It's better to believe that everything'll be all right than it is to worry that it won't."

UPSIDE DOWN PEAR COFFEE CAKE

Preheat oven to 350 degrees F., rack in the middle position.

Sweet Crumb Topping:

½ cup finely chopped pecans
⅓ cup brown sugar ***(pack it down in the cup when you measure it)***
¼ cup all-purpose flour ***(pack it down in the cup when you measure it)***
½ teaspoon cinnamon
1 and ½ ounces cold salted butter ***(that's 3 Tablespoons)***

Fruit Layer:

¼ cup salted butter ***(2 ounces, ½ stick, ⅛ pound)***
½ cup brown sugar ***(pack it down in the cup when you measure it)***
3 pears, peeled, cored, and thinly sliced, either fresh or canned
½ cup golden raisins

Coffee Cake Batter:

2 cups all-purpose flour ***(pack it down in the cup when you measure it)***
1 cup white ***(granulated)*** sugar
3 teaspoons baking powder ***(that's one Tablespoon)***
1 teaspoon salt
⅓ cup softened, salted butter
1 cup whole milk
1 large egg

Prepare your baking pan(s). You'll need a 9-inch by 9-inch square pan with 2-inch tall sides.

Hannah's 1st Note: If the only square pan you have is 8 inches square, use that and also use a standard-size bread pan. Baking times for alternate pans are different, so test for doneness by inserting a long toothpick or cake tester in the center of the pan. If it comes out clean, your cake is done. If not, give it a bit more baking time in the oven.

Spray your pan(s) with Pam or another nonstick cooking spray.

While your pan(s) are prepared, empty, and still cool, find a pretty, heatproof platter. Make sure that the platter is larger than the surface of the pan. It will also

help if the platter has slightly raised edges because the butterscotch liquid that will be formed in the oven will drizzle down when you invert the pan over the platter. ***And you won't want to lose a drop of that wonderful butterscotch taste!***

Prepare the Sweet Crumb Topping first.

Use a fork from your silverware drawer to mix the chopped pecans and the brown sugar together in a small mixing bowl.

Next, mix in the all-purpose flour and the cinnamon.

Use the fork or a pie crust blender to cut in the cold butter.

Continue to mix until the resulting mixture is crumbly.

Set the Sweet Crumb Topping aside on the counter while you prepare the fruit layer.

Place the butter in the bottom of your prepared baking pan(s). Set the pan(s) in the oven until the butter has melted. Use pot holders to take the pan(s) out of the oven and then move to a wire rack or a cold stove burner.

Sprinkle the brown sugar on top of the melted butter in the pan(s).

Arrange the thinly sliced pears in the pan(s).

Sprinkle the golden raisins on top of the sliced pears.

Let the pan(s) sit on the rack or cold burners while you make the Coffee Cake Batter.

Hannah's 2nd Note: This coffee cake is easier to make if you use an electric mixer. You can do it by hand, but it will take some time and muscle.

Combine the flour, white sugar, baking powder, and salt in the bowl of an electric mixer. Mix for a few seconds on LOW speed and turn off the mixer.

Add the softened butter, milk, and egg. Mix them in on LOW speed for a minute and then turn the mixer up to MEDIUM speed.

Mix for one minute, then shut off the mixer and scrape down the bowl.

Mix at MEDIUM speed for another 2 minutes, shut off the mixer, and scrape down the bowl again.

Take the bowl out of the mixer and give it another stir by hand with a rubber spatula.

Pour the Coffee Cake Batter over the fruit layer in your pan(s).

Remember that Sweet Crumb Topping? It's now time to use it.

Sprinkle the Sweet Crumb Topping over the Coffee Cake Batter in your pan(s).

Bake your yummy creation at 350 degrees F. until a cake tester, long toothpick, or thin wooden skewer inserted in the center of the cake comes out clean with no batter sticking to it.

Baking time for the 9-inch by 9-inch square pan should be approximately 50 minutes.

If you used an 8-inch by 8-inch square pan, baking time should be approximately 40 minutes.

If you also used a standard-sized bread pan, baking time should be approximately 40 minutes.

Hannah's 3rd Note: Start testing your Upside Down Pear Coffee Cake 5 minutes before the end of the baking time.

Use pot holders to remove the pan(s) from the oven, then immediately invert a heatproof serving platter over the top of your pan. Hold on to the pan(s) with pot

holders and invert the pan quickly. Leave the pan(s) in place, sitting on top of your Upside Down Pear Coffee Cake, for one or two minutes so that the butterscotch formed by the butter and brown sugar can drizzle down over the top of your coffee cake(s).

Yield: Approximately 9 servings unless you invite Mike or Norman.

Michelle's Note: The next time I make this, I'm going to try it with thinly sliced fresh peaches.

Chapter Thirteen

Promptly at nine o'clock, Hannah stood at the top of the steps of the Lake Eden First Mercantile Bank, waiting for Lydia Gradin, the head teller, to open the front door.

"Good morning, Hannah," Lydia said in her best customer service voice as she unlocked the door and ushered Hannah in.

"Hi, Lydia," Hannah responded, stepping inside the cavernous interior. The bank was built entirely of Minnesota granite, trucked here from the Cold Spring granite quarries.

"I'll help you in just a minute," Lydia told her. "Just let me open the safe and unlock my cash box."

"Take your time, Lydia," Hannah said, watching her walk away. Lydia was wearing a tight red pullover sweater that she must have purchased when she was two or three sizes smaller, and an extremely short black skirt that Delores would have termed "inappropriate" for a woman approaching sixty.

The only bank in town was nicely decorated with fake palm trees of a species that would never grow in the Minnesota climate. Comfortable chairs upholstered in a beautiful shade of lavender graced the waiting area, and Hannah chose one to occupy. There were small glass-topped tables between the chairs, and large colorful paintings of tropical flowers that would quickly wither and die if they had been planted in a local garden. The décor had been updated when Doug Greerson had taken over as president of the bank, and Hannah had once asked him why he'd chosen to decorate in fake trees and flowers that would be more at home on a tropical island. Doug had laughed and confessed that since he never had time for vacations, entering the newly decorated bank every morning gave him the illusion of tropical warmth and was second best only to taking a trip to Aruba.

"I'm ready for you." Lydia motioned to Hannah as she took her seat on the high swivel chair behind the first teller's window.

Hannah got up and hurried to Lydia's window. "I have a deposit for my personal checking account."

Lydia examined the check Hannah pushed through the grate that separated the tellers from the customers. Then she flipped it over and frowned slightly. "You have to endorse it, Hannah."

"Of course I do." Hannah felt like a fool as Lydia pushed the check back through the grate. "Sorry about that," she apologized as she quickly endorsed the check. "I know my account got really low, and this check should help a lot."

"Let's put it in and I'll give you your new balance," Lydia said, clicking some keys on her computer keyboard. A moment later, she began to frown.

"What is it, Lydia? I haven't reconciled my latest bank statement yet, but I'm not overdrawn, am I?"

"I should say not!" Lydia looked shocked at Hannah's question. "I'll write the current balance on your receipt of deposit."

It took a moment for the printer to generate the receipt,

and then Lydia flipped it over and wrote on the back of the slip. She pushed it through the grate to Hannah and watched as Hannah read the amount.

"But this says . . ." Hannah took a deep breath before she read off the amount. "Sixty thousand eight hundred and seventy-six dollars!"

"That's what my screen says. Did you make a big deposit to your personal account that should have gone in your business account?"

"No! I've never had that much in my business account. This is wrong, Lydia. Somehow my personal account was credited with someone else's deposit."

"Just let me see whose initials are on that large deposit." Lydia typed something on her keyboard and waited for a response. "Oh, dear!" she said, wincing slightly.

"Who is it?"

Lydia leaned closer to the grate. "It's Doug Greerson. Let me go see if he's in his office, Hannah. I'm not sure how this happened, but somehow a terrible mistake has been made."

Two minutes later, Hannah was seated in front of Doug's desk, a cup of cappuccino from his espresso machine in her hand. She sipped as Doug typed something on his keyboard and then he looked up at her.

"It's not a mistake, Hannah. That *is* your correct balance. Did you think you had more than that in your account?"

"Good heavens, no! I've never deposited that much money in my life, and now I have sixty thousand dollars more than I'm supposed to have. I was credited with someone else's deposit, Doug, and by now their checks are probably bouncing all over the place!"

Doug smiled. "It's not someone else's deposit, Hannah. It's yours. And I think I see the problem. Didn't Ross tell you that he was transferring money to your account before he left to go out on location?"

Hannah was so shocked that, for a moment, she couldn't speak. "No," she answered in a small voice. "I . . . I was at work and we didn't get a chance to talk before he left."

Doug pulled out his desk drawer and removed a folder. "Well, he certainly took care to make sure that you wouldn't need any money while he was gone. I have some signature cards for you to sign."

"Signature cards?"

"Yes. For his accounts. He listed you on all his accounts and he said he wanted to make them joint accounts. He told me he felt bad that he hadn't done that before you two were married."

Hannah watched as Doug pulled some cards from his folder. "There are three accounts, and here are three signature cards. Just sign your full name on the second line of each card and you'll be able to access any and all of them." Doug stopped speaking and stared at her across his desk. "You look pale, Hannah. Are you all right?"

"I . . . I . . . yes. It's just . . . a surprise, that's all." Hannah looked down at the signature cards so that Doug couldn't see how rattled she was. It appeared that Ross had left all of his assets to her, including his car. Was Cyril right and had Ross gotten a premonition that something bad was going to happen to him and he might not be able to come home? Or was this even more proof that he had planned to leave and never come back home to her? But Ross had taken his keys to the condo with him. Didn't that prove that he'd planned to come back?

As Hannah signed the first card, she tried her best to trust Cyril's advice about believing that everything would be all right instead of worrying about the worst. But faced with this new information about the man she had married, it was even more difficult not to worry.

"While you're signing, I'll print out the balances," Doug

said, turning to his keyboard again. "Ross told me he wanted you to know exactly what was in each of his accounts."

Hannah nodded. She was still too upset to try to speak. As she signed the second card, Doug's printer activated and a sheet of paper dropped into the tray.

Doug removed the paper and reached across his desk to hand it to her. "Here you are, Hannah."

"Thank you, Doug." Hannah signed the last card, stacked them in a neat pile, and pushed them across the desk to Doug. Then she folded the sheet of paper in half and stuck it in her purse. There was no way she could face any more surprises this morning. She'd look at it later, when she was alone in the kitchen at The Cookie Jar.

Hannah slipped the last pan of cookies onto a shelf in her industrial oven and closed the door. After she'd set the timer, she walked to the kitchen coffeepot and poured herself a cup. A moment later, she was sitting on her usual stool at the work station.

Her saddlebag purse seemed to loom large on the stool next to her. It drew her like a magnet, and her curious mind demanded satisfaction. *Go ahead and look*, it urged her. *You're alone and you've put it off long enough. Everyone else is in the coffee shop, and no one will notice if it upsets you. You want to know, don't you?*

She did want to know, and Hannah reached over to open her purse. She drew out the folded sheet of paper that Doug had given her and held it in her hand. Ross had spent the weeks preceding their marriage telling her not to worry, that they could afford it whenever he spent large sums of money, but was it true? Or would there be some huge credit card bills coming in the mail for her husband?

Hannah sent up a silent prayer that Ross had enough

money to pay any bills that would arrive, and then she unfolded the paper.

She was afraid to look at the paper. She eyed the swinging restaurant-style door instead, half hoping that someone would push through and she would have to stuff it back in her purse, but it was perfectly motionless.

Coward! Hannah's mind chided her. *You'll have to look, sooner or later. Do it right now while you have some privacy. Take a deep breath and just do it!*

She took a deep breath and looked down at the printout. The balance of the first account was a little over thirty thousand dollars, and it showed an interbank transfer of sixty thousand dollars. The transfer must be for the money that Ross had deposited in her personal checking account.

The second account was next, and Hannah noticed that it was a money market account. The balance on that account was close to a hundred thousand dollars!

Hannah was so shocked, she dropped the paper. She knew that KCOW paid Ross a good salary, but that couldn't account for this much money. No wonder he'd told her not to worry, that they could afford to pay for their honeymoon cruise!

She blinked to make sure her eyes wouldn't add any extra zeros to the balance of the third account. This one was an interest-bearing savings account, and it contained two hundred and twenty-six thousand dollars. Ross had over four hundred thousand dollars in the Lake Eden First Mercantile Bank!

Hannah stared down at the paper in awe. Maybe Ross wasn't in the same category as Bill Gates or Warren Buffett, but he had more money in the bank than she could ever hope to accrue in her lifetime.

She raised her coffee cup and took a sip. Then she looked down at the paper again. The totals were still the same. She hadn't imagined it. She pinched herself, just to make sure that this wasn't a very real dream, and looked again. Still the same. It was really true.

Hannah propped her head up with her hands. She felt slightly light-headed and just a bit dizzy with everything that had happened. Things were moving too fast, moving away from her and out of her control. She reminded herself to breathe deeply, and when she felt more in control, she examined the paper again. The totals were there, clearly printed in black ink.

The timer rang, and Hannah found she was grateful for the interruption. She needed to think about something besides wondering how Ross had accumulated all that money. She grabbed her oven mitts, moved the bakers rack closer to the oven, and took the trays from the shelves, one by one. The Maple Crunch Cookies would have to cool on the pans for a minute or two to crisp up before she placed the cookies on the bakers rack.

Several minutes later, the cookies and their parchment paper lining were on the racks. They smelled wonderful, and Hannah was glad she'd thought to make them. Now all that remained was to taste-test them. If they were good, she would bake more to take to the convention hall to sell as breakfast cookies.

Hannah was about to sit down at the work station again when there was a knock on the back door. It was a knock she recognized, and she hurried to let Norman in.

"Hi, Hannah," he greeted her, as he hung his parka on a hook by the back kitchen door. "Do I smell fresh cookies? Or are they . . . pancakes?!"

Hannah laughed. "They're not pancakes, but they do smell like that. They're Maple Crunch Cookies. Sit down, Norman. I'll get you a cup of coffee, and then I'll see if the cookies are cool enough to put on a plate."

While Norman sipped his coffee, Hannah walked over to the bakers rack to test the cookies. Since they were still warm but not hot, she filled a plate and carried it back to the work station.

"Try one, Norman," she urged as she set the plate down in front of him. "I've never baked these before and I want to know what you think of them."

Norman reached for a cookie and took a bite. Then he began to smile. "They're good," he told her. "I'd like to eat these for breakfast at least twice a week, maybe more. They're crunchy and sweet, and they taste like maple syrup. They're even better than pancakes. There's something else, too. It's something I like, but I can't quite figure out what it is."

"Corn flakes."

"That's it!" Norman nodded and reached for another cookie. "So it's cereal and pancakes, two of my favorites for breakfast. Are you going to try them out on your customers today?"

"Yes. They love it when we try out new cookies."

"Because they enjoy giving you their opinion?"

"That's part of it. The other part is taste-testing cookies for us means that they're free."

"That's always a bonus." Norman took another cookie and pushed the plate toward Hannah. "Put those away, please. They're addictive, and I'll eat them all if you leave them here."

Hannah was smiling as she removed the plate and placed it on the kitchen counter, but her smile faded as she approached the work station again. "I need to show you something, Norman. I need your advice."

"Okay. What is it?"

"Cyril gave me a check for five hundred dollars this morning. He said his profit from selling Ross's car was more than the cost of Michelle's car."

"That's great, Hannah!"

"Yes, but what happened after that wasn't so great. Or maybe it was. I need you to tell me."

"Okay. What happened?"

"I stopped by the bank to deposit Cyril's check to my personal account and I discovered that there could be a big problem."

"It's okay, Hannah. If you need money, I'll be glad to lend it to you."

"It's not *that*, Norman. As a matter of fact, it's exactly the opposite."

"Exactly the opposite?" Norman looked puzzled. "What do you mean? You'd better start from the beginning, Hannah."

MAPLE CRUNCH COOKIES

DO NOT preheat oven—dough must chill before baking.

2 cups white ***(granulated)*** sugar
1 cup salted butter ***(2 sticks, 8 ounces, ½ pound)***, softened to room temperature
2 large eggs beaten ***(just whip them up in a glass with a fork)***
½ cup maple syrup
1 teaspoon baking soda
1 teaspoon baking powder
1 teaspoon salt
1 teaspoon vanilla extract
4 cups all-purpose flour ***(pack the flour down in the cup when you measure it)***
½ cup crushed corn flakes ***(measure AFTER crushing – I used Kellogg's Corn Flakes)***
1 cup ***(6-ounce package)*** white chocolate or vanilla chips
½ cup white ***(granulated)*** sugar ***(for later, to coat the cookie dough balls you will make before baking your cookies)***

Hannah's 1st Note: To measure maple syrup, spray the inside of the measuring cup with Pam or another nonstick cooking spray. If you do this, the syrup will not stick to the inside of the measuring cup.

Hannah's 2nd Note: You can make these cookies by hand in a large mixing bowl with a wooden spoon, but using an electric mixer is a lot easier.

Place the white sugar and the softened salted butter in the bowl of an electric mixer.

Beat them together until they are smooth and creamy.

Add the beaten eggs and mix them in thoroughly.

Add the maple syrup and mix it in until it is well combined.

With the mixer running on LOW speed, beat in the baking soda, baking powder, salt, and vanilla extract. Mix until everything is well combined.

Measure out the flour and add it to the bowl in half-cup increments, mixing thoroughly after each addition.

Use a rubber spatula to scrape down the sides of the mixing bowl and remove it from the mixer.

Add the crushed corn flakes and white chocolate chips to your mixing bowl and stir them in by hand. Continue stirring until they are evenly distributed.

Give your Maple Crunch Cookie dough a final stir by hand with a wooden spoon.

Chill the dough for at least 1 hour before baking. ***(Overnight is fine, too.)***

When your dough has chilled, preheat your oven to 350 degrees F., rack in the middle position.

While your oven is preheating, prepare your baking sheets by spraying them with Pam or another nonstick cooking spray or lining them with parchment paper.

Measure out the ½ cup of white sugar and place it in a shallow bowl. You'll use this to coat your dough balls.

Roll the dough into walnut-sized balls with your hands.

Roll the dough balls in the bowl of sugar and then place them on the prepared cookie sheets, 12 to a standard sheet.

Flatten the dough balls just a bit with a metal spatula. ***(This will keep them from rolling off the cookie sheet as you carry it to the oven.)***

Bake your Maple Crunch Cookies at 350 degrees F. for 10 to 12 minutes or until they are golden brown.

Take the cookies out of the oven. Cool them on the cookie sheets for no more than 2 minutes. Then remove the cookies and place them on a rack to complete cooling. ***(If you leave them on the cookie sheets for too long, they'll stick.)***

Michelle's Note: Andrea says that Tracey and Bethie are trying to convince her to bring them down to The Cookie Jar so that they can eat these cookies instead of the bowls of cereal that Andrea usually gives them for breakfast.

Chapter Fourteen

"Here's what happened," Hannah said, sitting down on the stool across from Norman. "I put my personal checkbook in my purse because I didn't want Michelle to have to pay any extra money for whatever car she chose. I knew my balance and I was hoping that I had enough in my account to cover the difference."

"That was nice of you, Hannah."

"Thanks. I wanted to do it for her, Norman. She never lets me pay her for helping out at The Cookie Jar and I owe her a lot. I didn't have that much in my account, but I was hoping it would be enough. And if it wasn't, I was going to put the rest on time with Cyril and pay it off."

"I would have given you the money if it had been more, Hannah. All you had to do was let me know."

"Thank you, Norman." Hannah thought again about how sweet and caring Norman was, and then she went on with her explanation. "As it turned out, I certainly didn't need any more money!"

"Because of the check from Cyril?"

"That's just a small part of it. When I took Cyril's check to the bank and deposited it, I said something to Lydia about how I hoped I wasn't overdrawn. She checked my balance and she looked really shocked when she wrote the total on the deposit slip. It was sixty thousand dollars more than I thought I had."

"The bank made a mistake?"

"That's what I thought, and Lydia did, too. She looked at the teller's initials and said that Doug Greerson had handled that deposit."

"Doug?"

"Yes, and I went straight into his office to talk to him about it. It turned out it wasn't a mistake at all, that Ross had come in to see Doug right before he left town, and he'd deposited sixty thousand dollars in my personal account!"

Norman gave a low whistle.

"Don't whistle yet. That's not all. Doug said Ross had added my name to all of his accounts and he had the signature cards for me to sign so that I would have full access. Ross has a lot of money in the bank, Norman. It's much more than I ever would have guessed!"

Hannah had just given Norman that shocking news when there was a knock at the back kitchen door. It was rhythmic, three short knocks and then a louder one, almost like a snare drum cadence.

"Andrea," Hannah informed Norman. "If you go let her in, I'll pour a cup of coffee for her."

"You'd better put this back in your purse for safekeeping," Norman said, handing her the paper with the bank balances.

"Good idea." Hannah took the paper and slipped it into her purse. Then she walked to the coffeepot to pour coffee for Andrea.

By the time Hannah was back with a fresh mug of coffee, Andrea had seated herself on the stool next to Norman. "Sorry, Hannah," she said, looking very apologetic. "I've been out talking to people, and I couldn't find anyone who . . ." She stopped speaking and glanced at Norman. Then she gave Hannah a distressed look. "Sorry, Hannah. I'll tell you later."

"I don't have any secrets from Norman," Hannah reassured her. "Tell me now."

"Okay." Andrea turned to Norman. "Hannah asked me to talk to people to find out if anyone seemed to have a grudge against Ross or disliked him for any reason. She said she didn't know if that drugged candy was meant for P.K. or for Ross, and she didn't think anyone would tell her anything negative about Ross."

"I understand," Norman told her.

"But there was nothing," Andrea said. "I talked to everyone I could think of, even Irma York, and you know what a big gossip she is. Even Irma couldn't think of anything bad about Ross, and neither could anyone else. Everyone really likes him. He's very popular in Lake Eden."

"How about work?" Norman asked. "Is there anyone at KCOW Television who might feel it wasn't fair when Ross was hired and thought that they should have gotten his job instead?"

"I have to check that out later. I didn't get time to go out there today." She stopped and glanced at her watch. "I can't go now. I have an appointment. Is it all right if I do that tomorrow, Hannah?"

"You've done enough, Andrea. And believe me, I appreciate it. I'll run out to KCOW later and see if anyone there knows anything."

"I did find out one other thing, but it's not about Ross," Andrea told her. "Grandma Knudson told me that P.K.'s funeral is going to be held tomorrow."

Norman looked over at Hannah. "Are you planning to go?"

Hannah made an instant decision. "Yes, I want to go."

"I'll go with you," Andrea told Hannah. "Detectives always learn something at a murder victim's funeral. That's true in almost every detective show."

"You watch detective shows?" Hannah asked, knowing that Andrea preferred shows that involved fashion or interior decorating.

"Bill watches them. And since I like to spend time with him when he actually gets home at a reasonable time, I watch them, too. I'm definitely going to the funeral, Hannah. All those detective shows can't be wrong, and you never know who might talk to one of us and tell us something we need to know."

Once Andrea had left with a bag of Maple Crunch Cookies for Tracey and her friends, Norman turned to Hannah. "I'd better go. If I stay here, you'll never get any work done."

"Oh, yes, I will," Hannah said with a laugh. "All I have to do is bake some bar cookies and we can talk while I mix them up."

"Okay," Norman agreed, sitting back down again. "What are you making, Hannah?"

"Sweet and Salty Strawberry Bar Cookies. I love the combination of sweet and salty."

"So do I. I can remember my mother sprinkling sea salt on chocolate sundaes. She said it brought out the richness of the chocolate."

"And she was right." Hannah made a quick trip to the pantry and came out carrying the ingredients she needed. She softened some butter, mixed it in with the white sugar she'd already placed in the bowl of the industrial stand mixer, and gave a little sigh. "What do you think it means, Norman?"

"I can only guess, but it's clear Ross was worried he'd be gone for a while and he wanted to leave you with enough money."

Hannah smiled as she realized that Norman had correctly interpreted her ambiguous question. "You knew exactly what I was asking, didn't you," she said, and it was a statement rather than a question.

"Yes. I could see that it bothered you the entire time Andrea was here. You were listening to her, but you were thinking about what Doug Greerson told you."

"You're right," Hannah admitted, mixing the ingredients for the crust. Once the crust had been thoroughly mixed, she removed enough of the sweet dough for the crumble topping, wrapped it in plastic wrap, and stuck it in the walk-in cooler. Then she filled the bottoms of the pans she'd prepared with the remaining sweet dough, smoothed out the bottom crusts with the blade of a metal spatula, and slipped the pans onto the shelves in her industrial oven. She closed the oven door, set the timer, and came back to the work station to join Norman.

"Do you think he's coming back?" she asked.

Norman made a helpless gesture. "I really don't know, Hannah. Some things seem to point to it, and others don't."

"It's so frustrating! Sometimes I think . . ." The rest of her sentence was interrupted by an authoritative knock on the back kitchen door.

"Mike's here," Norman said, recognizing the knock.

"I know. I'll let him in."

"You have to tell him about the bank, Hannah."

Hannah gave a little sigh. "I know," she said as she walked toward the door to open it for Mike.

"He did *what*?" Mike stared at Hannah in shock.

"He signed everything over to me the day he left town. It's a lot of money, Mike." Hannah drew the printout Doug had given her from her purse and handed it to Mike. "See?"

Mike examined the printout. "Yes. This puts a different light on things, Hannah. We may have been looking for Ross in all the wrong places."

"What do you mean?"

"I need to find out if he withdrew any large sums of money. You say that you cosigned on all these accounts?"

"That's right. Doug told me that Ross wanted me to have full access to everything."

"Good! That'll save us a lot of time. I need you to go to the bank with me, Hannah."

"But I can't go now. I have bar cookies in the oven."

"How soon will they be baked?"

Hannah glanced at the clock. "I should be through in a little less than an hour."

"Okay. That'll do." Mike picked up his coffee and stood up. "I'm going back out to the cruiser. I have to check in with my detectives in the field, and then I'll give Doug a call. I need to tell him that we're coming in. I have to find out if there's any paperwork he needs from me."

When Mike had left, Hannah turned to Norman. "Do you have any idea why Mike needs me to go with him?"

"I think so. You cosigned on Ross's accounts and you can request information on deposits and withdrawals. Mike can't do that unless he gets a court order from a judge."

"But if I request those deposits and withdrawals, I can give the information to Mike so he can have it right away? And then Mike will know if Ross withdrew any large sums of money right before he left?"

"That's right."

"I get it now. And of course I'll cooperate. It just confused me when Mike said he could have been looking for Ross in all the wrong places."

"That puzzled me too, until Mike said he needed to take you to the bank. I think he needs to know how much cash

Ross took with him and whether Ross gave Doug any clue about how he was going to use the money."

"But . . . how could Ross give Doug a clue about . . ." Hannah stopped speaking for a brief moment, and then the answer popped into her mind. "Traveler's checks! If Ross bought traveler's checks, that might indicate he was planning to go to a place where he didn't want to carry a lot of cash."

"Exactly. And Ross may have asked about foreign currency. That would give Mike a clue. Mike's hoping something Doug tells him or something he sees on the bank records will point him in the right direction."

The timer buzzed, and Hannah got up to take the pans of sweet dough crust from the oven. She slipped them on the bakers racks to cool and went back to prepare her strawberry filling. Once that was done and the crusts had sufficiently cooled, she spread the filling on them, sprinkled it with sea salt, and topped it with crumbles of the refrigerated sweet dough.

"I'm almost done," Hannah said as she put the last pan of Sweet and Salty Strawberry Bar Cookies in the oven. "These will be baked in less than thirty minutes and then I can go to the bank with Mike."

"You can go now," Norman told her. "Just set the timer and I'll take the pans out of the oven and put them on the racks."

"Really?" Hannah asked.

"No problem." Norman started to grin. "I've watched you enough times to know what to do. It's not complicated. All I have to do is pull them out of the oven. And after all, Hannah, I'm a dentist."

Hannah stared at him for a moment. "What's that got to do with it?" she asked.

"Dentists are really good at extractions."

Hannah groaned and then she laughed. "You really reached for that joke."

"Maybe, but you laughed."

"That's true," Hannah admitted. "Are you sure you can stay long enough to finish the baking for me?"

"I'm sure. Doc Bennett's filling in for me for the rest of the day and the only thing I have waiting for me at the clinic is some boring paperwork. When Michelle comes back and you two are finished baking for the day, we'll all go out for that dinner I promised you."

"Thank you, Norman," Hannah said, patting his shoulder before she slipped on her parka. "I'll go tell Mike we can leave now, and I'll be back just as soon as I can."

"No hurry," Norman called after her.

Hannah thought about Norman and how much she liked him as she opened the door. She stepped out into the cold winter air and realized, once again, how lucky she was to have a best friend like Norman.

SWEET AND SALTY STRAWBERRY BAR COOKIES

Preheat oven to 325 degrees F., rack in the middle position.

The Crust and Topping:

2 cups ***(4 sticks, 16 ounces, 1 pound)*** salted butter softened to room temperature
1 cup white ***(granulated)*** sugar
1 and ½ cups powdered ***(confectioners')*** sugar
2 teaspoons vanilla extract
4 cups all-purpose flour ***(pack it down in the cup when you measure it)***

The Strawberry Filling:

11.75-ounce jar ***(net weight)*** strawberry ice cream topping or preserves
1 cup ***(6-ounce by weight package)*** white chocolate or vanilla chips
⅛ cup ***(2 Tablespoons)*** whipping cream
½ teaspoon vanilla extract
2 teaspoons sea or Kosher salt ***(the coarse-ground kind)***

Before you begin to make the crust and filling, spray a 9-inch by 13-inch cake pan with Pam or another nonstick baking spray.

Hannah's 1st Note: This crust and filling is a lot easier to make with an electric mixer. You can do it by hand, but it will take some muscle.

Combine the butter, white sugar, and powdered sugar in a large bowl or in the bowl of an electric mixer. Beat at MEDIUM speed until the mixture is light and creamy.

Add the vanilla extract. Mix it in until it is thoroughly combined.

Add the flour in half-cup increments, beating at LOW speed after each addition. Beat until everything is combined.

Hannah's 2nd Note: When you've mixed in the flour, the resulting sweet dough will be soft. Don't worry. That's the way it's supposed to be.

Remove the bowl from the mixer. With impeccably clean hands, take out a generous cup of the sweet dough, form it into a loose ball, and wrap it in plastic wrap. Stick that sweet dough ball in the refrigerator to

chill. You will use this chilled sweet dough for your top crumble crust.

Again, with impeccably clean hands, press the rest of the sweet dough into the bottom of your prepared cake pan. ***(If the dough seems a bit sticky, cover the dough with a sheet of waxed paper to use when you press it down.)*** This will form a bottom crust. Press it all the way out to the edges of the pan, as evenly as you can, to cover the entire bottom. Then remove the wax paper if you used it.

Bake your bottom crust at 325 degrees F. for approximately 20 minutes.

While the crust is baking, take the lid off your strawberry topping and place the jar in the microwave. Heat on HIGH for 20 seconds. Leave the jar in the microwave for 1 minute and then take it out.

Pour the slightly heated strawberry topping in a microwave-safe bowl on the counter. ***(I used a 4-cup Pyrex measuring cup.)*** Use a rubber spatula to get all the strawberry topping out of the jar.

When the edges of your crust have turned pale golden brown, remove the pan from the oven, but DON'T SHUT OFF THE OVEN! Set the pan with your

baked crust on a cold stovetop burner or a wire rack to cool. It should cool approximately 15 minutes.

After your crust has cooled, it's time to finish making your strawberry filling.

Add the cup of white chocolate or vanilla chips to the bowl with the strawberry topping. Mix them in with the rubber spatula.

Measure out ⅛ cup whipping cream and add that to your microwave-safe bowl. Mix it in with the rubber spatula.

Place the bowl in the microwave and heat the strawberry filling for 1 minute at HIGH power. Let the bowl sit in the microwave for an additional minute and then try to stir the mixture smooth with a heat resistant spatula or a wooden spoon. If you cannot stir it smooth, heat it for an additional 20 seconds at HIGH power, let it sit in the microwave for an equal length of time, and then try again. Repeat as often as necessary, alternating heating and standing times until the chips are melted.

Once your strawberry filling is ready, add the half-teaspoon of vanilla extract and stir it in. DO NOT ADD THE SALT YET.

Pour the strawberry filling over the baked crust in the pan as evenly as you can. Smooth it out with the rubber spatula.

Here comes the salt! Sprinkle the sea salt or Kosher salt over the strawberry filling in the pan.

Take the remaining sweet dough out of the refrigerator and unwrap it. It has been refrigerated for 35 minutes or more and it should be thoroughly chilled.

With your impeccably clean fingers, crumble the dough over the strawberry filling as evenly as you can, letting some of the strawberry filling peek through.

Return the pan to the oven and bake at 325 degrees F. for 25 to 30 additional minutes, or until the strawberry filling is bubbly and the crumble crust is light golden brown.

Take your pan of bar cookies out of the oven, shut off the oven, and place the pan on a wire rack to cool completely.

Hannah's 3rd Note: Do not be tempted to cut your Sweet & Salty Strawberry Bar Cookies until they are completely cool. That strawberry filling will stay hot and molten for at least 20 to 30 minutes.

When your bar cookies are completely cool, cut them into brownie-size pieces, place them on a pretty plate, and serve them to your guests. If you want to make them even prettier, add a few fresh strawberries around the edge of the plate.

Chapter Fifteen

Hannah and Mike sat in front of Doug Greerson's desk. She was sipping a cup of peppermint tea, something she usually didn't drink, but the butterflies in her stomach had been startled into flight by her fear that Ross might have done something illegal to have accumulated so much money.

Mike put down his cup of espresso and locked eyes with Doug. Hannah could tell that he was frustrated.

"Why didn't you call to tell me this when Ross didn't come back to town?"

Doug made a helpless gesture. "Number one, you didn't ask me. And number two, there's an issue of confidentiality here and federal regulations apply. I have to file a report if anyone deposits over ten thousand dollars in currency, but not if they withdraw large sums. If I called you every time one of our customers made a large deposit or took out a large sum of money, I wouldn't be a banker in this town for long!"

Mike didn't look happy, but he nodded. "Okay. You're right."

Doug turned to look at Hannah. "Besides, I thought Hannah would tell you when she reconciled her bank statement. That deposit was listed on her statement."

Hannah couldn't help feeling horribly guilty. "I'm sorry, Doug. I didn't even look at it when it came. I just put it on my desk to take care of when I had the time."

Doug sighed. "I know you keep a running balance, Hannah, but you should at least look at your statement every month. If you think there's a discrepancy, we want to know immediately."

"You're right, Doug," Hannah admitted. "I promise I'll do that when I get next month's statement."

"Statements," Doug corrected her with the plural. "You'll get a statement for your personal checking, your corporate account, and the three accounts you share with Ross. There are some large sums involved and it would be best if you showed more fiscal responsibility. If you need any help handling things, I'll be glad to be of assistance."

"I promise I'll take care of it, but thank you, Doug." Hannah was embarrassed, and she turned to Mike to change the subject. "Did you find anything helpful in the printouts Doug gave you?"

"Yes," Mike said, giving her hand a squeeze before he switched his attention to Doug. "I need to know if Ross made his last withdrawals in cash."

"Just a moment, Mike." Doug addressed Hannah. "Do I have your permission to discuss this, Hannah?"

"Yes," Hannah answered quickly.

"All right then. Ross wanted the cash in bills no larger than twenties and fifties. Normally, we don't keep that much cash on hand. There's no call for it. But we always start ordering more cash at the end of May and the end of November."

Hannah was puzzled. "Why then?"

"People want new, crisp bills for graduation presents and Christmas gifts. You'd be surprised at how many bills are requested over the holidays, especially after Jon Walker started to carry graduation and Christmas cards that have slots to hold cash at his drugstore."

"I remember getting a card from my aunt with little slots on a Christmas tree," Mike said with a smile. "It held dimes and it was so heavy, she had to put three stamps on the envelope."

Doug laughed. "It's quarters now, Mike. And they're even heavier. Bills are the way to go if you're mailing a cash card."

"So you had the amount of cash that Ross wanted on hand?" Hannah asked, attempting to keep them from getting sidetracked.

"Yes, we did. The armored truck had just delivered that morning and I went to the vault to get what Ross needed."

"Did Ross buy any traveler's checks while he was here at the bank?" Hannah asked.

The moment the question left her mouth, Mike turned to her with a smile.

"No. I get a record of traveler's checks sold every week, and there were none that week."

"Did Ross exchange any money for foreign currency?" Mike asked.

"No. I get a record of that, too." Doug reached into his center desk drawer, drew out a small padded envelope, and handed it to Hannah. "I'm sorry I forgot to give this to you earlier. Ross left it for you. I'm really not supposed to hand deliver anything in a sealed envelope from one customer to another customer, but if you'll open it in front of me so that I can see the contents are nothing illegal, that'll satisfy our internal bank regulations."

Hannah's hands were shaking slightly as she opened the envelope. Was it a note from Ross, explaining why he'd left? She was almost afraid to see what he'd left for her, but she steadied herself and looked inside.

"What is it?" Mike asked.

"Two keys on a key ring," Hannah answered, shaking them out of the envelope and onto the blotter on Doug's desk. "That's all. There's nothing else in the envelope."

"There's a tag with a number on it," Mike pointed out. "One thirty-seven."

"Do you mind if I pick them up?" Doug asked Hannah.

"No, go ahead. I know I've seen keys like that before, but I can't quite place them."

"They're safe deposit keys," Doug told her.

"Did Ross have a safe deposit box?" Mike asked him.

"I'll check. Give me a moment, and help yourself to more coffee while you're waiting. I'll be right back."

Both Hannah and Mike sat there and waited, each thinking their own private thoughts. Hannah was wondering why Ross had left her the keys to his safe deposit box. Did that mean he was never coming back to Lake Eden and to her? Was he gone forever? And if Doug was right about the keys, what was in Ross's safe deposit box? And would she be allowed to use the keys to find out? Or was there some banking regulation making that illegal?

Hannah took a deep breath, told herself to think positive thoughts about this new revelation, and turned to Mike. "What do you think this means?" she asked him.

"The envelope with his keys?"

"Yes. Does this mean that he's not planning to . . . to come back?"

Mike reached out for her hand again. "I don't know, Hannah. Maybe it's just a precaution."

"A precaution against what?"

Mike was silent for a moment and Hannah could tell he was thinking. Then he gave her hand a little pat, let it go, and spoke again.

"A precaution against loss. Or maybe against someone taking the keys against his will."

"But why would Ross be afraid that someone would . . ." Hannah stopped speaking as the door to the office opened and Doug came back in.

"Lydia checked the records. Ross's safe deposit box is here, and it's number one thirty-seven. As a matter of fact, she wrote out the receipt for him when he rented the box."

Hannah was almost afraid to ask, but she had to know. "Can I get into Ross's box?"

"Yes. Our bank has a self-service system for our safety deposit boxes. In other banks, a teller has to pull a signature card, check the customer's identification to make sure he or she is the customer who signed the card, let the customer into a secure area, and use the bank key *and* the customer's key to unlock the door that secures the box inside the vault. Once the box is removed from the vault, the teller carries it to a private room in the secured area and leaves. Then the customer lifts the lid on the box and either adds to, reviews, or removes the desired contents. When this is accomplished, the customer pushes a buzzer to summon the teller, the teller carries the box to the vault and replaces it, and the door is closed and relocked with both keys. No customer can get into his or her safe deposit box without the bank key, and no bank employee can get into the customer's safety deposit box without the customer's key. It's a very secure system."

"It certainly sounds like it," Hannah agreed. "But you don't have that system here?"

"No. We only have two full-time tellers and one part-time teller who comes in on busy bank days like Mondays, Fridays, and the first day and the last day of the month if those days don't happen to fall on a Monday or a Friday. The system I just described to you is labor intensive, and we don't have the personnel to do it. When I became bank president, we decided to remodel and use the self-service system."

"Is that why Ross had two keys?" Hannah asked.

"Yes. The safe deposit area is in the annex we built. It's in the back, right next to the employee break room. The customer uses one key to open the door, locks it behind him or her, and uses the other key to unlock the safe deposit box. There are two offices for our safe deposit box holders to use, again with locking doors. The customer uses one of them, completes whatever he or she came to do, carries the box back to the vault, and secures it behind the locked door."

"Is the annex open at night?" Mike asked.

"No, it's only available during banking hours and no one without a key can get in the door. The biggest advantage of the self-service system for a bank is that the bank is absolved of all responsibility for checking identification against signature cards, unlocking and relocking boxes with the bank key, and letting customers into the vault area."

"That makes sense to me," Mike said, giving a quick nod.

"It made sense to the board, too," Doug told him.

Hannah began to frown. "But . . . that means anyone with both keys can get into the annex and remove a safe deposit box."

Doug shook his head. "Not so, Hannah. The box number is not stamped on the keys and neither is the bank name. You'd have to know both of those things before you could go to the right bank and open the right box. It's one of the reasons why we write the box number on the receipt for the rental, but nowhere else."

"But there was a tag on Ross's keys with the box number," Hannah pointed out.

"The bank doesn't put a tag on the keys, so Ross must have added that tag specifically for you before he put them in the envelope."

Mike leaned forward and Hannah knew he had an important question to ask. "Does this solve the inheritance problem with safe deposit boxes and access for someone who's not on the signature card?"

"Yes. If you have both keys and you know the bank and box number, you have access during banking hours. It's that simple."

Hannah started to smile. She knew precisely why Mike had asked that question. "Then I could take someone with me when I looked inside Ross's box?"

Doug nodded. "Anyone of your choice, Hannah. It's all up to you."

"Mike?" Hannah turned to him. "Will you please look inside Ross's box with me?"

"Of course," Mike said, and he rose from his chair. "I was hoping you'd ask me that."

Both Mike and Hannah were speechless as they stared down at Ross's open safe deposit box. They gazed at each other in shock for what was probably only a brief moment but seemed like an eternity to Hannah.

"More money," she said.

"Yeah. A lot of it."

"How . . ." Hannah stopped to draw another shaky breath. "How much money do you think is there?"

"I'm not sure." Mike gave a little humorless laugh. "I've never seen that much money in one place before."

Hannah blinked and continued to stare down at the stacks of bills. "It's got white tape on it. Does that mean somebody counted it?"

Mike leaned down to read the inscription on the white band that was wrapped around one of the stacks. When he straightened up again, he made a sound that was halfway between a gasp and a chuckle. "It says ten thousand dollars, Hannah."

"Ross put ten thousand dollars in his safe deposit box?"

"No. Try ten times that, Hannah. There's a hundred thousand dollars in this box."

Both of them just stared at the contents for a moment longer, and then Hannah drew a deep, shuddering breath. "Do you think that Ross left all this money for me?"

"No question about it. Ross's intentions were clear when he put his keys in that envelope and asked Doug to give it to you the next time you came to the bank. He even attached the tag with his safe deposit box number. He was alive and well when he did that, and that's enough to prove that he wanted you to have it. It's every bit as clear as if he'd taken the time to draw up a will."

He was alive and well when he did that. The words echoed in Hannah's mind and she could feel her head start to spin. Did Mike believe that Ross was no longer alive and well? She didn't want to think about that, not now. It was too much to handle, too frightening to contemplate. Instead, she sat down in the chair in front of the desk holding the safe deposit box, and attempted to concentrate on the problem at hand.

"Are you okay, Hannah?" Mike asked her.

"Yes," Hannah said firmly. And surprisingly, once the affirmation had left her lips, she *was* okay. "Ross gave Doug those signature cards for me to sign. Why didn't he just open his safe deposit box and deposit this money in one of his accounts?"

Mike sighed, and it was clear that he didn't want to answer her question. "I don't know, Hannah. You'd have to ask him."

"I *can't* ask Ross if he's not here and I don't know how to contact him. You know that." Hannah could feel herself getting irritated with Mike for avoiding the intent of her question. "Let me rephrase that," she said, trying not to sound as frustrated as she felt. "What possible reasons could someone have for putting a hundred thousand dollars in cash in his safe deposit box when he could have deposited it in one of his bank accounts?"

Mike looked very uncomfortable. "Well . . . perhaps he couldn't have deposited it in one of his accounts, at least not all of it at once. You heard Doug tell us that he was obligated to file a report if someone deposited over ten thousand dollars in cash."

"I know what Doug said. But why didn't Ross deposit five thousand dollars at a time?"

"I don't know."

"Think of a reason, Mike. You're the detective."

Mike reached out to put his hand on her shoulders. "Calm down, Hannah. I can tell you're stressed to the max."

"I am," Hannah admitted and took a deep breath. "Let's start again. What reason would someone have to put a hundred thousand dollars in bills in a safe deposit box?"

"Well . . . he could have wanted to hide it from someone."

"Who?"

"There's no way of knowing that, but some people use safe deposit boxes to hide assets from a spouse."

"But *I'm* his spouse and Ross left me the keys. If he'd wanted to hide it from me, he wouldn't have done that. Give me some other possible reasons."

"Perhaps he didn't want to deposit it for some reason."

Hannah gave an exasperated sigh. "I know that, but *why* didn't he want to deposit it?"

"Well . . . there's the ten thousand dollar cash limit. The reason it's there is to prevent drug dealers and criminals from banking the profits of their crimes."

"I already thought of drug money, but what other crimes are you talking about?"

"There's extortion. This money could be extorted from someone. Or it could be the ransom from a kidnapping or bank robbery and the perp doesn't know if the bills are marked, or not. It could also be counterfeit and whoever put it in the safe deposit box wants to hide it and pass it off one bill by one to avoid detection."

"So it could be dirty money, or counterfeit money. Is that right?"

"That's right."

Hannah was silent for a moment, thinking it over. "Can you tell if this money is counterfeit?"

"No. I can give you a guess, but that's about it."

"What's your guess?"

"A couple of bills on the tops of the stacks look worn, and that makes me think that they, at least, are legitimate. But that's just my gut feeling, Hannah. I really don't know."

"Who would know if they're counterfeit?"

"I'm not sure, but I'll find out. I have a friend in the treasury department and I'll give him a call at home tonight. He's a good guy, and he'll put me in touch with someone who knows."

"Thanks, Mike." Hannah's mind was spinning with possibilities, and she latched on to one. "Would a bank robber be able to hide the money he stole in a safe deposit box?"

"Yes, under certain circumstances. If he had the proper identification, he could go to any bank and rent a safe deposit box. Then he could carry the money in, concealed in some kind of briefcase or travel bag, and put it in his box."

"And no one would know?"

Mike shook his head. "Once you rent a safe deposit box, you're given privacy to open it and put in anything that'll fit. It's just like when you used your keys to retrieve Ross's box.

No one from the bank can get in without you, and they leave you in privacy so that you're alone when you have access to the box. It's even easier with the kind of safe deposit boxes that Doug has here. No one even has to check your identification once you've rented the box."

Hannah could feel her frustration beginning to grow again. "So what you're telling me is that we really don't know anything about this money." She gestured to the stacks of bills. "It could have come from anywhere."

"That's right. Of course if this money is either counterfeit or from an illegal source, the person who tries to use it takes the risk of being apprehended."

Hannah thought about that for a moment. "Yes. And I certainly want to find out if that's the case." She bent closer to look at the stacks of bills again and gave a little gasp as she spied something. "What's that?"

"What's what?"

"There's something shiny under that third stack of bills." She pointed to the shiny object she'd noticed. "It's rounded on top and it looks like the edge of a coin."

Mike moved closer and leaned down to look. "I see it. It's something silver. Hold on a second and I'll get it out so we can find out exactly what it is. Do you have a nail file or anything thin, flat, and pointed in your purse?"

"I'm not sure. Let me look." Hannah set her saddlebag-size purse on the top of the desk and rummaged inside. Eleven pens, a paperback book she'd been meaning to read in her spare time, and a very old tin of breath mints later, she found something that met Mike's parameters.

"How about this?" she asked, holding up a rattail comb she'd dropped in her purse for Andrea when her sister's dress purse was too tiny to hold it.

"Perfect," Mike said, taking the comb. "It should work."

Hannah watched as Mike inserted the tip of the comb

under the stack of bills and poked against the object until it emerged from the other side. He shoved it out into the open area of the box without ever touching the contents of the box with his fingers.

"It's a key!" Hannah said, recognizing the shape immediately. She started to reach for it, but Mike grabbed her hand.

"Leave it there, Hannah," he told her. "We'll get it out without touching the inside of the box."

"How?"

"Do you have tweezers in that big purse of yours? That would do. Or maybe a pair of scissors?"

Hannah turned back to her open purse and began to search. There were no tweezers and no scissors that she could locate, but there was a set of chopsticks. "How about this?" she asked, handing the paper-wrapped packet to Mike.

Mike drew the chopsticks out of the packet and began to smile. "I'm pretty good with chopsticks, so let me give it a whirl. It'll be a tricky, but I think I can do it."

Hannah watched in fascination as Mike used the wooden chopsticks to lift the key and deposit it on top of the desk. "Can we touch it now?" she asked him.

"Yes. It's just the money that I didn't want you to touch. Pick it up, Hannah. Let's take a closer look at it."

Hannah picked up the key and flipped it over in her hand. "There's writing on this side," she said. "It's marked 'Superior Storage,' and there's a number on the other side. It looks like three-twelve."

"Let me see." Mike held out his hand and Hannah gave him the key. He turned it over in his hand, examining both sides. "You're right, Hannah. The two is a little worn, but it's definitely three-twelve. This is a key to a storage unit."

"Ross's storage unit?"

"Maybe. Either that or he was keeping it for someone. Do

you know if he wrote a monthly check to a storage company?"

"No. Ross paid his own bills, but Doug can give us a printout of all the checks he wrote." Hannah felt a rush of excitement so intense, it almost made her dizzy. "If we can locate his storage unit, there could be a clue to where Ross went."

Mike smiled at her. "Yes. It's the first lead I've gotten in my search for him. Let me keep this key, Hannah, and I'll research it on the department computer."

Hannah was about to agree when she thought better of it. "No. I'll keep it. You've got the name of the storage facility and the number of the unit. I'll keep the key."

"Why?"

"Because Ross is my husband and he left that key for me. I want to be there if you locate it. I need to unlock it myself."

"But . . . okay," Mike agreed. "If I find the unit, you can come along to open it."

"Thanks," Hannah said, dropping the key in her pocket. It might have been silly, but she felt as if she'd just won the lottery. She turned to look over at the safe deposit box again and frowned slightly. "I have one more question for you, Mike."

"What is it?"

"What do you think I should do with this money right now?"

"You should put it back in the vault. But before you do that, I think we should call Doug in to witness what's inside Ross's box. You haven't touched anything inside, have you, Hannah?"

"No. I just touched the outside of the lid when I opened it."

"Good. I want Doug to watch while I pick up one of the bundles and read off some of the serial numbers so you can copy them down for me. Then I'll put the bills back and he can substantiate that."

'Why?"

"Because I'll have to take money from the box to get the serial numbers. With Doug as a reliable witness, he can swear that I put the bills back if there's ever any question about that."

"That makes sense. And once you get the serial numbers, you'll call your friend to see if he can find out anything for us?"

"Yes. That's my plan."

"Okay. That all sounds reasonable to me. Do you want me to go and ask Doug to come in here?"

"No. I'll call him on my cell phone. I don't think that either one of us should leave the other in here alone."

"And that's just in case the money is counterfeit or illegal in some other way?"

"Right. And then, when we're finished, I want Doug to watch while you put the box back and lock it up." Mike moved closer and gave her a little hug. "It can't hurt to err on the side of caution, especially since we really don't know what we're dealing with here."

Chapter Sixteen

Hannah gave a little wave as Mike pulled away in his cruiser. Then she walked to the back door and stood there, wondering if she should go in. She had one more stop to make and she didn't want to take Michelle with her. It could be difficult for Michelle to be objective, hearing Hannah ask questions of P.K.'s coworkers.

She turned and took a few steps toward her cookie truck, but then she reconsidered. It was always easier getting people to talk if she brought some sweet treat with her to break the ice. She needed cookies to serve in the television station's break room. Anything chocolate would be good. Chocolate seemed to calm people down and make them more willing to be candid with her.

Hannah turned on her heel and reversed direction, walking quickly to the back door of The Cookie Jar. If luck was with her, everyone would be in the coffee shop handling the noon rush.

Cautiously, Hannah opened the door and peeked in. The kitchen was deserted. She rushed in, closing the door silently behind her, and went straight to the bakers rack where eight pans of Chocolate Cashew Bar Cookies were stacked, each on its own shelf. She hurried to cut a pan into brownie-sized pieces and place them on a platter. No more than two or three minutes later, she was stashing her platter in the back of the cookie truck and climbing behind the wheel.

It started to snow as she pulled out of the alley and Hannah sent up a little prayer that the snowflakes would remain light and sparse. She was really looking forward to dinner tonight at the Lake Eden Inn. Sally always had wonderful entrees, and breads, and sides, and desserts. Come to think of it, everything that Sally served was wonderful.

There weren't many cars on the road and Hannah made good time driving to KCOW Television's headquarters. The bar cookies she'd cut smelled enticing and her stomach gave a hungry growl as she pulled into the multi-level parking structure. She had spent a busy morning baking and she hadn't taken time for lunch. That meant she hadn't eaten anything since the breakfast that Michelle had made almost eight hours ago, not counting the cookies she'd tasted with Norman. She parked in a spot marked for visitors, retrieved her platter of bar cookies, and got out of the truck to walk across the concrete floor to the back entrance.

There was a buzzer by the back door and Hannah pressed it. A moment later a voice came over the intercom.

"KCOW-TV. Could I please have your name?"

"Betty?" Hannah asked, recognizing the tinny voice that floated out of the speaker. "Betty Jackson?"

"Yes. Hannah?"

"Yes. Are you working here now, Betty?"

"Yes, for a three-month job, and if I'm lucky, the lady who went out on maternity leave will decide to stay home with her baby. It's her first and her husband just got a promotion, so it could happen."

"If it does, do you think that you'll get her job?"

"That's what I'm hoping. Did you come out here to see anyone in particular, Hannah?"

"Actually . . . no, I didn't. I just dropped by with some Chocolate Cashew Bar Cookies for your break room."

"Right. Of course you did."

Even though the intercom didn't catch many vocal nuances, Hannah recognized sarcasm when she heard it. For a split second, she considered what she should do and she decided to act as if she hadn't understood. "Whatever do you mean, Betty?" she asked in the most innocent voice she could muster.

Betty laughed. "Don't play dumb with me, Hannah. Everybody knows that you're investigating. You always do."

Hannah decided that there was no reason not to admit it. "You're right, Betty. Do you think anyone will talk to me?"

"Sure, no problem with that, Hannah. People *like* you and that's all everybody out here's been talking about anyway. It's been the prime topic of conversation ever since it happened. There's even an office pool about when you'd get here to question us."

"You're kidding!" Hannah was shocked. As far as she knew, she'd never been the subject of an office pool before. "You *are* joking, aren't you, Betty?"

"Got me there, but there *could* be an office pool for that. They've all been wondering when you'd get around to us. Hold on a second and I'll buzz you in. Come up the stairs and through the first door on your left. That'll take you right into the reception area, and that's where I am. I have to taste those treats you brought to make sure they're suitable for everyone else."

Hannah laughed, and a second or two later, the buzzer sounded and the lock on the door clicked as it released. She pulled the door open, stepped through, and started up the steps. When she got to the top, she found Betty Jackson, resplendent in a stretchy gold blouse that had extended as far as its fabric would allow, and black slacks that actually made her more-than-plump legs look thinner.

"Hi, Betty," Hannah greeted her. "You look good. Have you lost weight?"

"Yes, twenty-two pounds. I'm on the one-zee diet."

"What's that?"

"Eat what you want, but only eat one. It works as long as you don't count a whole boatload of mashed potatoes and gravy as one."

Hannah laughed. "Obviously, you haven't done that. You really *do* look thinner, Betty. I noticed it right away."

"Thanks." Betty looked pleased as she ushered Hannah down the hall. Hannah noticed that she glanced at the platter of bar cookies every now and then.

It didn't take long for them to arrive at the break room door. Betty pushed it open, ushered Hannah inside, and motioned toward a table.

"Would you like to taste one now?" Hannah asked her, already knowing the answer.

"Yes, but whatever you do, don't let me have more than one. I bought all new clothes and they won't fit if I put any of that twenty-two pounds I lost back on."

"Okay, I won't let you have more than one," Hannah promised. "Do you want to eat it right now before anyone else comes in?"

"That's a real good idea." Betty went to the coffeepot and poured two cups. She handed one to Hannah and, once she'd added low-calorie sweetener to hers, she sat down across the table and watched expectantly as Hannah removed the foil wrap from the platter.

"Here, Betty." Hannah picked up one bar cookie with a napkin from the dispenser on the table and handed it to Betty. "Let me know how you like them."

"My pleasure," Betty responded, taking a bite. A moment later, a rapturous expression spread over her face and she was smiling as she swallowed. "Oh, my!" she breathed. "Everything you bake is great, but these are pure heaven!"

"Thanks. I'm glad you like them." Hannah unfolded another napkin and draped it over the platter, effectively hiding the bar cookies from Betty's sight.

"Smart," Betty said, reacting to Hannah's action. "Who would you like to see first, Hannah? Part of my job is covering for people when they go on break and I'll tell the person you choose to take a break now."

"I'm not sure who to choose. Will you recommend someone for me?"

"That's easy. Talk to Scotty MacDonald first."

"All right. But tell me why I should do that."

"Because there was bad blood between Scotty and P.K. Everybody could see that. I think it was jealousy."

"Why would Scotty be jealous of P.K.?"

"Scotty's been here longer than P.K. has, and Scotty was sure he'd get the job as head cameraman. It was a real surprise to everyone when P.K. got it instead. Scotty was mad about that, but he got even madder when Ross chose P.K. to be his assistant."

"And Scotty thought that he should have been Ross's assistant?"

"Yes . . . at least that's what everyone says."

"Were you working out here then, Betty?"

"No, not when P.K. got the head cameraman position. But people talk and I heard all about it from more than one person. When Scotty got passed over for the promotion, he started to resent the heck out of P.K."

"But you weren't actually here then?"

"No, but I was here when Ross took the job as head of

special programming. And I saw what happened when Ross and P.K. went out to the Lake Eden Inn to cover the Food Network Dessert Chef Competition."

"Scotty felt he should have gone with Ross instead?"

"I'll say! And it burned him even more when Ross went out on location with that special job they gave him a couple of weeks ago, and P.K. started using Ross's office. Every time Scotty went past the door, he glared at P.K. just like he wanted to kill him."

"Do you think Scotty actually did?"

Betty looked stunned by that question. "I didn't exactly mean it like *that*," she tried to explain, "but . . . to tell the truth, I don't know. I don't *think* it went that far, but I can tell you that Scotty criticized P.K. every chance he got. He didn't even warm up to P.K.'s girlfriend, and she was as sweet as sweet could be."

"Then you knew P.K.'s girlfriend?"

"Not well, but I met her a couple of times. She used to drive out to pick up P.K. so they could go to dinner."

"In her pink Jeep?" Hannah asked, remembering what Cyril had told her.

"Yes." Betty laughed. "Silliest thing I ever saw, but that girl loved her pink Jeep. She even found pink and white seat covers for the bucket seats. And P.K. gave her one of those vanity license plates that said 'PINKIE' on it."

"Do you happen to know Pinkie's real name?" Hannah asked.

Betty thought about that for a moment, and then she shook her head. "I don't think I ever heard it. P.K. always called her Pinkie and so did everyone else."

"How about Pinkie's last name?"

Betty shook her head again. "No, but maybe Carol would know. When I send her back to try one of your yummy bar cookies, you can ask her."

"Were Carol and Pinkie friends?"

"Not really, but Carol knows everything about everybody. She's been here from the beginning, and she's a walking encyclopedia of facts about the employees and their visitors. And even better, she doesn't mind telling anyone who'll listen."

"Can you send Carol in first?" Hannah asked.

"Sure, but why?"

"Because she can tell me about everyone else and then I'll know what to ask them."

"Makes sense to me," Betty said, rising from her chair. "Okay, Hannah. Carol first, and then Scotty."

Hannah waited until Betty left and then she removed the napkin from the platter. She attempted to think of the questions she wanted to ask Carol, and then she decided that it was better to simply let Carol talk about P.K.'s murder. Betty had promised that Carol wouldn't mind talking to anyone who would listen, and she was a good listener.

Hannah sipped her coffee as she waited. She really ought to tell Carol about the phone tree that Delores had established, the one Hannah and her sisters called the Lake Eden Gossip Hotline. Their mother could use someone like Carol as a resource.

Twenty minutes later, Hannah turned to a blank page in the stenographer's notebook she referred to as her *murder book*, and waited for Scotty to arrive. Carol hadn't known Pinkie's real name, but she'd been delighted to tell Hannah everything about everyone else who worked at KCOW Television. Carol had been sure that an employee named Martha might have wanted to kill P.K. at one time. She said that P.K. had dated Martha once, and then he hadn't asked her out again. According to Carol, Martha had been devastated by

P.K.'s apparent disinterest and she'd said several times that someone ought to show him what happened to a man who broke a woman's heart.

Hannah had written all this down dutifully, but then Carol had uprooted the suspicion that had been planted in Hannah's mind. She'd said that Martha was engaged now and everyone in the office, including P.K., had received invitations to the wedding.

There had been other employees, guests, and bosses that Carol had mentioned, but none of them had possessed a compelling reason to kill P.K. Even though Carol had been very forthcoming with the gossip she'd heard about everyone, nothing she'd said about anyone had convinced Hannah to add any of them to her suspect list.

"Hi, Hannah." Betty appeared in the doorway. "Here's Scotty. Give him a couple of those incredible bar cookies, will you? I don't dare even look at them or I'll leap across the table, grab the platter, and run to the nearest office with a door I can lock."

Scotty laughed, and Hannah could tell that he liked Betty. "And you'll eat every single one before anyone can unlock the door with the master key?"

"You got it," Betty said with a nod.

"Well, I won't stand in your way as long as you leave at least five for me," Scotty told her.

When Betty left, Scotty stopped smiling and faced Hannah squarely. "I know what you want, and you're barking up the wrong tree if you think that I had anything to do with what happened to P.K."

"But you didn't like P.K., did you, Scotty?" Hannah asked as she passed the platter of bar cookies to him.

"Not at first, no. But then we got to talking, and once I figured out what was going on, I liked him just fine." Scotty took a bar cookie from the platter and grabbed a napkin from the dispenser. "It's like this, Hannah. I just thought I got a raw deal from the bosses. I've been a cameraman here since KCOW Television went on the air, and I know that I'm a better cameraman than P.K. is." He stopped speaking and frowned. "Than P.K. *was*," he corrected himself. "Sorry, but it still doesn't seem real, you know? I keep waiting for him to come in every morning, and . . . he doesn't."

Hannah watched while Scotty took a sip of his coffee, gave a sigh, and blinked several times. "It just doesn't seem real," he repeated.

"I know," Hannah said, echoing his sigh.

"Is it always like this?" Scotty asked.

"I think it is."

"It's like, you turn around and somebody's not there anymore because something awful happened to them." Scotty took another swallow of his coffee, and then he bit into one of Hannah's creations. "These are good," he said.

"Thank you," Hannah accepted the compliment, but she wasn't about to let Scotty sidetrack their conversation. "You seem to have given people the impression that you didn't like P.K. And now you're telling me that you did?"

Scotty shook his head. "I didn't always like him, but I did after I found out that it wasn't P.K.'s fault he got the head cameraman job instead of me. Then I was okay with it. As a matter of fact, we had a drink together after work last Wednesday."

"You did?" Hannah frowned slightly. Was Betty wrong about the animosity between Scotty and P.K.? "Where did you go?"

"Out to the bar at the Lake Eden Inn. Dick makes his Pizza Dip on Wednesdays and P.K. was crazy about it. We were there for an hour or so, and both of us had a couple of drinks."

Hannah was puzzled. Michelle had mentioned that P.K.

didn't drink, and Cyril had said the same thing. "I thought P.K. didn't drink."

"He didn't. He told me he cracked up his dad's car when he was a teenager and he was just lucky he didn't get a DUI. He said he hasn't had a drop to drink since then."

"But he went out to Dick's bar?"

"Yeah, but that was for the Pizza Dip. I told you before, he was really crazy about it. I had a couple of beers, but P.K. stuck to Cokes with lime in them. Dick calls those Virgin Cuba Libres because real Cuba Libres have rum in them and he leaves out the rum for P.K."

Hannah made a mental note to check that out and went on with her questioning. "So you were on friendly terms with P.K.?"

"I wouldn't go quite that far. We sure weren't best buds or anything like that. But I know he didn't cozy up to the bosses to get that promotion. As a matter of fact, he was just as surprised as I was!"

"Really?"

"Yeah. He talked to me about it right after it happened. And he told me he didn't apply for it or anything like that."

"And you believed him?"

"Yeah. P.K.'s always been a straight shooter."

"But you resented the fact that P.K. moved up to be Ross's assistant?"

"No, not that. I didn't want *that* job."

"Why not?"

Scotty looked a bit surprised at the question. "It's the hours. You're always on call. And it's the travel. Maybe, if I'd been younger, I would have wanted it. But living out of a suitcase isn't for me. I resented the fact P.K. moved into that office, but that's it."

Hannah decided to be perfectly sincere. "I talked to two

people here and they both said you looked really angry every time you went past Ross's office and saw P.K. sitting there."

"That's true, but it was envy. That's a great office. It's cool in the summer and warm in the winter, and it's got a great view. I'm stuck in the back in a cubbyhole with one little window so high, I can't see out of it."

"Did you resent Ross when he got that office?"

"No. Ross was hired as an executive, and that's an executive office. But P.K. isn't. I know he's just using it while Ross is gone, but it still ticked me off when I saw him in there."

"Did you and P.K. ever discuss it?"

"Yeah, and that made me feel a little better about it. P.K. offered to share it with me until Ross came back."

"Did you take P.K. up on that?" Hannah asked.

"No. The fact that he offered counted for something. And, to tell the truth, neither one of us knew when Ross would be back and I didn't want to move all my stuff in there and then have to move it all back."

"I understand," Hannah said, and she did.

Scotty began to frown. "Ross is coming back, isn't he, Hannah?"

Hannah scrambled for an answer. She didn't want to lie about it, but neither did she want to admit that she really didn't know. Then the perfect response popped into her head, and she gave a little smile. "I'm not sure how you feel about it, but it can't be too soon for me!"

CHOCOLATE CASHEW BAR COOKIES

Preheat oven to 350 degrees F., rack in the middle position.

8-ounce ***(by weight)*** package brick-style cream cheese, softened ***(I used Philadelphia in the silver package)***
1 cup ***(2 sticks, 8 ounces, ½ pound)*** salted butter, softened
¾ cup white ***(granulated)*** sugar
¾ cup brown sugar ***(pack it down in the cup when you measure it)***
1 large egg
1 teaspoon vanilla extract
1 teaspoon baking powder
½ teaspoon salt
2 and ½ cups all-purpose flour ***(pack it down in the cup when you measure it)***
¾ cup chopped salted cashews ***(measure after chopping)***
1 cup ***(6-ounce package)*** milk chocolate chips

Prepare your baking pan. Spray a 9-inch by 13-inch cake pan with Pam or another nonstick cooking spray.

Alternatively, you can line the cake pan with heavy-duty foil, spray that and leave "ears" on the sides so that you can lift your bar cookies right out of the pan when they're baked and cooled.

Hannah's Note: If you forgot to take your cream cheese out of the refrigerator to soften it, there's an easy way to do it. Simply unwrap the brick of cream cheese, place it in the bottom of a small microwave-safe bowl, and heat it in the microwave on HIGH for 20 seconds. Let it sit in the microwave for 1 minute and then take it out and attempt to stir it smooth. If you can't, heat it for another 20 seconds, let it sit for another minute, and try again.

Aunt Nancy's Note: This recipe is a lot easier and faster to make if you use an electric mixer. You can also do it by hand, but you'll have to stir like the Dickens!

Place the softened cream cheese and the butter in the bowl of an electric mixer. Beat them together at MEDIUM speed until they are blended.

Add the white sugar and the brown sugar to the mixing bowl. Beat on MEDIUM speed until they are thoroughly combined and the mixture is light and fluffy.

Mix in the large egg and the vanilla extract. Beat until they are well incorporated.

Sprinkle in the baking powder and the salt. Mix it in at MEDIUM speed until the mixture is well blended.

Add the flour in half-cup increments, mixing at MEDIUM speed after each addition.

Shut off the mixer, scrape down the sides of the bowl with a rubber spatula, remove the bowl from the mixer, and give your bar cookie dough a final stir by hand.

If you haven't already chopped the salted cashews, do it now. Then measure out ¾ cup and add the nuts to your bowl. Mix them in thoroughly by hand with a spoon.

Mix in the milk chocolate chips.

Transfer your bar cookie dough into your prepared pan and spread it out with a rubber spatula or your impeccably clean hands. Pat the dough into the corners and cover the entire bottom of the pan. Press it down as evenly as you can.

Bake your Chocolate Cashew Bar Cookies at 350 degrees F. for 30 minutes or until the top is a light golden brown.

Let your bar cookies cool on the cold stovetop burner or on a wire rack until the pan is completely cool to the touch.

When your bar cookies are completely cool, frost them with Milk Chocolate Fudge Frosting, following the directions in the frosting recipe.

Let the frosted bar cookies cool completely. Then cover the pan with aluminum foil and either store them on the counter or refrigerate them until you'd like to serve them.

To serve, cut the bars into brownie-size pieces, place them on a pretty platter, and serve them with strong, hot coffee or cold glasses of milk.

Yield: Approximately 30 Chocolate Cashew Bar Cookies, but this depends entirely on how large you cut the pieces.

The Milk Chocolate Fudge Frosting recipe follows:

MILK CHOCOLATE FUDGE FROSTING
(microwave recipe)

2 Tablespoons ***(1 ounce)*** salted butter
2 cups milk chocolate chips ***(I used Nestle Milk Chocolate Chips, the 11.5-ounce package)***
1 can ***(14 ounces)*** sweetened condensed milk ***(NOT evaporated milk – I used Eagle Brand)***

Place the butter in the bottom of a microwave-safe bowl. ***(I used a quart Pyrex measuring cup)***

Place the milk chocolate chips on top of the butter.

Pour in the 14-ounce can of sweetened, condensed milk.

Heat on HIGH for 1 minute. Then remove from the microwave and stir with a heat-resistant rubber spatula.

Return the bowl to the microwave and heat for another minute.

Let the bowl sit in the microwave for 1 minute and then take it out ***(careful—it may be hot to the touch!)*** and set it on the counter. Attempt to stir it smooth with the heat-resistant spatula.

If you can stir the mixture smooth, you're done. If you can't stir it smooth, return the bowl to the microwave and heat on HIGH in 30-second increments followed by 1 minute standing time, until you can stir it smooth.

To frost your Chocolate Cashew Bar Cookies, simply pour the frosting over the top of your pan and use the heat-resistant rubber spatula to smooth the frosting into the corners.

Give the microwave-safe bowl to your favorite person to scrape clean. ***(If you're alone when you're baking these bar cookies, feel free to enjoy the frosting that's clinging to the sides of the bowl all by yourself.)***

Hannah's 1st Note: You can also make this recipe on the stovetop if you prefer. Simply heat the ingredients in a saucepan over MEDIUM-LOW heat, stirring constantly until the chips are melted. Then pull it to a cold burner, let it cool for one minute, and proceed to frost your bar cookies.

Hannah's 2nd Note: This frosting recipe is also enough for a 9-inch by 13-inch cake.

Chapter Seventeen

By the time she parked in her spot in back of The Cookie Jar again, Hannah's head was swimming with information. Carol had been a font of second-hand gossip, telling Hannah details about P.K. that Hannah probably didn't need to know. Although most of it seemed to be immaterial to her investigation, Hannah had taken the time to cull through the data and write down a few facts that might be useful.

Even though it was cold once she'd shut off her cookie truck, Hannah paged through her murder book and arranged what she'd learned. "Pinkie" was not P.K.'s girlfriend's real name, but no one at KCOW had known her true identity. Carol had mentioned, however, that she thought that Pinkie had gone to high school with P.K. Hannah flipped to Pinkie's name on her suspect list and wrote down that information. She knew that Pinkie and P.K. had broken off their engagement and no longer saw each other. Michelle had told her that, but Mike had once mentioned that anyone who'd had a close personal relationship with the murder victim was automatically a suspect until they'd been cleared.

Next, Hannah flipped to the page she'd set aside for Scotty. Her instincts told her that Scotty probably wasn't the killer, but she still had to investigate him. Luckily, she knew where to start. Scotty had mentioned that P.K. had joined him at the bar in the Lake Eden Inn. Hannah planned to interview Dick, the co-owner and bartender, when they went out there for dinner with Norman tonight.

Then there was Betty Jackson. She'd told Hannah that she liked P.K., but Betty had been very quick to mention that she thought there had been bad blood between Scotty and P.K. If that turned out to be false, either Betty wasn't as observant as Hannah thought she was, or Betty had deliberately attempted to steer suspicion away from the real culprit. The real culprit could even be Betty. It seemed unlikely, but Hannah wasn't even close to having all the facts. Digging for more information might either substantiate or disprove that theory.

The final suspect Hannah had added was the unnamed suspect with an unknown motive. That suspect always had a separate page on her suspect list. In some of her investigations, the name was actually filled in and so was the motive, but not usually this early in an investigation. That could be the case in P.K.'s murder. There was no way she could know that yet.

Hannah closed her murder book, stuck it back in her purse, and got out of her cookie truck. A few moments later, she was stepping inside the kitchen at The Cookie Jar.

"Hannah! You're back!" Michelle greeted her with a big smile. "Norman went down to the clinic to check on his mail and he's coming back at five-thirty to pick us up for dinner. Is that okay with you?"

"It's fine," Hannah responded, hanging her parka on a hook by the door. "Something smells good. What are you baking?"

"Chocolate Butterscotch Crunch Cookies."

"Is that a new recipe?"

"Yes. It's a variation of your Chocolate Chip Crunch

Cookies and your Chocolate Sugar Cookies. I made a couple of batches of bar cookies, and I wanted to do something in a regular cookie. You had some corn flakes in the pantry, and I found some butterscotch chips, so I decided to try these."

"They smell great!"

"This is the second batch I made. The first batch is on the bakers rack if you'd like to taste one."

"Yes. Thanks!" Hannah hurried to the bakers rack and plucked a warm cookie from one of the shelves. She took a small bite, just to taste, and then she took another much larger bite because the first had been so delicious.

"Sit down, Hannah. You look tired." Michelle motioned toward the work station. "I'll pour us both a cup of coffee and we can decide what to bake next."

"Please get more of these cookies, first," Hannah said, taking another bite as she turned and headed for her favorite stool. When she reached it, she sat down, finished her cookie, and accepted the coffee and plate of cookies that Michelle brought to her.

"Do you think the customers will like them?" Michelle asked.

"They'll love them. Try one and you'll see."

Michelle smiled as she sat down on the stool across from Hannah. "Norman told me about all the money in those accounts that Ross left for you. It's a *lot* of money, Hannah!"

"I know," Hannah said, but her mind added a second sentence. *Just wait until you tell her about the safe deposit box!*

"Did Mike get any idea of where Ross is from the bank records?"

"He didn't really tell me if he did or he didn't and I didn't want to ask in front of Doug. Doug did tell us that Ross requested the money he withdrew that day in bills no larger than twenties and fifties."

"Is that important?"

"I don't think so. Most people who are going on a trip take money with them, and they usually take denominations that are easy to spend."

"That makes sense."

"I asked Doug if Ross had purchased any traveler's checks."

"Smart!" Michelle was clearly impressed. "Did he?"

"No. Mike followed up by asking if Ross had changed any money into foreign currency, and Doug told him no to that, too."

"No clues there, right?"

"I don't think so." Hannah took a sip of her coffee and picked up another cookie. It was time to tell Michelle about the contents of Ross's safe deposit box.

"What?" Michelle asked, noticing that Hannah's expression had changed.

"Something else really unusual happened. I found out that Ross had a safe deposit box, and since it was one of those self-service ones and he left me the keys, Mike went with me to open it."

Hannah described how amazed she'd been to see the stacks of bills and how they'd discovered the key that had slid under one of the stacks. When she was through, Michelle just shook her head.

"This gets stranger and stranger," Michelle said. "Were you able to identify the key?"

"It looks like a padlock key, and we think it's the key to a storage unit because it says Superior Storage on one side. Mike says he's going to check it out, but he's pretty busy with P.K.'s murder right now. And that's one of the reasons I insisted on keeping the key."

"Can I see it?"

"Yes." Hannah drew the key from her pocket and handed it to Michelle.

"You're right, Hannah. It's a key to a storage unit and the number's stamped on the back. Superior Storage is a really big chain of storage units and they're all over the place."

"How do you know that?"

"There's a storage facility marked Superior Storage in St. Paul. I walk by it every day on my way to the campus. One of my college roommates wanted to put some things in storage so she went to the office and rented a unit. She said the lady told her that they had facilities all over Minnesota, Wisconsin, and Iowa."

"I wonder if Ross's storage unit is in the St. Paul building."

"I can find out right now," Michelle said, reaching for her cell phone.

Hannah listened as her sister made the call. It only took a moment to discover that Ross didn't have a storage unit in the St. Paul building.

"Sorry," Michelle said after she'd ended the call. "The lady told me his name isn't on unit three-twelve."

"Oh, well. That really would have been too good to be true. Thanks for trying."

"I can get a list online and call some of the other buildings," Michelle offered.

"That's a good idea, but do it tomorrow. That storage unit isn't going anywhere." Hannah got up to get more coffee for both of them. When she'd topped off their cups with hot coffee, she said, "I have something else to tell you. I didn't spend all that time at the bank."

"Where did you go?"

"I drove out to KCOW. I stopped by here, but everybody was in the coffee shop so I didn't bother to tell anyone where I was going. I just picked up some cookie bars and dashed out there."

"Tell me all about it," Michelle said, leaning forward. "Did you find any new suspects?"

"Yes, and I learned a little more about Pinkie."

"Her name?"

"No. Everybody at KCOW just called her Pinkie. Nobody I talked to knew her real name. But I did find out that P.K. and Pinkie went to high school together."

"Oh, good! Then we can find out where. We're going to the funeral and P.K.'s parents will be there. All we have to do is ask them where he went to high school."

"Isn't that a little . . ."

"Rude?" Michelle supplied the word.

"Not exactly rude, but perhaps a bit inappropriate considering that we're not close family friends. If we get the chance to talk to them, we should offer our condolences, not ask them questions."

"We don't have to ask them questions."

"We don't? Then how are we going to find out?"

"Mother knows them, and she loves to help you investigate. We'll get *her* to ask them."

Hannah thought about that for no more than a split second. "That could work. Mother's a genius in social situations. She'll figure out a way to work it into her condolences."

"Did you run into anybody else at KCOW?" Michelle asked.

"Yes. Betty Jackson works out there now."

"Great! Betty's one of the biggest gossips around. Who did she think did it?"

"She didn't hazard a guess, but she did suggest that I talk to the guy who thought he'd be head cameraman until they promoted P.K. to the job. His name is Scotty, and he claims he wasn't that angry at P.K."

"But Betty thinks it could be a workplace rivalry that was taken to the extreme?"

"She backtracked a little when I asked her if she really thought that Scotty killed P.K., but it's still possible. I just don't know, Michelle. I talked to Scotty, and my gut feeling is that he had nothing to do with it."

"Then you're probably right."

"But I can't assume that my gut is correct. I have to investigate Scotty anyway."

"I understand. Tell me about everyone else you saw at KCOW and how you feel about them."

Hannah told Michelle about Carol, describing her in detail. When she was through, Michelle looked thoughtful.

"Did Scotty have an alibi for the time of P.K.'s death?" she asked.

"I didn't ask him because it doesn't matter. P.K. died because he ate the drugged candy. The candy was the murder weapon, and it was mailed and delivered days before P.K. ate any."

"Right. And we don't know when the killer sent it because the mailer was thrown away."

"That's true. And even if we knew when it was mailed, we wouldn't know who mailed it. P.K.'s killer could have been hundreds of miles away at the time of his death."

"Or he could have been right here in Lake Eden when P.K. died," Michelle speculated.

"That's true, too. This is the only murder case I've ever tried to solve where the time of death doesn't relate in some way to the crime. And to make things even more complicated, the victim might not have been the intended victim."

Michelle thought about that for a moment. "You're right. We really can't assume anything!"

Both sisters were silent for a long moment, and then Michelle spoke again. "Let's say you really wanted someone dead. You wouldn't have gone through all the trouble to lace that candy with tranquilizers if you hadn't wanted them to die. After all, there are easier ways to kill someone. And then you went to the trouble to figure out a way to get the candy delivered to your intended victim without being implicated. At least we know that the killer was very determined to kill without being caught."

"That's true," Hannah agreed. "You're describing a person who was *driven* to commit murder."

"And if you were so driven to kill that particular person in that particular way and you knew it might not happen immediately, wouldn't you want to stick around to make sure everything eventually happened the way you planned?"

Hannah stared at her youngest sister for a moment and then she smiled. "You're absolutely right, Michelle. If I were the killer, I'd want to make sure that I was successful and I wouldn't want to just read about it in the papers. I'd need to know how, and when. And then I'd want to find out how the investigation into the murder was developing, how close the detectives were coming to figuring out the truth."

"Exactly. And don't forget about *you*, Hannah. The killer's going to want to know how *your* investigation is developing."

Hannah gave a little shiver. "You're right, of course. But what if the killer *didn't* succeed? What if the wrong person died?"

Michelle considered that for a moment. "Then the killer would want to get as far away from Lake Eden as fast as he or she could."

"Right. So we're right back where we started. We still don't know if the right person died or if the killer is still in Lake Eden."

Michelle sighed deeply. "That's true and I'm fresh out of theories. Investigating P.K.'s murder is terribly frustrating, isn't it?"

"Yes. And we're not even taking into account the fact that our emotions are involved."

"I didn't even think of that!" Michelle began to frown. "I guess that means we have to try to be dispassionate. If we think about it too much, our emotions will color everything. We're both upset over what happened to P.K. and . . . I can't decide if it's better or worse if we discover that P.K. was the intended victim."

"And I can't decide if it's worse or better if it turns out that Ross was the intended victim."

"I know." Michelle reached across the table to give Hannah a hug. "There's only one thing I know for sure."

"What's that?"

"That we have to catch the killer."

"I agree," Hannah said. "We have to catch P.K.'s killer, and that's doubly complicated this time."

Both sisters sat there staring down at their coffee cups as if, by some sort of magic, the answer to the killer's identity might suddenly appear there.

"There's got to be some way we can cope with this," Michelle said, looking up at Hannah. "Do you know how we can do that?"

"Yes, I do. We have to be intuitive and logical. And be both of those at the same time. And we have to be perfectly neutral about how we want this case to turn out. We can't even think about that aspect of it."

"Right. Anything else?"

"We have to be suspicious of everyone who had any sort of quarrel or resentment toward either P.K. or Ross, or disliked either one of them for any reason, real or imagined."

"That makes sense, but . . . how do we do that?"

"We have to interview everyone who had any kind of relationship with either one of them. And we need to learn about their lives from birth to the present. All we really know is that we have to collect all the information we can, listen to everyone attentively and critically, and wait for something to make some kind of sense."

"*That's* a tall order. Will it help us catch the killer?"

"Not necessarily, but that's the only way I know to proceed. It could take us a while, but it's like a giant jigsaw puzzle. Once we shake all the pieces out of the box and figure out how they fit together, we'll get a clear picture of the killer."

"I hope so! It sounds almost impossible, but I promise I'll do my best to help."

"I know you will. You always do. There's just one more thing, a very important thing, that we have to do."

"What is it?"

"We have to eat a lot of chocolate so we don't get discouraged."

Michelle just stared at Hannah for a moment, and then she began to laugh. "*That* I can do!" she declared, jumping up to get more cookies from the bakers rack.

CHOCOLATE BUTTERSCOTCH CRUNCH COOKIES

Preheat oven to 350 degrees F., rack in the middle position.

1 cup salted butter ***(2 sticks, one-half pound)***
6 one-ounce squares semi-sweet chocolate ***(I used Baker's)***
1 cup powdered sugar ***(not sifted – pack it down when you measure it)***
1 cup white ***(granulated)*** sugar
2 large eggs
1 teaspoon vanilla extract
1 teaspoon baking soda
1 teaspoon salt
3 cups flour ***(pack it down in the cup when you measure it)***
1 cup ***(6-ounce by weight package)*** butterscotch chips
2 cups crushed corn flakes ***(measure after crushing)***

Melt the butter and chocolate squares in a saucepan over low heat, stirring constantly, or in the microwave.

(I melted mine in a quart measuring cup in the microwave on HIGH for 3 minutes.) Once the butter and chocolate are melted, stir them smooth, transfer them to a large mixing bowl, and add the powdered and white sugars. Stir thoroughly and set the mixture aside to cool.

When the mixture is cool enough that it won't cook the eggs, add the eggs, one at a time, stirring after each addition. ***(You can use an electric mixer at this point if you like.)***

Mix in the vanilla, baking soda, and salt. Mix it all up together.

Add flour in half-cup increments, mixing after each addition. You don't have to be precise. ***(One very important reason for adding flour in increments is so that the whole mountain of flour won't sit there on top of your bowl and spill out all over the place when you try to stir it in.)***

Scrape out the bowl, take it out of the mixer if you used one, and give it a good stir by hand with a wooden spoon. Then add the cup of butterscotch chips and the cups of crushed corn flakes. Mix them in thoroughly.

Once the dough has been thoroughly mixed, roll one-inch dough balls with your fingers. ***(You can also use a 2-teaspoon scooper to form the dough balls)***.

Place the dough balls on a greased cookie sheet ***(I usually spray mine with Pam or another nonstick cooking spray,)*** 12 dough balls to a standard-size sheet. Flatten the dough balls a bit with your impeccably clean palm so that they won't roll off the cookie sheet on the way to the oven.

Bake the Chocolate Butterscotch Crunch Cookies at 350 degrees for 10 to 15 minutes. ***(Mine took 12 minutes.)*** Cool them on the cookie sheet for 2 minutes and then remove the cookies to a wire rack to finish cooling.

Yield: Approximately 5 to 6 dozen delicious chocolate butterscotch cookies that everyone will love.

Chapter Eighteen

Ten batches of assorted cookies and bar cookies later, Hannah and Michelle sat down at the work station again. "We did it," Hannah said, smiling at her sister. "You really helped a lot, Michelle."

"It was fun. Do you think that Sally will let us into the conference center to check out our booth?"

"I'm sure she will. I talked to her on the phone today and she's really excited about having us there. She said that having refreshments and setting up tables and chairs in the center like a food court will make a huge difference in how much longer people will stay and shop."

"She's right about that. Airports and malls have food courts. And so do county fairs. People need to rest, to re-energize."

"That's right. I can't think of a single large company that doesn't have a break room for their employees. Just look at us. We're sitting here at the work station drinking coffee right now."

"And waiting for Norman." Michelle glanced up at the clock on the wall. He should be here any minute."

As if on cue, there was a knock on the back kitchen door.

Michelle laughed and rose to her feet. "There he is. I'll go let him in."

"Thanks, Michelle," Hannah heard Norman say as he hung his parka on the hook by the back kitchen door. A moment later, he walked over to the work station. "Hi, Hannah."

"Hi, Norman."

Norman gave her a little hug. "I hope I'm not too early. Are you getting hungry?"

Hannah laughed. "I'm starved."

"That's exactly what Michelle said when she opened the door. Is there anything you want to take out to the conference center tonight? My trunk's practically empty."

"I don't know." Hannah turned to Michelle. "Can you think of anything we should take?"

"Not really."

"Okay then." Norman held out his hand for Hannah. "Let's go eat. When I called, Sally said to go ahead and come out early. She can't fit us into the dining room until seven, but Dick's making his Pizza Dip in the bar and it's not karaoke night until after nine."

"That's great!" Hannah exclaimed, and then she laughed. Norman was staring at her as if she'd gone stark, raving mad. "I'll tell you why it's so wonderful on our way out to the Lake Eden Inn."

After a smooth, cozy ride through the cold, snowy night, Norman pulled into a parking spot marked DELIVERIES ONLY in back of the Lake Eden Inn. "Sally said to park back here," he told them. "She left the back door open for us. All we have to do is lock it behind us when we come in."

"This is perfect," Michelle said, slipping out of her boots and switching to her shoes. "It's only a couple of steps to the door, and we don't have to wear our boots."

"It might be snowing when you come out," Hannah warned her youngest sister.

"I know, but I'll take the chance. It's so nice not to have to switch from boots to shoes and then back again."

"You're right," Hannah agreed. "I'll take the chance, too. How about you, Norman?"

"I'll play it safe. That way I can wade out here to get your boots if a blizzard blows in . . . unless, of course, you think I have absolutely no spirit of adventure. If that's the case, I'll go in barefoot!"

Hannah laughed and so did Michelle. "Wear your boots, Norman," Hannah told him. "That's the gentlemanly thing to do. And if there happens to be an unseasonable heat wave, you can always throw down your parka for us to walk over."

All three of them were smiling as they went inside, locked the door behind them, and walked down the narrow hallway that passed Sally's gigantic kitchen. As they went through the lobby and approached the bar, Norman turned to Hannah.

"Go ahead and get a table unless you'd rather sit at the bar. And save a chair or a barstool for me. I'll take our parkas and hang them up, switch to my shoes, and come right back."

Hannah and Michelle shrugged out of their parkas, handed them to Norman, and went through the swinging saloon-style double doors to Dick's bar. There were already quite a few people at the tables, but only a few customers at the bar.

"Where do you want to go?" Michelle asked Hannah.

"The bar. Dick's bartending, and it'll be easier to talk to him there."

"You're going to ask him about Scotty and P.K.?"

"That's my plan. Dick's a very observant guy. I told him that once, and he said that good bartenders had to be observant, that it was part of the job. I want Dick to tell me his impression of the way Scotty and P.K. were getting along the last time they were here."

"Okay," Michelle agreed. "I'll follow your lead, Hannah."

Hannah walked up to the bar and motioned to a stool. "Take this one, Michelle. I'll put my purse on the barstool on the other side of me to reserve it for Norman."

When Hannah and Michelle were seated, Dick hurried over to them. "Hi, girls," he greeted them both with a smile, and then he turned to Hannah. "You're a little early for karaoke, Hannah."

"You'd better thank your lucky stars for that, Dick. Have you ever heard me sing?"

Dick thought about that for a moment, and then he shook his head. "I don't think so, at least not that I can remember."

"Oh, you'd remember!" Michelle told him emphatically. "Hannah's really loud, and she can't carry a tune in a bucket. Believe me, I know. When I was young, she used to try to sing me to sleep."

"And it didn't work?"

"It worked just fine," Hannah said. "Michelle listened for about thirty seconds, and then she went to sleep to get away from my singing."

Dick laughed. "I think you're both pulling my leg, but I'll consider myself warned. Actually Hannah, your singing might be a big relief tonight."

There was a grin on Dick's face and Hannah knew that she was about to be the recipient of his leg-pulling. "What makes you so sure we won't stop in for an after-dinner drink?"

"Alice Vogel and Digger Gibson are coming in. They always sing duets."

"Digger can't sing?" Michelle guessed.

"And neither can Alice?" Hannah added her question to the mix.

"You can say that. But since I'm their bartender, my lips are sealed . . . along with my ears."

"Ear plugs?" Hannah asked him.

"Far be it from me to say anything unkind about a paying customer. Let's just say that Digger and Alice love to . . ." Dick paused, searching for the right word. "They love to *perform* together."

The two sisters exchanged glances. It was obvious to both of them that Dick was avoiding use of the word *sing*.

"We get it," Michelle told him. "Do Digger and Alice think they're really good . . . uh . . . *performers*?"

"They think they're a terrific duo, especially when people applaud much longer and louder than they do for anyone else. Neither one of them realizes that their audience is applauding the fact that they're finished with the song."

"That sounds like me," Hannah admitted. "I thought I was good until my class was singing a song for a school program, and the teacher asked me not to sing, but just to whisper the words instead."

Dick's grin grew wider. "That wouldn't work with Alice and Digger. They're firmly convinced that they're incredibly musical."

"And no one's ever told them they're not?" Hannah asked.

Dick shook his head. "Everybody likes Alice and everybody likes Digger. And no one wants to hurt their feelings. To tell the truth, there's only one good thing about their performance."

"What's that?" Hannah asked, aware that she was falling into Dick's trap, but unable to resist hearing the punch line.

"It's like this. When Digger and Alice push back their chairs, everybody in the bar knows that they're going to get up on stage. That makes everybody in the bar order doubles of whatever they're drinking, even if they are drinking beer!"

"How do you double a beer?" Michelle asked.

"You order two bottles at once."

"I wonder if that helps," Hannah wondered aloud.

"It sure does! And it doesn't hurt that all of my waitresses pass out disposable ear plugs with every double."

Hannah and Michelle had just finished laughing when Norman pushed through the swinging doors of the bar. Hannah waved at him and Norman walked over to sit down on the stool she'd saved.

"Sorry that took so long," he apologized. "I ran into one of my patients and she asked me to tell her all about implants."

Hannah was curious. "I thought implants were highly specialized. Do you do implants?"

"No, but I told her to come in for an exam to see if she was a good candidate. And I said that if she was, I'd give her the name of a good oral surgeon."

"What'll it be, everybody?" Dick asked, placing blue and green striped cocktail napkins with the words LAKE EDEN INN in bold black letters in front.

"I'll have a glass of your house chardonnay," Michelle said. "I had it the last time I was here, and it was good."

"It's Clos du Bois," Dick told her, and then he turned to Hannah. "And for you, Hannah?"

"I'd like an Arnold Palmer, heavy on the iced tea," Hannah said.

"You're not drinking?" Norman asked her.

"Not until dinner. I've been running around all day, and if I have more than one glass, it'll probably put me to sleep."

Dick looked over at Norman. "What about you, Norman?"

"Hot lemonade with cinnamon, please."

"Good choice," Dick said, smiling at him.

"Dick?" Hannah claimed his attention before he could

leave to prepare their drinks. "Later, when you get a chance, I'd really like to talk to you for a couple of minutes."

Dick leaned a bit closer to her. "About P.K.'s murder?"

"Yes. I have a couple of questions for you."

Dick smiled. "Of course you do, Hannah. You always do. Let me get your drinks and check the rest of the people at the bar. Then I'll come over and we can talk." He glanced at his watch and continued. "We're having Hockey Playoff Pizza Dip at the bar tonight, and it's almost ready to come out of the oven. Would you like to try it?"

"I don't know about them, but I would," Norman said. "I'm really hungry."

"I'd like to try it," Hannah agreed. "Michelle?"

"Count me in." She turned to Dick. "You said it was a dip, right?"

"That's right."

"What do you dip in it?"

"Almost anything. It's my friend John's recipe. We rented rooms in the same house when we were in college, and we used to all get together to watch hockey games on television. John always made his dip and the girls brought something to use as a . . ." he paused and glanced at Hannah. "What do you call potato chips when you have them with a dip?"

"Potato chips," Hannah said with a perfectly straight face.

Everyone laughed and Dick gave a little sigh. "I should have known better than to ask it like that, but I still want to know."

Hannah thought about that for a moment, and then she shrugged. "I'm not really sure. I guess you could call them *dippers* or *scoops*, but that doesn't sound very appetizing. And if there's a culinary term for them, I've never heard it. Why don't you just sidestep the problem by putting whatever you're using in a bowl or a basket and serving it along with the dip? People are used to eating dips, and they'll know how to use whatever it is. You could even say something like, 'Here's a bowl of whatever-it-is to use for dipping.'"

"Okay, that's easy," Dick said, glancing at his watch again. "I'll get your drinks now, and then I'll serve your dip."

JOHN'S HOCKEY PLAYOFF PIZZA DIP
(An Appetizer)

Preheat oven to 350 degrees F., rack in the middle position.

8-ounce package brick cream cheese, softened to room temperature ***(I used Philadelphia in the silver rectangular package)***
½ teaspoon dried oregano
½ teaspoon dried parsley
¼ teaspoon dried basil
1 cup ***(about 4 ounces)*** shredded mozzarella cheese
1 cup ***(about 4 ounces)*** shredded Parmesan cheese
½ teaspoon onion powder ***(or 1 Tablespoon finely minced fresh onion)***
½ teaspoon garlic powder ***(or 1 teaspoon finely minced fresh garlic)***
1 cup spaghetti sauce with meat ***(I used Prego)***
2 ounces of pepperoni slices
2 to 3 Tablespoons sliced black or green pitted olives
1 small can of button mushrooms

1 loaf store-bought garlic bread ***(the kind wrapped in foil) (or 2 packages of refrigerated soft breadstick dough)***

Prepare your pan(s) by lining a pie plate with foil. ***(If you chose to use the tubes of refrigerated breadstick dough, also line a cookie sheet with foil.)***

In a small bowl, combine the softened cream cheese, oregano, parsley, and basil. Mix the ingredients together thoroughly.

Hannah's 1st Note: If you've just taken your package of cream cheese out of the refrigerator and you need to soften it in a hurry, simply unwrap it, place it in a small, microwave-safe bowl and heat it in the microwave on HIGH for 20 seconds. Let it sit in the microwave for a minute and then try to stir it smooth. Repeat as often as necessary until you achieve a smooth texture. Then take the bowl out of the microwave and mix in the oregano, parsley, and basil. Mix thoroughly.

Spread the cream cheese and herb mixture out in the bottom of your prepared pie pan.

In a separate bowl, mix the shredded Parmesan and shredded mozzarella cheeses together.

Hannah's 2nd Note: You can use your impeccably clean fingers to mix the cheese together.

Sprinkle HALF of the shredded cheese mixture on top of the cream cheese and herb mixture.

Measure out the cup of spaghetti sauce and place it in a small bowl.

Mix the onion and the minced garlic ***(or the onion powder and garlic powder)*** into the spaghetti sauce.

Spoon the spaghetti sauce mixture over the top of the contents of the pie pan. Use a rubber spatula to spread it out evenly, but DO NOT MIX it in.

Sprinkle the remaining cheese mixture over the top of the spaghetti sauce mixture.

Arrange the pepperoni evenly on top of the cheese.

Place the sliced olives on top of the pepperoni.

Pat the button mushrooms dry with paper towels and then arrange them on top of the olives.

Bake your Hockey Playoff Pizza Dip at 350 degrees F., for a total of 25 to 30 minutes.

After your pizza dip has been in the oven for 5 minutes, place the garlic bread in the oven and bake according to package directions.

If you've decided to make the soft breadsticks instead of the garlic bread, cut each breadstick in 2 pieces, and follow the package directions to bake them. Coordinate baking times so that everything comes out of the oven at approximately the same time.

Slice your garlic bread, put the slices in a napkin-lined basket, and serve it with your dip. Since you've already cut the soft breadsticks in 2 pieces, simply place them in a napkin-lined basket.

Hannah's 3rd Note: You might want to bake the soft breadsticks a bit longer so that they will hold their shape when your guests dip them in the Hockey Playoff Pizza Dip. Both the soft breadsticks and the garlic bread should be on the crispy side for ease in dipping. You can also use chips in place of the bread.

Chapter Nineteen

They had almost finished their drinks by the time Dick was through refilling glasses and delivering his dip. Hannah, who had been keeping an eye on the time, gave a relieved sigh. She wanted to interview Dick tonight and she really hadn't wanted to come back to the bar with karaoke going full swing.

"Okay, Hannah," he said leaning over the bar toward the three of them. "I've got at least five minutes before anyone's going to want a refill."

"Thanks, Dick. And before I forget to tell you, your pizza dip was wonderful."

As Norman and Michelle took turns complimenting Dick on his college friend's creation, Hannah drew her murder book out of her purse and grabbed one of the numerous pens that had dropped down to the bottom. Then, when there was a lull in the conversation, she began to ask the questions she'd thought of on the drive out to the Inn. "Please tell me about the last time you saw P.K."

"Of course. P.K. came in after work with Scotty. I'd never seen them together before, so I was a little curious. They ordered drinks, beer for Scotty and a Virgin Cuba Libre for P.K."

"Did they seem to be friendly?" Hannah asked.

"Not exactly. Polite, yes. Friendly, not when they first came in the bar."

"But they were friendly later?" Michelle asked the obvious question.

"Yes. P.K. was okay from the beginning, but Scotty was a little reserved. It's hard to tell with him, but I've known him long enough to read his body language."

"Was it different than it usually is when he comes in here?" Norman asked.

Dick nodded. "They sat down at a table and Scotty sat up straight, not relaxed at all, and he didn't prop his elbows on the table the way he usually does."

"Anything else?" Hannah asked him.

"Yes. Scotty didn't touch his beer right away, and he likes to drink off the layer of foam on top." Dick stopped and gave a little shrug. "I know these things are little things, but they tell me what kind of mood my regulars are in."

"And Scotty didn't behave the way he usually did?" Hannah asked.

"No. Something was different with him. He looked at his beer, but he didn't pick up the glass to drink it. And he didn't dig into the pizza dip until after he'd talked to P.K. for a couple of minutes."

"Did you overhear anything they said?" Michelle asked.

"No. I wasn't that close. I was curious because Scotty wasn't his usual self, but I didn't want to be obvious. I just watched to see what was going to happen because I could tell they were talking about something serious."

"How could you tell?" Hannah followed up.

"Because Scotty locked eyes with P.K. and he didn't look away for a couple of minutes. And then both of them took a sip of their drinks and dug into my pizza dip. There were other things too, things that told me everything was okay between them."

Hannah didn't say anything. She just raised her eyebrows in an unspoken question, and Dick went on.

"Scotty came out here almost every week with five or six friends, and he was buddy-buddy with them. They laughed a lot and kidded each other the way good friends do."

Norman looked curious. "And Scotty acted like that after he had the conversation with P.K.?"

"Not exactly. They still weren't buddy-buddy, but I could tell that they were getting along. Scotty's elbows went up on the table and he took a big swallow of his beer. And he smiled at P.K. for the first time since they sat down. There was another thing, too. They were passing the basket of chips back and forth. That's when I figured out that whatever had been bothering Scotty had been resolved."

"You notice a lot about people, Dick," Michelle told him. "Did you take psychology courses in college?"

Dick shook his head. "Never. But I've been a bartender for a long time. That's how I paid for college. It's a skill a good bartender picks up because it's needed."

"Needed?" Michelle looked confused. "I know you have to pay attention to people so you notice when they need something, but it sounds as if you notice a lot more than that."

"That's true. Bartenders need to become familiar with the people they serve. It's a matter of self-preservation."

"How so?" Norman asked.

"As a bartender, you don't want to serve another drink to someone who's about to cross the line between having a good time and becoming too drunk to drive. If you do that, it's actionable. A good bartender knows when to cut someone off, and that means you have to watch for all sorts of little signs that will tip you off."

"Did Scotty ever get . . ." Hannah paused. She'd been about to ask if Scotty had ever gotten drunk, but Dick probably wouldn't tell her.

"Did he get a little tipsy?" Dick supplied the rest of her question.

"Yes."

"Only once that I can remember. He usually had no more than three glasses of beer. The only time I saw him drink more was when he was in here with his wife. It was his birthday and they were celebrating with a bunch of their friends. I was wondering if I should stop serving him, but his wife came up to the bar and assured me that she was driving home. She even showed me the car keys."

Hannah checked another item off her mental checklist. She knew that occasionally, when someone had one too many drinks, resentments flared. "So Scotty wasn't a heavy drinker?"

"No." Dick shook his head. "I never saw Scotty order a mixed drink. He was a beer man, but only tap beer. He never drank bottled beer and a glass of beer would last him at least an hour, sometimes longer. Heavy drinkers generally go for something with more alcoholic content, like hard liquor or fortified beer or wine. I know what you really want to know, Hannah, so I'll cut to the chase. There's no way Scotty left here drunk the night he was here with P.K."

Dick's phone rang and he turned around to answer it. A moment later, he was back. "That was Sally. Your table's ready and she wants to know if it's all right to join you for dessert. She said she has some information for you."

Once they'd assured Dick that it would be fine if Sally joined them for dessert, Hannah, Michelle, and Norman left Dick's bar. They walked down the hallway to the restaurant and entered the alcove that contained the receptionist's stand.

Dot Larson was working as the hostess and she greeted them warmly. "Hi, guys! Sally said you were coming out for dinner. She saved a private booth for you and she asked me to take you there." Dot turned to Hannah. "Did Dick tell you that Sally wants to join you for dessert?"

"Yes, he did, and we told him that was just fine. Thanks for asking, Dot. How's the baby?"

"He's not a baby anymore. If you ask him, he's a big boy now. And that means he gives my mother a run for her money!"

"Your mom is still babysitting for you?" Michelle asked her.

"Yes. She wants to babysit until Jamie gets in preschool. Then it'll be only half-days. That'll be two years from now, Lord willing and the creek don't rise."

Hannah smiled. "You always say that."

"That's because my grandmother came from delta country and they were flooded out every four years or so. And before I forget, Sally wanted me to remind you to enter our Christmas decorating contest. All you have to do is join a committee, bring your favorite ornament from home, and hang it on your tree. All employees vote and the three best Christmas trees win a trophy." Dot turned to Norman. "Follow me, and I'll show you which booth Sally chose for you tonight and introduce you to your waitress. She's new, but she's really good and I know you'll like her."

With Dot in the lead, the three of them climbed up the steps leading to the raised area on the far side of the dining room. They walked past the curtained booths and stopped at the one on the far end.

"Sally saved this one for you," Dot told them. "She told me that she had something important to tell you. I'm thinking that it's either about the convention, or P.K.'s murder."

Hannah just smiled. She doubted very much that the bulk

of Sally's conversation would be about the convention. She wouldn't have needed to put them in a curtained booth if that were the case. Hannah was almost certain that Sally wanted to tell them something about P.K. that might relate, in some way, to the murder investigation. Hannah's curiosity was piqued, but she knew it wouldn't be satisfied until after they'd finished their entrées and it was time for dessert, coffee, and whatever Sally had to impart.

"Just one more thing before I leave," Dot said after they were seated. "Sally says she really wants you to try her new appetizer."

Hannah almost groaned. She knew she'd eaten far too much of Dick's pizza dip and now there was another appetizer to try.

"It's called Crunchy Salty Cheesy Prosciutto and Asparagus Rolls, and they're very light and not at all filling," Dot said, as if she'd somehow read Hannah's mind.

"They sound great!" Michelle commented, taking a sip of the wine that she'd brought with her from the bar. "I love asparagus. I think it's my favorite vegetable."

"And it goes so well with prosciutto," Norman added.

Hannah felt her appetite beginning to return. "What does Sally use for the wrapper?" she asked.

"Puff pastry rolled out thin," Dot told them. "They're great with phyllo dough too, but it's a lot harder to work with. They're baked in a hot oven so they turn out nice and crisp and they're served hot."

Yes, her appetite was definitely coming back, Hannah decided as she thought about Sally's new creation. Perhaps she could have an entrée after all and still have room for dessert.

Their waitress arrived and poured more wine for Michelle and a glass for Hannah. She was carrying a glass of iced tea for Norman, and she set it down in front of him. She whisked away his nearly empty glass, handed it to her busboy, and turned to them again. "Dot told me you wanted to try Sally's new appetizer, and that's baking right now for you. Have you thought about what you'd like for an entrée, or would you like a little more time?"

"I'm ready with my entrée order," Michelle told her. "I'll have the center-cut pork chop with fingerling potatoes. I know that comes with carrots in sweet mustard sauce, but could I have creamed spinach instead?"

"Certainly," their waitress responded. "All of the entrées tonight come with Piccadilly Cheese Mini Muffins that we include in the bread basket. Is that all right, or would you rather have sourdough soft rolls?"

"I'll try the mini muffins. I've never had those before." Michelle turned to Hannah and Norman. "Would you two excuse me for a moment? I have to make a phone call to see if Lonnie can drop by the condo later, and the reception isn't very good in these curtained booths."

"Sally's got a hotspot in her office," their waitress told her. "If you stand in the hallway outside the office door, the reception's really good. I always duck out there when I need to make a call."

"Thanks," Michelle said and rose to her feet. "I'll be back as soon as I can."

"Go ahead, Michelle," Hannah said with a nod. Perhaps Michelle's cell phone didn't work well in this curtained booth, but their sister-to-sister radar was working just fine. She knew exactly why Michelle wanted Lonnie to drop by to see them tonight.

"I'd better tell you what I want now before I forget," Norman said to the waitress. "You can leave the iced tea, but could I please have a glass of ginger ale, too? I'm really thirsty tonight."

"I'll bring one now and another with your entrée," their waitress promised. "Did you have any of Dick's pizza dip?"

"We all did," Hannah answered her.

"Then that's probably why you're thirsty. Dick loves to spice it up." She turned to Hannah. "And for you, ma'am?"

"I have a question before I order my entrée. What are Piccadilly Cheese Mini Muffins? I don't believe I've ever seen them on the menu before."

"That's because they're a new item tonight. We're trying them out with our customers. Sally got the recipe from her grandmother, and they were very popular in her grandfather's pub."

"Then I'd like to try one, also," Hannah decided. "And for an entrée, I'll have the half Cornish game hen with sautéed button mushrooms and wild rice."

"Very good," their waitress said, jotting it down on her pad before she turned to Norman. "And for your entrée, sir?"

"I'll have the duck with raspberry sauce, and the braised snow peas."

"Would you care to try the Piccadilly Cheese Mini Muffins?" their waitress asked him.

Norman looked over at Hannah and smiled. "Absolutely. I don't want to be the only holdout."

"I'll send my busboy over with the muffins and the rest of tonight's bread basket," their waitress said, pulling aside the curtains and stepping out of the booth. She closed the curtains behind her, and Hannah turned to face Norman. "Michelle is calling Lonnie to come over tonight so that we can try to find out how Mike is coming along with his investigation."

"I guessed that."

"Then will you please come over after you drop us at The Cookie Jar?"

"Of course I will. I'll stay at your place for as long as you need me, Hannah."

At that exact moment, the curtains were pulled aside and Delores stood there glaring. She glanced behind her and stepped in quickly, pulling the curtains shut behind her. "Hannah Louise Swensen! How dare you? And you, Norman. You should know better than this!"

Both Hannah and Norman stared at Delores with puzzled expressions. "Norman knows better than *what*, Mother?" Hannah asked her.

"I heard what you said to my daughter, Norman! It's simply scandalous!"

It took a moment, but then Hannah realized what her mother had overheard. The last thing Norman had said to her before Delores had jerked back the curtains was, *I'll stay at your place for as long as you need me, Hannah.*

"But, Mother. You don't understand," Hannah began to explain. "Norman didn't mean . . ."

"I know precisely what Norman meant!" Delores interrupted her. "And I can tell you right now that I do not approve!"

"Calm down, Mother," Hannah pleaded. "You *don't* know what Norman meant. If you'll listen to me for a moment, I'll tell you."

"You want me to listen to *you*?" Delores looked completely outraged. "I'm ashamed of you, Hannah! You should know better than to come out here with Norman and sit in a private booth with him. It fairly shouts to the whole world that you have something to conceal!"

"But, Mother . . . you just don't understand!"

"Oh, I understand perfectly and let me tell you what *you*

should understand. Married women do not hide behind curtains with men who are not their husbands! Ross hasn't even been gone for three full weeks and you've already found someone to replace him!"

At that exact moment, the curtains were pulled back and Michelle stepped in. "Sorry that took longer than I thought. I had to wait for Lonnie to call me back so I just stayed close to . . ." She stopped speaking as she spotted her mother. "Hello, Mother. What are you doing out here tonight?"

CRUNCHY SALTY CHEESY PROSCIUTTO AND ASPARAGUS ROLLS
(An Appetizer)

Preheat oven to 450 degrees F., rack in the middle position.

2 sheets of frozen puff pastry dough (***I used Pepperidge Farm***)
20 slices prosciutto in long thin strips
20 spears asparagus, cleaned and trimmed ***(either fresh or frozen)***
Parmesan cheese, finely grated

Prepare your baking sheet by either spraying it with Pam or another nonstick cooking spray or lining it with parchment paper.

Hannah's 1st Note: I used a cookie sheet lined with parchment paper.

Thaw your frozen puff pastry dough according to package directions.

Spread out your thawed dough on a lightly floured surface and roll it out until it's slightly thinner than pie crust dough.

With the blade of a sharp knife, cut the sheets into rectangles the same size as the length of your asparagus. Make sure that the rectangles are high enough to wrap around the prosciutto-covered asparagus spear twice.

Wrap one slice of prosciutto around an asparagus spear.

Roll the prosciutto-covered asparagus spear in the shredded Parmesan cheese.

Place one puff pastry rectangle out a clean surface.

Hannah's 2nd Note: I used a sheet of wax paper for my clean surface.

Spray the inside surface of the rectangle with Pam or another nonstick cooking spray.

Place the prosciutto-covered asparagus spear on the bottom of the rectangle. Roll the spear up from the bottom and press down the top of the rectangle slightly so that it will stay in place when you bake it.

Place the completed roll on the prepared baking sheet.

Repeat until all the asparagus spears are wrapped with prosciutto, rolled in shredded Parmesan cheese, and encased in puff pastry rectangles.

When all of your appetizers are on the baking sheet, bake them at 450 degrees F. for 10 minutes, or until they are golden brown.

Serve these delicious appetizers warm.

Yield: 20 delightful appetizers that will make any party a success.

Hannah's 3rd Note: Lisa wants to make these appetizers ahead of time and freeze them. She's going to thaw them for 15 minutes on the kitchen counter, spray them with Pam or nonstick baking spray on the outside, and bake them until they are golden brown. I think it will work just fine, but she hasn't tried it yet.

Chapter Twenty

Delores had apologized profusely for leaping to conclusions, laughed with them about her misinterpretation of the situation, and joined them to enjoy the appetizer. When Doc arrived, she'd left to have dinner with him, and shortly after that, their entrees had been served. Once those had been eaten, the busboy had cleared away their dishes, and now they were waiting for the coffee they'd ordered.

"Here's your coffee," their waitress announced, coming in with a tray containing coffee cups, cream and sugar, and spoons. Once all three of them had their coffee, she said, "Sally wants me to tell you that she'll be with you in less than five minutes and she's bringing the dessert. It's something she tried today and she'd like your opinions."

"What is it?" Hannah asked.

"Almond Custard Pie with Raspberry Jam Glaze. The waitstaff always tries out new things, and everyone thought it was delicious."

"I believe you," Hannah told her. "Everything Sally makes is delicious."

When their waitress had left, Norman leaned forward and lowered his voice. "What do you think Sally has to tell us?"

"I don't know," Hannah admitted. "It could be something

about almost anybody. Everyone in Lake Eden comes out here to eat when they want a fancy dinner or it's a special occasion."

"People from the neighboring towns come here, too," Michelle added.

"It could be something about the convention," Norman reminded them.

"Somehow, I don't think so, but I guess we'll just have to wait and see," Hannah said, taking a sip of her coffee.

Sally arrived at their table within five minutes, just as their waitress had promised. She was followed by one of her busboys, who was carrying dessert plates, forks, a bowl of something puffy and white that Hannah guessed was sweetened whipped cream, and a whole pie cut into six pieces.

"Thanks for the feedback on my appetizer," Sally said, sliding into the booth and nodding to the busboy to serve their dessert. "How did you like the Piccadilly Cheese Mini Muffins?"

"All three of us loved them!" Hannah responded immediately. "They're different than anything I've ever tasted before and they're delicious. Could I have the recipe?"

"Of course. I'll print it out before you leave."

"And could we have the recipe for the new appetizer, too?" Michelle asked.

"I'll give you both of them," Sally promised. "And once you taste my new pie, you'll want that, too. Both Loren and Brooke raved about it and asked me how to make it. They're going to serve it to the vendors on the last day of the convention."

"Our waitress said it was an almond custard with a raspberry glaze, and she told us that it was delicious," Norman told Sally.

"Yes. It's a smooth, creamy custard. Just wait until you taste it. My grandmother used to make it, and the recipe was in her recipe box. Back then, they didn't have almond butter and she had to make her own before she could mix up the rest of the pie."

"Did she include a recipe for the almond butter?" Hannah asked, wondering if it was the same as the one she had.

"No. It wasn't included in the pie recipe and I was too young to remember how she made it. Since Florence carries almond butter in the peanut butter and jelly aisle, I just used that. It worked really well in the custard."

Sally waited until the busboy placed a slice in front of each of them. Then Sally picked up the bowl of sweetened whipped cream and garnished the top of their slices with a generous dollop. "You can decorate the whipped cream with fresh raspberries if you like. It makes the pie look a little dressier."

She picked up her fork, and the three of them quickly followed suit. When they tasted the pie, smiles spread across everyone's face.

"Well?" Sally asked as they each went for a second bite.

"I'm just not sure, Sally," Norman said, cutting off another, much larger bite. "I may have to try another slice to make sure."

"I agree," Michelle told Sally. "It wouldn't be fair to judge it on just one slice."

Sally laughed and turned to Hannah. "Will *you* give me an opinion?" she asked.

"Yes, but I want to make sure the custard is consistent so I'd better have a second piece, too. So far, it's incredibly delicious. I love the texture, and the almond flavor reminds me of marzipan with only one difference."

"What's that?" Sally asked.

"Your pie is more delicious and I like it a lot better than marzipan. And the raspberry glaze complements the almond flavor perfectly. Put it on the dessert menu, Sally. It's definitely a huge winner."

Their waitress brought a second pie, and everyone ate another slice. The busboy arrived with a fresh carafe of coffee, and after he had left, closing the curtains behind him, Sally leaned forward so that she could lower her voice.

"Are you ready to hear what I know about the murder case?" she asked Hannah.

"The three of us are all ears," Hannah told her, letting Sally know that it was fine to share this information with Michelle and Norman.

"P.K. and Pinkie came out here quite a bit," Sally told them. "It was their favorite place to eat. Dot got to know them quite well since they were here so often."

Hannah held up her hand to stop Sally. "Just a minute, Sally. This is important. Do either you or Dot know Pinkie's real name?"

"No. I was curious and I asked Dot. She checked around for me, and she said no one here had ever heard her called anything other than Pinkie. Dick doesn't know either. I asked him."

"How about Pinkie's last name?" Michelle asked. "Was it ever on a credit card she used?"

Sally shook her head. "P.K. always paid so we don't know that, either. Let me give you a little background about their relationship."

Hannah drew her murder book out of her purse and found a pen. "Please do," she told Sally.

"Pinkie didn't eat red meat, but she loved my chicken and fish entrees. P.K. always had some kind of red meat, but he always asked Pinkie if that was okay. She would tell him that it really didn't bother her to see him eating red meat and he should order whatever he wanted."

"Did Pinkie drink wine with dinner?" Norman asked.

"No. Neither one of them drank alcohol, at least not out here. I asked Dick about that and he said both of them ordered Virgin Cuba Libres when they came to the bar. They'd come out here after P.K. got off work, sit in the bar with their drinks for a while, and then they'd come into the dining room for dinner."

"Did Pinkie ever eat any of Dick's pizza dip?" Michelle asked.

Sally smiled. "Dick told me that Pinkie loved it, but she made P.K. eat off all the pepperoni slices before she'd have any. He also told me that P.K. used to kid her about how he had to save her from temptation, and then they'd both laugh about it. Dick thought they were a really cute couple and he congratulated them on their engagement. He was about to offer them a bottle of champagne on the house, but then he remembered that they didn't drink alcohol so he brought a chilled bottle of sparkling apple juice instead."

"Did you see Pinkie or P.K. after they broke up?" Hannah asked.

"Yes, I saw her and she was desperately unhappy. It was shortly after the breakup. I could ask Dot to look up the exact date if you want it."

"No, that's okay," Hannah told her, "but please keep it handy. If I need it for any reason, I'll let you know."

"It'll be right there in the monthly reservation books. I keep all of them in a file box, just in case."

"In case of a murder?" Michelle asked.

"That could be one reason I guess, but there are others."

"Please tell us." Norman was clearly curious.

"I started keeping the reservation books in case my tax returns were ever audited and they wanted to know who was working on a particular day. Dot writes the names of everyone's server right under their reservation. It could also be useful if one of my diners is involved in a court case."

"To prove that they showed up for dinner and what time they came in?" Hannah guessed.

"Yes. Anyway, as I said, when Pinkie came in alone, she told Dot she missed P.K. and she didn't understand why he'd broken off their engagement."

Michelle's mouth dropped open in surprise. "But . . . I thought it was the other way around and Pinkie broke up with *him*!"

"Let's just say it was mutual and there were bad feelings on both sides. I'm almost positive that there's no way they could have patched it up and gotten back together."

Hannah really didn't want to ask the follow-up question, but this was a murder investigation and she was obligated to ferret out the truth. "Do you know the reason they broke up?"

"Oh, yes. Everyone who was in the dining room that night knows. Their breakup was very contentious."

"Did it involve another woman?"

"No. That wasn't it at all."

Hannah had been holding her breath, and she let it out in a soft sigh of relief. She'd been hoping that the words *other woman*, or Michelle's name, wouldn't come up in their conversation.

"You said everyone who was here knew the reason they broke up," Hannah followed up again. "Tell us about it."

"Of course. You have the background now. Just remember that everyone here thought they were a perfect couple and they never did anything to make us think differently. That's why it was so shocking."

Hannah leaned a little closer, and then she realized that Michelle and Norman were also leaning forward toward Sally. It was as if their action would cause Sally to hurry and tell them. But instead of continuing, Sally reached for the coffee carafe and filled everyone's cup.

Sally could give Lisa a run for her money, Hannah thought. *She's got all three of us on pins and needles, waiting to hear what she's about to tell us.*

"Pinkie decided she wanted the Maine lobster with drawn butter that night, and P.K. ordered my tenderloin tips with wild mushrooms. When their entrees came, Pinkie took only one bite of her lobster, put down her fork, and started to argue with P.K."

"Was it a bad argument?" Michelle asked.

"I'll say! It went on for at least ten minutes and that's a long time to fight, especially in a public place with people listening. And my lovely Maine lobster sat there getting as cold as icicles. The drawn butter had already started to congeal before they were through arguing."

"Do you know who started the argument?" Hannah asked in an effort to bring Sally back to the subject of the argument itself.

"Pinkie did. P.K. was about to take his first bite of tenderloin when she began to accuse him of all sorts of things."

"What things?" Norman asked.

"Everything under the sun," Sally said. "She started by accusing P.K. of not really loving her, and then she told him all the things he did wrong."

"Like what?" Michelle asked.

"She said he was mean to her, he never remembered to call her from work, he couldn't possibly be too busy to take a second to tell her he loved her, and on, and on, and on. She became positively unhinged and it all ended badly. Very badly."

Sally stopped, drew a deep breath, and then she went on. "We've had some squabbles in here, but this one was legendary. I've never seen anyone carry on the way Pinkie did. P.K. tried to calm her down, but their fight got louder and louder."

"P.K. got loud?" Michelle sounded surprised, and Hannah knew why. P.K. had been very soft-spoken and they'd never heard him say a harsh word about anyone.

"Not him, *her*. P.K. never raised his voice, not even when she got totally ridiculous. Pinkie was the one who started yelling and screaming at him. Would you like my opinion on this?"

"Yes, please," Hannah said quickly.

"All right. I think Pinkie was just trying to start a big public fight with him, and she got madder and madder when he stayed calm and refused to fight with her."

"Did P.K. attempt to answer her accusations?" Norman asked.

"Yes, he did. And he did it in a nice, calm voice. But that seemed to infuriate her even more. She kept carping at him and he kept trying to calm her down and reassure her. It seemed to go on forever, but eventually P.K. reached the end of his patience."

"What did he do?" Norman asked.

"He said that if she was going to be like that and throw a tantrum in front of a whole roomful of people, he didn't want to marry her."

"Was P.K. really angry?" Michelle asked her.

"He didn't sound angry. He just sounded very definite, as if he'd just reached a logical conclusion. And then Pinkie told him that was fine with her, she wouldn't marry him even if he was the last man on earth. And she yanked off that engagement ring that she was so proud of."

"And did she give to him?" Michelle asked.

"And how! She threw it at P.K. so hard, it bounced off the

water glass and ended up two tables away. And then she stomped out of the dining room, out to the parking lot, and drove away."

"That's . . . awful," Michelle looked shocked and upset. "What did P.K. do?"

"He got up from the table, apologized to everyone here for her behavior, collected his engagement ring from the lady who held it out to him, and stopped at the desk to pay his bill. And then he left."

"But . . . how did he get back to KCOW to pick up his car?" Michelle asked.

Sally shrugged. "I don't know. I guess he called a taxi."

"I have to ask you a hard question, Sally," Hannah addressed her directly. "Do you think that Pinkie was deranged enough to kill P.K.?"

Sally thought about that for a long moment, and then she sighed. "I just don't know, Hannah. I thought about that. The argument was quite a while before P.K. died, but I guess it's possible that Pinkie could have held a grudge against him that long. I know people do. And it could have kept building and building inside her until finally she was driven to take action."

ALMOND CUSTARD PIE WITH RASPBERRY JAM GLAZE

Preheat oven to 350 degrees F., rack in the middle position.

The Crust:

1 and ½ cups of crushed soda or Ritz Crackers ***(measure AFTER crushing)***
6 Tablespoons ***(¾ stick)*** salted butter, melted
⅓ cup brown sugar ***(pack it down when you measure it)***

The Almond Custard:

¾ cup whole milk
1 cup heavy cream ***(that's whipping cream)***
⅔ cup smooth almond butter ***(I used Jif)***
¼ cup white ***(granulated)*** sugar
¼ cup brown sugar ***(pack it down when you measure it)***
4 large eggs

sweetened whipped cream to garnish pie slices
chopped, blanched almonds to garnish or fresh raspberries

You will use a 9-inch pie plate for this recipe.

Mix the cracker crumbs, butter, and brown sugar thoroughly.

Press into bottom and sides of a 9-inch pie plate.

Bake at 350 degrees F. for 10 minutes or until lightly toasted. Then remove it from the oven, but DON'T TURN OFF THE OVEN.

Let the crust cool on a wire rack or a cold burner while you make the filling.

Combine the milk and cream in a medium saucepan and bring it to a simmer.

Add the almond butter and allow it to sit for a minute. Then whisk it smooth.

In the bowl of an electric mixer, mix the white sugar, brown sugar, and eggs until the mixture is fluffy and light yellow. This will form part of your custard mixture.

With the mixer running on LOW, add the hot milk mixture slowly to your bowl, mixing all the while.

Hannah's 1st Note: If you add the hot milk mixture too fast, it may cook the eggs!

Set the pie crust on a drip pan ***(that's any larger pan with sides)***.

Pour only HALF of the custard mixture into the crust. You will add the second half of the custard mixture once your pie is on the oven shelf.

Hannah's 2nd Note: The unbaked pie may be difficult to carry to the oven without spilling it. If you pour half of the custard into the pie shell first, pull out the oven rack just a bit, stick in the pie and drip pan and THEN fill the pie with the rest of the custard mixture and carefully push in the oven rack, the custard mixture won't spill on the way to the oven.

Bake your pie at 350 degrees F. for 30 minutes.

Test your pie while it's still in the oven by inserting the blade of a table knife one inch from the center. ***(You may have to pull out the rack a bit to do this.)***

Pull out the knife and if there is still milky liquid clinging to the blade, your pie needs at least 5 minutes more in the oven.

After the 5 minutes are up, test your pie with a clean table knife again. Repeat as often as necessary until the blade of the knife comes out clean.

When your pie has set, remove it from the oven and place it on a cold stove burner or a wire rack for 15 minutes. Don't forget to shut off the oven.

When the time is up, refrigerate your pie until it is completely cold. ***(You can tell by feeling the bottom of the pie pan. If it's still warm, your pie hasn't been refrigerated long enough.)***

When your Almond Custard Pie has thoroughly chilled, make the Raspberry Jam Glaze and pour it over the top of your pie. Then refrigerate it. When the pie and glaze are completely chilled, slice the pie. Garnish each slice with a dollop of sweetened whipped cream and a sprinkling of chopped almonds or fresh raspberries if you desire.

(Raspberry Jam Glaze recipe can be found on the following page.)

Yield: This pie is very rich and delicious. I usually cut it into 8 pieces and serve it with plenty of strong, hot coffee.

RASPBERRY JAM GLAZE

1 cup seedless raspberry jam
½ teaspoon dry unflavored gelatin ***(I used Knox)***
¼ cup cold water

Hannah's 1st Note: The original glaze was made with jelly, not jam. Jelly does not have pieces of fruit in it. I've modified it so that you can use either jam or jelly, which gives you a wider choice of flavors.

Measure out one cup of seedless raspberry jam and place it in the bowl of a food processor.

Process the jam with the steel blade until it is smooth and completely pureed.

Put the water in a small bowl and sprinkle the dry, unflavored gelatin over the cold water. Let it stand for 1 minute.

Stir and let stand another 10 minutes. This will allow it to "bloom."

Hannah's Note: When gelatin "blooms," it means that soaking the gelatin in liquid will cause it to become tender and dissolve more readily. Both sheet gelatin and dry gelatin granules will usually "bloom" in any liquid.

Mix the gelatin and water mixture with the pureed raspberry jam in a small saucepan.

Cook the mixture over MEDIUM heat until it bubbles, stirring the mixture constantly with a wooden spoon or a heat resistant rubber spatula.

Pour the Raspberry Jam Glaze over the cooled Almond Custard Pie and refrigerate it until the glaze has set.

Chapter Twenty-one

Sally paused at the open door to the convention floor so that all three of them could drink in the scene. Then she turned back to them. "Do you like it?"

"It's stunning," Hannah told her, gazing at the giant Christmas tree in the center of the food court. Round tables with red and green tablecloths were set up on the length of the center space, and there was a white picket fence, decorated with colored Christmas lights, defining the rectangle that was designated as the food court. Statues of reindeer and elves were placed along the inside of the fence, and there was a golden throne at one end with a sign announcing the hours that Santa Claus would be there.

"Very impressive," Norman said, walking over to examine one of the statues. "Where did you get these, Sally? I'd like to get a couple to decorate my front lawn for Christmas."

"They're from a place called Christmas Joy. It's located in Avon and they delivered the statues and set them up for me. Take a look at their website. I'll give you the address before you leave. The statues are sturdy and they're indoor-outdoor and they're okay up to thirty below. I thought I'd put a few of them outside when the convention's over."

"I love the throne," Michelle said. "Who's playing Santa this year?"

"Gene Hickman from Jordan High. He's been playing Santa out here for the past two years, and all the kids love him." She motioned them forward. "Come with me and I'll show you your booth."

Hannah was amazed when she saw their booth. The Cookie Jar was spelled out in letters made of linked candy canes and the outside was decorated with garlands and lights. The inside was lined with counters and shelves, and two giant coffeepots sat close to the front service window, but not so close that someone could touch them and burn themselves. There were brightly colored cardboard cutouts of Christmas trees, holly, snowflakes, reindeer, and Christmas stars tacked on the walls, and a giant wreath with red and green bells hung in the center, above the service window.

"It's beautiful, Sally!" Hannah smiled happily. "I might just move in here and forget about going back to The Cookie Jar."

"Brooke and Loren decorated it. They helped to set everything up yesterday."

A man waved from the doorway, and Sally motioned him in. "Come over and meet your new neighbors, Gary," she called out to him.

The man hurried over to Sally with a friendly smile on his face. "These two ladies are the Swensen sisters, Hannah and Michelle. And this is Norman Rhodes. They're manning The Cookie Jar booth." She turned back to Gary. "And this is Gary Fowler. He's taking care of his sister's booth, and it's the one on your right."

"Hello, Gary," Hannah greeted him. While Norman and Michelle did the same, she turned to look at Gary's booth. It was filled with Christmas decorations of every type conceivable. "You have a lot of product," she said.

"My *sister* has a lot of product," he corrected her. "She's in the hospital and couldn't be here so I volunteered to take over for her."

"That's nice of you," Michelle commented, walking over to look at a little toy rocking horse. "This is really cute."

"I think she told me that it was a replica of a Swedish horse, or maybe it was Norwegian. It's homemade."

"She made this?" Michelle was surprised. "It's really beautiful."

"She didn't make it," Gary told them. "My sister's selling the horses for the man who made them. That's what she does. She sells things on consignment that other people make."

"Are all the decorations homemade?" Norman asked him.

"Yes. She doesn't handle anything commercial."

"I'll be here helping Hannah and Michelle. When I take a break, I'll come to look at your decorations. I'm decorating for Christmas this year and I don't have a thing."

"Drop by anytime. I'll give you a discount if you buy more than five things." He turned to Sally. "I'd like to stay and talk, but I'd better continue unpacking. I didn't get a chance to finish it today." He smiled at them. "I'll see you all on Friday."

"Gary's my early bird," Sally said, leading them back to the door. "He's a really hard worker. He must have made six trips back to the Cities to pick up more product. He told me he wants everything to be perfect for his sister. Remember when I told you that one of my vendors came in a week early, Hannah?"

"I remember."

"Well, that was Gary. I'll introduce you to your neighbor on the other side when you get here on Friday morning. They're a bit flaky, but very, very nice. They own a small bookstore and card shop in Princeton, and they're selling all kinds of Christmas books and cards."

"I wonder if they have any how-to books on homemade Christmas gifts," Michelle said.

"I don't know, but that sounds like something they might carry," Sally replied. "You'll have to check out their booth while you're here."

"What time should we be here on Friday morning?" Norman asked.

"Eight o'clock. That'll give you time to make the coffee and put out the cookie display before we open at nine." Sally stopped and looked slightly worried. "That's not too early, is it?"

Hannah and Michelle began to laugh and Norman joined in.

"What did I say?" Sally asked them.

"I usually get up at four-thirty," Hannah told Sally, "and Michelle gets up even earlier than I do."

"Of course you do." Sally looked a bit embarrassed. "I knew that. You mentioned it once, but I just forgot. I guess I did you a huge favor."

"How so?" Michelle asked her.

"Coming out here at eight will be a real vacation for you two!"

Hannah was in the lead as the three of them climbed the outside staircase to her condo. The recipes Sally had given them were tucked in her purse and she was careful not to dislodge them as she pulled out her keys to open the door. "Who wants to catch Moishe?" she asked.

"I will," Norman volunteered. "Michelle is carrying the rest of the pie that Sally gave us for Lonnie."

"For Lonnie and Mike," Michelle corrected him. "You're forgetting that when food is involved, Mike just seems to materialize out of thin air."

Norman chuckled. "You're right. I forgot all about Mike's food-dar. They'll arrive together."

Hannah stepped up to the door with the keys in her hand and turned around to Norman. "Are you ready?"

"I'm ready," Norman said, bracing himself for the twenty-three pound onslaught that was about to land in his arms.

Hannah unlocked the door and pushed it open, but there was no furry missile, no sound of a frantic rush down the hallway from the bedroom, and no Moishe at all, even though they stood there for several long moments and waited for him to appear.

"Uh-oh!" Hannah said, beginning to worry. "I hope nothing's wrong."

"He's probably sleeping," Michelle told her. "It's like Great-Grandma Elsa used to say, *Don't borrow trouble or it'll find a home with you.*"

"Right," Hannah agreed, leading the way inside. Everything looked perfectly normal in the living room. The RoboVac was parked in its corner the way it always was, the dining room window was closed and locked, and the dim light in the laundry room was on the way she always left it.

"I'll check the bedrooms," Michelle offered, walking down the carpeted hallway.

"How do you like our wedding present?" Norman asked her, pointing toward the RoboVac.

"I love it. I haven't had to vacuum since you and Mike gave it to me and there's no cat hair on the carpet, even though Moishe is shedding."

A moment later, Michelle came back, followed by Moishe. He jumped up on the couch and purred. His eyes were still half-lidded with sleep and Hannah thought he looked a bit embarrassed that they'd caught him taking a nap.

"I'll get you a treat," Hannah told him, rubbing the area below his ears in a way that he seemed to particularly like.

"Moishe was out like a light," Michelle said when Hannah came back to the living room with the fish-shaped, salmon-flavored kitty treats that he loved.

"I suspected that," Hannah said as she placed four treats on the back of the couch. "Moishe's been sleeping a lot lately. I really should call Sue at the vet's office tomorrow. She can ask Bob if that's a warning sign of something and call me back."

"Good idea," Norman told her. "Even better, why don't I pick up Moishe tomorrow morning and take him in for a checkup. Then I'll bring him over to visit Cuddles at my place for a while and take him back home later. You'll feel much better if Doctor Bob calls to say that everything is normal."

Hannah took a moment to consider that. It was true that she'd feel relieved if she found out that there was nothing wrong with her pet. "If you're sure you don't mind, I'd really appreciate that," she told him.

Just then, there was a knock on the door, three staccato raps in an authoritarian summons that demanded entry.

"It's Mike," Hannah said.

"Told you!" Michelle informed Norman. "Hannah taught me how to recognize his knock."

"Me, too," Norman said with a grin, and then he turned to Hannah. "Better go let him in before he teams up with Lonnie and they start practicing how to break down a door."

Hannah laughed and opened the door. Mike stepped in, followed by Lonnie, and assumed a stern look as he faced Norman. "We heard that!" he said. "And we don't need any practice. We *know* how to break down a door."

"Sorry," Norman apologized. "I was just kidding."

"So am I." Mike grinned to show that he hadn't taken offense. "Actually, we've never had occasion to break down a door, and Hannah's door is pretty solid. I checked it out the first time I came here." He turned to Hannah. "Good for you, Hannah. You looked through the peephole."

Michelle and Lonnie greeted each other, and then Michelle turned to Mike. "Do you two have time to eat a piece of Sally's Almond Custard Pie with Raspberry Jam Glaze?"

"That sounds interesting," Mike responded. "Sure, we have time. We're off work unless we get a call. We're always on call when we're working on a murder investigation."

Michelle and Lonnie began talking and Hannah turned to Mike. "I don't suppose you had a chance to call your friend about the money yet?"

"Yes, I did. He checked out the serial numbers and they're still in circulation. That means they're not reported as stolen. And he thinks it's really doubtful that they're counterfeit."

"I'll put on the coffee and get the pie," Michelle said to Hannah. And then she turned to Lonnie. "Why don't you help me in the kitchen, Lonnie?"

Very sneaky, Hannah thought. Her sister had found a perfect way to get Lonnie away from Mike so that she could ask him questions about their investigation.

Norman exchanged glances with Hannah, and Hannah knew he'd figured out exactly what Michelle was doing.

"She's probably going to pump Lonnie about our investigation," Mike commented, sitting down at Hannah's dining room table. "I warned him about that."

Well, so much for being sneaky! Hannah thought, chuckling inwardly. *Michelle should have known that Mike would catch on.*

Because Mike knew exactly what was going on, Hannah decided to take the bull by the horns. She motioned Norman to a chair and addressed Mike. "Speaking of investigations, how *are* you coming along?"

"Things are proceeding normally," Mike said, narrowing his eyes at her. "And how are *you* doing?"

"I've developed a suspect list in view of their motives."

"Good for you. Who's on it?"

"Scotty MacDonald, for one."

Mike didn't look at all surprised. "Okay. What's his motive?"

"Jealousy. He wanted the job as head cameraman."

"That's all?"

"No. He got over that when he found out that P.K. wasn't trying for the job. But Scotty always wanted the office that they gave to Ross. He understood when Ross got it, but he hated seeing P.K. take it over while Ross was gone."

Mike smiled. "Good for you! I assume you went out to the Lake Eden Inn and talked to Dick at the bar?"

"Yes, we were there tonight. Norman took us out to dinner and we all stopped at the bar to ask Dick about Scotty."

Mike turned to Norman. "Did you know that Hannah was going to ask Dick about Scotty?" When Norman nodded, Mike faced Hannah again. "So, Norman is your Lonnie on this case?"

Hannah laughed. "I guess you could say that. And Michelle's helping me, too."

"And you're pretending to be me, the law enforcement authority and lead investigator?"

Hannah was taken aback slightly. When Mike was investigating a murder, it was more difficult to read his intent. And perhaps that was what made him such a good interrogator. Her great-grandmother's phrase popped into her mind. *You can catch more flies with honey than you can with vinegar.* She smiled at Mike. "Sorry, Mike. I didn't mean to step on your toes."

"You didn't. I just wanted to give you a hard time before I told you anything. I figure you'll appreciate it more now."

Hannah bristled. "That was . . ." She paused as she recalled the phrase she'd remembered and decided to change what she'd originally intended to say. "That's understandable, I guess. It's just that I'm emotionally involved in this case. Not only was P.K. my friend, but if Ross were going to contact anyone at KCOW, it would have been P.K. I know P.K. would have told me if he'd heard from Ross. And now . . . P.K. is gone." Hannah felt tears come to her eyes and she blinked them away. "It's a little like I lost my last link with Ross."

"I'm sorry, Hannah." Mike reached out to pat her hand. "I didn't think of it that way. I've had people accuse me of not being empathetic enough and maybe they're right."

"It's okay," Hannah told him, wondering if she'd gone a bit overboard. She'd told Mike the truth, but she didn't want to be the type of person who played on someone's sympathy.

"Anyway," Mike continued, "Lonnie and I spent the day driving to all the candy company's retail outlets in a fifty-mile radius. They don't keep the names of their customers, but they do have a code for the type of boxed candy that P.K. ate. We found some hits, but if the customer pays cash, the store isn't required to keep a record of the name."

Norman looked sympathetic. "So you didn't find anything useful?"

"No, not a thing. We worked all day on a wild goose chase, and we still don't have any idea who purchased that candy and when it was sent."

"This case is incredibly frustrating," Hannah stated the obvious. "We've got the method and the time of death, but we can't alibi anyone the way we usually can by knowing where a suspect was when the victim was killed."

Mike looked a bit surprised. "That's exactly right, Hannah! There's no sure way to clear anyone."

"So what can we do?" Norman asked him.

"We have to just keep at it until we get a break. Either someone says something to incriminate himself, or points us to someone else. Sooner or later, something's going to lead us to the killer."

"We can do that," Hannah promised. "Can you take time to relax with a beer, Mike? I've got some in the refrigerator."

Mike nodded. "Just one, though. And I'd better follow it with coffee. Lonnie and I are on call."

"I'll ask Michelle to get it," Hannah said, getting up from the couch and walking to the kitchen doorway. Their backs were to her and they couldn't see that she hadn't stepped into the kitchen yet.

"Is she holding up okay?" Hannah heard Mike ask Norman.

"She's okay," Norman responded. "To tell the truth, Mike, I don't know how she does it. I was a wreck when I was in Seattle and Bev left me."

"Was I too hard on her?" Mike asked, and Hannah thought he sounded a bit contrite.

"No. She was baiting you a little."

"And I took the bait," Mike admitted. "But I was serious, Norman. Is she really okay?"

"I think so. There's a harder edge to Hannah lately, and I think it's because she doesn't dare let her emotions show. She's got to be devastated about Ross."

"Yeah, you're right. So help me, Norman, if I ever find that guy and he doesn't have a good reason for leaving the way he did, I'm going to beat him to a pulp."

"Not without me, you're not," Norman said. "After what he did to Hannah, I dream about using him as a punching bag."

Hannah stepped into the kitchen. She really didn't want

to overhear any more. On one hand, it made her feel special and loved to have two men ready to defend her. On the other hand, she loved Ross and didn't want to listen to anyone talk about causing him harm.

Michelle and Lonnie were standing by the coffeepot talking, and she gave them a little wave before she opened the refrigerator. The beer was on the bottom shelf, and she grabbed a bottle. She retrieved the magnetic opener that was stuck to the side of the refrigerator, opened the bottle and replaced the tool that the boys in her class had called a *church key*, wondered about that for a split second, and went back into the living room.

"Thanks," Mike said, taking the beer when she handed it to him. "Look, Hannah . . . I guess I was a little hard-nosed tonight. That's because I'm not getting anywhere with this case. Will you please tell me if you get any kind of a break?"

"Of course I will," Hannah promised. "Maybe it'll help if we go at this investigation from different directions and contribute any leads we get. Something we discover might fit with something you discover and add up to a clue."

Mike nodded. "It could help," he agreed. "The ball's in your court, Hannah. I still don't have any idea who put the drugs in that candy."

"Neither do we, but I do have a couple of suspects. Let me get my list, and you can tell me if you investigated them already."

A few minutes later, Michelle and Lonnie emerged from the kitchen with pie and coffee. Michelle looked surprised when she saw Mike reading Hannah's suspect list. "What's going on?" she asked.

"Since we're not getting anywhere with our investigation and Mike and Lonnie aren't getting anywhere either, we decided to try sharing information. We're hoping that something that we discover and something that Mike and Lonnie discover will combine into an actual clue to the killer's identity."

"You're sharing our information with them?" Michelle was clearly shocked.

"That's right."

"Well, this is a first!" Lonnie exclaimed, looking as shocked as Michelle did. "Mike and I have never really worked with you before."

"Sometimes it takes a radical move to get results," Mike told him. "This case is so complicated, it just might take all five of us to solve it."

Chapter Twenty-two

Hannah and Michelle dabbed at their eyes when the funeral service ended.

"No wonder he went by P.K.!" Hannah said to Michelle.

Michelle dabbed at her eyes again, and then she managed a smile. "He told me he didn't want to be called a cross between a steak and a vacuum cleaner."

Hannah smiled back, even though she still felt like crying. They'd gone out to Hannah's cookie truck to compose themselves after the formal service was over. The burial at the graveside was private, attended only by P.K.'s parents and his aunt and uncle.

"Ready?" Hannah asked Michelle.

"Ready," Michelle responded. "We'd better go in and find Mother and Doc."

Hannah retrieved the platter of cookies they'd baked for the funeral buffet. It was always held after the formal church service, and it was a tradition in Lake Eden. Usually, it was held in the church basement, which was equipped with a kitchen and a large reception area.

Both sisters walked to the side door that led to the basement of St. Jude's. Michelle pushed it open and they began to descend the stairs.

The sound of subdued voices greeted them as they reached the bottom of the staircase and opened the inner door to the largest basement meeting room. It was the venue where church suppers and potluck fundraisers were held. The scents of coffee and a mixed bouquet of casseroles, salads, breads, and desserts were compelling, and Hannah realized that she was hungry. She really didn't feel like going through the buffet line and eating at one of the long tables where she would be obligated to make polite and meaningless conversation with the other mourners.

"What's wrong?" Michelle asked, noticing the frown on Hannah's face.

"I really don't want to stay long enough to eat," Hannah told her. "I'd rather find Mother and Doc and see if they need our help to get the information we need. Then I'd like to leave."

"I'm with you," Michelle said. "I'm hungry, but I don't want to socialize for very long either."

Hannah looked around at the crowd of people who had taken seats at the tables. "Everyone else must have come straight down here after the church service."

"There's Mother and Doc." Michelle gestured toward one of the tables. "It looks like they saved places for us."

"That's good. Most of the tables are already filled. Let's drop off these cookies and go sit with them."

They gave Doc and Delores a wave to indicate that they had seen them, and then the two sisters headed straight for the kitchen in the rear to deliver the cookies they'd brought.

"Hello, girls!" Father Coultas's long-time housekeeper, Immelda Griese, greeted them. "What did you bring?"

"Raisin Almond Crunch Cookies," Hannah told her.

"Sounds great. I might just have to eat one or two as I put them out," Immelda said, smiling at them. "Thank you, girls. I'm sure everyone will enjoy the cookies."

Hannah and Michelle backed out of the kitchen as quickly as they could. The ladies were rushing around, and they didn't want to get in the way of the food preparation. They entered the meeting room again and dodged the women who were carrying platters, bowls, and covered casserole dishes to the table that had been moved to the front of the room to hold the after-service buffet.

"Hello, Mother," Hannah said, sitting down next to her. "Hi, Doc," she greeted Doc Knight, who sat across from Delores.

"Hi, girls," Doc said to both of them. "Are you two all right?"

"Yes," Michelle answered for both of them. "Thank you for asking, Doc."

"Funerals are always a strain," Delores said, looking properly solemn. "I thought Father Coultas gave a lovely eulogy, didn't you?"

"Very nice," Doc agreed, "but I wish he hadn't given P.K.'s full name. No wonder he went by his initials!"

"He said that he didn't want to be known as a cross between a steak and a vacuum cleaner," Michelle told him.

Delores gave one sputter of startled giggles, but she composed herself again quickly. "I shouldn't have done that," she said. "This is a grave occasion."

Both Hannah and Michelle began to shake with silent laughter, even though they tried to hold in their mirth and look serious.

"What *is* the matter with you two girls?" Delores asked them.

"They're trying to keep from laughing," Doc explained.

"But why?"

"This is a *grave* occasion?" Doc repeated. "Please stop with the puns, Lori. You know they crack me up. I'm having enough trouble maintaining after the cross between steak and the vacuum cleaner."

"I *did* say that," Delores admitted. "I just never thought that . . ." she paused and took a deep breath. "It was totally unintentional, but I'd better not say another word." She slapped her hand over her mouth to show that she was serious, and there was a very determined look in her eyes. When she removed her hand, her lips were closed tightly.

Hannah, Michelle, and Doc exchanged glances. They all knew that Delores would never be able to hold her tongue for long.

There was silence at their end of the table. No one spoke, including Delores. Her promise of silence lasted for at least twenty seconds, fifteen seconds more than Hannah had expected. Then Delores turned to Hannah and opened her mouth.

"When Edith gets here, I'll take you girls over to meet her and we'll offer our condolences."

"Do you have a plan to get the information we need?" Hannah asked her.

"Yes, and I'm almost certain it will work."

"Do you want us to do anything to help you?" Michelle asked.

"Yes. Michelle, you should just stand there and look solemn."

"But what should I do if P.K.'s mother or father asks me a question?"

"Respond politely, of course. And Hannah?" Delores addressed her. "I'll take the lead, but I'll need you to play along with my plan. You're exactly the right age for it."

"What *is* your plan?" Hannah asked.

"We don't have time to go into it now. P.K.'s parents are back. You'll catch on, I'm sure."

Everyone quieted as P.K.'s parents, accompanied by his aunt and uncle, stepped into the meeting room. Father Coultas led them to the private table that had been reserved for the family, and two of the parishioners rushed over with coffee for them. Hannah noticed that P.K.'s mother was shaking slightly, but she couldn't tell if it was from grief, or from the exposure to the cold weather at the graveside. Hannah had attended enough local funerals to know that Digger Gibson, their local funeral director, always made sure that his driver delivered the family to a spot that was as close to the gravesite as possible. In the winter and in any other inclement weather, a long runner of all-weather carpeting was stretched down a shoveled walkway, all the way to the graveside. Even though a canopy was always erected over the grave and surrounding area, the wind was blowing today and heavy, wet snow was falling. Although P.K.'s family had been standing under the canopy, it would not have completely protected them from the elements.

"Let's go," Delores said, once P.K.'s parents and relatives had warmed themselves with the coffee. "I want us to be first in the condolence line. Follow me, girls."

Hannah and Michelle stood up obediently and followed their mother past tables of people who were eating the funeral food. Hannah glanced at the buffet table as they walked by and spotted the cookies she'd brought. She didn't have to squelch the urge to reach out and take one, an urge she usually felt when she took sweets to a buffet. As a matter of fact, she wasn't even hungry any longer. Perhaps that was because she was anxious about responding incorrectly when her mother broached the subject of P.K.'s high school and spoiling their chances of following that line of inquiry.

"Edith? Arnold?" Delores sounded very solemn. "I know I've said this before, but I am so terribly sorry for your loss."

"Thank you," P.K.'s mother responded. "It was so kind of you to come out to see us the day after we received the news. You have been a great comfort to us."

Mother's been a comfort? Hannah's mind inquired incredulously. *How ever did she pull that off?*

Hannah shut off the critical part of her mind and gave a polite smile. But perhaps smiling was not a polite thing to do at a funeral. She wiped the smile off her face and assumed a solemn expression again and did her best to concentrate on what Delores was saying.

"This is my oldest girl, Hannah." Delores gestured toward Hannah. "And this is my youngest, Michelle." She turned to them. "Girls? I'd like you to meet Edith Alesworth, P.K.'s mother, and Arnold Alesworth, P.K.'s father."

"I'm so sorry for your loss," Hannah said quickly.

"And I'm sorry, too," Michelle said. "P.K. made the commercials for the plays I'm directing. He was wonderfully talented."

"Thank you," P.K.'s mother said.

"I think Hannah went to high school with P.K.," Delores told his mother, giving Hannah a look that said, *Pay attention! This is important!*

It was her cue and Hannah took it. "He would have been a year behind me," she said. "I thought I knew everyone at Jordan High, but I don't remember P.K."

"No wonder, dear," P.K.'s mother said. "P.K. attended Clarissa High. We didn't move to Lake Eden until the year after he graduated."

Bingo! Hannah's mind chimed in. *You got it!*

Delores cleared her throat. "We really must go. People are starting to line up behind us, and I know they all want to offer their condolences. The next time you're free, please do drop by to see me. I'm in the penthouse at the old Albion

Hotel. There's a lovely little garden under that dome on top. It's climate controlled, and we can sit there in comfort and watch the snow fall." She turned to Hannah and Michelle. "Come along, girls. This is a very trying day for Edith and Arnold, and we mustn't take up any more of their time."

When they got back to their table, Hannah remained standing and motioned for Michelle to do the same. "We have to go, Mother. We have to get back to work. We have tons of baking to do."

"Of course, dears. But you didn't get anything to eat."

"We'll pick up something on the way," Hannah told her. "Don't worry about us, Mother. And thank you very much for the opening you gave me with P.K.'s parents."

"It worked, didn't it!" Delores said proudly.

"It certainly did!" Hannah agreed. "You're a real genius, Mother. I never would have thought to do that."

"You're wonderful at situations like that, Mother," Michelle complimented her.

"Why thank you, dears," Delores said graciously, and then she turned to Doc. "Would you like to get in the buffet line, dear? Or would you rather go somewhere else to eat?"

Since their mother was busy, talking to Doc, Hannah nudged Michelle, gave a little wave to Delores and Doc, and they made their escape.

"Did you mean what you said about going for something to eat?" Michelle asked as Hannah pulled out of the church parking lot.

"Yes. I thought we'd run out to the Corner Tavern for a hamburger."

"And fries."

"And maybe even onion rings."

"And just so we don't feel that we're ignoring our vegetables, we could always order a small dinner salad," Michelle added.

"Only if we get our blue cheese dressing on the side," Hannah told her.

"So we can dip our fries and onion rings in the dressing?"

Hannah smiled. "Exactly."

They rode a few miles in silence, and then Michelle spoke again. "You have something you want to check out at the Corner Tavern, don't you?"

Hannah laughed. "I should have known I couldn't put anything past you. Of course I do. That comment Sally made about Pinkie just keeps running through my mind."

"The one about how devastated Pinkie was after the breakup, even though she deliberately caused it?"

"That's right."

"And you're wondering if Pinkie could be carrying a grudge against P.K., a totally irrational grudge that could have somehow led to P.K.'s murder?"

"Exactly."

"But how will going out to the Corner Tavern help you find out?"

"I called this morning, and I found out that Georgina is working this afternoon."

"She works at the Red Velvet Lounge too, doesn't she?"

"She does. And Georgina has a way of knowing everything about her customers."

"That's what you said about Carol out at KCOW."

"I know I did, but when Pinkie went out there to pick up P.K., she was probably on her best behavior. And Georgina might have seen her at other times of the day, like nights or weekends when P.K. wasn't around. Everyone at KCOW seemed to think that Pinkie was a very sweet person. And so did Sally and Dot, until the night she threw P.K.'s engagement ring at him and stormed out."

Michelle thought about that for a moment. "That's true and it's worth checking out. The Corner Tavern is an after-event place. People go out there late at night after they've seen a movie, or gone to a sports event at Jordan High. It's the best place to go at night if you want a burger."

"They have a fish burger, too. And I know there's a barbecued chicken burger. And remember that Pinkie only took one bite of her lobster. She was probably hungry after spending all that energy fighting with P.K. and she might have stopped there to get something to eat. I'm curious to know Pinkie's demeanor after that awful breakup."

Traffic was light, and Hannah and Michelle arrived at the Corner Tavern a few minutes later. Since it was too early for dinner and too late for lunch, the parking lot wasn't crowded. Hannah found a spot very close to the front door, and they hurried inside to get out of the cold.

"Hi, girls," Nona Prentiss, the owner's wife, greeted them.

"Hi, Nona," Hannah responded. "We didn't expect to see you here this time of day."

"My regular hostess had a doctor's appointment and I told her I'd fill in. She should be back soon. Are you here to eat, or just to see if you can find out something about P.K.'s murder?"

"Both," Hannah admitted. "I called earlier and your regular hostess told me that Georgina was working. Could Michelle and I please sit in her section?"

"Sure thing," Nona said. "And I understand completely. Georgina's a great source of information about everyone who comes in here. Follow me, and I'll take you to one of her tables."

Hannah stopped to pet Albert, the stuffed grizzly bear.

Albert stood upright on his rear legs, almost as if he were guarding the patrons who entered the dining room. Michelle, who had been fascinated with Albert when she was a child, also gave him a pat as she walked by. Albert was a fixture at the Corner Tavern. The story was that Nick had inherited the restaurant and Albert from his grandfather, Nicholas. He was the man who'd opened the restaurant, shot the grizzly in the woods, and had gone to a taxidermist to have Albert preserved. Albert had been standing at the door to the dining room for three generations, and since Nick and Nona had a son named Nicky, it was entirely possible that Albert would stand guard for another Nicholas.

People who studied Minnesota history had doubts about Albert's origin since grizzly bears weren't known to frequent the woods in Minnesota. Despite that, no one wanted to doubt how Albert had come to the Corner Tavern, and the story had become a local legend.

"I'll see if I can find a four-top open in Georgina's section," Nona told them. "That way, you girls will have the extra chairs for your purses."

Hannah smiled. "We'd love a four-top. Michelle and I are so hungry, we're going to cover the whole tabletop with food."

Nona laughed as they followed her past the bar and through the arch that separated the bar from the area reserved for tables, chairs, and booths. She gestured to a table in the center of the room and asked, "How's this one?"

"It's just fine," Hannah said, taking a seat at the table. "If you see Nick, say hi for us."

"I will if he doesn't notice you out here and come over to say hello himself. Enjoy your late lunch, girls."

Georgina saw them almost immediately and rushed over to them. "I was wondering when you'd get around to me," she told Hannah.

"Then you have some information that might help us?"

Georgina shrugged. "I don't know. On one hand, maybe it will. On the other hand, maybe it won't. You can decide that for yourselves after I tell you."

"When will that be?" Hannah asked the important question.

"A few minutes after I deliver your food. I'm due for my break in twenty minutes and I'll come and sit down with you."

RAISIN AND ALMOND CRUNCH COOKIES

Preheat oven to 350 degrees F., rack in the middle position.

½ cup salted butter, softened ***(1 stick, 4 ounces, ¼ pound)***
½ cup almond butter ***(I used Jif)***
1 cup white ***(granulated)*** sugar
1 cup brown sugar ***(pack it down in the cup when you measure it)***
2 teaspoons vanilla extract
1 teaspoon baking soda
2 large eggs, beaten ***(just whip them up in a glass with a fork)***
2 cups crushed salted potato chips ***(measure AFTER crushing) (I used regular thin unflavored Lay's potato chips)***
2 and ½ cups all-purpose flour ***(pack it down in the cup when you measure it)***
1 cup regular or golden raisins

Hannah's 1st Note: 5 to 6 cups of whole potato chips will crush into about 2 cups.

Mix the softened, salted butter with the almond butter. Beat until they form a smooth mixture.

Add the white sugar and the brown sugar. Beat them until the mixture is light and fluffy.

Add the vanilla extract and the baking soda. Mix them in thoroughly.

Break the eggs into a glass and whip them up with a whisk or a fork. Add them to your bowl and mix until they're thoroughly incorporated.

Put your potato chips in a closeable plastic bag. Seal it carefully ***(you don't want crumbs all over your counter)*** and place the bag on a flat surface. Get out your rolling pin and roll it over the bag, crushing the potato chips inside. Do this until the pieces resemble coarse gravel. ***(If you crush them too much, you won't have any crunch left.)***

Measure out 2 cups of crushed potato chips and add them to the mixing bowl. Stir until they're incorporated.

Add the flour in half-cup increments, mixing after each addition. ***(You don't have to be exact – just eyeball it and add what you think is a half cup at a time.)***

If you're using an electric mixer, take the bowl out and scrape it down the sides with a rubber spatula.

Add the cup of raisins to your cookie dough. Mix them in by hand with a wooden spoon.

Let the dough sit on the counter while you prepare your cookie sheets.

Spray your cookie sheets with Pam or another non-stick cooking spray, or line them with parchment paper, leaving little "ears" at the top and bottom. That way, when your cookies are baked, you can pull the paper, baked cookies and all, over onto a wire rack to cool.

Drop your cookie dough by rounded teaspoons onto your cookie sheets, 12 cookies on each standard-sized sheet.

Hannah's 2nd Note: Lisa and I use a 2-teaspoon cookie scoop when we bake these at The Cookie Jar. It's faster than doing it with a spoon.

Bake your Raisin and Almond Crunch Cookies at 350 degrees F. for 10 to 12 minutes or until nicely browned. ***(Mine took 11 minutes.)***

Let the cookies cool for 2 minutes on the cookie sheet. Then remove them with a metal spatula to wire

racks to finish cooling. ***(If you used parchment paper, simply pull the paper over and onto the wire rack.)***

Yield: Approximately 5 dozen chewy, sweet and salty cookies that are sure to please everyone who tastes them.

Hannah's 3rd Note: This recipe can be doubled if you wish, but do not double the baking soda. Just use the 1 teaspoon it calls for in the original recipe.

Hannah's 4th Note: These cookies are Norman's favorite. Of course he always says that any new cookie he tastes is his new favorite. Andrea likes them too, even though she claims to hate raisins.

Chapter Twenty-three

The hamburgers were just as juicy and delicious as they always were, the fries and the onion rings were crispy, and the small dinner salads they ordered was cold and crunchy. They had two sides of blue cheese dressing apiece, one to spoon over their salads, and the other to use as a dip for their French fries and onion rings.

Hannah gave a satisfied sigh as she swallowed her last French fry and leaned back in her chair. "I'm full," she declared.

"So am I, but I've got one onion ring left and I can't let it go to waste." Michelle picked up the final onion ring, dipped it in the blue cheese dressing, and munched until it was gone.

"I think that last onion ring turned a late lunch into lunch and dinner combined," Michelle said.

"I hope you feel differently around six-thirty tonight."

"Why?"

"I put dinner in the slow cooker before I left the condo this morning. Since Norman bought us dinner last night, I thought I'd invite him for dinner with us tonight."

"Oh, so *that's* what delayed you this morning! I was beginning to worry that your cookie truck had broken down or something. I was going to ask you why you were late, but we were so busy in the coffee shop, I forgot to ask. What did you make?"

"Lick Your Chops Pork, and I thought I'd try Sally's Piccadilly Mini Muffins to go with it."

"Yum! I'll make dessert. Butterscotch Marshmallow Bar Cookies only take a couple of minutes to put together. I can run down to the Red Owl and get what I need. I just love those bar cookies."

Hannah noticed that a surprised expression had crossed Michelle's face right after she'd mentioned the bar cookies. "What is it?" she asked.

"I didn't think I'd want any dinner, but now I think I may be able to eat after all!"

Hannah laughed and just then, Georgina arrived with the coffee carafe and three cups. "I'm on break," she announced. "Is it all right if I join you for coffee?"

"It certainly is!" Hannah said, and Michelle reached out to grab her purse from the extra chair closest to her.

"Sit here, Georgina," Michelle told her.

"Thanks." Georgina poured them all a cup of coffee, and then she sat down. "Are you interested in hearing some things about P.K.'s fiancée, Pinkie?" she asked them. "Or maybe I should call her P.K.'s *former* fiancée."

"We're definitely interested," Hannah told her. "We're looking into their relationship as part of our investigation."

A satisfied smile crossed Georgina's face, but it disappeared quickly. "I can tell you that things were a lot different than they looked from the outside. She was in here the night they broke up, and Pinkie was a real piece of work!"

"What makes you say that?" Michelle asked her.

"Whenever she came in here with P.K., she seemed so nice. She always had the fish sticks or the chicken burger and she always told him that she didn't mind if he had red meat, that it didn't really bother her, but she didn't want to eat it. I thought that was very nice of her because P.K. just loved our double-doubles. You know what those are, don't you?"

"Oh, yes," Hannah told her. "Two patties, two pieces of cheese."

"Right. Anyway, the night they broke up, Pinkie came in here and ordered a double-double. It just about shocked me right out of my shoes. And then she ordered a double Bloody Mary to go with it."

"What did you say?" Hannah asked, knowing that Georgina could be outspoken.

"I just stared at her and she laughed. And then she pointed to her ring finger. *He's gone*, she said. *I don't have to do that stuff anymore. Now I can be myself so I'm celebrating. Hurry with that drink, will you, Georgina? I really need it tonight.*"

"Wow!" Michelle said. "I can see why you were shocked."

"There was no way I was going to say anything critical to her, not when she was in that kind of mood. I just went to the bar, got her drink, and brought it right back to her. She drank almost half of it right there in front of me, and then she smiled. *That's better*, she said."

Michelle just shook her head. "If that was the first drink she'd ever had, it must have put her under the table!"

Georgina shook her head. "Nope. She handled it just fine. And once her Bloody Mary was gone, she told me that P.K. was so straight-laced that every once in a while she needed to cut loose and be herself."

Hannah wasn't as shocked as Michelle appeared to be by that revelation. She'd almost expected something like that. "Did she eat her double-double?"

"Yes, all of it. And then she paid the bill and left. I have a suspicion, though."

"What's that?" Hannah asked her.

"I think she went to the bar to have another couple of drinks before she went home. You should stop there and ask Bobby. He's our night bartender now, and I know he was working that night."

"What'll it be, ladies?" the bartender asked as Hannah and Michelle slid onto two vacant stools. The bar was almost deserted this time of day. It was too early for a drink after work and too late for a drink at lunch.

"I'll have a Virgin Cuba Libre," Michelle said, smiling at him.

"And for you, ma'am?" The bartender turned to Hannah.

"A virgin Bloody Mary."

The bartender looked a bit confused. "You're sitting at the bar, but neither one of you drinks?"

Michelle laughed. "We drink, but we have to get back to work and we wanted to talk to you first."

"That's right," Hannah followed up. "You're Bobby, aren't you?"

"That's me. What did you want to talk about?"

"Georgina told us that you were the night bartender," Hannah explained. "We're trying to locate a woman named Pinkie, and Georgina thought she might have come in here for a couple of drinks after she ate at Georgina's station in the dining room."

"Georgina's right. What do you want with Pinkie?"

"We want to ask her about her former boyfriend."

Bobby nodded. "P.K. I heard about his murder. What are you, cops?"

"No," Hannah said, "but we're working with them. It's a really complicated case. That's why we'd like to talk to Pinkie."

Bobby began to frown. "Do the cops think she did it?"

Hannah knew it was time to tread carefully. Bobby might have some reason to try to protect Pinkie. "Not really. They just want to know if she has any information that might relate to the case."

"Like what?" Bobby asked.

"Like whether she knew if P.K. had any enemies that might have wanted to harm him," Michelle answered him. "They want to know if Pinkie suspects anyone of killing P.K."

"Okay. I guess that makes sense." Bobby gave a quick nod. "She might know something. One night she told me that they were together a long time and their romance started way back in high school. She probably knew him better than anybody else."

"So can you help us find Pinkie?" Hannah asked the most important question.

Bobby shook his head. "I would if I could, but I can't help you there. I haven't seen Pinkie for over a month, maybe longer. She might have been around, but she didn't come in the bar while I was working."

"Do you know where she lives?" Hannah asked him.

Bobby shook his head. "No. She never said, not exactly. Except . . ."

"What?" Hannah and Michelle asked, almost simultaneously.

"I heard her mention something about paying her rent. And if she owned a house, she would have said house payment instead of rent. It was probably an apartment somewhere because she complained that her neighbors downstairs played their music so loud, she couldn't sleep in on Sunday mornings. That's all I know, though."

"Thanks, Bobby," Hannah said.

"Sorry I couldn't help you more," Bobby told them. "I'd

kinda like to know what happened to Pinkie. She was here a lot and then she just dropped out of sight."

"I'm curious," Michelle said. "When Pinkie came in here, did she drink a lot?"

"Oh, yeah! Pinkie always had doubles and she had more than one, that's for sure. The guys in here used to buy her drinks to get on her good side so they could dance with her. Pinkie loved to dance."

"Did she . . . uh . . . go home with any of them?" Hannah asked.

"Nope. She just danced with them and flirted a little, but that's it. And then she drove home alone in her pink Jeep."

Chapter Twenty-four

The sisters were silent as they went out to Hannah's cookie truck and began the drive back to The Cookie Jar. Both of them were busy mulling over what Bobby had told them. They were just turning at Main Street and First when Michelle spoke. "I don't know about you, but I think Pinkie was drinking all along and she just pretended not to drink around P.K."

"I agree. And after a while, the pretense got to her and she just couldn't do it anymore. It really wasn't a good relationship. That much is clear."

"Do you think that one night, when Pinkie was drinking a lot, she might have plotted to kill P.K.?"

"I think it's possible," Hannah said, "but there's no way of knowing for sure. Pinkie could be just another red herring."

"*Pink* herring," Michelle corrected her.

"Or, if what Georgina and Bobby told us about Pinkie's drinking is true, Pinkie could have been a *pickled* herring."

Michelle laughed. "That's awful, Hannah!"

"I know, but I thought we needed a little levity."

There was a long moment of silence before Michelle

spoke again. "We've got to find her, Hannah. Pinkie *could* be the killer."

"I know." Hannah pulled into her parking spot in back of The Cookie Jar. It was cold outside, and she gave a fleeting thought to plugging her car into the strip of electrical outlets that ran along a wooden strip in front of the parking spaces, but she decided that it wasn't quite cold enough to bother.

"Aren't you going to plug in your truck?" Michelle asked.

"No, not yet. We're planning to leave again soon."

"Where are we going?"

"The library's not open this afternoon, but Marge always carries the keys with her. I'm going to ask her if she still has a shelf with all the yearbooks from the high schools in our area. If she does, I'll get the keys to the library from her and we'll go down to look at the Clarissa High yearbook to see if we can identify Pinkie."

"That's a good idea," Michelle said, "but neither of us has ever seen Pinkie and we don't know her real name. How are we going to identify her?"

"I'm not sure, but Pinkie went to school with P.K. And a school yearbook usually contains some student photos."

Michelle looked excited. "You're right. I didn't even think of that. There may be a photo of P.K. and Pinkie together!"

"And maybe, if it's a student photo, she might be called *Pinkie* in the caption under the photo."

"And then all we have to do is go through the official class pictures, find her there, and we'll know her real name!" Michelle gave Hannah a huge smile. "You're brilliant, Hannah! Let's go see Marge."

The two sisters gathered their things and got out of Hannah's cookie truck. They walked together to the back of the building, and Hannah opened the back kitchen door. As they stepped in, they wiped their feet on the mat just inside the door and hung their parkas on the hooks on the wall. But before they could make their way to the swinging door that separated the kitchen from the coffee shop, Aunt Nancy pushed it open and rushed into the kitchen.

"Oh, good!" she said. "I thought I heard you come in. Do you have a minute, Hannah? I really have to talk to you!"

"I'll go find Marge," Michelle told Hannah, making herself scarce by hurrying through the swinging door that Aunt Nancy had just entered.

"Coffee?" Hannah asked, noticing that Aunt Nancy looked worried about something.

"Yes, thanks, but I'll get it," Aunt Nancy offered. "You sit down. I'll be right with you."

Hannah took her usual stool at the work station and watched Aunt Nancy rush to the kitchen coffeepot. As she poured two cups, Hannah noticed that her hands were shaking. Something was wrong with Aunt Nancy and Hannah hoped that it wasn't anything serious.

Once Aunt Nancy had added cream and sugar to her coffee, she carried both cups back to the work station. "Here you go," she said, setting one cup down on the stainless steel surface in front of Hannah. Then she went to the opposite side, put down her coffee cup, and sat down.

"What's the matter?" Hannah asked her, not waiting for Aunt Nancy to broach the subject that was bothering her. "You look upset."

"I am! I've never had a situation like this before in my life, and I don't know what it means."

Hannah smiled to set her at ease, and took a sip of her own coffee. "Tell me about it," she invited.

"It's Heiti. He dropped by to see me a few minutes ago. He said that Bill had offered him a job at the Winnetka

County Sheriff's Station. Bill said that they really need him and they want Heiti to start right away."

"But that's good, isn't it?" Hannah asked.

"I don't know! Heiti told me all about it, how he'd be working to update some of their equipment and maintain it, and then he asked me if I wanted him to take the job and stay in Lake Eden." Aunt Nancy gave a quivering sigh. "Why did he ask me that, Hannah?"

Before she answered, Hannah had something she wanted to know. "Do you want Heiti to stay here?"

"Of course I do!" The answer came without hesitation and emphatically. "I like Heiti very much, and I'd miss him dreadfully if he left town. But why did he ask *me*, Hannah?"

"I suspect it was because he wanted to hear you say exactly what you told me. Heiti needed reassurance that you wanted him in your life."

Aunt Nancy thought about that for a moment and then a smile spread across her face. "Really?" she asked in a soft voice.

"Really. I can't think of any other reason why he would ask you."

"Then . . ." Aunt Nancy stopped and took a deep breath. "Then do you think that Heiti really likes me?"

"Without a doubt. A man doesn't ask a woman if she wants him to stay unless he's hoping she'll say she does."

"That's . . . well . . . it's wonderful!"

Hannah noticed that Aunt Nancy looked as if she'd pulled the handle on the giant slot machine in the lobby of the Twin Pines Casino and won the million-dollar prize.

"Thank you, Hannah!" Aunt Nancy said, jumping up from her stool. "I'd better get back to work."

Hannah smiled as Aunt Nancy ran to the swinging door and pushed through without even looking through the diamond-shaped window to see if anyone was coming from the other side. She'd obviously heard precisely what she'd hoped to hear and even though Hannah could no longer see her, she knew that Aunt Nancy was smiling from ear to ear.

Her coffee was fresh and hot, and Hannah decided to finish it. She would need a little energy to get through the rest of the day.

"I'm back!" Michelle announced, coming through the door and hurrying over to the work station. "Marge gave me the keys. She said the lights are on the wall, on our right as we come in and we should be sure to lock the door when we leave." Michelle sat down on the stool that Aunt Nancy had just vacated and when she noticed the almost full cup of coffee, a puzzled expression crossed her face.

"What happened with Aunt Nancy?" she asked. "She came back in the coffee shop with a huge smile on her face."

"I told her what she wanted to hear," Hannah said.

"What was that?" Michelle looked curious.

"I don't have time to go into it now, but I'll tell you all about it on the way to the library."

"Here it is," Michelle said, handing Hannah the slim volume with the words *Clarissa High* on the front in gold lettering. This is the year that P.K. was a junior, and he told me that he started dating Pinkie after they were in the junior play together."

"Did he have a part in the play?"

"No, he was the head of the technical crew and he ran the light board. He told me it was ancient and it always needed repair."

"And Pinkie was in the crew, too?"

"I don't know. He didn't say." Michelle sat down next to

Hannah at the long library table so that they could look at the yearbook together.

The front pages of the yearbook were filled with class photos. There was the freshman class, the sophomores, and the juniors. The names were listed, but since they didn't know what Pinkie looked like, they couldn't identify her.

"Here's the official photo of the play," Hannah said, and Michelle leaned closer.

"It gives the names, but that doesn't do us any good." Michelle sounded very disappointed. "It just says it's the cast and crew of *Adam's Rib*. That must be the play they did."

Hannah drew in her breath sharply. "*Adam's Rib*! So *that's* where Pinkie got it!"

"Got what?"

"Her nickname. She must have had the female lead, the one Katharine Hepburn had in the movie. It was about two married lawyers and they both had red hair. Spencer Tracey's character and Katharine Hepburn's character were both called *Pinkie*, except they were spelled differently. The play is based on a true story about a couple who was getting a divorce. And after the divorce was final, the real couple ended up remarrying. She married her lawyer and he married his lawyer."

"That's interesting, but we still don't know Pinkie's real name," Michelle pointed out.

"Let's try the following year, when both of them were seniors," Hannah suggested. "Senior pictures are usually head shots and the names are listed. Maybe Pinkie will be wearing pink."

Michelle nodded. "Okay. If we're lucky, Pinkie's high school published the senior photos in color. We did that at Jordan High, but I was on the yearbook staff and I know it cost a lot more. We won't be able to tell if Pinkie is wearing pink unless Clarissa High went for the color photo option."

"You're right." Hannah felt a bit foolish for not realizing that. When she'd graduated from Jordan High, her senior photo had been published in black and white. "Even if Pinkie's high school didn't go for the color option, they may have listed the nicknames under the senior photos."

"That's true," Michelle agreed. "I'll get the yearbook for the next year and put this one back."

"Leave it here, Michelle," Hannah said when her sister reached for the yearbook. "We'll compare the photo of the cast and crew of *Adam's Rib* to the senior photos in the next yearbook. At least we'll be able to identify the senior photos of the girls who were in the cast and crew of the play."

"But we still won't know which one of them is Pinkie," Michelle pointed out.

"That's true, but it's a way of narrowing it down a little. We can eliminate the girls who weren't in the photo."

"You're right. I'll get the next yearbook."

Michelle walked to the yearbook section of the library and examined the books that were there. The yearbook for the following year was out of place, and it took her a minute or two to locate it. When she did, she pulled it down, walked back to Hannah to hand it to her, and sat down in her chair again.

"Thanks," Hannah said, flipping straight to the individual senior photos near the end. "We're in luck. They're in color."

As Hannah paged through the senior photos, Michelle groaned. "There are at least ten girls wearing shades of pink. It must have been a really popular color that year."

"It must have been," Hannah agreed, and then she began to smile. "I think I found a match, Michelle!"

Michelle leaned over and studied the photo that Hannah

had chosen. "I think you're right. She has different glasses, but her hairstyle is the same. And she's wearing a light shade of pink. That's the girl at the far end of the top row, isn't it?"

"I think so. Her name is Misty Franklin."

The two sisters agreed on four more matches, and Hannah wrote them down in her murder book. She'd just finished when Michelle let out a whoop of excitement.

"There's Pinkie, Hannah!" she exclaimed.

Hannah studied the photo for a moment, and then she turned to the cast and crew photo. "It's the girl in the center of the front row, and the two photos match. But there are other matches, too. Why do you think that this particular girl is Pinkie?"

"Because she's short and P.K. mentioned that he could hold out his arm and Pinkie could walk right under it."

"But how do you know that the girl in the senior photo is short?"

"I can't tell from her senior photo, but she's in the front row in the cast and crew photo and almost everyone there is taller than she is. And when they take group photos, the photographer always puts the shortest people in the front row."

"Good point." Hannah turned back to the senior photo. "Her name is Mary Jo Hart. Does that sound familiar to you?"

"No, but P.K. never mentioned her by name."

Hannah turned back to the senior photos. "I think you could be right about Mary Jo Hart, Michelle."

"What makes you say that?"

"Under her credits, it lists both the junior and senior class plays. None of the other girls wearing pink were in both plays."

"Okay. Let's assume that Pinkie is Mary Jo Hart. How do we find out for sure?"

Hannah looked down at her wrist and realized that she'd forgotten her watch at The Cookie Jar. "What time is it, Michelle?"

Michelle looked at the display on her cell phone. "Almost a quarter after four."

"On a Thursday," Hannah began to smile. "We've got a chance of finding out more if you call Clarissa High and there's someone who's still in the office."

"Got it." Michelle found the number of the office on the high school's website. She punched in the number and switched to speaker phone mode so that Hannah could hear it ringing.

The phone rang five times and Hannah began to frown. "I think the office is closed."

"Maybe not. Let's give it ten rings before we give up."

The phone rang three more times, and then a woman answered. "Clarissa High. This is Lila speaking."

"Hi, Lila. I have Miss Swensen on the phone for the principal. Is he still in?"

"No. I'm sorry, but he had to leave early today. Is there anything I can do to help you?"

Michelle handed the phone to Hannah. "Hello, Lila. This is Hannah Swensen from Swensen Enterprises. I'm calling to see if the school has a current phone number and address for one of our job applicants, Mary Jo Hart. The address and phone number on her resume are no longer current and we'd like to speak to her about an opening in our corporation."

"Oh, dear!" Lila sounded very distressed. "I'm afraid that . . . well . . . Miss Hart is no longer . . . uh . . . available."

An expression of surprise crossed Hannah's face, and it was mirrored on Michelle's. "Oh, I see. If you don't mind me asking, has Miss Hart found another position?"

There was a long pause, and then Lila spoke again. "No, not exactly. Miss Hart is no longer . . . with us."

Hannah felt her hopes sink. If Lila meant what Hannah feared she meant, Mary Jo Hart was dead.

"We *are* speaking about the same person, aren't we?" Hannah continued. "The Mary Jo Hart who applied with us gave her nickname as Pinkie."

"Yes, that was Pinkie," Lila responded. "She had the lead in the junior play and after that, everyone began to call her Pinkie. And now both of them are gone. They were two of our most promising students, and it's so terribly sad. I read about what happened to Porter in the papers."

"Oh my," Hannah said. "Was Pinkie murdered, too?"

Lisa hesitated and then she sighed heavily. "Pinkie committed suicide. I'm not exactly sure how, but someone told me it was pills."

"That must have been devastating for her family!" Hannah said, hoping to get even more information. "How long ago was that?"

"A little over a month. Such a waste. She was a lovely girl. I think poor Pinkie went into a terrible depression when Porter broke off their engagement. Porter was the love of her life and a real stabilizing influence on her in high school."

"Stabilizing?" Hannah asked, trolling for more clarification.

"Yes. I knew Pinkie quite well, and it had a profound effect on her life when her parents died. A terrible accident on the freeway coming from the airport in the Cities. Her brother did all he could to help her, but he had to work to support them. He had a very good job in the Cities and he came home every weekend to be with her."

"So Pinkie lived alone in her parents' house?"

"Her parents' farm," Lila corrected her. "But it's hard to be all alone in a farmhouse way out in the country. Pinkie's brother ended up selling the farm, and renting a two-bedroom apartment in town for them."

"Was Pinkie glad to move to town?" Hannah asked her.

"Yes. It saved her a long bus ride to school. I never personally met her brother, but she talked about him all the time."

"Do you remember his name?" Hannah asked.

There was a long silence and then Lila sighed. "I just don't recall. It was something simple, like Bob or Tom, but I can't remember it. He sounded like a really nice man. I know he tried very hard to take care of Pinkie, but he was gone all week and I think Pinkie was lonely. She had Porter, but he worked part-time after school and he couldn't spend all of his time with her."

"Didn't Pinkie have any friends?"

"The rest of the girls liked her, but she didn't have a best friend or anything like that. Except for Porter, Pinkie was a bit of a loner. You know the type. Friendly enough, but subdued. I think that was why she liked to hang around the office and help me after school. To tell the truth, I think that's why she got a good job when she graduated. She had front office experience." There was a pause, and then Lila spoke again. "Here I go, running off my mouth again. I think that's because the whole thing is so sad. I can't believe that Pinkie and Porter are both gone."

"Thank you for telling me all this," Hannah said. "And I want you to know that I'm sorry, too. I really wanted to hire Pinkie as a high-level secretary."

"Oh, that would have been much better than the job she had!" Lila said. "She worked for Dr. Benson and I don't think he utilized her skills well enough. She took bookkeeping, typing, filing, and computer science here at Clarissa High. She passed all those business classes with A's, and all Dr. Benson wanted her to do for him was answer the phone and keep his appointment book. Believe me, Pinkie was capable of a more demanding job than that!"

BUTTERSCOTCH MARSHMALLOW BAR COOKIES

Preheat oven to 350 degrees F., rack in the middle position.

10-ounce package Lorna Doone shortbread cookies (***if you can't find them, you can use Pecan Sandies, or Nilla Wafers***)
2 cups miniature marshmallows (***white, not colored***)
6-ounce package butterscotch chips (***approximately 1 cup – I used Nestle***)
1 cup chopped pecans
2 teaspoons Kosher or sea salt
½ cup butter (***1 stick, ¼ pound***)
½ cup brown sugar, firmly packed
1 teaspoon vanilla extract

Spray a 9-inch by 13-inch cake pan with Pam or other nonstick spray. ***(If you like, buy a disposable foil pan at the grocery store, place it on a cookie sheet to support the bottom, and then you won't have to clean up. You can also avoid clean up by lining***

your regular cake pan with heavy-duty aluminum foil.)

Line the bottom of the pan with a layer of Lorna Doone shortbread cookies. ***(It's okay to overlap a little.)*** Alternatively, crush the round cookies, and spread the cookie crumbs out over the bottom of the pan. Make enough cookie crumbs to completely cover the bottom and press them down with a metal spatula when you're through.

Hannah's 1st Note: If you couldn't find the shortbread cookies and you need to use round cookies instead, crush the cookies by putting them in a sealable plastic bag and rolling them with a rolling pin or dropping them into a food processor and processing in an on-and-off motion with the steel blade. The crumbs should be the size of coarse gravel.

Sprinkle the shortbread cookies ***(or the cookie crumbs)*** with the marshmallows.

Cover the marshmallows with the butterscotch chips.

Cover the butterscotch chips with the chopped pecans.

Sprinkle the chopped pecans with 2 teaspoons of Kosher or sea salt.

In a small saucepan over low heat, combine the butter and brown sugar. Stir the mixture constantly until the sugar is dissolved.

Hannah's 2nd Note: Alternatively, you can place the butter and brown sugar in a microwave-safe container and melt it on HIGH for 1 minute. If you choose to do it this way, let the mixture sit in the microwave for another minute and then take it out and stir it to see if the brown sugar has melted. If it hasn't, process it for another 20 seconds, let it sit in the microwave for another minute, and try again. Repeat as often as necessary.

Once you have melted your butter and brown sugar and stirred the mixture smooth, add the vanilla extract and stir it in thoroughly.

Drizzle the butter, brown sugar, and vanilla extract mixture over the contents of the cake pan as evenly as you can.

Bake your Butterscotch Marshmallow Bar Cookies at 350 degrees F. for 10 to 12 minutes or until the bar cookies are golden brown on top.

Remove the pan from the oven and cool it on a wire rack.

When the bar cookies are completely cool, cut them into brownie-sized pieces and serve.

If there are any leftovers ***(which there won't be unless you have less than three people),*** store them in the refrigerator in a covered container. They can also be wrapped, sealed in a freezer bag, and frozen for up to two months.

Yield: 2 and ½ to 3 dozen yummy treats that will please adults and kids alike.

Hannah's 3rd Note: Tracey loves to make these with me and take them to class for a treat. Since her little sister, Bethie, wants to help, her job is to take the marshmallows out of the bag, one by one, and put them in the measuring cup. Bethie does a really good job doing this and Tracey and I pretend not to notice if she eats a couple of marshmallows while she's doing it.

PICCADILLY CHEESE MINI MUFFINS (PICKLE-DILLY)

Preheat oven to 350 degrees F., rack in the middle position.

1 and ½ cups dry biscuit mix ***(I used Bisquick)***
¾ cup grated cheddar cheese ***(I used Kraft sharp cheddar)***
¼ teaspoon garlic powder
¼ teaspoon onion powder
¼ teaspoon salt
1 Tablespoon white ***(granulated)*** sugar
¼ teaspoon dry mustard
⅛ cup ***(2 Tablespoons)*** whole milk
1 large egg, beaten ***(just whip it up in a glass with a fork)***
¼ cup dill pickle relish ***(I used Vlasic Dill Relish)***

Hannah's 1st Note: Do not mix up these mini muffins with an electric mixer. Any time you make muffins, they should be mixed by hand for best results.

Hannah's 2nd Note: This recipe can be doubled, but only use one egg, not two.

Prepare your baking pans by filling 2 mini muffin pans ***(6 cups apiece)*** with mini muffin papers.

Measure out one and a half cups of biscuit mix and place it in a medium-size bowl. ***(Press it down in the cup when you measure it.)***

Sprinkle the sharp grated cheddar cheese on top of the biscuit mix.

Sprinkle on the garlic powder.

Sprinkle on the onion powder.

Sprinkle on the quarter-teaspoon of salt.

Sprinkle on the Tablespoon of sugar.

Sprinkle on the dry mustard.

Mix all the dry ingredients together with a wooden spoon.

Pour the whole milk in a small bowl and add the beaten egg. Mix with a fork ***(you can use the same fork you used to whip up the egg)*** until they are thoroughly blended.

Pat the dill pickle relish with paper towels to get off some of the moisture. Then add it to the bowl with the milk and egg. Mix well with the fork.

Pour the contents of the small bowl ***(the wet ingredients)*** into the medium-size bowl ***(the dry ingredients)***. Mix them with the wooden spoon just until they are blended. Do not overmix. There are supposed to be some small lumps.

Using a small melon baller, or a teaspoon from your silverware drawer, fill the mini muffin cups almost but not quite to the top of the cups.

Hannah's 3rd Note: These mini muffins don't rise very much, just enough to get rounded on the tops.

Bake your Piccadilly Cheese Mini Muffins at 350 degrees F. for 12 to 15 minutes or until they are golden brown on the tops.

You can test your mini muffins for doneness by inserting a toothpick into the center. If the toothpick comes out without sticky dough clinging to the sides, your mini muffins are done.

Hannah's 4th Note: You can also make this recipe as regular-size muffins using a cupcake pan. If you do this, you'll need to bake your larger muffins for 20 to 25 minutes.

Yield: approximately 3 dozen mini muffins.

Chapter Twenty-five

"Great meal, Hannah!" Norman said, leaning back in his chair. "I don't think I could eat another bite."

"Not even my Butterscotch Marshmallow Bar Cookies?" Michelle asked him.

"Oh boy!" Lonnie said, before Norman could respond. "Butterscotch and marshmallows are two of my favorite things. They sound great, Shelly!"

"I might try one," Norman admitted with a smile. "I don't think I can handle more. I ate two pork chops and three of Hannah's Piccadilly Mini Muffins."

Mike just smiled as he chewed and then he held up his thumb and forefinger in an *okay* sign. Hannah could understand why Mike was currently speechless. He was too busy eating his fourth pork chop and his fifth mini muffin.

Hannah stood up, intending to clear the table, but Michelle waved her back down. "Lonnie and I will clear the table, put up the coffee, and cut the bar cookies," she said. "Just relax and try not to trip over Moishe if you go down the hallway for anything. He did the *Moishe flop* again and he's in the middle of the hallway, stretched out and sleeping."

"What's the *Moishe flop?"* Mike asked, popping the last bite of pork chop in his mouth and putting down his fork at last.

"That's Michelle's term. Sometimes, if we're walking down the hallway and Moishe is walking ahead of us, he just flops down in the middle of the carpet and goes to sleep." She turned to Norman. "Does Cuddles do that?"

"She does something similar when I decide to go up to bed and I climb the stairs."

"She flops on the stairs?" Mike asked.

"That's right. And a second later, she's asleep."

"Doesn't she roll off the step when she does that?"

Norman shook his head. "No. She's small and she stretches out lengthwise. I used to go up the stairs in the dark because I always leave a light on in my bedroom and there's a glow from that at the top of the stairs. Now I have to turn on the hanging light over the stairs so I don't trip over Cuddles."

"Was this before or after Doctor Bob ran his tests?" Hannah asked.

"Both before *and* after. I told him about it, and he was concerned until all her tests came back in the normal range."

"What did he say then?" Mike asked.

"He told me to be very careful not to trip over Cuddles."

"Because you might injure her?"

"Not exactly. He said to be careful because he wasn't qualified to put a cast on me unless I had four legs."

"That sounds like Doctor Bob," Hannah said with a laugh. Then she sobered and turned to Mike. "How are you and Lonnie coming along with your investigation?"

"Slowly. We did eliminate Scotty MacDonald for lack of motive. He really didn't want P.K.'s job that much, and since P.K. offered to share Ross's office, there was no reason for Scotty to kill P.K."

"Right," Hannah said. "Did you talk to anyone else?"

"We interviewed everyone at KCOW and we talked to P.K.'s parents and his aunt and uncle. We came up with a big, fat zero for that." Mike looked very disgruntled. "How about you, Hannah?"

"We tried to talk to P.K.'s former fiancée, Pinkie. She was our prime suspect. We managed to find out some information about her, but this afternoon we learned that she was dead."

"Yes, the suicide," Mike said. "We learned about that from P.K.'s aunt. Did you cross Pinkie off your suspect list?"

Hannah shook her head. "No. I might have if I hadn't done some research on her boss, Dr. Benson. He's a vet, and Pinkie could have taken some animal-grade tranquilizers from his office to use in the drugged candy."

"Do you know how Pinkie killed herself?" Mike asked.

"No, but we heard it was pills. Was it an overdose of tranquilizers?"

"Yes. Doc called the doctor that did her autopsy and he said they were powerful and they might have been animal tranquilizers."

"Then it's a good thing I didn't cross her name off my suspect list. Pinkie could have drugged the candy with tranquilizers before she committed suicide."

"But the candy didn't arrive until a couple of weeks after her death. How do you explain that?"

There was an amused expression on Mike's face, and Hannah decided to set him straight. "After Pinkie died, someone could have gone through her things, found the addressed, pre-paid mailer with the candy, and put it in the mail."

"Yes. That was our conclusion, too. So do you have anyone else on your list?"

Hannah made a helpless gesture. "Yes, but most of them are pretty far-fetched. It seems that every time we think we have someone promising, we're wrong. We really don't know where to turn next."

"We're in the same boat," Mike admitted. "I have two of my team interviewing P.K.'s friends to see if any of them has a possible motive. I hate to be a defeatist, but I don't expect any positive results."

"Have you given up on the theory that Ross might have been the target instead of P.K.?" Norman asked him.

"No, but we've been concentrating on P.K. up until now. We're not discarding the notion that the candy may have been intended for Ross, but since we thought that was a longshot, we haven't done much on it yet. I do have one thing I want to check out, though. Will you let me have that storage locker key, Hannah? I can spare a couple of guys to put on that. There's a slim chance that there may be something in Ross's storage locker that will help us figure this out."

Hannah frowned slightly. She really didn't want to give up the storage locker key. Storage lockers could contain a glimpse into someone's past, and that key was her last link with Ross. It seemed almost wrong to let someone else go through his storage locker before she did.

"Hannah?" Norman asked, noticing her frown. "Is there some reason why you don't want Mike to have the key?"

It took Hannah a moment to frame her answer. "I guess I wanted to be the first one to look inside."

"I can understand that," Mike told her. "You were thinking that there might be personal stuff there. But think of it this way, Hannah. There could be something that'll help us find out where Ross is and why he left."

Hannah sighed. Mike had dropped a dilemma in her lap. "You're right. I'll go get the key. But if you don't find anything helpful there, you have to return the key to me."

"I'll see to that personally," Mike promised.

Hannah got up from the table and went down the hallway to her bedroom to get the key. It was right where she'd placed it in her top drawer, and she carried it back and handed it to Mike. "We already checked the storage facility next to the MacAlister campus so you don't have to go there. Unit three-twelve doesn't belong to Ross."

"Did you check anywhere else?"

"No. We were too busy getting ready for Sally's gift convention." She sighed heavily and shook her head. "In retrospect, perhaps we should have concentrated on finding the right storage facility."

"That could be a wild goose chase, too," Mike told her. "It's just that I have two guys that can spend time doing it so we might as well turn over every stone we can find. Sometimes that's the only way to solve a complicated murder case."

Hannah nodded agreement, but in her mind she was thinking, *There are way too many stones in his case, practically enough to build a wishing well. And it might take a lucky coin in a wishing well to learn who killed P.K. and why.*

Hannah knew that she had never seen so many oranges. They were stacked in a pyramid reaching almost up to the sky. Florence, from the Red Owl Grocery, was standing in front of them in her white cap and butcher's apron. There was a gun belt around her waist and what looked like silver revolvers with pearl grips in both side holsters.

"No oranges for you," she said to Hannah.

"But why? I love oranges."

"Not enough. You have to take care of your orange, say that it's handsome, and hold it like you'll never let it go. You have to tell your orange that you adore it, that you think it's wonderful and that it's the best orange in the world. You can't invite other oranges to your condo and treat them like friends. If your orange doesn't think that it's your most desirable orange, you know what will happen."

"No. Really I don't." Hannah was puzzled. "Please tell me what will happen, Florence."

"It's simple, and you've been through it before. The orange you chose will leave you. It'll roll away from you one day when you're not at home. And you'll never see it again!"

"But why?"

"Your chosen orange has to be your *only* orange. It's that simple."

"If my orange rolls away, I'll just choose another." Hannah reached out for another orange, but Florence pushed her hand away. "Oh no, you don't, Hannah Swensen!"

"But I *need* another orange!"

"Need, schmeed," Florence snorted derisively. "You don't *deserve* another orange after the way you treated your first one!"

"But . . . it wasn't my fault that my first orange rolled away!" Hannah could feel the tears gather in her eyes. "Really it wasn't!"

"I should have known you wouldn't believe me. Your kind never does. You treat your orange badly and then you're surprised when it doesn't want to stay with you."

"Please, Florence. I love oranges! Can't you please let me have another? I promise I'll do better with the next orange."

Florence shook her head. "I can't give you another orange. You knew the rules. Your orange gave you the key to its heart and you didn't appreciate what your orange had given you."

"But I promise that I won't do it again!"

"I don't believe you. I let you have not one, but two oranges who wanted to stay with you forever. Both of them were willing to give you the keys to their hearts, and you rejected both of them. I really thought you'd changed your attitude, that you were ready to appreciate citrus, but you haven't changed one bit! It's clear to me that you don't know how to treat the oranges you say you love!"

"But I do! And I want one! Please! I love oranges and I've got to have one!"

"Hannah?" a voice asked, but it didn't sound like Florence. Perhaps Florence had developed a cold.

"I want an orange! I *need* an orange! I can't *live* without an orange!"

"Hannah! Wake up. You're dreaming," the new voice said. "Open your eyes and look at me."

Hannah opened her eyes. At first, everything was hazy, but then she realized that Michelle was sitting on the edge of her bed. Florence was gone, the pyramid of beautiful oranges was gone, and the nightmare began to dissolve. "I was dreaming?"

"You certainly were! Now I know that I need to stop baking anything with fruit in the morning. You did it again."

"Oh," Hannah said, waking up enough to sit up and rub her eyes, but she still felt a bit out of touch with reality. "I remember now. What did you bake today? It smells scrumptious."

"Orange Marmalade Muffins. You still had that big jar of marmalade in your pantry. I made three batches so we can take some with us to our booth at the convention."

"Just smelling them makes me hungry," Hannah told her. "I'll take a quick shower, get dressed as fast as I can, and come out to the kitchen to taste one."

"Do you want me to bring you a wake-up cup of coffee?"

"No thanks. I can wait. The shower will wake me up."

"Just as a precaution, please remember not to tip your head up toward the bathroom ceiling."

"Why?"

"Because if you fall asleep in the shower that way, you'll probably drown!"

Hannah was true to her word. She showered and dressed as fast as she could, and she was in the kitchen only a few minutes past the ten-minute mark. She started to walk toward the coffeepot, but Michelle waved her down into a chair at the kitchen table.

"I'll get it," she said. "I can see you're ambulatory, but I don't think you're ready to carry a hot cup of coffee quite yet."

Hannah sank down in the chair at the Formica-topped table that was soon to become an antique, along with the matching chairs and the apple-shaped clock that hung on the wall. "Thanks," she said, when Michelle set the coffee mug in front of her. "Muffins?"

"Coming right up," Michelle reassured her. She tipped two muffins out of the tin, put them on a plate, and carried it to the table. "I haven't had one yet, either," she said, fetching another cup of coffee and sitting down across from Hannah.

Hannah peeled off the cupcake paper and split the muffin in half. The warm orange marmalade was pooled in the center, and she breathed deeply. "I love oranges," she said, biting into the muffin without benefit of butter.

"What do you think?" Michelle asked her.

"I think these are winners." She took another bite and looked thoughtful. "Is that oatmeal I taste?"

"Yes. These are Orange Marmalade Filled *Oatmeal* Muffins. I thought the orange and the oatmeal would be a good combination."

"You thought right." Hannah reached for the dish of salted

butter on the table and buttered the other half of her muffin. Then she took another bite and smiled. "They're great with salted butter, too."

"Let it cool and see how that tastes," Michelle advised.

Hannah shook her head. "Not on a bet! They're too good warm. I'll let my second one cool . . . if I can wait that long."

Just then, the phone rang, and since Michelle was closer, she reached up to the wall phone and grabbed the receiver. "Hello?" she answered.

There was a moment of silence while Michelle listened to the caller, and then she stretched out the cord and handed the receiver to Hannah. "It's Sue from Doctor Bob's office."

"Hi, Sue," Hannah greeted her. "Are you calling with the results of Moishe's tests?"

"Yes, I am."

"But it's more than an hour before you open. Are you at the office already?"

"No, we're having our first cup of coffee, but I knew you'd be up and Bob wanted me to call. He says that Moishe is a very healthy kitty. All his levels are perfect and there's no sign of any infection or disease. Moishe's even lost a little weight, and Bob says to tell you that you must be doing something right with his diet."

"But why is Moishe so tired all the time?" Hannah asked her.

"Bob wants me to remind you that Moishe is getting older and he'll be sleeping more now. There's another thing, too. Cats tend to nap when they're bored. There's also another possibility."

"What's that?"

"Moishe is staying awake because something has engaged his interest during the day while you're gone and that makes him tired and want a nap."

"Like what?"

"Perhaps a mouse somewhere in your condo, or a bug he wants to catch, or even something he sees outside the window. Bob suggests that you leave the television or radio on for him to keep him company while you're at work."

"I already do that, Sue."

"Then don't worry about it. Cats go through phases, just like people do. Their sleep habits aren't always the same. Moishe may be prowling around at night because he hears something moving in the walls, or a noise in the attic, or something happening in another unit. Bob ran every test in the book on him. If there were anything wrong with Moishe, he would have found it."

"Thanks, Sue. That's a big relief. See you soon." Hannah handed the receiver to Michelle to hang up. "Moishe's fine," she reported. "Sue said there's nothing wrong with him."

Hannah had no sooner picked up her muffin again when there was a knock on the door. The two sisters exchanged glances, and then both of them laughed.

"Mike?" Michelle guessed.

"Probably. It sounded like his knock. I guess his food-dar is working early this morning."

Michelle got to her feet and hurried to the door. "Hi, Mike," she said, pulling it open.

"You didn't look through the peephole," Mike said, frowning slightly. "Always look through the peephole to make sure you know who's knocking."

"I knew," Michelle told him. "Both of us knew. Come in and have a muffin, Mike. Hannah's in the kitchen."

Mike looked as if he wanted to give her a short lecture about taking precautions before opening the outside door, but the lure of muffins was too great. He just said, "Well, please be more careful in the future," and went to join Hannah at the table.

"What are those?" he asked, watching as Hannah put the last bite of muffin in her mouth.

"Orange Marmalade Filled Oatmeal Muffins."

"I don't know if I like orange marmalade, or not."

"You'll like it in these muffins," Hannah promised, getting up to pour him a mug of coffee. She took two more muffins out of the pan, wrapped them in a napkin, and delivered the coffee and the muffins to Mike. "Try them," she advised. "You'll like them."

"They smell great, but I tried one of those little packets of orange marmalade on some toast when I went out for breakfast at the Corner Tavern, and I didn't like it."

"This is different."

"How is it different?"

"It's different because you're going to love it. All you have to do is take a bite and you'll see."

"Okay, if you say so." Mike bit into the muffins, and a surprised expression crossed his face. "It's good!"

Michelle came into the kitchen just in time to hear Mike's comment. "Of course it's good. I made them. Where's Lonnie? I thought you two were working together today."

"We are. He's going to meet . . ." Mike stopped speaking as there was another knock at the door. ". . . me here," he finished the sentence. "That's probably him now." As Michelle turned to go to the door, he called after her, "Look through the peephole or Lonnie will give you an even longer lecture than the one that I gave Hannah."

ORANGE MARMALADE FILLED OATMEAL MUFFINS

Preheat oven to 400 degrees F., rack in the middle position.
(That's four hundred degrees F., not a misprint.)

1 and ⅓ cups all-purpose flour ***(pack it down in the cup when you measure it)***
¾ cup rolled oats ***(not instant – I used Quaker's Quick 1-Minute)***
⅓ cup white ***(granulated)*** sugar
¼ teaspoon salt
2 teaspoons baking powder
1 large egg, beaten ***(just whip it up in a glass with a fork)***
¾ cup whole milk
¼ cup vegetable oil ***(I used Wesson Vegetable Oil)***
6 Tablespoons orange marmalade

Prepare a 12-cup muffin tin by spraying the cups with Pam or another nonstick cooking spray, or lining them with cupcake papers.

Place the flour in a large bowl.

Add the rolled oats and mix them into the flour with a fork from your silverware drawer.

Add the white sugar and mix it in thoroughly.

Use the fork to mix in the salt and the baking powder.

In another bowl, combine beaten egg, whole milk, and vegetable oil. Mix them together thoroughly. ***(I used a whisk to do this.)***

Add the wet ingredients ***(egg, milk, vegetable oil)*** in the second bowl to the dry ingredients ***(flour, oats, sugar, salt, baking powder)*** in the first bowl.

Stir until the dry ingredients are moistened. ***Don't over-stir! This will make the muffins tough!***

Drop 1 Tablespoon of batter into each muffin cup and spread it out with a rubber spatula to cover the bottom of the cup.

Drop ½ Tablespoon of orange marmalade on top of the batter. Try to drop it in the center of the cup so that it is surrounded by the batter you spread on the bottom.

When you have done this in every muffin cup, fill each cup with batter, distributing it as evenly as you

can. ***(Lisa and I do this with a scooper down at The Cookie Jar.)***

Gently run the blade of a table knife around the edge of the batter in each muffin cup to seal the orange marmalade in the center of the muffin. There may be some leakage, but as long as you used cupcake papers, you will be able to get the muffins out of the tin.

Bake your Orange Marmalade Filled Oatmeal Muffins at 400 degrees F. for approximately 20 minutes or until they are a nice golden shade of brown on top.

These muffins are best served warm. You can also bake them, store them, and reheat them in the microwave to warm them later.

Make sure you have plenty of softened, salted butter for those who want it and lots of coffee or cold milk.

Yield: 12 delicious muffins. If you invite Mike for breakfast, you'd better mix up 2 batches!

Chapter Twenty-six

Twenty minutes later, after the consumption of a total of a dozen muffins by Michelle, Hannah, Mike, and Lonnie, the two sisters were in their respective cars on their way to The Cookie Jar to pack up the cookies and cookie bars they'd baked for Sally's Holiday Gift Convention.

"Looks like Lisa's here already," Hannah said, gesturing toward the sporty red car that Lisa's husband, Herb, had given her the previous year as a surprise Christmas gift.

"Marge and Aunt Nancy are here early, too," Michelle told her. "I went around the block and I noticed that their cars were parked in front. I wonder what time they all got here."

Hannah unlocked the back kitchen door, and the two sisters stepped into the warmth. Once they'd hung their parkas on hooks by the back door and walked into the main part of the kitchen, they stopped and stared in disbelief.

"Good heavens!" Hannah breathed, staring at the racks of cookies and cookie bars that filled the two bakers racks. Additional baked goods were spread over every flat surface in the kitchen and, as they watched, Marge and Lisa carried racks of cooled cookies into the coffee shop.

"Hi, girls!" Aunt Nancy greeted them.

"Hello, Aunt Nancy," Hannah managed to say, and then she pointed to the filled bakers racks. "What's all *this*?"

"The cookies and cookie bars you're going to take to the convention hall."

"But . . . what time did you get here?" Michelle asked.

"We all met in the kitchen at three-thirty. We talked about it on the phone last night and we decided to give you two a good send-off. You'll be working hard all day, and since you had some dough mixed up, we decided to bake it for you."

Hannah looked at the bakers racks again. "But it looks like you baked a lot more than we mixed up before we left last night."

Aunt Nancy laughed. "Of course we did! There were a couple of recipes we wanted to bake and one new recipe we needed to try."

"Which recipe is new?" Michelle asked.

"We're calling it Chocolate Caramel Bar Cookies, and it's based on my friend Lyn Jackson's Salted Caramel Bar Cookies. We got the idea the last time we made Lyn's recipe and Lisa was unwrapping the caramels. She said there used to be a couple of chocolate caramels in with the rest of the plain caramels and her mother saved those for her."

"So you decided to make up a recipe with chocolate caramels?" Hannah asked the obvious question.

"Yes. All three of us worked on it, and that's why we wanted to try it this morning. Will you test it for us to see if you like it?"

"Of course!" Michelle said quickly.

Hannah nodded. "We've already had breakfast so one of the new bars can be dessert."

Aunt Nancy laughed. "Dessert for breakfast. I like the concept. Go pour yourselves some coffee and get one for me, too. I'll see if our new bar cookies are cool enough to cut."

Michelle and Hannah seated themselves at the work station with fresh cups of coffee for themselves and one with cream and sugar for Aunt Nancy. A few moments later, Aunt Nancy walked over with a plate of bar cookies.

"Here they are," she said. "Please take one and taste it. We want to know if you think we should add them to the coffee shop menu."

Hannah took one bite and nodded. "Please add them," she said, and then, rather than go into detail, she took another bite.

"I agree," Michelle said.

Aunt Nancy took a bar cookie from the plate she'd filled and tried it herself. "Me, too!" she said with a smile. "The customers will love these."

"Are they difficult to make?" Hannah asked her.

"Not at all. As a matter of fact, you save a little time because you don't need to unwrap as many caramels. On the first batch, we used caramel ice cream topping mixed with a six-ounce by weight bag of chocolate chips. And on the second try, we used thirty-five caramels instead of the fifty in the original recipe, the same amount of chocolate chips, and a quarter cup of whipping cream. Both ways worked just fine."

"Then you didn't have to look for actual chocolate caramels?" Hannah asked.

"No. And both ways work and save time, too. We don't think it gets any better than that."

After they each had another Chocolate Caramel Bar Cookie apiece, Aunt Nancy helped Hannah and Michelle pack up the cookie truck. They had decided to leave half of the new cookie bars at The Cookie Jar so that Lisa, Aunt Nancy, and Marge could try them out on the customers. Hannah and

Michelle took the other half with them and headed off to the Lake Eden Inn.

"It's a beautiful morning," Michelle said as they turned off on the road that led around Eden Lake. "Just look at the sun glinting off the snow."

"Michelle, it's a yard light. It's winter. The sun's not up yet."

"Oh. I think I might need more sleep. But look at the *yard light* glistening on the branches of the pine trees. I wonder if that's where they got the inspiration for tinsel."

"Dad told me that, way back in Great-Grandma Elsa's day, tinsel was actually made from shiny lead. They used to call them icicles."

"Why did they stop making them out of lead?" Michelle asked her.

"I'm not completely sure, but I'll bet it had something to do with lead poisoning, or maybe the fact that people were supposed to save scrap metal for the war effort."

"I remember Great-Grandma Elsa telling us about the old rusty tractor that they hauled out from behind the barn and gave to a scrap metal drive."

"Yes, farm equipment was heavy, and there were shortages of metal to make tanks, and ships, and all sorts of things. Some people even removed non-essential parts from their cars and donated those."

"Like what?"

"Bumpers and in some cases, even fenders. People went through their homes to donate anything made out of metal, and some families tore down wrought iron fences and donated those. Most families had someone close to them fighting in the war, a neighbor, a son, a nephew or cousin. Scrap drives became very important to them because everybody wanted to help the soldiers."

"Were there scrap drives for other things besides metal?"

"Oh, yes. There were scrap drives for rubber, too. Big trucks came to collect old tires because they could be recycled and used on troop trucks and Jeeps. New tires were in very short supply here at home, and people did all sorts of things to patch them up and use them longer. Paper was another thing that was in short supply, and schools held paper drives to collect old magazines, newspapers, and anything made out of paper. There were drives for anything that was in short supply, and everything that could be recycled was recycled."

Michelle looked thoughtful. "We're doing that again now. We separate glass, and metal, and paper in our trash so that it can be recycled. We have a special can for recyclables at the house in St. Paul."

"And we have a separate Dumpster in the garage at the condo," Hannah told her. "We started that a couple of months ago. It's the blue Dumpster."

"I saw that and I was going to ask you about it. I figured it wasn't for regular trash."

"We're here!" Hannah said as they pulled up by the back door to the convention center. "Sally said we can use this spot to unload."

"Great! Back in, Hannah, but leave enough room for you to open the back and stand there. If you hand things up to me, it'll go a lot faster."

"Now it'll go twice as fast," a male voice shouted out, and Hannah and Michelle turned to see Loren standing on the loading dock.

"Hi, Loren," Hannah said as she backed up the truck and got out. "Are you sure you have time to help us?"

"I've got time. Just hand things up to me. I brought a cart and we can push it to your booth."

The loading dock wasn't that high, and it was a simple matter to hand things up to Loren so he could stack them on the cart. When they were through, Michelle went with Loren to help him unload at their booth, and Hannah moved the cookie truck to their designated parking spot.

With all three of them working, it still took a while to unload at the booth and arrange things for display. Sally had already filled the two thirty-cup coffeepots with water, and she'd even filled the baskets with coffee grounds. Hannah found the eggs they'd brought, cracked one into the grounds and stirred it in, and started one pot of coffee while Michelle finished writing the names and prices of their bakery items on the big whiteboard that Sally had provided.

"Done!" Michelle said, just as Hannah turned on the coffee.

Hannah glanced at her watch. "Perfect," she said. "It's twenty to nine and we're all ready to go. Let's walk over and greet our neighbors."

They started with Gary, the man that Sally had introduced when she had shown them their booth. Gary was busy unpacking another box of handmade Christmas ornaments, but he put the box down in order to greet them.

"Good to see you again, Hannah," he said, and then he turned to Michelle. "You two are here bright and early."

"That's only because we had help unpacking," Michelle told him. "Otherwise, we'd still be setting out cookies."

"How about a cup of coffee?" Hannah asked him. "It should be ready in about five minutes."

"Thanks for the offer, but I don't drink coffee."

"We have orange juice and apple juice," Michelle offered him an alternative.

"I really like apple juice. Let me pay for it now."

"Oh, there's no charge for neighbors," Hannah said quickly, as Gary reached in his pocket. "Come over and get more any time you want it."

"Or holler over at us and one of us will bring it to you,"

Michelle added. "After all, there are two of us and you're handling your booth all by yourself."

"We'll give you cookies, too," Hannah told him. "Do you like raisins and almonds?"

"Yes. Almonds are my favorite nut."

"Then we'll bring over two of our Raisin and Almond Crunch Cookies to go with your apple juice."

Once they'd delivered the cookies and a paper cup of apple juice to Gary, Hannah and Michelle walked over to the booth on the other side of theirs.

"Hello," Hannah said to the two women who were arranging holiday patterned scarves in a colorful array on one of their shelves. Their books were already displayed on shelves, and there was a rack at the side of their booth for samples of their boxed Christmas and Thanksgiving cards.

"We're your neighbors in The Cookie Jar booth," Michelle told them.

"Hello!" one of the women turned to greet them with a smile. "You must be Hannah Swensen. Sally told me all about you." She turned her smile on Michelle. "And you must be Hannah's sister Michelle."

"That's right."

"Well, I'm Dorothy and this is my sister, Faye."

Faye turned around to give a friendly wave. "Nice to meet both of you. Are you girls all ready to open?"

"Yes, and we've already made coffee. Would you like us to bring you a cup?"

"Oh, yes!" Dorothy responded quickly. "We didn't have nearly enough coffee this morning, right, Faye?"

"Right."

"Do you take cream or sugar?" Michelle asked them.

"Yes, both please." Again, Dorothy was the one to respond.

"How about a couple of our Chocolate Chip Crunch Cookies?" Hannah asked them.

"Yes, but just one for me," Dorothy said. "I'm watching my calories."

Michelle turned to Faye. "One, or two?"

"Two, please. I'm watching my calories, too." She paused and gave a little laugh. "I'm watching them very carefully as they go straight to my hips."

Both Hannah and Michelle laughed, and Dorothy just shook her head. "My sister, the comedian," she commented.

"We'll be right back with cookies and coffee," Michelle promised, and the two sisters walked back to their booth.

Once Hannah and Michelle had delivered Dorothy and Faye's coffee and cookies, they went back to their own booth to start the second big pot of coffee. It was cold outside, and the people who arrived at the convention would want something to warm them up, especially if they hadn't had time for a leisurely breakfast before they drove to the Lake Eden Inn.

As it turned out, it was a very good thing that they'd made advance preparations. When Sally unlocked the wide door to the convention hall, there was a line of customers, waiting to get in. People entered in droves, starting at one side of the huge space and stopping at any booth that caught their interest until they got to The Cookie Jar booth.

The smell of fresh coffee must have been enticing, because almost every shopper stopped for coffee and cookies, carried them to Sally's decorated food court, and munched and sipped until they regained their energy for more shopping. Then they walked past the booths beyond The Cookie Jar booth, crossed to the other side and didn't stop again until they'd reached the halfway point. That was when they went back to get their second cup of coffee and more cookies from Hannah and Michelle.

The line at The Cookie Jar booth seemed endless, controlled only by the speed with which customers finished examining and purchasing from the booths that caught their interest. Of course they needed something to go with the beverage of their choice, and dozens of cookies and bar cookies were consumed. When the line finally diminished, Hannah glanced at her watch.

"It's only five minutes to twelve!" she exclaimed. "I thought it was much later than that."

"So did I." Michelle reached up to straighten her apron. "Wave, Hannah. There's Andrea across the way from us. She's here with Tracey. They must have had a half-day at school today. And there's Grandma McCann with Bethie."

"I hope they come over to say hi. I want Andrea to taste one of our new bar cookies."

"Which one?" Michelle asked. "We have several."

"We'll give them all a different one and they can compare them. Do I need to put on more coffee just in case we get a noon rush?"

"I just made it. Do you realize that we've gone through eight large pots of coffee and I don't know how many cookies and bar cookies? We sold all my Orange Marmalade Filled Oatmeal Muffins, too."

Hannah turned around to assess the packaged cookie and bar cookies that they had left. "We've gone through over half of our baked goods already! I'd better call Lisa and see if they have any extras they can spare."

CHOCOLATE CARAMEL BAR COOKIES

Preheat oven to 325 degrees F., rack in the middle position.

The Crust and Topping:

2 cups ***(4 sticks, 16 ounces, 1 pound)*** salted butter softened to room temperature
1 cup white ***(granulated)*** sugar
1 and ½ cups powdered ***(confectioners')*** sugar
¼ cup cocoa powder ***(I used Hershey's)***
½ teaspoon salt
1 Tablespoon vanilla extract ***(Tablespoon is not a misprint)***
3 and ¾ cups all-purpose flour ***(pack the flour down in the cup when you measure it)***

The Caramel Filling:

12 and ¼-ounce ***(by weight)*** jar caramel ice cream topping (***I used Smucker's)***
⅛ cup whipping cream
1 cup ***(6-ounce bag by weight)*** semi-sweet chocolate chips (***I used Nestle)***
½ teaspoon vanilla extract

2 teaspoons sea or Kosher salt ***(the coarse-ground kind)***

Before you begin to make the crust and filling, spray a 9-inch by 13-inch cake pan with Pam or another nonstick cooking spray. Alternatively, you can line the pan with heavy-duty foil and spray that. ***(Then you can lift the bar cookies right out of the pan when they have baked and cooled.)***

Hannah's 1st Note: If your store doesn't carry jars of caramel ice cream topping, you can still make these bar cookies by using an 11-ounce bag of square Kraft caramels, counting out 35 pieces, unwrapping them, and adding a 6-ounce by weight bag of semi-sweet chocolate chips. Drizzle with ¼ cup whipping cream and heat in the microwave for one minute, followed by another minute standing time. Try to stir the mixture smooth and if you can't, heat for another 30 seconds, followed by 30 seconds standing time, and try again. Repeat heating and standing times until you can stir the mixture smooth.

Combine the softened butter, white sugar, powdered sugar, cocoa powder, and salt in a large bowl or

in the bowl of an electric mixer. ***(This crust is easier to make if you use the mixer.)***

Beat at MEDIUM speed until the mixture is light and creamy.

Add the vanilla extract. Mix it in until it is thoroughly combined.

Add the flour in half-cup increments, ***(the last increment can be ¾ of a cup)***, beating at LOW speed after each addition. Beat until everything is thoroughly combined.

Hannah's 2nd Note: When you've mixed in the flour, the resulting sweet chocolate dough will be soft. That's the way it's supposed to be.

Measure out one rounded cup of the sweet dough. Wrap it in plastic wrap and put it in the refrigerator to chill.

With impeccably clean hands, press the rest of the sweet dough into the bottom of your prepared cake pan. This will form a bottom crust. Press it all the way out to the edges of the pan, as evenly as you can, to cover the entire bottom.

Bake your bottom crust at 325 degrees F., for approximately 20 minutes or until the edges are beginning to turn a deeper brown color.

While the crust is baking, open the jar of caramel ice cream topping, take off the metal lid, and place the open, lidless jar in the microwave. Heat the contents on HIGH for 20 seconds.

Use pot holders to take the jar out of the microwave. Depending on the power of your microwave, it could be too hot to handle. Dump ***(yes, indeed. Dump is a recognized cooking term, at least in my house!)*** the warm caramel topping in a microwave-safe bowl.

Hannah's 3rd Note: when I bake these at home, I always use my quart Pyrex measuring cup.

Sprinkle the semi-sweet chocolate chips over the top of the caramel ice cream topping and pour the whipping cream on top of that.

Give the contents of your microwave-safe container a stir with a heat resistant rubber spatula.

Listen for your stove timer. When your crust has browned a bit around the edges, remove the pan from the oven, but DON'T SHUT OFF THE OVEN!

Set the pan with your baked crust on a cold stove-top burner or a wire rack to cool. It should cool approximately 15 minutes, so set the oven timer for that length of time.

After your crust has cooled approximately 15 minutes, place the microwave-safe bowl with the mixture of caramel topping, chocolate chips, and whipping cream in the microwave.

Heat the caramel mixture for 1 minute at HIGH power. Let the bowl sit in the microwave for an additional minute and then try to stir the caramel, cream, and chocolate mixture smooth with the heat resistant spatula or a wooden spoon. If you cannot stir the mixture smooth, heat it for an additional 20 seconds at HIGH power, let it sit in the microwave for an equal length of time, and then try again. Repeat as often as necessary, alternating heating and standing times until you achieve a smooth mixture.

Once your chocolate caramel mixture is melted, add the half-teaspoon of vanilla extract and stir until smooth. **DO NOT ADD THE SALT YET.**

Hannah's 4th Note: At this point, I always want to dip a spoon into all that rich goodness and taste.

Resist that urge. You'll be able to scrape out of the bowl after you've added the mixture to your baking pan.

Pour the chocolate caramel mixture over the baked crust as evenly as you can. Spread it out with the heat resistant spatula so that it reaches the very edges of the pan.

Here comes the salt! Sprinkle the two teaspoons of sea salt or Kosher salt over the chocolate caramel layer in the pan.

Take the remaining sweet dough out of the refrigerator and unwrap it. It has been refrigerated for 35 minutes or more and it should be thoroughly chilled.

With your impeccably clean fingers, crumble the dough over the caramel layer as evenly as you can, leaving little spaces for that yummy chocolate caramel to peek through.

Return the pan to the oven and bake at 325 degrees F. for 25 to 30 additional minutes, or until the caramel layer is bubbly and the crumble crust is golden brown.

Take the pan out of the oven, turn off the oven, and place the pan on a cold stovetop burner or a wire rack to cool. Resist the urge to cut just one Chocolate Cara-

mel Bar Cookie to taste it. It will still be molten hot for at least another 25 minutes.

When your Chocolate Caramel Bar Cookies are completely cool, cut them into brownie-size pieces, place them on a pretty platter, and serve them to your guests. I can practically guarantee that everyone will rave about them!

Chapter Twenty-seven

"I'm here!" Norman walked up to The Cookie Jar booth at twelve noon, the exact time that Hannah and Michelle had asked him to come.

"Oh, good!" Hannah said, beaming at him. "Where did you park your car?"

"Right by the back door in the spot for deliveries. Sally said there wouldn't be any more deliveries today so I could park there. Just teach me the ropes and I'll handle the booth alone so you two can go to lunch. Sally has a great buffet lined up in the dining room."

Hannah and Michelle exchanged glances. "It's okay. I don't need lunch right now," Michelle said.

Michelle's response made Hannah smile. The sisterly radar was working, and they were definitely on the same wavelength. "Neither do I," she told him. "Michelle and I have something more important than manning the booth for you to do if you're willing."

"I'm willing," Norman said, without even asking what it was.

"Could you drive back to The Cookie Jar to pick up the extra cookies that they baked for us? We've already gone through over half of our supply, and the doors don't close until five."

"I can do that. But how about your lunch break?"

"We'll take it once you get back and we unpack the cookies. It's not like there's nothing to eat here."

"That's true," Norman agreed, looking around at the display of partially-filled cookie jars. "I'll head for town then."

"Wait a second!" Hannah called out as Norman turned to go. "How about a go-cup with coffee for the road?"

"Great idea!" Norman stood by the counter until Hannah filled a cup of coffee and clamped on the lid. "Thanks for thinking of that, Hannah. I'll be back as soon as I can."

The noon rush hadn't hit yet, and the two sisters relaxed for several minutes on the stools that Sally had brought for them. Michelle erased several items that were sold out from the menu she'd written, and Hannah wiped down the counter and put out more sugar, cream, and low-calorie sweetener. Now that there was no line, she was beginning to realize how tired she was from the morning's work, and she looked around at the decorations that Sally, Brooke, and Loren had done so beautifully.

Two huge Christmas trees sat in all their lighted splendor just inside the door to the convention hall entrance, one on either side. Tinsel hung from the branches, multicolored ornaments were strategically placed for maximum effect, and brightly hued mini lights created a lovely glow that captured the spirit of the season to come. She was just wondering how Sally and her crew had moved such huge trees inside when she heard a soft giggle.

"Hi, Aunt Hannah! Were you sleeping with your eyes open?"

It was Tracey and Hannah laughed. "I might have been. I was concentrating on those beautiful Christmas trees by the door."

"I do that all the time when I'm reading," Tracey confessed. "My teacher calls it *out to lunch*."

"That's a good description."

"Hi, Hannah," Andrea said, arriving at the counter. "Tracey ran ahead of me."

"That's because I'm a sprinter, Mom. There's no way you can keep up with me. Grandma McCann said she thinks I could run a mile in less than four minutes." Tracey turned to Hannah. "That's pretty good, isn't it, Aunt Hannah?"

"That's very good. It was the record for a long time. Roger Bannister did it first in nineteen fifty-four."

"How old was he?"

"Well . . . he was born in nineteen twenty-nine, so . . ."

"Twenty-five," Tracey gave the answer almost immediately. "He was twenty-five, Aunt Hannah."

Hannah was amazed, especially because Tracey was only in second grade. "How did you subtract that so fast?"

"It's easy. All I did was say to myself, *Twenty-nine is almost thirty, and thirty from fifty-four is twenty-four. Then, because you made him a year younger than he actually is, you add that year to your answer*. It's easy, Aunt Hannah, because you can go up or down, whichever way is easiest. All you have to remember is to add to or subtract from your answer."

Andrea looked proud. "Tracey's doing very well in math," she said quite needlessly. "Tell your aunt Hannah your idea, Tracey. She might let us do it."

"Mom and I want to take care of your cookie booth for an hour while you and Aunt Michelle go to the lunch buffet," Tracey said. "We already went, and we really want to do it, Aunt Hannah. I need the practice."

Hannah didn't dare look at Michelle. She was almost sure her youngest sister was biting her lip, trying not to laugh. "Why do you need the practice, Tracey?"

"Because it's a career path. I don't know what I want to do when I grow up, but I like to bake and maybe I can open a cookie shop someday. If I do that, it'll be good practice for me to wait on your customers today."

"I see." Somehow, Hannah managed to maintain a straight face. Tracey was unique. She'd never met any other second-graders who wanted to practice for a career path. "Well . . ."

"Mom says you have to eat, so it's a perfect opportunity for me. And you and Aunt Michelle don't have to worry that I'll do something wrong because Mom will be right here with me."

"What do you think, Michelle?" Hannah asked, hoping that Michelle had recovered at least part of her equilibrium.

"I think we should help Tracey out with this," Michelle said. "And I *am* hungry."

"So am I," Hannah said, silently praising Michelle for her serious demeanor. "If it's okay with your mom, it's fine with us, Tracey."

"Oh, goody!" Tracey turned to Andrea. "I told you they'd let us, Mom." Then she turned back to Hannah. "I bought something for Grandma McCann for an early Christmas present. I'm going to give it to her as a consolation prize when we hold the gumdrop Christmas tree contest. Bethie and I are going to do it together this year, so we're bound to win."

"You have a gumdrop Christmas tree contest?" Michelle asked.

"Yes. It's really fun. Mom bought us a plastic gumdrop tree with little protru . . . portrus . . ." Tracey struggled for the word and Hannah decided to help her.

"Protrusions?" Hannah asked her.

"Yes! That's it. Good for you for knowing such a big word, Aunt Hannah. Anyway, Bethie is going to hand me the gumdrops and I'm going to put them on the pro-tru-sions on the ends of the branches. Grandma McCann has a plastic tree too, and she's going to race against us."

"That sounds like fun," Michelle commented.

"It will be if Bethie doesn't eat all the gumdrops when she takes them out of the bag. She won't eat the purple ones. She doesn't like those, but I don't think we can win with a tree that's all purple. Take a look at Grandma McCann's consolation prize, Aunt Hannah. I want to know if you and Aunt Michelle think she'll like it."

Hannah took the bag that Tracey held out to her and peeked inside. Then she lifted the tissue-wrapped contents from the bag.

"It's a cookie ornament for our real Christmas tree," Tracey told them. "I thought it was supposed to be a raisin cookie at first, but the man in the booth told me that it's a chocolate chip cookie. Grandma McCann bakes those for us, and they're really good. . . ." Tracey stopped speaking and looked a bit anxious. "They're not as good as your cookies, Aunt Hannah, but that's to be expected because you're a professional."

Hannah was careful not to laugh. "I'm sure they're very good, Tracey." She unwrapped the ornament and held it up so Michelle could see it. "It's pretty, Tracey."

"Yes, and it's handmade in Minnesota. The man who sold it told me that handmade things are even more valuable."

Hannah held the ornament in her hand and turned it from side to side. She happened to look at the bottom as she was turning it and she noticed something that made her curious. There was a tiny label stuck on the bottom of the cookie ornament. She pulled it off, assuming that it was the price tag, but it wasn't. The label read *Made in China* in tiny red letters. "Where did you buy this, Tracey?" she asked.

"From your neighbor, over there." Tracey pointed to Gary's

booth. "He was really nice to me, and he gave it to me for half-price when I told him it was for Grandma McCann."

"That was nice of him," Hannah said, sticking the label deep in her apron pocket. Tracey was clearly delighted with her purchase, and Hannah wasn't about to disillusion her. She'd decide what to do about the sticker later.

"All the ornaments he sells are handmade right here," Tracey told her. "He said his sister sells them in her shop on consignment. That means the person who makes the ornament agrees to let her sell it in her shop and to give her a commission, doesn't it?"

"That's exactly right." Hannah rewrapped the ornament in the tissue, put it in the bag, and handed it to Tracey. "You can keep it on the shelf behind the counter while you're working."

"Thanks." Tracey turned to Andrea again. "Let's take their aprons and let them go to lunch, Mom. All the prices are on the whiteboard and we know which cookies they are."

Several minutes later, after some basic instructions and tying a towel around Tracey's waist because the aprons were too big, Hannah and Michelle walked away to go to lunch.

"I saw you take something off that ornament," Michelle said when they were far enough away so that Tracey and Andrea couldn't hear her. "What was it?"

"A label that read, *Made in China.* Gary did tell us that all his sister's ornaments were handmade in Minnesota, didn't he?"

"He did." Michelle began to frown. "I wonder why he lied about that?"

"I don't know. I wonder about that, too. But that's not all that concerns me."

"What else concerns you?" Michelle stepped inside the dining room, and led the way to an empty table.

"I'm wondering what other things he's lying about. People who lie generally have something to hide. So even more important, what does Gary have to hide?"

Only seconds passed until Dot, who was working in the dining room, saw them and came rushing over. "How's it going in the convention hall, girls?"

"It's going well," Michelle told her. "We're close to running out of cookies. We had to send Norman back to The Cookie Jar for more."

"Who's taking care of your booth?"

Hannah smiled. "Tracey and Andrea. Tracey said she needed a career path and it was a good opportunity for her."

Dot laughed. "That sounds like Tracey. I really enjoy it when they come out here for dinner. She's precious and so is Bethie. Are you two here for the buffet?"

"We are," Michelle told her.

"Plates are up there and I'll get you silverware and napkins. Just help yourselves when you're ready. What would you like to drink? Drinks are included unless it's wine or beer. Then it costs extra."

"I'll have club soda with a wedge of lime," Hannah told her.

"The same for me. I've had enough coffee to float a battleship."

"Is Sally around?" Hannah asked Dot.

"She's around here somewhere. Would you like me to locate her and tell her you want to see her?"

"Yes, please. I have a question to ask her and it may be important."

Dot's eyebrows shot up. "You mean it's about the . . ." She stopped speaking. "Never mind. I think I know what it's about. I'll go find Sally while you fill your plates."

* * *

Sally came up to their table just as they had almost finished their lunch. "Dot said you had something important to ask me?"

"We do." Hannah glanced around. The people at the table closest to them had finished their lunch and left, and there was no one else within earshot. "It may have to do with P.K.'s murder, but we're not sure yet."

"What is it?"

"Gary mentioned that his sister was in the hospital in the Cities. You don't happen to know which hospital that is, do you?"

Sally shook her head. "Gary didn't say when he called to reserve the booth for his sister."

Hannah stored that information away for future reference. "So you've never spoken to Gary's sister?"

"No. I do know her name and the name of her store, though. Gary gave it to me over the phone. Will that help?"

"Yes," Michelle told her.

"Her first name is Violet and her store is called Many Hands. Violet sells local handmade items on consignment."

"Is Violet's last name the same as Gary's?" Hannah asked.

"I think Gary said she was married and when they divorced, she kept his last name. I don't remember it, but I might have written it down on the booth application. Do you want me to look it up for you?"

"Yes, please," Michelle answered. "You don't know where Many Hands is located, do you?"

Sally started to shake her head, but then she stopped. "It's in Minneapolis, but Gary didn't give me the street address. I could ask him if you want it."

"No, that's okay," Hannah said quickly. "If we need it, we can get it from directory assistance. It sounds like an interesting store, and I was thinking of dropping by there the next time I get to Minneapolis."

"Does Gary run Many Hands with Violet?" Michelle asked Sally.

"I asked him that and he said no, that Violet has an assistant who comes in part-time and the assistant was keeping the store open for Violet until she got out of the hospital."

"Thanks, Sally," Hannah said. "You've helped a lot already."

Sally looked a bit uncomfortable. "You don't suspect Gary of sending that drugged candy to KCOW, do you?"

"Gary's not on my suspect list," Hannah said quite truthfully. "Michelle and I were just interested in learning more about him."

"Yes," Michelle said. "Both of us think it's very nice of him to come here and run his sister's booth."

"He seems like a nice enough guy," Sally said.

"Nice enough?" Hannah questioned Sally's choice of words. "Do you have some reservations about Gary?"

"Well . . . not really. It's just that . . . some things about him are slightly . . ." She stopped and began to frown. "I was going to say *odd*, but that's not really the right word. *Curious* is closer to what I mean."

"What do you find curious?" Hannah asked her.

"Well . . . he came here a week before I asked my vendors to arrive. He said he just wanted a little respite before he began to unload his sister's ornaments and prepare her booth for the convention."

"Did you ask him why he needed a respite?" Michelle asked.

"No, I didn't want to pry into his personal life, but when I thought about his situation, I could understand why he might need a respite."

Hannah thought she knew what Sally's reasoning was, but she was silent, waiting for Sally to explain.

"I think Gary wore himself out staying with his sister in the hospital. And now that she's recovering, he needed a little time to himself."

"Was Gary his sister's only visitor?" Michelle asked.

"Heavens no, but I think Gary felt obligated to be there. He told me that all her friends and clients came to see her, and she had so many visitors that the charge nurse had to limit the time they could spend in her room."

Hannah nodded. "I can understand that. Too many visitors can exhaust a patient. How about Gary and Violet's parents? Did they visit her, too?"

"No. They were in Europe, visiting his aunt, and since Violet's injury wasn't life-threatening, Gary didn't want to tell them and spoil their overseas visit."

"What was Violet's injury?" Michelle asked.

"She fell on the ice and broke her leg. Gary told me that he didn't leave her until she was moved to the rehabilitation center. Then she told him that everything was okay and she had plenty of people who would come to visit. She said she wanted him to take some time for himself before the convention started and he had to take care of her booth."

"So he came here early," Hannah concluded.

"Yes. I gave him a nice suite with a view of the lake, and he stayed to himself for the first day or two, ordering meals from room service and just sitting in an easy chair by the window."

"He was probably tired from taking care of Violet," Michelle said.

"Yes, I think so. But then he seemed to recover and he started coming down to the restaurant for meals. He's fine now that he got his energy back. And he calls his sister at the hospital every day."

"From the phone in his suite?" Hannah asked, hoping that she could get the number of the hospital from the phone records.

"No, there are no charges to his room for phone calls, so he must use his cell phone." Sally paused and looked at her watch. "Go get some dessert, girls, and I'll tell Dot to clear your table and bring you coffee. I've got several things on the dessert buffet that you might want to try."

Hannah laughed. "I *might* want to try them all, but I don't think I'd better do that. I'll limit myself to three samples."

"A wise decision. We'll have the same choices tomorrow and you can try another three. I'll run back to the office to get a copy of Violet's booth application and bring it out to you. That way, if I wrote it down, you'll know her last name."

Chapter Twenty-eight

"Thanks for packing up, Norman," Hannah said, as Norman came back to The Cookie Jar booth. He'd carried the leftover cookies out to Hannah's cookie truck for them and left two dozen behind in case there were last minute sales to handle.

"It's almost five o'clock," Michelle told them after checking the time on her cell phone. "Let's throw out the trash on our way to our cars."

"I'll do it," Norman offered, lifting the bag out of the container under the counter. "Do you two have any plans for dinner?"

Hannah shook her head. "Not really. I thought we'd pick up some takeout on the way home. Would you like to join us, Norman?"

"Yes, but let's not do takeout. I have another idea. I've never eaten in at Lan Se Palace. All we ever do there is pick up Chinese takeout. Instead of takeout tonight, let's actually eat in their dining room."

"That sounds good," Hannah said, and then she turned to Michelle. "Do you want to have dinner there?"

"Yes. I've never been in their dining room, either. Andrea described it, and it sounded nice."

Norman looked pleased. "Then I'll meet you there in a few minutes, unless you have to go home first and feed Moishe?"

Hannah shook her head. "Moishe doesn't expect his dinner until after six at night. That's the earliest I usually get home from work."

"Okay then. I'll drive straight there and get us a table. Do you want me to put in an order for an appetizer?"

"Yes!" Michelle looked delighted. "Let's have shrimp rolls. I've always wanted to order those, but the woman at the takeout desk told me they don't travel well."

"Hannah?" Norman turned to her.

"I'll have a shrimp roll, too," Hannah told him.

"How about drinks? Shall I order those for you?"

"That would be nice. Iced tea for me if they have it," Hannah decided. "And if they don't, I'll have lemonade or any other fruit drink."

"Same for me," Michelle told him. "We'll just wipe down the counters, and then we'll close up and meet you there."

Hannah pulled up in front of Lan Se Palace less than fifteen minutes later. Traffic had been light and it had stopped snowing, so visibility was good.

"I think it turned colder," Michelle commented as she got out of Hannah's Suburban.

"It *does* feel colder than it did this morning," Hannah agreed. "I'd better plug in my cookie truck."

Michelle waited, stomping her feet to stay warm, as Hannah attached the cord she'd wound around her front bumper to the electrical strip that ran all the way around the side of the building. Then the two sisters walked to the entrance and opened the outside door.

"I love the blue mirrors on the front," Michelle said, stepping into the warmer area between the outer door and the door to the interior of the restaurant.

"So do I," Hannah said, chuckling a bit as she hung up her parka and switched her boots for the moccasins she'd carried in with her. "Do you remember when Andrea told us that she'd been here when she was in high school and it was called the Watering Hole?"

"Yes, and Mike asked her why she was there when she was underage, and Andrea had to make up that ridiculous story about just coming in to call for help because Bill's car had broken down."

Once Michelle had switched to her street shoes, they walked into the toasty warm interior of the restaurant itself. They spotted Norman sitting at a booth by the window and went over to join him.

"Just in time," Norman said as they slid into the horseshoe-shaped booth. "Adam came by to say the shrimp rolls would be here in a minute or two."

As they sipped their drinks and waited for the shrimp rolls to arrive, Hannah told Norman about the ornament that Tracey had shown her and how they'd gotten Gary's sister's name from Sally.

"Are you going to call Violet at the hospital and ask her why she has ornaments in her store that aren't handmade?" Norman asked.

"No," Hannah said. "That's not really the important thing. The real question is why Gary lied to Tracey and to us when he mentioned the ornaments."

"Did you ask him about that?"

Michelle shook her head. "We decided not to. Hannah didn't want him to know that we'd stumbled on his lie."

Norman's eyes narrowed slightly as he turned to Hannah. "So Gary's about to join the other suspects on your list?"

Hannah shrugged. "Maybe. I have a couple of things to check out first."

"Like what?"

"Like whether his sister is really in the hospital. But first, we have to find out which hospital it is. All we know is that it's in the Cities."

Norman smiled. "I can do that for you if we stop by my place. I've got a really fast online connection, and I'll print out a list for you. Or, if you'd like, I can help you call the hospitals to ask."

"That would really save time," Michelle told him. "Then there'd be three of us calling."

"Michelle's right," Hannah agreed. "If you'll get that list for us and come to the condo with it, we'll all work on making those phone calls. And bring Cuddles. Doctor Bob said that all Moishe's tests came back just fine and he's perfectly healthy. He even lost a pound and a half, and that's good."

"So Doctor Bob wasn't worried about the Moishe flop?"

"Not at all. Sue said that if there were anything wrong, Doctor Bob would have found it."

"I'm sure that's right," Norman agreed. "I'll bring Cuddles, and with all three of us calling, it shouldn't take long to locate the right hospital."

"*If* she's actually *in* the hospital," Hannah reminded him.

"Right." Norman looked up to see Adam Wang coming out of the kitchen door. "Here comes our order of giant shrimp rolls."

"Are the rolls with shrimp giant, or does giant refer to the shrimp?" Michelle asked.

"I posed that same question to Adam when I ordered them," Norman told her. "The shrimp are giant shrimp. And I'm going to order two giant shrimp without the rolls to take back for Moishe and Cuddles."

Once she'd ordered the rest of her meal, Hannah glanced

around at the décor. The dining room was lovely with pale green booths lining the walls and ebony tables in the center. A chandelier hung from the center of the ceiling, casting a soft light over the interior. It was made of cylinders covered with something that reminded Hannah of rice paper. Some cylinders were longer and others were shorter, and they were arranged in a pattern that made them resemble the petals of a mammoth flower. The muted light cast a soft glow on the honey-colored floor. Even the window treatments added to the serene feel. The plate glass was covered with ebony wooden-framed panels of printed silk so thin that it was almost possible to see outside, but not quite. The print on the silk was done in muted colors and the design was of pink cherry blossoms with pale green leaves. There were large prints of flowers on the walls, soft music was piped into the room, and the serving dishes picked up the color of the cherry blossoms in the panels that covered the windows.

"Lovely," Hannah breathed, not even realizing that she'd spoken aloud.

"Yes, isn't it," Michelle agreed. "I'm glad we finally came in to eat here. It's very relaxing."

Their main dishes arrived, delivered by Adam and his wife. Hannah felt a sense of déjà vu as the succulent food was placed on the table. "It's just like at home when we unpack the takeout," she commented once Adam and his wife had left the table.

"We ordered too much food?" Michelle guessed.

"Right. We won't have to worry about dinner tomorrow. There's no way we can finish all this food, and we'll be taking it home to enjoy tomorrow night."

* * *

"Let's see if Moishe will be more active today," Hannah said, motioning for Michelle to stand in front of the outside door to the condo.

Michelle braced herself and prepared for Moishe to race out the door and jump into her arms. "I bet he will be. He's been waiting at least half an hour for his dinner."

Hannah retrieved her keys from her purse and inserted the door key in the lock. She turned it, opened the door, and stepped quickly to the side.

Nothing, absolutely nothing happened. There was no sound of Moishe rushing down the hallway, no welcoming yowl, and no leap into Michelle's waiting arms.

"Looks like you were wrong," Hannah said. "Let's go wake him up and give him his dinner. He'll perk up when Cuddles comes."

After Michelle had closed and locked the door behind her, they heard a noise from the bedroom. Then there was a thump as Moishe jumped off the bed and, a moment or two later, he padded into the living room, yawning.

"Were you sleeping?" Michelle asked the obvious.

"Rrrroowww!" Moishe answered her. Then he jumped up to the back to the couch and looked at Hannah expectantly.

"Okay," Hannah told him, reaching out to pet his soft fur and giving him a scratch behind his ears. "Michelle will get your kitty treats and then I'll feed you. How's that?"

The answer this time was a loud purr, and Hannah thought, not for the first time, how Moishe truly appeared to understand what she was saying. "You're going to have shrimp later tonight. Norman is bringing Cuddles to play with you."

"Rrrroowwwww!"

The response was loud and prolonged, and Hannah laughed. "That's right. Cuddles and shrimp, your favorite combination. You two can eat and play until Norman, Michelle, and I finish making phone calls."

Moishe turned to Michelle, who was coming in from the kitchen with a canister he recognized. It contained the fish-shaped, salmon-flavored kitty treats that were his favorites.

"I'll put some food in his bowl and then I want to take a quick shower," Hannah told Michelle. "It'll only take me a few minutes, and then you can shower if you want to."

"I want to," Michelle said. "I feel a little grubby after working all day. Go ahead, Hannah. When you leave, I'll put on a pot of coffee and check the answering machine to see if Mike called. Fingers crossed, his team has found Ross's storage locker and discovered some clue to where Ross went and why he left in the first place."

The smell of fresh coffee was an incentive to hurry as Hannah emerged from her shower. She dressed in a clean pair of sweatpants and a sweatshirt, ran a brush through her hair, and went down the hallway to the kitchen to get a cup.

"My turn," Michelle said, gesturing toward the kitchen. "I poured a cup for you and set it on the counter."

"Anything on the answering machine?" Hannah asked.

"No calls. If you want to do something, cut that pan of bar cookies on the counter."

"You baked bar cookies in fifteen minutes?" Hannah asked, clearly astounded.

"Of course not. I baked them this morning before you got up and stuck them in the refrigerator in case we needed a dessert for tonight."

"And you think we need a dessert after that huge meal?"

"Yes, definitely. I don't know about you, but an orange cut up in fancy pieces just doesn't do it for me."

"Are you ready?" Norman asked, standing by the cat carrier, his hand on the grate.

"I'm ready," Hannah said.

"Me, too," Michelle added.

"Rrrroowwww!" Moishe confirmed it.

"Okay. She's going to come out like a rocket. Here goes!"

Norman was right. Cuddles shot out of the crate like a circus clown shot out of a cannon. The first thing she did was make a sharp right and race down the hallway with Moishe in close pursuit.

"Where are they going?" Michelle asked.

Hannah laughed. "Probably to the bedroom, where they'll launch themselves up to my bed, congratulate each other for startling us, burn what we used to call a *wheelie* in high school, hop down again, and sprint back here."

"You're probably right," Norman said quickly. "I think I just heard them hit the floor again. Head for the couches and feet up! Quick!"

Hannah, Michelle, and Norman made a beeline for the sofas and got their feet up just a split second before the two cats came roaring through the living room.

"Okay," Michelle said. "Let's get to work making those . . ." She paused and stared at Hannah and Norman. "Why are you two shaking your heads?"

"Norman and I have seen this game more than you have," Hannah told her. "We figured out the pattern, and the cats always do this three times."

"Oh!" Michelle said, lifting her feet again. "But I don't hear any . . ." She stopped speaking again and gave a little nod. "Yes, I do. They just jumped down from your bed."

When the second race was over, Hannah got up and hurried to the kitchen for the treat canister. She got back just in time to watch the third race. When it was over, both cats jumped up on the back of the couch and watched while Hannah took the lid off the small canister. "That was a good show," she told them, placing an equal number of treats in front of each cat. Then she turned to Norman and Michelle.

"If we're right about the number of races, it should be over now. And that means that we can get to work."

Fueled by strong coffee and an occasional Lovely Lemon Bar Cookie, they made calls to each of the hospitals on Norman's list. He'd also made another list of rehabilitation and physical therapy facilities attached to hospitals, and Hannah called those. Since Norman had numbered his initial list, he took the even numbers and Michelle took the odd. They worked until they'd called every place on both lists, and then they just sat there and looked at each other in consternation.

"She's not there," Norman said, telling them what they already knew.

"That's right, unless she checked in under her married name," Michelle said.

"We can check for that," Norman said. "What was her married name?"

"We don't know," Hannah told him. "We might be able to find out tomorrow, but we've done all we can for tonight. Thank you for helping us tonight, Norman. And thanks for dinner. It was fun."

"Yes, it was," Michelle agreed.

"I thought so, too. We'll have to do it again instead of always getting takeout." Norman got up. "I'd better let you two get some sleep."

Norman was just getting ready to put Cuddles in her kitty carrier and leave when Michelle's cell phone rang. She reached out to answer it, listened for a moment, and then she put out a hand to stop him.

"Don't leave yet," she said. "This is important."

There was no way either Hannah or Norman could figure out who Michelle's caller was or the subject of the call from Michelle's side of the conversation. It consisted of *yes*, *no*, *not really*, and *I'll check*. When Michelle got off the phone,

Hannah could contain her curiosity no longer. "Who was that?" she asked.

"The lady on night shift at the Superior Storage facility that I called, the one close to my campus. She said I spoke to someone new, but the woman had written everything down. June, the supervisor I talked to tonight, was going over the new employee's work, and she found the record of my phone call. She checked the list of rental units for the name, Ross Barton, and it wasn't there, but there was a name that was very similar."

"What was the name?" Norman asked.

"Russ Burton."

Norman looked hopeful. "That's pretty close."

"That's what she thought. And then she told me that they were about to put the contents up for auction because the rent was three months in arrears. And she said that if we wanted to come there to look at the contents, that would be fine with her."

"And it's unit three-twelve?" Hannah asked.

"No, but the contents could still belong to Ross. I think we should go and take a look."

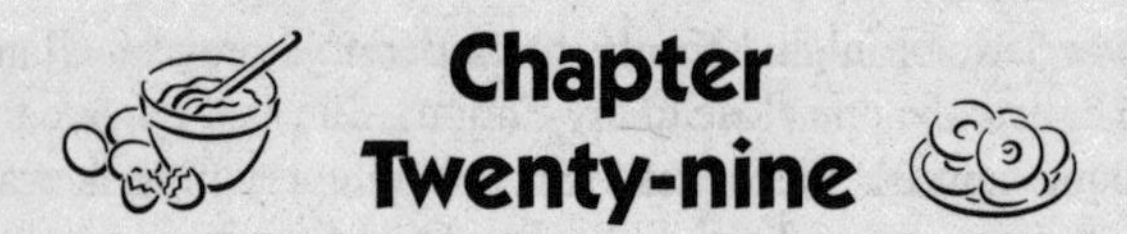

Chapter Twenty-nine

Hannah sat in the front seat of Norman's car, clutching a thermos of coffee. "More coffee, Norman?"

"No, thanks. I'll wait until we stop for breakfast. We have an hour to eat. June doesn't get to work until nine."

"I wonder how everyone's doing down at The Cookie Jar," Michelle said from the back seat. "Lisa said that Marge and Aunt Nancy were going to meet her there at four to do the baking."

"That's right. And then Marge and Jack will handle the customers at The Cookie Jar while Lisa and Aunt Nancy take care of the booth at the convention."

"I hope they can handle all that," Michelle said, sounding a bit worried.

"I'm sure they can," Hannah said, but she began to feel guilty at taking the day off. She'd have to make it up to them somehow. "We should have met them there at four. We could have helped with the baking."

"Stop feeling guilty," Michelle told her. "Aunt Nancy said she was looking forward to it. And we'll be back early and we can help out. We can even bake more cookies if they run short."

"But I could have gotten up an hour earlier," Hannah argued.

"No," Norman said firmly. "You need your sleep, Hannah."

"Not as much as Michelle. She thought a yard light was the sun."

"You promised you wouldn't say anything about that."

"Oops. Sorry about that, but it was so funny, I had to tell Norman."

They rode in silence for several miles and then Norman cleared his throat. "Seriously, Hannah . . . I meant what I said about getting more sleep. You have to keep your mind sharp to solve P.K.'s murder. Both Mike and Lonnie said they weren't getting anywhere."

"Neither are we. The only lead we have is Gary, and that's really tentative."

"But he lied," Norman pointed out.

"Maybe not if Violet used her married name. And lying about his sister and the hospital doesn't really make him an automatic suspect. People lie, and you can't prosecute them for lying unless it's under oath. We need a lot more than lying to link Gary to the murder case."

"Maybe we can get more tomorrow," Michelle said. "You know . . . bring things up in casual conversation and hear what he has to say."

"Yes. It has to be tomorrow. We've only got one more day with Gary," Norman said, turning off the interstate and taking the exit road. "This is right, isn't it, Michelle?"

"Yes," Michelle told him, and there was a big smile on her face. "I'm going to have a Reuben omelet. They're really good here. Or maybe I'll have the chopped liver and corned beef on rye. And afterwards, I'm going to buy a loaf of rye to take home with us. It's the best I've ever tasted."

* * *

Fifty-five minutes later, they were walking back to Norman's car. They were heavier than they'd been walking into the deli, but it wasn't entirely from the huge breakfasts they'd consumed. Norman was carrying two bags, Hannah was carrying one, and Michelle was carrying three. They'd walked past the strategically placed deli section on their way out and the delicious scents coming from the long, refrigerated glass case had prompted them to buy even more. Then they'd passed the bakery section, which had sung a siren's song to Hannah. She had six chocolate rugalach, four different kinds of hamantaschen, some mandelbread, and a loaf of egg challah. She also had a container of chopped liver, a container of fish salad, a half-pound of sliced corned beef, a half-pound of lox, and two huge containers of pickles, one half-sour and the other sour.

The Superior Storage building wasn't far from the deli, and they pulled up in the parking lot at five minutes after nine. They sat there for a moment, still digesting their breakfasts, and then Norman opened his car door.

"Let's go see that unit," he said.

"We're ready," Hannah told him, and since she knew that Norman always opened the car door for her, she waited until he walked around the back of his car and opened her door and Michelle's door.

The small rental office was clean and bright. There was an older woman with short brown hair sitting at a desk, and Norman walked up to her. "Are you June?" he asked.

"Yes." June smiled as she spotted Michelle and Hannah. "You came to see the Russell Burton storage unit, right?"

"Right," Hannah said.

"The unit isn't far from the office. I'll show you where it is."

They followed June past several large buildings. She stopped at another building that was identical to the others, and pointed to the door. "All the units in this building are inside units."

"You have units that are outside?" Norman asked.

"I know what you're thinking, so let me explain," June said. "All the units are inside units, but the door to an outside unit is a big aluminum door that rolls up. It's wide enough for large items like cars and boats."

June opened the door to one of the buildings, switched on a bank of lights, and led the way down a wide hallway to a door. "Here it is," she said. She chose a key on the ring she carried, unlocked the padlock, and opened the door. "There you go," she said. "You can't go in and touch anything, but take a look and see if these are your husband's things."

Hannah stood just outside the open door and stared at the things that were stored inside. "It looks like everything is in cases of some sort." She turned to Norman. "I see a few that look like camera cases. Am I right?"

"Yes. I'm not sure what's in the larger, suitcase-like cases, but they could be some sort of video equipment."

"You're welcome to go in and look if you're willing to pay the back rent," June told them.

"I'm willing," Hannah told her. "My husband studied photography and filmmaking in college so these things could be his. I'll definitely pay the back rent."

"But you didn't even ask how much the rental is," Michelle pointed out.

"It's okay, Michelle," Norman reassured her. "I'm sure it's worth it."

"The back rent isn't that expensive," June told them. "This unit was rented five years ago when this facility first opened, and they had a special deal for anyone who rented in the first month. The original rent remains the same for the first five years and then it goes up to the current rate. This particular until is only forty-five dollars a month."

"That's fine with me," Hannah told June. "And I saw some trucks parked outside. You rent them, don't you?"

"Yes. We're partners with a national chain. You can rent a truck and drop it off at any of the approved locations."

"I don't suppose there's an approved location in Lake Eden, Minnesota," Norman said.

"As a matter of fact, there is. We just opened a branch office out by the community college. You could rent a small truck here and drop it off there if you'd like."

"We'd like to do that," Norman told her. "I'll rent the truck."

"Then let's go to the office and take care of the paperwork," June told him.

"Thank you, June," Hannah said as June locked up the unit again and they all followed her to the door.

"Okay then." June led the way back to the office. "Who's going to drive the rental truck? I'll need a driver's license."

"I am," Norman said, and then he turned back to Hannah and Michelle. "Who's going to drive my car?"

"I will," Michelle volunteered. "Hannah can ride with you in the truck. And don't worry, Norman. I'm a good driver. One of my former roommates had a car just like yours and I used to drive it all the time."

The arrangements with June at the rental office were made very quickly. She handed Hannah a key to the unit and gave Norman the truck keys. Norman, Hannah, and Michelle drove the truck down to the building that contained the rental unit and worked together to load the contents. Since everything was already packed in cases and boxes, it didn't take long, and within thirty minutes the truck was loaded and ready to go.

"I'm not sure where I'm going to put all this," Hannah confessed, looking at the contents in the back of the truck.

"I can store it at my place," Norman offered. "I've been doing some work on the house and I enlarged the garage. It's heated now, and there's plenty of storage."

Hannah drew a relieved breath. "Thanks, Norman. I don't think the storage above my parking spots would hold it all."

"I know it wouldn't," Michelle told her. "I tried to put my suitcase up there and it wouldn't fit."

Norman turned to Michelle. "Then we'll all meet at my place. And once we unload, you can drive my car to the rental office by the college. We'll drop off the truck and then I'll take you two back to The Cookie Jar."

Sooner than they expected, Norman turned into his driveway and pulled the truck up to the garage. "We can store all this equipment in the annex I built out here."

Hannah stared at the garage in surprise. "You really enlarged this garage!"

"Yes. It's triple the size it used to be. I'm planning to make several guest rooms on one side and we'll use one of those as a storage place for now."

The unpacking didn't take long, and then Hannah and Michelle followed Norman to the truck rental place so that Norman could drop off the truck. While they waited for him to finish at the truck rental office, Michelle called Marge at The Cookie Jar to see if they needed to bake more cookies.

"Marge says no, they have enough," she reported to Hannah.

"At the convention booth, too?"

"Yes. Marge checked with Lisa and she said they had plenty."

It didn't take long for Norman to finish at the truck rental office. "Do you have to go back to The Cookie Jar?" he asked them.

"Not today," Hannah replied. "You can take us back to the condo."

"Dinner tonight?" he asked them.

"Yes, but we'll cook," Hannah answered. "You took us out last night and it's our turn."

"Aren't you tired after loading and unloading the truck?"

Michelle shook her head. "Are you kidding? Today's a short day for us."

"But I can take you out tonight, too."

"No, Norman," Hannah told him. "You've done enough for us today. We want to make dinner for you."

"Yes, we do," Michelle agreed. "Just take us back to the condo, drop us off, and come back at seven for dinner. And bring Cuddles with you."

This is almost like old times, Hannah thought as she climbed the covered staircase with Michelle. *Dinner with Norman, and Mike is bound to show up with Lonnie. All we have to do is figure out what to make*. She did a mental inventory of the supplies she had in the freezer and began to smile. "How does Chicken Paprikash sound to you?"

"It sounds great. I love your Chicken Paprikash and I can bake something easy for dessert."

Chapter Thirty

As they climbed the covered staircase past her living room window, Hannah glanced into her living room. No Moishe. But perhaps he was waiting by the door to greet them by jumping up into her arms.

"You or me?" Michelle asked her when they reached the second-floor landing.

"I'll catch him this time," Hannah answered, bracing herself as Michelle unlocked the door and pushed it open.

The expected feline missile did not launch and land in Hannah's arms. There was no sound of rushing feet and no orange and white blur as Moishe went airborne. Hannah sighed. Moishe was probably sleeping again, and as they went inside and shut the door behind them, she wished she knew why he was always so tired.

As they stepped into the living room, Hannah heard a whining noise. "What's that?" she asked Michelle.

"I don't know, but it sounds like it's coming from my room."

For a moment, Hannah was puzzled, but then she realized that they were home much earlier than they usually were and the RoboVac was still vacuuming the wall-to-wall carpeting. "It's the RoboVac," she told Michelle.

"I've never seen it operate," Michelle replied. "Let's go look."

Hannah led the way as they walked down the hallway to watch her new vacuum do its job. They looked in the open guest room door and the sight they saw both amazed and amused them. The RoboVac was whirring away, twisting and turning around the furniture in the guest bedroom. And right behind the robotic vacuum was Moishe. The hair was bristled on his back, and his ears were flat against his head.

The vacuum turned and Moishe leaped back, startled. He gave the round case a swipe with his paw, but it didn't stop moving. Instead, it turned again and Moishe reacted again. Then the RoboVac moved toward Moishe, and Moishe sprang out of the way as it headed toward the door. Hannah and Michelle stepped aside and left the room.

"So *that's* why you're so tired!" Hannah said, startling her feline roommate even more than the RoboVac had. "Come here, Moishe. I'll pick you up and Michelle will go get the kitty treats."

Contrary to his usual reaction to that invitation, Moishe walked past them as if they were invisible and followed the RoboVac down the hallway, stalking it as it made its way back to the living room. Only when the vacuum had gone back to its corner and shut itself off did Moishe rush back to them.

"Just wait until I tell Norman and Mike about this," Hannah said as she picked Moishe up and carried him to his favorite spot on the back of the couch. "I'll bet that Cuddles stalks Norman's RoboVac, too."

Dinner was tasty and, just as Hannah had expected, Mike and Lonnie arrived shortly before they were ready to sit down to eat. Hannah had already told Norman about watching Moishe stalk the RoboVac, and he'd laughed and promised to set both of their machines on a schedule that wouldn't exhaust their pets.

"This is really good," Mike said as he took a third helping from the slow cooker crock in the center of the table. "I'm glad we dropped by."

"Michelle and I knew that you would if your food-dar was working," Hannah told him. "By the way, we found out that Ross had a storage unit at the Superior Storage location in St. Paul."

Mike dropped his fork with a clatter, even though he'd barely begun to eat his third helping. "But you gave me the key! How did you get in?"

"The rent was three months in arrears, so all we had to do was pay the back rent and the manager let us in," Norman told him.

"They're not supposed to do that unless . . . was the unit in Ross's name?"

"Not exactly," Michelle explained, "but the manager thought it was close enough. The name on the application was Russ Burton."

"You lucked out," Mike said. "The manager must have thought that someone got the name wrong."

"That's exactly what she thought," Hannah said. "She said they'd hired a part-time worker to type the names of the tenants in the computer when they'd switched over to a new system and the worker must have misread the name on the application."

"Amazing!" Mike said, shaking his head in disbelief. "She shouldn't have done that, you know."

"I know, but it turned out that the things stored inside *did* belong to Ross. I recognized a couple of the luggage tags that Ross's fiancée made for him while we were in college."

"And the unit was number three-twelve?" Mike asked Hannah.

"No. It was in the building marked five hundred and the unit was five-twenty. Everything inside was from our college years. Ross must have rented it after he graduated and moved out of the apartment building. The manager told us the unit was rented almost five years ago."

"Did you leave the stuff there?" Mike asked.

"No," Norman told him. "Hannah paid the back rent on the unit, and we got a small truck to move everything into my garage."

"Is there anything interesting there?" Mike asked Hannah.

"I don't think there's anything personal, if that's what you mean. Everything was in cases, and it all looked like camera or video equipment."

"I don't suppose you talked your way into checking unit three-twelve," Mike said.

"No. She wouldn't have let us do that,"Hannah told him.

"Okay, then here's what I'm going to do, we're not going to bother going through those cameras and equipment right now. And I'll give the guys out there one more day to come up with something. Then I'm going to pull them back here and give them another assignment. Rick's good at interviewing people, and they can do some legwork for us."

Hannah's sleep was deep and peaceful. No problems plagued her and no nightmares haunted her night. She woke up in the morning without the alarm, cuddled with Moishe for a moment or two, shut off the alarm so that it wouldn't ring while she was in the shower, and got out of bed to begin her morning ritual.

Fifteen minutes later, when she came out of the shower,

she smelled the tantalizing aroma of freshly brewed coffee and she dressed as quickly as she could. Michelle was up early too, and she'd put on their morning coffee. No mouth-watering baking scents were in the air, probably because they'd told Norman that they'd meet him early at the Lake Eden Inn to take advantage of Sally's excellent breakfast buffet.

When Hannah walked down the hallway, Moishe at her heels, she felt better than she had in a long time. She was actually looking forward to the day and the work that awaited them. Selling cookies wasn't work; it was fun. And baking was always enjoyable.

"Good morning, Michelle," Hannah greeted her sister as she stepped into the kitchen. "How are you today?"

Michelle smiled. "I'm fine, and you look a whole lot better than you have in a while. I guess some time away from work restored your positive attitude."

Hannah poured herself a cup of coffee and thought about that. Michelle was right. She'd lost her positive attitude when she'd lost Ross. She hadn't realized that his disappearance had affected her personality as deeply as it had.

The winter sky was just beginning to lighten slightly as Hannah drove to town. Marge, Aunt Nancy, and Lisa were already at The Cookie Jar, and Michelle was just parking when Hannah pulled into her spot. Hannah was smiling as she met Michelle at her car, and they walked in the back kitchen door together. With all five of them working, the baking would be done in record time.

"Hannah? Do you have a minute before we start packing up the cookie truck?" Aunt Nancy asked her.

"Sure. What is it?"

"Not here. I don't want Marge or Lisa to hear. I'll go in the coffee shop. Do you think you can follow me in a couple of minutes without them noticing?"

"Let's try it. Go ahead, Aunt Nancy. And give me a minute or two to follow you."

"What's going on?" Michelle asked Hannah when Aunt Nancy had left.

"Aunt Nancy wants to speak with me personally in the coffee shop. Could you distract Marge and Lisa so they don't miss us while we're talking?"

"I can do that. Just watch."

Hannah watched as Michelle picked up a tray of unbaked cookies and headed toward the oven, where Lisa and Marge were standing.

"Oh, no!" Michelle exclaimed as she pretended to stumble and the unbaked cookies went flying all over the counter. "I'm so sorry. I just lost my balance for a second."

"That's okay, honey," Marge said, hurrying over to help Michelle. "You go sit down and catch your breath. There's no harm done. Isn't that right, Lisa?"

"Marge is right," Lisa agreed. "None of the cookies hit the floor so they're perfectly usable. You just sit and relax. Marge and I will reshape the dough and put it back on the cookie sheet."

Hannah reminded herself to compliment Michelle on her quick thinking and made her escape through the swinging door to the coffee shop. Aunt Nancy was sitting at a table near the plate glass window and she motioned Hannah over to her.

"It's Heiti," Aunt Nancy said as soon as Hannah sat down with her. "I think he's going to give me an engagement ring!"

Hannah was puzzled. "But that's good, isn't it?"

"Oh, yes! It's wonderful! But I think that Lisa might feel hurt if I don't confide my suspicions to her."

Hannah smiled. "That's easily solved. All you have to do is tell Lisa."

"But what if I'm wrong? Heiti said something about good things coming in small packages and I know he went out to the jewelry store at the Tri-County Mall. If he's giving me a necklace or a bracelet instead of a ring, I'll be horribly embarrassed."

She's making a mountain out of a beaver dam, Hannah thought. It had been one of her father's favorite sayings, but she didn't repeat it aloud. Instead she said, "Just act surprised at whatever it is and don't let Lisa and Herb know that you expected anything else."

Aunt Nancy thought about that for a moment. "You're right! I shouldn't tell them unless I know for sure, and I don't."

"Then you solved your own problem, Aunt Nancy."

Aunt Nancy thought about that for a moment and then she smiled. "I did, didn't I?"

Hannah stood up. "We'd better get back to work before anyone misses us. And if they noticed that we were gone, we'll just say we were checking to make sure everything was ready in here. And, Aunt Nancy?"

"Yes, Hannah."

"Heiti's a wonderful man, and I really hope that you're right!"

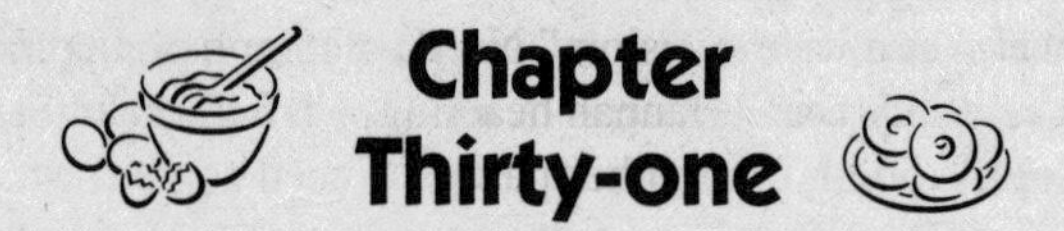

Chapter Thirty-one

It seemed that everyone and their cousin had turned out for the final day of Sally's Holiday Gift Convention. From their vantage point in the center of the convention hall, Hannah, Michelle, and Norman could tell that every booth was doing booming business. The Cookie Jar booth was no exception. Norman had driven back to town twice to pick up more cookies. Now, at four in the afternoon, their supply was getting low again.

"Do you want me to go to town again?" Norman asked them.

"No." Hannah made an executive decision. "It'll take you twenty minutes to get to town and twenty minutes to drive back here. By that time, it'll be almost a quarter to five and the convention closes at five."

"You're right," Norman agreed, "but I hate to see you run out."

Michelle smiled, and it was the smile that Delores described as *the cat that got into the cream pot* in the Regency romances she wrote. "We won't run out," she said.

"How can you be sure?" Hannah asked her.

"I stuck four pans of bar cookies in a cooler in the back

seat of your cookie truck. I decided to bring them just in case."

"That was a wise decision," Norman complimented her.

"It certainly was." Hannah headed toward the chair in the back of the booth to grab her parka. "I need some fresh air. I'll go get them."

As she passed by Gary's booth, Hannah stopped to say hello. "We're almost sold out. How are you doing today?"

"It's the same here. I just sold my last handmade sleigh ornament and everything else is in short supply. Today was my best day."

"I'm sorry to hear that you're out of the sleighs," Hannah told him. "I was going to buy one for Mother for her Christmas tree."

"I have another box, but it's in the passenger seat of my Jeep," Gary told her. "I was going to go out to get it earlier, but I got busy before I could do it and I haven't had time since."

"I'm going out there anyway," Hannah told him. "I can bring the box back for you."

"That would be great!" Gary said, reaching in his pocket to pull out his car keys and hand them to her. "Use the driver's side door. The lock on the passenger's door doesn't work very well in the winter. It's the black Jeep Wrangler with a small trailer hitched to the back."

"I know which one it is. I'm parked right next to it. I'll bring back your sleighs if you'll sell me one."

"I'll *give* you one," Gary promised, turning to smile at the customers who were approaching his booth. "Thanks, Hannah."

"No problem," Hannah said, leaving him to his customers. She walked down the row of booths to the back door, waving at the vendors she'd met. The back door was unlocked, and she pushed it open and stepped outside, breathing deeply of the still, cold air. She coughed once, and immediately held her winter scarf over her mouth, breathing through that to warm the air slightly. The temperature outside was so cold that taking a deep breath hurt her lungs.

Hannah unlocked the driver's side of the Jeep, pulled it open, and spotted the small box on the passenger's seat. It had the word SLEIGHS written on the side, and she leaned across the driver's seat to lift it out.

There was a Styrofoam cup of coffee in the cup holder between the seats, but Hannah didn't notice that as she lifted the box and pulled it toward her. The corner of the box hit the cup, which contained only an inch or two of coffee in the bottom. The impact caused the cup to come out of the holder and upend, splashing the cold coffee all over the tan leather covering the driver's seat.

"Oh, great!" Hannah said sarcastically, setting the ornament box on the roof of the Jeep and reaching across the seat to open the glove box. It was where most people stored tissues, paper napkins, or rags, and she rummaged for something she could use to dry the seat.

There was a box of tissues, and Hannah grabbed the box, placed it on the passenger's seat, and pulled out several tissues. She used them to wipe up the spill and was about to replace the box in the glove box when she noticed that the interior of the glove box was a vivid shade of pink.

"Pink!" Hannah gasped, completely startled by the color. Gary's Jeep was black. Why was the interior of his glove box pink?

It was a great paint job, Hannah. They even painted the inside of the glove box and the wheel wells, Cyril's words describing Pinkie's Jeep came back to Hannah. This was Pinkie's Jeep! There was no doubt about that. She had to ask Gary where he'd bought his Jeep.

Hannah remembered her promise to Mike. She'd promised to notify him if she came across an important clue. She took out her phone and snapped a photo of the interior of the glove box before she closed it again.

Better check the wheel wells, her mind told her. *That's even more proof that it's Pinkie's Jeep.*

It was a good idea, and Hannah shut the door of the Jeep, locking the door behind her. She crouched down as far as she could near the driver's side wheel well and held her cell phone out to snap another photo. One glance at her photo told her that it was even more proof that Gary's Jeep had once belonged to Pinkie. Hannah was smiling as she typed a text message to Mike.

My neighbor at the convention, Gary Fowler, owns Pinkie's Jeep. Then she attached the two photos. As she walked back toward the door to the convention hall, Hannah felt very virtuous for fulfilling her promise and letting Mike know what she'd just discovered.

There was a line of waiting customers at Gary's booth, and once Hannah delivered the box with the sleighs and took one for herself, she went back to The Cookie Jar booth with Michelle's bar cookies. She would wait to talk to Gary until he finished with his customers.

Michelle immediately cut up the bar cookies she'd brought, and since Norman was there to help wait on customers, Hannah grabbed a cup of coffee and took a moment to sit down at a table in the food court to sip it. She had just begun to relax when her cell phone rang. She glanced at the display and was surprised to see a number from Clarissa High displayed there.

"Hello, this is Hannah," she answered.

"Oh, good! I got you! This is Lila from Clarissa High. I

just thought of the name of Pinkie's brother. Remember when I told you that it was a common name?"

"I remember," Hannah said.

"Well, it's Gary."

"Gary?"

"That's right, or at least I'm pretty sure it is. He's the one who sold the farm and rented that apartment in town for Pinkie."

There was a pause, and then Lila said, "I've got to go. I've got another call. Good-bye, Hannah."

The phone clicked off, and Hannah just sat there for a moment with a puzzled expression on her face. Pinkie's brother's name was Gary. She reminded herself that there were a lot of men named Gary in the world and the fact that one of them had Pinkie's Jeep didn't necessarily mean that her neighbor, Gary, was Pinkie's brother. Actually, now that she thought about it, Lila had said that she was *pretty sure*, not completely sure. Gary had told her that his sister, Violet, had given him the Jeep. Violet could have bought it from a car lot. And all this could be a coincidence. Things like that happened, didn't they?

Hannah wiped down the counters of their booth for the sixth time as she waited for everyone to leave so that she could talk to Gary alone. Norman had gone home to shower and change clothes, and Michelle had gone off to Dick's bar to have a glass of wine and meet her friend, Trish, who was working the afternoon shift today. Trish would take Michelle to The Cookie Jar to get her car, and then all three of them—Norman, Trish, and Michelle—would meet at Hannah's condo at seven to have leftover Chinese food and fresh pizza that Norman had promised to bring.

There were only a few vendors left in the convention

hall, and Hannah took heart. It wouldn't be long now. She told herself again that all she had was circumstantial evidence linking Gary to Pinkie and there really wasn't any reason to be overly suspicious. Even if Pinkie's brother's name happened to be Gary, he might not be the Gary who'd been Pinkie's brother. And even though Gary had told Hannah that everything Violet sold was handmade on consignment and she'd found a label that said the cookie ornament Tracey had bought was made in China, that could have been Gary's mistake. Perhaps Violet had ordered the ornaments for a friend, or even for her personal Christmas tree at home, never intending to sell them at her shop. Actually, even the fact that Violet's name hadn't been on the patient list of any hospital or rehabilitation facility that they'd called could be explained. Violet could have been discharged before they'd called and now she was at home, being cared for by her part-time assistant who worked at the store.

Then there was the fact that Violet's store, Many Hands, wasn't listed in the telephone directory or with the Better Business Bureau. This could also be easily explained. Violet could be following the lead of so many businesses and was using her cell phone number for business. And the fact that she wasn't listed with the Better Business Bureau wasn't that unusual either. If there had been no complaints about her business, Violet might not have chosen to pay to be listed with them. The last and final piece of circumstantial evidence could also be explained quite easily. Pinkie's brother, whatever his name, could have sold Pinkie's Jeep after she died, the car lot could have had it repainted black so that it would sell more easily, and Violet could have purchased it for Gary. Michelle had a used car, and they had no idea who the previous owner was. They hadn't even thought to ask Cyril. Most people who bought used cars checked the history of the car itself, but not the history of ownership. Everything Hannah had that pointed her to Gary as Pinkie's brother was entirely circumstantial.

The coffee Hannah had poured for herself before she'd cleaned out Sally's coffeepots was sitting in a large Styrofoam cup on the counter. It was still almost full and she picked it up and took a sip of the lukewarm brew while she waited.

Finally, Gary's last customer left. Hannah knew that somehow she needed to trip Gary up and catch him in an outright lie. And she'd need proof of Gary's outright lie for Mike. Hannah used the app on her cell phone to record her upcoming conversation with Gary, picked up her coffee, and walked over to Gary's booth.

"It was nice having you for a neighbor Gary," she said, hoping to get him completely off-guard for the probing questions she planned to ask.

"And it was nice talking to you," Gary told her. "If you're ready to leave, I'll walk you out to the parking lot."

"Thanks," Hannah said politely. "I just wanted to ask you a couple of questions and it's too cold to talk outside."

"Ask away," Gary told her, shrugging into his parka and pulling on his winter driving gloves.

Hannah glanced at his gloves. They were black, padded leather gloves. *All the better to choke you with, my dear!* the suspicious part of her mind cautioned. *You'd better be very careful now.*

"Michelle and I felt sorry for your sister, Violet, and we were going to send her some cookies," Hannah gave him the excuse she'd rehearsed in her mind. "You didn't mention where she was hospitalized, so we called around but we couldn't find her."

"When did you call?"

"Last night."

"*That* explains it," Gary said with a smile. "The doctor released Violet yesterday morning. She's home now."

"Oh, no wonder," Hannah pretended to believe him. "We also thought about sending cookies to her business address, but it's not listed with the Better Business Bureau."

"Violet never bothered to do that, and everyone's always been happy with anything they've gotten at her store."

"But she doesn't have a business phone, either."

"Sure, she does. She uses her cell phone number. She had a landline for a while, but the only calls she got were from salesmen. Anything else you want to know? Or can I leave for the Cities now?"

Back off! the rational part of Hannah's mind warned. *He's getting suspicious, and that's dangerous if he's the killer.*

"Just one thing," Hannah told him, deciding to go for broke. "Why are you driving Pinkie's Jeep?"

"Who?" Gary asked, looking completely puzzled.

"Pinkie. Her real name was Mary Jo Hart. Your Jeep was pink before you had it painted black."

The expression on Gary's face changed from slightly suspicious to icy cold and menacing. "You think you got it all figured out, don't you, Hannah?"

"Maybe, maybe not," Hannah said quickly. "There is no Violet, is there, Gary?"

"Of course not," Gary admitted, giving her a hard look. "I heard you were a good detective, and it's true."

"Thank you," Hannah said quickly, "but there's still something I don't know. Did you drug that candy and send it to P.K.?"

"You bet I did! He ruined Mary Jo's life! She killed herself because of him. Did you know *that*?"

"I heard about her suicide. Did she get the pills from Dr. Benson?"

"Of course! She had some left, and I wanted P.K. to die the same way. It was only right! He killed her, you know. He made her crazy enough to take those tranquilizers and kill herself. It's the same as if he'd put a gun to her head and shot her!"

"But weren't you afraid that Ross might get that candy instead of P.K.?"

"He was long gone. And even if there'd been some collateral damage, it didn't matter. I did it for Pinkie. It's what P.K. deserved!"

Hannah felt her mouth go suddenly dry as Gary leaned forward and glared at her.

"And now you know too much."

"Don't worry," Hannah said quickly. "Everyone will understand why you did it. You were grief-stricken about Pinkie. They'll understand."

Gary laughed. It was an insane laugh, almost hysterical, and Hannah knew she'd reached the end of the line. Then he sobered, and his eyes began to glitter with deadly intent.

"This time it won't be drugged candy. I'll be putting out your lights personally! And it'll be a real pleasure for me!"

Hannah gasped as Gary reached down and picked up a large hammer, the kind that people in construction used for framing a house. Then he looked up with the most evil expression Hannah had ever seen.

Get out of here! both parts of her mind, the rational and the suspicious, warned her. *He's going to kill you!*

It was the first time that both parts of her mind had agreed about anything, but Hannah didn't waste time thinking about that. She raised her coffee cup and threw the contents straight into Gary's face. And then she whirled and ran toward the open door to the hallway as fast as she could.

As she approached the doorway, Hannah heard a thud, but she didn't turn around to see what it was. She just kept on running, hoping that the splashed coffee had done its job and Gary had slipped and fallen.

Hannah sprinted down the long hallway that separated the convention center from the main part of the inn. The hallway was dimly lit and completely deserted. Everyone else who'd worked at the convention hall had already left. The huge floor-to-ceiling windows on one side of the hallway looked out on the lake, and the other side had a lovely view of the pine forest. But Hannah had no time to appreciate the beauty of nature tonight, not when she was being chased by P.K.'s killer!

Hannah's eyes were focused straight ahead, scanning the carpeting for any obstacles she might encounter in her headlong dash to the safety of the inn. And then she saw it in the distance, her goal, the open door that led into the restaurant. Panting heavily from the unaccustomed exertion, Hannah raced to the doorway and dashed through.

Soft dining music was playing, but Hannah didn't hear it. Waiters and waitresses in stylish uniforms were serving their guests, but Hannah barely noticed them. Behind the plate glass windows in the front of the dining room, kitchen workers were busily stirring, pouring, and mixing the contents of various-sized cooking pans over huge, professional stoves. Hannah noticed none of it. She was too focused on saving her life.

She was almost ready to drop from exhaustion when she spotted a table in the center of the room and recognized Bill and Andrea. She rushed toward them, too out of breath to shout, and grabbed the first thing she saw on their table, the silver cover that their waiter had just removed from Andrea's entrée.

Hannah turned to see Gary coming at her, the hammer raised high in his hand, and she jammed the silver entrée cover into his face.

Things happened very fast as the waiter stepped out of the way and Gary fell backwards to the floor, dropping the hammer as he clawed at the silver cover that was jammed over his face. Hannah grabbed the heavy hammer and hit the entrée cover as hard as she could.

Andrea gasped. "Hannah! What are you . . . ? Oh!"

"Cuff him!" Hannah managed to gasp out, hammering away to keep Gary on his back on the floor. "Hurry! He killed P.K.!"

Bill motioned to two of his off-duty deputies who were sitting at a neighboring table, and they sprang into action to flip Gary over on his stomach and cuff him. Bill relieved Hannah of the hammer and slipped an arm around her shoulders. "He killed P.K.?" he asked her.

"Yes! He sent that drugged candy! I've got his whole confession on . . . on my phone!"

"Deputies?" Bill motioned to them. "Does either one of you have a phone like Hannah's?"

"I do," one of them said, examining Hannah's phone.

"Do you know how to send that taped confession to me?" Bill asked him.

"Sure. It's an app. I can do it right now, if you want me to."

"Yes," Bill told him.

"There's an unsent text with photos. Do you want me to send that, too?"

"That's up to Hannah." Bill turned to her. "Do you want him to send it?"

Hannah nodded, too shocked to speak. She hadn't sent the photos of Gary's car to Mike. No wonder he hadn't responded!

"Hannah?" Bill prompted her again.

"Yes, but it doesn't matter now," she managed to say,

glancing at Gary, handcuffed on the floor. "Everything turned out all right in the end."

A moment or two later, the confession arrived on Bill's cell phone. "Good work," he said, glancing at the display. "Take him down to the station. Leave the cuffs on, lock him up, enter that hammer and entrée cover into evidence, and I'll take it from there. And then come back here and have a nice dinner on me, anything you want."

Once the deputies had left with their prisoner, Bill leaned down to kiss Andrea. "Sorry about date night," he said. "I know you were looking forward to seeing that movie."

To Hannah's surprise, instead of looking disgruntled or disappointed, Andrea just laughed. "It's okay, honey. I'm glad we both drove. Right now, all I want to do is go home and have a glass of wine. I've already had all the entertainment that I can handle for one date night."

Chapter Thirty-two

As Hannah took the familiar road home, she began to relax. P.K.'s killer was behind bars, and now they could work on finding Ross's second storage locker. Except for missing Ross and wishing that he would come home, everything was back to normal again. They'd lucked out and caught P.K.'s killer, the daily profits from selling cookies at Sally's convention had netted at least three times the daily profit they made at The Cookie Jar, and they had found one of Ross's storage lockers and rescued the contents before they'd gone up for public auction. On the whole, it had been a good outcome. And to cap it all off, Andrea wasn't even upset that Bill had cut their date night short. She'd been too busy laughing about the sight of Hannah straddling Gary and hammering away at the entrée cover that was stuck on his face.

Snow was gently falling as Hannah turned into her condo complex, used her key card to open the wooden slat that served as a gate, and drove down the pretty lane that led to her condo building. If Ross were here right now, they'd put on their parkas and walk down the path that led around the man-made lake inside the condo complex. They'd hold hands to keep warm, and they might even stop under one of the tall pines and share a kiss.

As she imagined that kiss beneath the sheltering branches of the pine, a phrase popped into her mind. *It's better to have loved and lost than never to have loved at all.* Would it have been better if she'd never seen Ross again and fallen in love with him? Or was it better to have experienced his love, even for such a short while? Hannah wasn't sure. All she knew was that she'd never felt so alone and abandoned.

As she passed the guest parking lot, Hannah noticed Mike's car. And a little further down, she spotted Norman's car, too.

She smiled. She might have known that Mike would be here. His food-dar had probably told him the moment Norman had called to order the takeout pizza. Since neither Mike nor Norman had been sitting in their cars, Hannah continued to the end of the lane and drove down the ramp into the garage she shared with the other condo owners. Since Norman had a key, they must be inside.

When she climbed up the covered staircase to her condo on the second floor, Hannah noticed that Moishe was perched on the living room window sill. That was a good sign. It meant that the RoboVac hadn't tired him out too much today. She waved at him, and to her delight, he raised his paw to wave back.

Hannah unlocked the door, braced herself, and pushed it open. Moishe hurtled out, just as she'd anticipated, and landed in her outstretched arms. And then he did something new, something he'd never done before. He extended his paws, claws retracted, and patted both of her cheeks at once.

"That's sweet," Hannah said, smiling at him. And then, just as she was about to step inside, Moishe licked her cheeks with his rough tongue and started to purr.

Hannah hugged him to show that the feeling was mutual, and carried him inside. She placed him on the back of the couch in his favorite spot and rubbed the base of his ears. Only then did she turn to greet Norman and Mike.

"Hi, guys," she said, still smiling from Moishe's unexpected show of affection.

Mike nodded to acknowledge her presence, and then he said, "Sit down, Hannah."

Alarm bells clanged in Hannah's mind, and she hurried to sit down on the sofa. Norman took the seat next to her, and she was glad he was here. Mike had used his command voice, and that meant something was happening. "What's wrong?" she asked him.

"We found Ross," Mike told her. His voice was flat, and that didn't bode well. "It's bad news, Hannah."

Hannah could feel her tightly controlled composure slip alarmingly. "Is he . . . ?" she stopped to swallow, her throat suddenly dry. "Is he . . . dead?" She managed to force out the word.

"No."

Hannah drew a deep breath of relief, but then another dreadful possibility occurred to her. "Injured?"

"No, he's perfectly okay."

Hannah started to smile, but Mike wasn't smiling and neither was Norman. That left her completely puzzled and her fear began to build again. "But . . . if Ross isn't dead, or injured, why did you tell me that it was bad news?"

Mike nodded to Norman and Norman sighed. "Mike meant that it's not bad for Ross, but it *is* bad news for you, Hannah."

"What? Mike needs an interpreter?" Hannah felt her irritation grow by leaps and bounds. Getting bad news should be like ripping off a Band-Aid. If you dragged it out, it hurt more than if you gritted your teeth and yanked it off quickly. She turned to look directly at Mike. "What is it, Mike?"

"Well, Hannah . . ." Mike winced slightly. "I'm not quite sure how to tell you this . . ."

"Just spit it out, Mike!" Hannah's irritation took wings. "Don't drag it out! Tell me!"

Norman reached out for her hand, and even though she had the urge to yank it back, Hannah let him hold it. She knew that Norman was only trying to help her get through whatever it was that Mike was about to tell her.

"It's like this, Hannah . . ." Mike stopped and an expression of pain crossed his face. "The reason Ross left you is because . . ." Mike took a deep breath and let it out again. "Ross went back to his wife."

Hannah shut her eyes. Of course she was dreaming. She must be dreaming. It had to be another crazy nightmare like Florence and the oranges and the perfect pear, and . . . but she could feel Norman holding her hand. She could actually *feel* it. And Michelle wasn't baking because Michelle wasn't here. She had to wake up somehow. This couldn't be happening to her. It didn't make sense. It was a dream and she had to open her eyes and wake up!

Through a supreme effort of will she hadn't known she possessed, Hannah managed to open her eyes. But they had been open all along, hadn't they? There were tears on her face and they were falling from her eyes. Was it raining in her living room? That's where she was. She could see it. She was sitting on the couch and Norman was holding her hand. And her whole face was wet. It must be raining. And that meant this was just another crazy dream.

"Wha . . . what did you say?" Hannah asked Mike.

"I said Ross went back to his wife," Mike repeated.

Oh yes, Hannah decided, this was definitely a dream because that was crazy. She had to tell Mike she knew that she was dreaming. Then she would wake up from this nightmare.

"That's not right," she said. "It's just not right, Mike. It makes no sense at all. Ross couldn't go back to his wife because *I'm* his wife!"

"Hannah. Please listen to me and try to understand." An expression of sympathy crossed Mike's face and for one brief moment, Hannah thought she saw unshed tears in his eyes. "Hannah . . . you're not married. Ross was never your husband. He's married to someone else."

Raspberry Danish Murder Recipe Index

Baking Conversion Chart

These conversions are approximate, but they'll work just fine for Hannah Swensen's recipes.

VOLUME

U.S.	*Metric*
½ teaspoon	2 milliliters
1 teaspoon	5 milliliters
1 Tablespoon	15 milliliters
¼ cup	50 milliliters
⅓ cup	75 milliliters
½ cup	125 milliliters
¾ cup	175 milliliters
1 cup	¼ liter

WEIGHT

U.S.	*Metric*
1 ounce	28 grams
1 pound	454 grams

OVEN TEMPERATURE

Degrees Fahrenheit	*Degrees Centigrade*	*British (Regulo) Gas Mark*
325 degrees F.	165 degrees C.	3
350 degrees F.	175 degrees C.	4
375 degrees F.	190 degrees C.	5

Note: Hannah's rectangular sheet cake pan, 9 inches by 13 inches, is approximately 23 centimeters by 32.5 centimeters.

Here's a special treat from *New York Times* bestselling author Joanne Fluke!

Two bonus recipes, plus a letter letting readers know what Hannah is going to be up to in her next book!

PINEAPPLE DREAM CUPCAKES

Preheat oven to 350 degrees F., rack in the middle position.

Hannah's 1st Note: You can mix up these cupcakes by hand, but it's much easier to use an electric mixer. Lisa and I have a large stand mixer and several hand mixers down at The Cookie Jar. We usually use the stand mixer to make these.

8-ounce ***(net weight)*** can of crushed pineapple ***(I used Dole)***
½ cup golden raisins ***(Regular raisins will also work in this recipe.)***
¼ cup pineapple juice ***(I used Dole)***
½ cup chopped pecans ***(measure AFTER chopping)***
11- or 12-ounce ***(by weight)*** bag of white chocolate or vanilla chips ***(I used Nestle)***
4 large eggs
½ cup vegetable oil
8-ounce container sour cream
½ teaspoon pineapple or coconut extract ***(If you***

don't have either of those and don't want to buy them, use vanilla extract.)

Box of yellow Cake Mix, with or without pudding in the mix, the kind that makes a 9-inch by 13-inch cake or a 2-layer cake ***(I used Duncan Hines)***

5.1-ounce package of instant vanilla pudding mix ***(I used Jell-O, the kind that makes 6 half-cup servings.)***

Open the can of crushed pineapple and pour the contents into a strainer sitting over a measuring cup to catch the juice.

Let the pineapple drain while you prepare your cupcake pans.

Line 2 cupcake pans ***(12 cupcakes per pan)*** with cupcake papers.

Use folded paper towels to pat your crushed pineapple dry. You don't want to add too much liquid to your cupcake batter.

Place the crushed pineapple in a bowl on the counter.

See how much pineapple juice has been caught in your measuring cup. If it's ¼ cup, you have enough. If it's not, add water until you do.

Put your half-cup of golden raisins in a microwave-safe bowl. Add the quarter-cup of pineapple juice and heat the bowl in the microwave for 1 minute on HIGH. Leave the bowl in the microwave for an additional minute and then use potholders to take it out of the microwave and set it on a folded dishtowel on your counter to cool. The hot pineapple juice will plump your raisins.

If you did not buy chopped pecans, put the pecans in your food processor with the steel blade and chop them using an on and off motion. Take them out of the processor bowl, but put the steel blade back in place. ***(You'll use it to chop the white chocolate chips.)***

Measure out a half-cup of pecans, bag the rest for the next time you bake something and need chopped pecans, and add the quarter cup you need for your cupcakes to the bowl with the crushed pineapple.

Hannah's 2nd Note: Chopped nuts freeze beautifully. Bag the leftovers when you chop them, label the freezer bag, and stick it in the freezer. Chopped nuts will last for a year in your freezer. If you just

bag them and leave them on a shelf in your cupboard, they will turn rancid.

Put the white chocolate chips in the bowl of your food processor. Use the steel blade in an on and off motion to chop them into pieces approximately the size of coarse gravel.

Add the white chocolate chip pieces to the bowl with the pineapple and chopped pecans.

Hannah's 3rd Note: The reason why you chop the white chocolate chips into smaller pieces is to keep them from sinking to the bottom of your cupcakes.

Crack the eggs into the bowl of your mixer.

Pour in the half-cup of vegetable oil and mix it in with the eggs on LOW speed. Continue to beat at LOW speed until you achieve a smooth mixture.

Use a rubber spatula to transfer the contents of the sour cream container to your mixer bowl. Mix that in on LOW speed. Then mix in the pineapple extract.

With the mixer running on LOW speed, open the box of dry cake mix and slowly add it to the ingredi-

ents in the bowl. Continue to mix until everything is well combined.

Let the mixer run on LOW and sprinkle in dry instant vanilla pudding mix. Beat until that's thoroughly incorporated.

Use your rubber spatula to scoop the pineapple, chopped pecans, raisins, and white chocolate chip pieces out of their bowl and into the bowl of your mixer. Mix them in at LOW speed.

Mix until everything is well combined. Then turn off the mixer, scrape down the sides of the bowl, and take it out of the mixer. Set it on the counter next to your prepared cupcake pans and give your batter a final stir by hand.

Fill your cupcake papers ⅔ full of batter. ***Lisa and I use a scooper to do this at The Cookie Jar. It's a lot faster than doing it with a spoon.***

Bake your Pineapple Dream Cupcakes at 350 degrees F. for 20 to 25 minutes or until they test done. If you don't know how to test your cupcakes, read the 4th note below.

Hannah's 4th Note: Before you take your cupcakes out of the oven, test for doneness by inserting

a cake tester, thin wooden skewer, or long toothpick in the center of a cupcake. If the tester comes out clean, your cupcakes are done. If there is still unbaked batter clinging to the tester, shut the oven door and bake your cupcakes longer, in 5 minute increments, until the tester comes out clean. Make sure to test one cupcake in each of the 12-cup pans.

Once your cupcakes pass the doneness test, take the pans out of the oven and set them on cold stove burners or wire racks. Let the cupcakes cool in the pans until they are completely cool.

Hannah's 5th Note: When the cupcake are cool, you can cover and refrigerate if you wish. Cupcakes are easier to frost when they're thoroughly cold. Either leave them right in the pans, or remove them to another container, that's your choice. Make sure to cover them with plastic wrap or foil so that they don't dry out.

When you're ready to frost your cupcakes, prepare the Cream Cheese Frosting. ***(The recipe and instructions follow.)***

Yield: 24 tasty cupcakes that both adults and kids will love to eat.

CREAM CHEESE FROSTING

½ cup ***(1 stick)*** softened, salted butter
8-ounce ***(net weight)*** package softened, brick-type cream cheese ***(I used Philadelphia in the silver package.)***
½ teaspoon pineapple or coconut extract ***(You can substitute vanilla extract if you don't have pineapple or coconut.)***
4 cups confectioner's ***(powdered)*** sugar ***(no need to sift unless it's got big lumps)***

Mix the softened butter with the softened cream cheese and the pineapple or coconut extract until the mixture is smooth.

Hannah's 1st Note: Do this next step at room temperature. If you heated the cream cheese or the butter to soften it, make sure it's cooled down to room temperature before you continue.

Add the confectioner's sugar in half-cup increments until the frosting is of proper spreading consistency. ***(You'll use all, or almost all, of the powdered sugar.)***

Hannah's 2nd Note: When Lisa frosts cupcakes, she grabs one at the bottom of the paper and dips it

into the frosting up to the top edge of the paper. Then she twists it and pulls it up, out of the frosting. This method is lightning fast. When I tried it, I got the cupcake too deep in the frosting and I ended up with frosting on the cupcake paper. I tried to correct for that and I didn't dip it in far enough and there was an unfrosted space all the way around the top. I went back to using the method described below.

Using a frosting knife ***(or rubber spatula if you prefer)*** spread frosting from the center of your cupcakes out to the edges. Let the frosting "set" at room temperature and then refrigerate the cupcakes.

If you have frosting left over, spread it on graham crackers, soda crackers, or what Great-Grandma Elsa used to call store-boughten cookies. This frosting can also be covered tightly and kept in the refrigerator for up to a week. When you want to use it, let it sit on the kitchen counter for an hour or so until it reaches room temperature and it is spreadable again.

You can also color this frosting with a drop or two of food coloring. If you make these cupcakes at Halloween, a drop of yellow and a drop of red will make a nice orange frosting. On Valentine's Day, use just

one drop of red and your frosting will be pink. Use green for St. Patrick's Day, and alternate between red and green for Christmas.

This frosting also works well in a pastry bag.

A Letter to Hannah Fans

Dear Hannah Fans,

Have you ever wondered exactly why Hannah decided to open The Cookie Jar and what it was like for her at the very beginning? Or are you curious about Michelle's teenage years at Jordan High? Then there's Andrea, who's currently a successful, married real estate agent with two young daughters. Who helped Andrea get started in her career? There's Lisa, Hannah's partner at The Cookie Jar. As Hannah would tell you, hiring Lisa was the best decision she ever made. But when did this successful duo get together? And then there's Delores, the mother that makes readers wince and laugh at the same time. What was she like before the Hannah series opened?

If you're as curious about these things as most Hannah fans seem to be, I have wonderful news for you. I just finished writing another Christmas book and it goes back in time to answer all those questions and then some. It's called, ***Christmas Cake Murder***, and some of your favorite Lake Edenites are in it.

Christmas Cake Murder is now available so you won't have to wait a whole year to read about Hannah and Lake Eden again. I had so much fun writing this Christmas book and the recipes are yummy. I always test recipes three times, but I'll admit that I tested the Ultimate Lemon Bundt Cake a lot more than that!

I hope you'll all go back in time with me to enjoy the Christmas Ball with its Christmas Cake Parade at the Albion Hotel in the heart of Lake Eden. Fond hugs and happy baking to all of you!

Love, Jo

Not even Lake Eden's nosiest residents suspected Hannah Swensen would go from idealistic newlywed to betrayed wife in a matter of weeks. But as a deadly mystery unfolds in town, the proof is in the pudding . . .

When The Cookie Jar becomes the setting of a star-studded TV special about movies filmed in Minnesota, Hannah hopes to shine the spotlight on her bakery—not the unsavory scandal swirling around her personal life. But that's practically impossible with a disturbing visit from the shifty character she once believed was her one and only love, a group of bodyguards following her every move, and a murder victim in her bedroom. Now, swapping the crime scene in her condo for her mother Delores's penthouse, Hannah and an old flame team up to solve a case that's messier than an upended chocolate cream pie. As suspects emerge and secrets hit close to home, Hannah must serve a hefty helping of justice to an unnamed killer prowling around Lake Eden . . . before someone takes a slice out of her!

Please turn the page for an exciting sneak peek of Joann Fluke's next Hannah Swensen mystery CHOCOLATE CREAM PIE MURDER coming soon wherever print and e-books are sold!

Chapter One

It was a cold Sunday morning in February when Hannah Swensen left the warmth of her condo and drove to Lake Eden, Minnesota. A frown crossed her face as she traveled down Main Street and passed The Cookie Jar, her bakery and coffee shop. It had snowed during the night and Hannah and her partner, Lisa Beeseman, would have to shovel the sidewalk before they could open for business in the morning.

Hannah gunned the engine a bit as she began to drive up the steep hill that led to Holy Redeemer Lutheran Church. The church sat at the very top of and it overlooked the town below. Hannah pulled into the parking lot and came very close to groaning as she realized that her whole family was standing at the bottom of the church steps, waiting for her to arrive. Perhaps their intent was to allay her anxiety about what she planned to do, but it didn't work and Hannah was sorely tempted to turn around and put things off for another week. Of course she didn't do that. Hannah was not a quitter. Somehow she had to gather the resolve to carry on with as much grace and dignity as she could muster.

The first person to arrive at her distinctive cookie truck

was Hannah's youngest sister, Michelle. Hannah resisted the urge to tell Michelle that she ought to be wearing boots and plastered a welcoming smile on her face. "Michelle," she said, by way of a greeting. "Get in the back seat. It's cold out there."

"I'm okay. I just wanted to be the first to talk to you, Hannah. Are you completely sure that you want to do this?"

Hannah shook her head. "Of course I don't *want* to, but I don't really have a choice. It's only right, Michelle."

"But you *don't* have to do it, not really," Michelle argued, sliding onto the back seat and shutting the door behind her. "Word gets around and everyone's probably heard what really happened by now."

"That's doubtful, Michelle. Nobody in our family has said anything to contradict our cover story for Ross's absence. And I know that Norman and Mike haven't mentioned it to anyone. You haven't heard any gossip about it, have you?"

"No," Michelle admitted.

"And you know the whole town would be buzzing about it if anyone knew."

"Well . . . yes, but we can figure out another way of telling them. You don't have to put yourself through the pain of getting up in front of the whole congregation and talking about it."

"Yes, I do. They deserve an explanation. And they also deserve an apology from me for lying to them."

The front door opened and Hannah's mother, Delores, picked up the heavy cookie platter that was nestled on the passenger seat and got in. "I heard what you just told Michelle and you're wrong, Hannah. No one here expects you to apologize. What happened is no fault of yours."

The other back door of Hannah's cookie truck opened and Hannah's middle sister, Andrea Swensen Todd, got in. "And nobody here wants to see you upset. If you think we owe anyone an apology, let *me* do it. I can get up there and tell them what happened."

"Thanks, but no. It's nice of you to offer, Andrea, but this is something I have to do myself."

"I understand, dear," Delores said, "but I wish you'd told me your plans earlier. We could have gone shopping for something more appropriate for you to wear."

Hannah glanced down at her blue pantsuit. "A lot of women wear pantsuits to church, especially in the winter. What's wrong with mine?"

"Nothing's wrong . . . exactly," Delores explained. "It's just that the color washes you out. At least you're here early and we have time to fix your makeup. A darker color lipstick would do wonders and you need some blusher on your cheeks."

Andrea opened her purse and glanced inside. "Mascara and eye shadow couldn't hurt. I've got something that would bring out the color of Hannah's eyes."

And I can do something with her hair," Michelle offered.

"Hold it right there!" Hannah told them. "My appearance doesn't matter that much. What really matters is what I'm going to say. I've worn this same outfit to church at least a dozen times and you've never criticized my appearance before."

"Today is different," Delores pointed out. "Grandma Knudson told me that you asked to stand in the front of the church right after Reverend Bob makes his announcements. Everybody's going to see . . ." Delores stopped speaking and a panicked expression crossed her face. "You're not planning to wear your winter boots, are you?"

Hannah had the urge to laugh. She had never, in her whole life, walked down the aisle of their church wearing winter boots. She came very close to saying that, but she realized that the root of her mother's concern was anxiety about how the congregation would receive what Hannah had to tell them.

"Relax, Mother," Hannah told her. "I brought dress shoes with me and I'll change in the cloakroom as soon as we get inside."

Delores still looked worried. "Your dress shoes aren't brown, are they?"

"No, Mother. I know how you feel about wearing brown shoes with blue. These are the black shoes we bought at the Tri-County Mall last year."

"Oh, good!" Delores drew a relieved breath and glanced at the jeweled watch her husband, Doc Knight, had given her. "Then let's go, girls. It'll take us a while to get Hannah ready."

Hannah wisely kept her silence as she walked to the church with her family. Once the cookies she'd brought for the social hour after the church service had been delivered to the kitchen next to the basement meeting room, Hannah suffered her family's attempt to make her into what Delores deemed *church appropriate*.

"It's time," Delores declared, glancing at her watch again. "Follow me, girls."

As they walked down the center aisle single file, Hannah spotted her former boyfriend, Norman Rhodes. Norman was sitting on one side of his mother, and Carrie's second husband, Earl Flensburg, was sitting on her other side. Norman smiled at Hannah as she passed by and he held his thumb and finger together in an *okay* sign.

Hannah swallowed the lump that was beginning to form in her throat and reminded herself that she knew almost everyone here. The Holy Redeemer congregation consisted of friends, neighbors, and customers who came into The Cookie Jar. They would appreciate her apology and no one would be angry with her . . . she hoped.

She was beginning to feel slightly more confident when she noticed the other local man she'd dated, Mike Kingston. He was sitting with Michelle's boyfriend, Lonnie Murphy, and both of them smiled and gave her friendly nods. Mike was the head detective at the Winnetka County Sheriff's Department and he was training Lonnie to be his partner. Both men usually worked on Sundays, but they must have traded days with a pair of other deputies so that they could come to hear Hannah's apology.

Doc Knight saw them coming up the aisle and he stepped out of the pew so that they could file in. Hannah went first so that she would be on the end and it would be easier for her to get out and walk to the front of the church when it was time.

"Are you all right?" Michelle asked her as they sat down.

It took Hannah a moment to find her voice. "Yes, I'm all right."

"But you're so pale that the blusher on your cheeks is standing out in circles." Michelle reached for the hymnal in the rack and flipped to the page that was listed in the church bulletin.

"Is something wrong?" Andrea asked in a whisper.

"Everything's fine," Hannah told her, pretending to be engrossed in reading the verse of the familiar hymn they were preparing to sing.

The organist, who had been playing softly while people filed into the church, increased the volume and segued into the verse of the hymn. This precluded any further conversation and Hannah was grateful.

If there had been a ten question quiz about the sermon that Reverend Bob delivered, Hannah would have flunked it. She was too busy worrying about what she wanted to say to pay attention. There were times during the sermon that

Hannah wished Reverend Bob would hurry so that she could get up, apologize, and go back home. At other times, she found herself wishing that the sermon would go on forever and she'd never have to walk to the front of the church and speak.

When Reverend Bob finished, stepped down from the pulpit, and went into the room at the side of the nave to hang up his vestments, the butterflies of anxiety in Hannah's stomach awoke and began to churn in a rising cloud that made her feel weak-kneed and slightly dizzy. She concentrated on breathing evenly until Reverend Bob reappeared in the black suit he wore once the sermon was over.

The announcements Reverend Bob made were short and sweet. There was a request for donations of canned food from the Bible Church for their homeless shelter in the church basement, an announcement of the nuptials scheduled on Valentine's Day, a reminder that the lost and found box in the church office was overflowing with forgotten mittens, gloves, and caps, a notice of a time change in Grandma Knudson's Bible study group, and two notifications of baptisms to be held after church services in the coming month.

"And now we have a special request from Hannah Swensen," Reverend Bob told them. "She'd like to say a few words to you before the social hour."

Hannah stood up and slid out of the pew. She walked up the aisle at the side of the church on legs that shook slightly to join Reverend Bob. She cleared her throat and then she began to speak.

"Almost everyone in the congregation today attended my wedding to Ross Barton in November. Most of you were also at the Lake Eden Inn for the reception."

There were nods from almost everyone in attendance and Hannah went on. "I asked to speak to you today because I need to apologize." I think you all know that Ross is gone and my family and I told you that he was on location for a new special that he was doing for KCOW Television. That is *not* true. I'm sorry to say that we lied to you and we owe you an apology for that."

"If Ross isn't out on location for a special, where *is* he?" Howie Levine asked.

Hannah wasn't surprised by the question. Howie was a lawyer and he always asked probing questions. "Ross is in Wisconsin."

"Is he filming something there?" Hal McDermott, co-owner of Hal and Rose's Café asked.

"No. I'll tell you why he's there, but first let me tell what happened on the day Ross left Lake Eden."

Haltingly at first, and then with more assurance, Hannah described what had happened on the day Ross left. The words were painful at first, but it became easier until all the facts had been given.

"Did Ross leave you a note?" Irma York, the wife of Lake Eden's barber, asked.

"No. There was nothing. His car was still there, his bill-fold was on top of the dresser where he always left it when he came home from work, and he'd even left his driver's license and credit cards behind. It was almost as if he'd packed up his clothes and . . . and vanished. "

"You must have been very worried," Reverend Bob said sympathetically.

"Not at first. I was upset that he hadn't called me to say he was leaving, but I thought that he had been rushed for time and he'd call me that night. Then, when I didn't hear from him that night or the next day, I got worried."

"Of course you did!" Grandma Knudson, Reverend Bob's grandmother and the unofficial matriarch of the church, said with a nod.

"After three days," Hannah continued, "I was afraid that something was very wrong and I asked Mike and Norman to help me look for him."

Mike stood up to address the congregation. "It took us weeks of searching, but two of my detectives finally found Ross. Right after I verified his identity, Norman and I went to Hannah's condo to tell her." He turned around to face Hannah. "Go on, Hannah."

"Yes," Hannah said, gathering herself for the most difficult part of her apology. "When I came home that night, Mike and Norman were waiting for me. Both of them looked very serious and I knew right away that something was wrong. That's when Mike said that they'd found Ross, and . . ." Hannah stopped speaking and drew a deep, steadying breath. "Mike told me that Ross had gone back to his wife."

"His *wife*?" Grandma Knudson looked completely shocked. "But *you're* his wife, Hannah! We were all right here when *you* married Ross!"

There was a chorus of startled exclamations from the congregation. Hannah waited until everyone was quiet again and then she continued. "Ross was already married when he married me. And that means my marriage to him wasn't legal."

"You poor dear!" Grandma Knudson got up from her place of honor in the first pew and rushed up to put her arm around Hannah. Then she motioned to her grandson. "Give me your handkerchief, Bob."

Once the handkerchief was handed over, Grandma Knudson passed it to Hannah. "What are you going to do about this, Hannah?"

"I . . . I don't know," Hannah admitted truthfully. "I just wanted to tell all of you about this today because my family and I lied to you and we needed to set the record straight."

"Hannah could sue Ross for bigamy," Howie pointed out. "And since bigamy is a crime, Ross could be prosecuted. Do you want to press charges, Hannah?"

"I'm not sure. All I really know is that I never want to see him again." There was a murmuring of sympathy from the congregation as Hannah dabbed at her eyes with the borrowed handkerchief. "I know all of you thought I was married. I thought I was married too, but . . . but I wasn't. And since you gave me wedding presents under false pretenses, I'd like to return them to you."

"Ridiculous!" Grandma Knudson snorted, patting Hannah's shoulder. And then she turned to face the worshippers. "You don't want your wedding gifts back do you?"

"I don't!" Becky Summers was the first to respond. "Keep the silver platter, Hannah. Consider it an early birthday present."

"The same for me!" Norman's mother chimed in. "You keep the crystal pitcher, Hannah."

Several other members of the congregation spoke up, all of them expressing the same wishes, and then Grandma Knudson held her hand up for silence. "If anyone here wants a wedding gift back, contact me and I'll make sure you get it. And in the meantime, I think we've kept Hannah up here long enough." She turned to Hannah. "I know you brought something for our social hour, Hannah. I saw Michelle run down the stairs with a big platter. What wonderful baked goods did you bring today?"

Hannah felt a great weight slip off her shoulders. It was over. She'd come and accomplished what she'd set out to do. Now she could relax and spend a little time with the people she knew and loved.

"I brought Valentine Whippersnapper Cookies," she told them. "They're a new cookie recipe from my sister, Andrea.

Since we're about ready to start baking for Valentine's Day at The Cookie Jar, Andrea and I really want your opinion. Please try a cookie and tell us what you think of them."

Grandma Knudson turned to the congregation. "I'll lead you downstairs so you can start in on those cookies. And then I'm coming back up here for a private word with Hannah." She took Hannah's arm, led her to the front pew, and motioned to her to sit down. "I'll be right back," she said. "Just sit here and relax for a few moments."

Hannah watched as the church emptied out with Grandma Knudson leading the way. Then she closed her eyes for a moment and relished the fact that the tension was leaving her body. She felt good, better than she had for a long time. Perhaps Reverend Bob was right and confession was good for the soul.

Hannah turned around when she heard the sound of footsteps. Grandma Knudson was coming back. "Thank you," she said, as Grandma Knudson sat down next to her.

"You're welcome. I heard some very interesting things down there, Hannah. I'm really glad I got those fancy new hearing aids."

"I didn't know you had hearing aids!"

"Neither does anyone else except Bob, and I swore him to secrecy. I've changed my opinion about a lot of people in this town. Why, the things I've heard could fill a gossip column!"

"But you wouldn't . . ."

"Of course not!" Grandma Knudson said emphatically. "But I may not tell anyone about my hearing aids for a while. It's a lot of fun for me."

Hannah gave a little laugh. It felt wonderful to laugh and she was grateful to Grandma Knudson for giving her the opportunity.

"Seriously, Hannah," Grandma Knudson began, "you haven't heard from Ross since Mike and his boys located him, have you?"

Hannah shook her head. "No, not a word."

"All right then. If Ross calls you, tell him that if he knows what's good for him, he'd better never show his face in Lake Eden again. I heard Earl say he wanted to run Ross down with the county snowplow, and Bud Hauge asked Mike and Lonnie to give him five minutes alone with Ross if they picked him up. And Hal McDermott claimed he was going to leave out Rose's heaviest frying pan so he could bash in Ross's head."

Hannah was shocked. "But do you think they'd actually do it?"

Grandma Knudson shrugged. "If I were Ross, I wouldn't chance it. And I can tell you one thing for sure. If Ross comes back and winds up dead, you're going to have a whole town full of suspects!"